ISOLATION

DENISE R. STEPHENSON

Mill City Press
Minneapolis, MN

Mill City Press, Inc.
322 First Avenue N, 5th floor
Minneapolis, MN 55401
612.455.2293
www.millcitypublishing.com

ISBN-13: 978-1-62652-760-7
LCCN: 2014904172

Cover Design by Alan Pranke
Typeset by Sophie Chi

Printed in the United States of America

From watermelon red to pretty, pretty white
you've colored my life with more than family lies.
Without you, Boo, there would be far less art,
and I would be far more isolated.

CONTENTS

Bacteria are not going to be destroyed. They've been here, they've seen dinosaurs come and go... so any attempt to sterilize our home is fraught with failure.

—Stuart Levy

The world will soon break up into small colonies of the saved.

—Robert Bly

UNSUSPECTED SOURCES

No one expected her to die. It was a simple kitchen accident.

Rebecca's small dinner party had gone off without a hitch. She had the red wine open and breathing and the white on ice when the guests arrived. A simple meal of curried veggies with lime-marinated tri-tip and fresh bakery bread. As Rebecca served, one of the guests inquired about her Band-Aid.

"Oh, just nicked my finger while chopping the onion."

"Should we look for blood?" asked Reg, her neighbor. "Is that why you chose a curry?"

The next evening, Rebecca noticed a thin red line running up her arm from the cut. She removed the Band-Aid and found the wound surrounded by a white ring with grey pus oozing out. She looked in her medicine chest but couldn't find any antibacterial ointment. She realized the local pharmacy had already closed, so she poured a bit of alcohol on the wound and then put on a clean Band-Aid, intending to dress the wound better the next day.

In the middle of the night, she awoke to a burning sensation. She turned on the light. The red line had lengthened. Pus oozed out of the bandage. The clock read 1 a.m. Not the best time to need medical attention, but what could she do? She wrapped a couple of paper towels gently around her hand in the hope of not getting pus on anything. Then she dressed and knocked on her neighbor's door.

Reg saw her through the peephole. He cracked the door open. "What's up, Beck?" Then he saw her hand. "Whoa, girl, did you hurt yourself?"

"Remember, I cut myself prepping dinner?"

"Yesterday."

"It's infected. I need to go to emergency."

"For a finger? Can't it wait till morning?"

"It's hot and nasty. I'm scared."

Reg walked Rebecca into Emergency and then took a seat in the waiting room. Rebecca told the attending nurse she'd cut her finger. The staff moved slowly until they discovered the red line emanating from the wound and learned she'd cut herself in a kitchen accident. Rebecca insisted it was onions she was chopping, not steak, when the knife had sliced across her finger. The nurse looked skeptical but didn't argue.

When she was alone in the curtained space, Rebecca suddenly got nervous. She felt cold, even though she was wearing a winter parka. Her finger still felt hot, like the burning when you'd stayed outside too long in the snow. She put up her hood and wrapped her arms tightly around herself. The nurse's questions got her wondering.

She could have been cutting the tomato when she did it, but it was definitely tomato or onion, not steak. She didn't think about germs in her mouth even though she'd immediately sucked on the cut. She didn't consider that she hadn't washed the vegetables before cutting them. She didn't worry that she left the same Band-Aid on when she cooked the steak, served the meal, showered, and slept. Since it hadn't been deep and didn't need stitches, she had simply ignored the cut after covering it.

By the time the doctor arrived, Rebecca was shivering. She asked for a blanket, but instead, the doctor ordered ice to try to lower Rebecca's temperature, which had spiked to 104 degrees. The doctor feared sepsis. She sent for a white blood count.

"What's wrong with me?"

"I can't be sure yet, but it appears you may have blood poisoning."

"From a simple cut?"

"From bacteria most likely. Were you working with meat?"

"That's what the nurse asked. I used a fork on some steak, but I was slicing an onion or maybe a tomato when I cut myself."

"Could be your immune system has been compromised by a cold or flu. Could be a virulent form of bacteria on the food. Could just be bad luck. But we'll get you taken care of."

Reg couldn't comprehend what the doctor told him. He drove home in a daze, crawled into bed in the middle of the day and pulled the covers over his head. Rebecca dead? From food poisoning? How could that be?

***

Tomás had just returned from Europe. On his way home from the airport, he stopped at a fruit stand and bought produce. It was summer and the peaches, plums, and berries were gorgeous. Some of the melons were already ripe, so he grabbed a small one of those as well. Plus he bought everything for salads, including the spinach he couldn't get while traveling. As he paid, he felt a sudden urge to take a dump. He was looking forward to going home and crapping in his own toilet, so this was a welcome sensation. He drove straight home, the urge intensifying en route. Suddenly it didn't feel normal. His stomach gurgled and the urge was so intense he almost released right there in the car. He grabbed his produce and wobbled into the house, keeping his knees together as a precaution. He hoped he hadn't picked up a bug. He'd been careful not to drink the water abroad.

When he saw blood, he wasn't surprised at first, because he had hemorrhoids. Then he noticed his toilet was dark red. Blood was slowly dripping down his leg. He sat back down so as not to bleed all over the floor, but quickly realized he couldn't just sit there.

Without hesitating, he dialed his ex-wife, the nurse.

"Sara?"

"Tomasíto, good to hear from you. Are you back on this continent?"

"I am. Look, I have a problem. I need some advice."

"Shoot."

"I'm bleeding."

"From?"

4

"My ass. But it's not the hemorrhoids. I had diarrhea, but now there's just blood, a fair amount of blood. I'm standing here with a towel..."

"Call 911."

"Really? I just drove—"

"Tomás, don't hesitate. This could be serious. You've been out of the country."

"You're the paranoid one, I'm not."

"This isn't paranoia and it's not a nightmare. You don't mess around with anal blood loss. The membranes are thin there so it can be a sign of many kinds of illness. Call 911. Or just call an ambulance, but get to the hospital. I'll meet you there."

He thought Sara was being a bit reactionary, she'd always been that way. It was one of the things that made him notice her initially, and one of the things that made him leave. *But he'd called her first. He trusted her medical knowledge.*

He started to look for the number for an ambulance when he felt something warm on his hand and looked down to see the towel soaked through. He dialed 911, went to the bathroom for a clean towel, wrapped it so his genitals were covered, and waited by the door.

"Whoa, buddy!" said the first paramedic as he approached Tomás. "Yowsa!" exclaimed the second.

"Thanks a lot, guys. Guess I was right to call."

"Yes, sir. Good move," said the first, regaining his professional composure. "Just lie down on our stretcher, and we'll take it from here."

"I'm just gonna take a look," said the second as he snapped on a glove and reached toward Tomás.

"Fine," said Tomás releasing his grip on the towel. "But I don't think you'll see anything. The blood started with diarrhea and won't stop."

He watched the paramedics exchange a look. They stopped and put on masks before touching him again. In the ambulance, he overheard them talking with the hospital. He couldn't understand everything, but he could tell it was bad. He felt a little faint. Blood loss must do that, he thought as he slipped from consciousness.

***

Yaku was an aide in the clinic in Klawosk. Jo, Yaku's partner, was one of the few non-Tlingits in the small village. She'd lived in Alaska for 15 years, but knew she'd always be an outsider.

In parts of the country, outbreaks were becoming commonplace, but in this small island village of southeastern Alaska, an outpost of health and safety, food-borne illnesses had been minimal. Everyone believed the dangerous antibiotic-resistant *Staph* known as *MRSA* had gotten off a cruise ship, probably riding on one of those damn little dogs rich people carried with them like pocket change. Yaku was in attendance when discussions with the family of victim zero had revealed she'd petted a dog and shaken hands with the passenger carrying it. He'd talked with other clinic workers during the first days, exchanging stories about the early victims who'd all had contact with ship passengers and often with dogs. It could never be proven, but the truth rarely was.

Klawosk had been safe from food-borne bacterial outbreaks for several reasons. Fresh produce was rare and when it did arrive, it had usually been nuked for preservation. Oddly, that had become protection against many of the bacterial strains that were so problematic elsewhere. Then there was the fact that very few people ate salads, as produce was rarely fresh enough to be served that way. And finally, the small population had meant that the few times *E. Coli O157:H7* or *Listeria* made it to shore in a contagious condition, the person who became sick was able to be quarantined quickly and there had been little spread of contagion.

When *MRSA* arrived, however, it arrived full force. Klawosk's clinic didn't have the necessary updated testing available to find out quickly that it was *Staph*, let alone that it was Community *MRSA* or *CA-MRSA*. By the time it was identified, not only had the initial patients been dosed with useless broad-spectrum antibiotics, which only made the bacteria that much more resistant, but several health workers were overcome with the illness and the makeshift hospital started churning out Hospital *MRSA* or *HA-MRSA* faster than rabbits reproduce. Luckily, they hadn't evacuated the first cases to the hospital in Juneau. If they had, the consequences for the rest of Alaska might have been much worse.

As it was, the strain ran rampant through Klawosk, taking out half of the residents in the first wave of a month's time and then, over the next year, diminishing the population to a mere 85, one-tenth its former size. The CDC eventually identified the novel strain, a mutation that combined characteristics of *MRSA* with *E. Coli*, involving both flesh and organs. This strain was labeled *Cha-Cha MRSA*, echoing the former designations and acknowledging with a dark irony, the fast-moving dance of death in which this *Staph* engaged.

First the governor shut down the island, then the president forgot about the state. After the first month, when *Cha-Cha* killed half the population, Jo and Yaku moved away from the scene of the disaster, away from the harbor, away from the clinic, away from the dead.

***

Hosuk Lee, the man seated in 13A on the small jet bound for Kauai, wore a mask. So did the man next to him, his best friend and roommate, Cho Luck. The masks were simple antibacterial-treated cloth with a metal nose piece and thin white elastics around the ears. Both men wore over-the-counter blue masks rather than the designer ones with decorative colors, which were all the rage in their Chinatown neighborhood. They didn't stay in the masks 24-7, but wore them often in public. They wore their masks today because airplanes were notorious for distributing dangerous contaminants brought aboard by passengers from all over the globe.

Hosuk and Cho waited tables in a busy Asian fusion restaurant in San Francisco. They started as busboys, worked their way up to waiters, and now Hosuk sometimes stepped in as host or manager when needed. He was building his skill set and his resumé. He wanted a future beyond the community his parents and relatives had always occupied and now, at 23, he believed it would be possible.

Cho, on the other hand, was shy and content with his lot in life. At 21, he would never have dreamed of this vacation, but Hosuk's dream became his, and the two had saved for three years to afford this trip.

As the plane descended, rain pelted the window. Hosuk worried it did not bode well. The woman in the aisle seat told them it had been raining for a week. She said the island was a rainforest that received more rain than anywhere on Earth. Cho's eyes got wide trying to imagine what that meant. The woman asked about their plans. Hosuk listed a series of outdoor activities: kayaking, hiking, learning to surf. As they landed, the woman said, "Hope the weather clears for you. Sounds like a great vacation."

Outside the terminal, they stood under the airport cover to avoid getting soaked until their bus came to take them to their hostel near the beach. They were used to rain in San Francisco, but neither of them brought an umbrella for Hawaii.

Once at the hostel, they settled into their semi-private room. Hosuk decided they should get drinks and maybe some munchies and asked at the desk where they should go. The attendant directed them to an ABC Store, the ubiquitous Hawaiian quick stop. He also suggested they might want umbrellas.

Hosuk thought the attendant was offering to loan them umbrellas. He said they were just going across the street, they'd be fine. The attendant insisted they should *buy* umbrellas at the store. Hosuk asked about the weather report.

The attendant said, "You'll want an umbrella. You can't trust weather reports, you're on an island, brah."

Back in the room with snacks and beverages, Hosuk peeked out the window and saw that the rain had stopped. He breathed deeply, stretched, and got into bed. Cho had already fallen asleep.

Unbeknownst to Hosuk, a small cockroach, less than a half-inch long, crawled on the bamboo table next to his bed. It came directly from a trash bin filled with discarded food wrappers, cigarette butts, used Kleenex, and soda cans deposited by guests throughout the hostel. It walked across Hosuk's book, then on the rim of his water bottle. It would be gone before he moved from bed in the morning.

***

Sara arrived at the ER before Tomás did. She watched as the paramedics wheeled him directly to a room. The paramedics reported they hadn't been able to take a history before Tomás passed out. The doctor ordered several blood workups: blood clotting, a complete blood count and a comprehensive metabolic panel. He also did a suprapubic tap to get urine for analysis to check for protein or blood.

Sara had come directly from the doctor's office she worked in, so she was wearing her medical whites. When the doctor asked Sara to help with the tap and she refused, he discovered that rather than a nurse, she was the patient's ex-wife, and the questions began:

"Has he consumed raw meat?"

"I doubt it, he's nearly vegetarian."

"Does he have a history of clotting problems?"

"I don't know of any."

"How long has he had rectal bleeding?"

"Not long, I think he called me first thing, about 75 minutes ago."

"Does he take any medications?"

"Last I knew, he took an analgesic, but that was it besides supplements."

"What kinds of supplements?"

"Nothing weird. Vitamins, fish oil, occasionally zinc and extra C if he felt a cold coming on."

"Does he take any illegal substances?"

"No."

"Does he drink excessively?"

"No, maybe a beer in the evening."

"Has he been out of the country recently?"

"He just got back from Europe."

"Where in Europe? Exactly."

"I'm not sure. He usually goes to France, Spain, Italy. I think I recall him mentioning that Germany was on this itinerary."

Sara felt a little odd—she was the ex-wife, not the wife anymore. But Tomás hadn't remarried. She knew most of the answers. Still, it seemed a bit intimate, not something she wanted to be involved in. And yet, he'd called. She appreciated that. It wasn't really like him to seek her advice. If he'd only done that more during the marriage, maybe they'd still be together.

Sara realized she should call the family. Tomás was close to his sister and her kids. They needed to be told. She stepped outside to make the call.

"Hi Cathy, is your mom home?"

"Mooooom!"

"No need to shout. This is your...this is Sara. I used to be married to your Uncle Tomás."

"Hi, Sara. M-o-m, Sara's on the phone. Sara of Tomás and Sara, but not, you know."

"Hi Sara, sorry about Cathy."

"Maria, Tomás is in the hospital. He's at St. Mark's in Emergency."

"Was there an accident? What happened? Is he OK?"

"No accident. But I'm not sure if he's OK. They're doing tests. You'll want to come."

"Were you on duty? How do you...?"

"He called me. He had blood in his stool, a lot of blood, and he wanted my opinion."

"Oh. Of course. I have to wait for Jorge to get home to watch Cathy and her brother, but I'll be there as soon as I can."

As Sara reentered the ER, she noticed blood on the sheeting below Tomás was pooling. It must still be flowing out of him. She pointed it out to a nurse.

The blood tests hadn't told them a thing. The urinalysis wasn't back yet, but they were going to have to try something else. They asked Sara to step out of the room.

"Get a fecal sample, stat," ordered one of the doctors. "Increase the coagulants, check his levels and prepare for a transfusion. Someone talk to the family about blood donation. And place a call to the CDC to find out if there are any outbreaks we need to know about."

***

Hosuk and Cho awoke to the sound of air raid sirens. Both men jumped out of bed and stumbled for the door. Others were standing in the hallway equally perplexed. Panic was visible behind the drowsy eyes of the hostel guests. The clerk called from the lobby, "Flash floods, brah."

"Will the hostel flood?"

"Not likely, brah. But if yah gotta da rental car, check for road closures, especially da bridges, yah?"

"So we don't have to worry?" Hosuk asked.

"No brah, go back to bed."

Later, on the way to breakfast, Hosuk and Cho ran through the rain to the ABC Store, hopping over puddles. Plenty of umbrellas. Nothing cheap and nothing fancy, but their new purchases allowed them to walk the rest of the way to breakfast.

Hosuk took the rain as an opportunity to re-plan their week. During a let-up, he and Cho went to a frog-named shop and picked up snorkel gear cheap, investigated surf boards, and talked to someone about lessons, even though they expected to just rent boards and try on their own. Cho liked the mesh bags they got for the snorkel gear. Seemed ingenious to him the way it kept the gear together but allowed sand and water to sift through.

On the way back to the room, they got caught in a deluge that drenched them, even with umbrellas.

Just before evening, the throbbing rain stopped. The sky lightened a bit, though the cloud cover was as solid as ever. They walked outside near the ocean. It was calming to finally hear its rhythm. Cho heard a rooster crow. Hosuk snuck up from behind. The rooster turned and pecked Hosuk's hand sharply before fluttering away from them.

On day two, as the rain continued, they lounged around the hostel. They commiserated with other travelers. They felt sorry for themselves. They phoned home and tried to get sympathy. Their friends and family told them they were in paradise, it couldn't be *that* bad.

While hanging the mesh bag of snorkel gear on the wall, Hosuk cut the edge of his hand on a rusty screw head. He washed the cut and asked for a first-aid kit. The attendant got him a Band-Aid but no antibacterial ointment. Hosuk thought that odd, but realized he was living cheap, at a hostel. What did he expect? He considered buying AB ointment at the ABC store, but couldn't see spending all that money for a single use.

By the end of the third day, Hosuk and Cho were sick and tired of each other. They had never traveled together before. Their interests and styles didn't sync, and the small room and drenched landscape weren't helping.

The ocean mural painted on the wall of their tiny room— an idyllic ocean scene, faded but heartening with its splash of local colors—had provided an optimistic icon of their journey at first, but now, as the storm continued to rage, it mocked them every time they entered.

***

Yaku and Jo gathered their tools and traditional Chilkat blankets made of cedar bark and retreated to a small cabin in the woods.

It belonged to Yaku's clan, not to him alone. The second week they were there, his cousin, Taglish, had shown up. Yaku and Jo came to the window when Taglish knocked. He asked to join them, saying he didn't feel well. Yaku told Taglish he would take care of him, but asked him not to enter the cabin, to keep it safe from the plague. If Taglish got well, he could join them. Taglish understood.

Yaku built a lean-to at the side of the cabin, away from doors and windows. Jo immediately cleaned the areas Taglish had touched at the front. She gathered soft bark to make a place for Taglish to rest, but she let Yaku put it in the lean-to. Jo had been near her share of death, but both she and Yaku were more confident in his immunity. She offered a blanket and cooked broth and ferns for the men.

Taglish had boils on his flesh, dark red welts with yellowing pus in the centers. Yaku never touched the sores. In fact, he tried never to touch Taglish at all, at least not with his bare hands. He no longer had surgical gloves, but he used small pieces of cloth when he had to touch Taglish. After any exposure to Taglish's skin, Jo washed the cloths in water boiled over a small fire pit out back. She never touched the cloths until they had boiled for at least 30 minutes.

For more than a week, the boils stayed the same in size and number. Yaku told Taglish this was a good sign and he hoped it was. But he knew that once infected, the bacteria was unlikely to go away. He hadn't seen anyone healed since *Cha-Cha* arrived on the island. A few lingered, but none survived.

Taglish hadn't been a favored cousin, but in a small community, Yaku knew him well. They'd played catch even though Taglish was a decade younger. Yaku was fond of Taglish's mother, who made the best salmon berry pie he'd ever tasted. Taglish told Yaku he was the last of his immediate family. All the others had died. Taglish had tended his mother until the last, bringing her water and mopping her forehead when she got fevers.

When Taglish became feverish and the boils began to grow, Yaku asked him what he wanted. They had both seen too much death and none of it had been peaceful. Taglish said he wasn't afraid of dying, but he couldn't bear suffering. He knew what was ahead and he saw no reason to endure the pain and agony. Yaku consulted Jo and all three agreed on poison.

Jo had collected mushrooms when she'd gathered ferns since they tended to grow in similar dark, misty areas. She'd gotten several Amanita Regalis, a reddish-brown toadstool with white spots that she knew to be dangerous. She also knew them to be hallucinogenic in small doses. She wasn't sure why she'd kept them, maybe because the ferns were fewer than expected or maybe because gathering things was becoming a primary pastime and an important one. Maybe she had foreseen this need, but she doubted it. She wasn't very in tune with this new universe.

"Will the Amanita do the trick?" Jo asked Yaku.

"How many?"

"Less than a dozen, but some of them good-sized."

"Taglish isn't healthy. It will do."

"I could go look for more."

"He's decided. Can you make them into a soup?"

"Absolutely." Jo went inside. She washed the toadstools and cut them quickly. She chopped them as tiny as she could and placed them in a pot with water. She covered the pot, uncertain whether escaping fumes could carry away the toxin. She doubted it. Uncertainty was the one thing she was sure of. When it was drinkable, she called Yaku to the back door.

"Thank you." He said. "I'll stay with him. Can you keep digging?"

"You don't think that will be a sound he doesn't want to hear? It would make me sad. Or crazy."

"He knows."

Jo waited until she knew Taglish would have consumed most of the mushrooms, then she went out and worked on the grave. She was glad it was still summer. She was glad the cabin was far enough from the muskeg that the body wouldn't contaminate their drinking water. Jo had a strong upper body but a grave was a huge undertaking. She dug steadily and slowly, piling the dirt close enough to save energy now and later. The gravesite was close to the lean-to, on the same side of the cabin to make the journey with the body easier for Yaku, but far enough away to not see it as a contaminant. What a safe perimeter entailed was unclear, but Jo and Yaku were both confident that mentally as well as physically, they would want Taglish's body out of immediate proximity.

***

Sara sat in the waiting room. Finally, a nurse walked in and announced "Tomás Hernandez?" Both Sara and Maria stood.

Sara had been in the bathroom when Maria arrived so they hadn't noticed each other. Maria glared at Sara as if this were all her fault.

"Family?" inquired the nurse.

Both women answered, "Yes."

Sara saw Maria's glare and immediately explained to the nurse that she was the ex-wife.

"I need blood relatives only," the nurse said and stepped away with Maria. Sara stood there a little stunned. She had waited, hoping to talk to Maria. "He's lost a lot of blood," the nurse told Maria.

"What's wrong? Can I see him?"

"No, they're working on him now. We're doing several tests. But the blood loss is already substantial, he'll need a transfusion. Has your family got blood in storage?"

"What?"

"Storage. Many people donate regularly so they'll have family blood when health situations arise."

"No, no we haven't done that."

"Do you know if you're the same blood type?"

"No, actually..."

"Would you and your family like to be typed? If you're a match, you could donate."

"Yes, certainly. There's just me, and my children. Can they donate?"

"How old?"

"Cathy's 10 and Jake is 14."

"Yes, in this situation. Cathy would need to donate platelets rather than whole blood. At her age, we wouldn't want to decrease the volume. It's a longer process, but perfectly safe. If she's a match, we have videos for her to watch during the process."

"I'll have my husband bring the children over. Should I wait for them or do you want to test me now?"

"Let's start right away. Tomás needs blood."

As the nurse led Maria out of the ER, Sara reached out to touch Maria's arm.

"I'm going to donate blood," Maria said to her. "You needn't wait."

Sara felt adrift. She couldn't say goodbye to Tomás, he was unconscious. But she didn't feel right leaving now. If she left, she wouldn't know what was happening, and she was the one with medical knowledge, not Maria. Sara stood in the waiting area several moments, then walked out the door. She phoned a friend, hoping someone would tell her she was doing the right thing.

***

On day four, Cho wanted to return the snorkel equipment and see if they could get an earlier flight home. Hosuk suggested Cho do just that. He, on the other hand, expected the rain to break so he'd get at least one chance to snorkel. He couldn't believe the fates would be so cruel as to not grant him that small favor. Nearly once an hour he found himself adding in his head how much this horrid trip had cost him. He no longer thought of it as a vacation, he wouldn't use that word. Three years he had saved...for this!

Cho avoided Hosuk and the stultifying hostel by going to the library. In the Hawaii section, he looked at pictures of gorgeous flowers, most of which were canoe plants brought to Hawaii by the Polynesians. He discovered they used plants for clothes, fishing line and medication. A plant was even used to stun fish so they would float to the surface for an easy catch. He'd never been interested in plants, though he knew herbs were big in Chinese medicine. His father only went to Chinese doctors, not believing in Western science. Cho always thought this old-fashioned. But maybe the Chinese were smart like the Polynesians.

Cho returned to the room to find that Hosuk had piled everything on the top bunk, Cho's bunk. "What are you doing?" Cho asked as casually as he could manage, feeling rage rising inside him. He noticed Hosuk was wearing his mask. With so few human interactions, neither had been bothering with masks.

"Cockroaches!" Hosuk yelled. "I found cockroaches in the room. Fomites. They carry bacteria. After all we've been through, I'm not letting big ugly bugs infect us."

"How is piling everything on my bed gonna stop cockroaches?"

"As I cleaned, I put things out of the way up there. Sorry. Didn't mean to take over."

"You could have put the stuff on your bed."

"I was just trying to get as much distance as possible between the floor and our stuff."

"Uh-huh."

"Are you flying out or what?"

"Too expensive."

"We're both here for the duration?"

Cho nodded, turned and headed for the bathroom before Hosuk could make him angrier. "I'll have everything back where it belongs when you return," offered Hosuk. Cho didn't acknowledge the statement, but took his time in the bathroom.

***

Yaku and Jo didn't speak of Taglish as they didn't speak of the overpowering death that had raged through their world. There was too much to do. They knew they must store as much food as possible before the equinox. After that, light would be scarce, the cold could arrive unexpectedly and it would stay. They saw no reason to avoid the *Cha-Cha Plague* only to die of hunger.

Winters were long on Alaskan islands, the darkness always intense and oppressive. There was little snow that winter, which made the daily trek for water and use of the outhouse more manageable. During the five or so hours of daylight, Jo and Yaku got water, took walks to stretch their legs, and chopped firewood. They filled those few hours of light as fully as possible so they slept well. The more time they spent cuddled in bed, the less wood they needed for heat, the fewer candles they burned, the less food they ate. They thought of it as their winter of hibernation, like the bears, who, upon reflection, they hoped were doing the same. They'd seen no bears since moving to the cabin, which they were most grateful for, yet they were ever watchful, knowing the past doesn't predict the future.

They'd recycled an old calendar and used it to track time. By late January they felt the increase in daylight. Their island gained six minutes a day, so they had gone from less than five hours of light to more than eight in the last month. It lifted their spirits.

But it didn't compensate for their dwindling food supply. Yaku hunted in hopes of squirrel or deer but hadn't been lucky since late fall, a kill they'd long since finished eating. They wondered if any of the animals were susceptible to *Cha-Cha*. They'd come to believe there were fewer creatures about. They realized that might be paranoia. They hoped it was, since an infected animal could infect their food supply.

They contemplated a hike to the ocean, where they were certain of food sources. Unfortunately, they couldn't see storm fronts from the woods, so they couldn't be sure what the weather might hold. A snowstorm could be deadly. They couldn't risk it yet.

Though the hours of daylight grew, their activities shrank to match their food supply. They'd been good at rationing. They had reduced their portions yet again hoping it would last long enough.

***

On the final morning of their vacation, the sun finally shone. They didn't have to leave the hostel until 11, so Hosuk put on his swimsuit and grabbed the snorkel gear. Cho followed, in his travel pants and shoes, just to watch. Hosuk ran into the brown water up to his knees. The waves knocked against him. Maybe the clear blue he expected was out farther. He put on the mask and snorkel but he couldn't see anything through the murk. He swam out. Nothing. In utter frustration, he took off the gear and screamed at the top of his lungs. He trudged in, falling once into a sinkhole hidden in the churning brown water.

Cho thought the rains were to blame. Weren't there rivers all over the island? Wasn't that where they were going to kayak? He looked down the length of the beach. Not a single person in sight. Maybe locals knew something they didn't. The waves were crashing. Cho wandered down the beach. He could see a great distance but couldn't spot a single soul. Maybe it was too early.

Hosuk stamped up the beach. Cho knew better than to speak to him. As they walked by the front desk, the attendant looked at Hosuk and shook his head. He was thinking about ignorant tourists who knew nothing about how heavy rains caused sewage to overflow into rivers and, eventually, the ocean. If he'd seen the Asian guy leave the hostel in swimwear, he'd have let him know about the warnings that suggested people not even go barefoot on the beaches because of possible contamination from *Staph* and *Salmonella*.

***

Maria was sitting in the ER waiting room. Her husband was with the children while Cathy donated platelets. A doctor called "Tomás Hernandez?" and walked toward her as she stood. He directed her away from other waiting families.

"The tests showed *E. Coli*, but it's not a strain we've seen before. The symptoms are mirroring *O157:H7*, the dangerous form. We're treating him as if this strain will also result in hemolytic uremic syndrome, HUS for short, but we can't be sure."

Maria wanted to ask what that meant, but she could tell the doctor didn't want to explain.

"We have to move quickly," he said. "We've already wasted time. He's still bleeding and now he's turning yellow. We need to do a complete transfusion in hopes that we can stop his kidneys from shutting down."

"I've donated blood," offered Maria, "and my daughter Cathy is giving platelets right now. My son isn't a match..."

"We'll use reserve blood for the first transfusion, including your donation." The doctor began to walk away.

"Will he be OK?" Maria asked.

"It's too soon to tell. I must warn you, HUS is a killer, ma'am. We'll try to save him."

Maria breathed in sharply. She choked and coughed into her open hand, stunned by the doctor's stark admission. *This can't be happening, she thought. Tomás lives a healthy lifestyle. He does all the things a person is supposed to do. This isn't fair!*

The doctors moved Tomás to isolation. They began the transfusion as soon as the diagnosis was made. The moment they started the line, he leaked blood more profusely, first out his anus, then out of his ear and nose. At that point, they stopped. There was no reason to waste good blood on a dying man. No reason to continue to contaminate the hospital. No reason to continue to endanger medical staff.

They called time of death. Everyone left the room except the nurse who posted notification of possible contagion.

The CDC was contacted again, to inform them of the death and to send, by special courier, the sample with the unidentified strain of *E. Coli*. Hazmat was on the scene within the hour to begin the cleanup. When the family asked about scheduling a funeral, they were told to proceed because suspicious contagion would prevent the body from being released for burial.

Maria screamed, and collapsed into her husband's arms. Cathy began to sob audibly.

No one thought to call Sara.

***

Jo longed for the give and take of conversation. Her intimacy with Yaku was more intense than ever with the two of them working together on such an important goal: survival. Yet as his speaking all but stopped, Jo found the growing silence oppressive. She tried humming, then talking to herself, but she knew her own mind, she wanted another voice.

"Yaku, do you remember any of the stories your father used to tell?" He nodded. "Can you tell me one?" He shook his head. "You mean you're not good at stories?" He nodded. "But if you don't tell them, they'll die, too." Yaku looked at Jo. He hadn't thought of that and he didn't like that Jo had said it aloud. He got up from his chair, kissed her on the forehead, as he always did in the evening, and got into bed.

***

Hosuk and Cho flew back to San Francisco, returning to their jobs and their everyday lives. Cho made light of the rain-logged week on the islands, joking that maybe he hadn't made the proper offerings to the gods. People hardly believed that their vacation could have been so unlucky. Hosuk tried not to talk of the trip at all. He just kept focusing on how much the trip cost and how horrible it was. He couldn't seem to let go.

A week later, Hosuk noticed he didn't feel well. He was a little nauseous. Perhaps he'd eaten more than he should have for lunch. He tried to relax and breathe, but he felt an urge rising in his throat. He ran to the toilet in time to heave his lunch into it. He bent over, shuddering and spitting, trying to clear the taste from his mouth. He walked to the sink, rinsed and immediately headed to the toilet again.

Hosuk had heard reports that the rain in Kauai was called "Red Rain" because it carried bacteria. He didn't believe rain could be a fomite. Rain could be seeded with chemicals, sure, but not bacteria. Could it? He assured himself this was part of the government's propaganda to persuade people to follow mandated precautions and stay inside when they were told to. Still, he wondered. Could rain make him sick? He thought the cockroaches were more likely to blame. But it didn't matter, he realized as he left work for the clinic.

Because Hosuk gave the intake nurse details of his travels in Hawaii, they quickly determined he had *Salmonella*. But they also found an unhealed wound on his hand with a red ring around it. He had contracted a virulent form of *Staph* that caused necrotizing fasciitis. The clinic staff explained to him that both infections probably came from sewage contamination. They asked if he'd had any open wounds when he went swimming. He wasn't sure. Who looked for cuts before a swim? He'd had no idea of the dangers.

When he told Cho, a knowing look came over his friend's face. Cho nodded his head and said, "Ah, that's why no one was on the beach. We were alone when you went snorkeling."

The incubation was a long one, and though Hosuk was young, the bacteria did a great deal of damage. For months he was on machines meant to clean his various systems: digestive, circulatory, lymphatic, respiratory. He had multiple surgeries cutting away flesh to remove the *Staph* so his body would stop eating itself. In the end, his kidneys were beyond saving. He was put on dialysis. They'd already removed fingers and so much of his side that his organs were compromised. Before they had to take a lung, Hosuk succumbed.

Cho didn't become ill, but many restaurant customers did. It appeared that Hosuk himself had acted as a fomite. He became the carrier, like the cockroach he worried so much about. There was no way for the restaurant to notify people since most of their business was take-out. Some became ill quickly and called the restaurant to ask about possible food poisoning. When the calls came, the manager referred them to the Department of Health. It wasn't his job to break the bad news.

Cho told people that Hosuk's vacation killed him. He was grateful his parents gave him good luck money before he traveled. As the months elapsed, Cho found he wore his mask more often, washed his hands with greater frequency, and started bowing like the ancients rather than shaking hands.

DON'T TOUCH

Habits learned early are habits for life. Gary heard the words echo in his head just as his hand touched his cheek to catch his cough. Even though he was in his own bedroom, Gary double-checked: no one in sight. He wiped his hand on the bottom of his jeans, but then immediately went to the bathroom and washed his hands with AB wash and threw the jeans into the washer.

His father's voice droned in his head, "Habits learned early, Gary, that's the thing." In front of them a billboard had proclaimed the mantra as they'd driven to the babysitter. "You can do it, son. You'll see." Gary hadn't protested, but he also didn't see the importance. Now, years later, he'd learned to hide his infractions. He could keep from touching his face when others could see him, but when he was alone, he didn't bother. It was that simple. No one knew—not his best friend Frank, not his mom, and certainly not his dad.

"So much shit," Gary muttered as he entered the garage. He looked around to make sure his mom was gone. At 12, he wasn't allowed to swear. "Shit," he said again, delighting in his daring.

The dreary day led Gary to dig around for entertainment. He climbed to the shelves that overhung the car. He was still small enough to crawl up amid the boxes and poke around in the cage-like space.

Toward the center, where no one but he could reach, Gary found a bright red plastic box. It had come from his grandfather's house when he'd been placed in care. Supposedly it had held his mother's toys. "Legless" he thought they were called because, though there were faces amid the small primary-colored rectangular plastic blocks, there were no other body parts.

He pried open the lid to discover a jumble of childhood bits. Besides the "Legless," there was a slender doll with large, pointy breasts, which he ran his fingers across lightly. He was old enough to know breasts were untouchable, but not old enough to be genuinely interested.

He poked through a bunch of miniature metal cars, but most had chipped paint or missing wheels. The race games on his handhelds were far superior to these. Why pretend to make a tiny car go fast when he could be in the driver's seat?

He started thumbing through a stack of books. He picked up one with a large man in a red and white fuzzy suit. Inside, he found a picture with the man touching his nose! His mother would be shocked to know this was in her own garage.

Immediately, he secreted the book under his shirt, tossed the lid lightly back on the box and slid down the ladder onto the cement floor. His mom had walked to the market where she bought produce directly from independent farmers in hopes of getting safer veggies, fruit, and eggs. She wouldn't be gone long, so he quickly made his way into the house and back to his bedroom.

He heard the front door even before he closed his, so he rapidly stuck the book under his mattress and nervously yelled, "Hey Mom, is that you?" as he trotted into the kitchen, expecting a treat from the market.

It was several days before he remembered his treasure. When he finally extracted it, everyone else in the house was asleep. He turned on his bedside lamp with its low-watt gray-lit bulb. It was hard to make out the words, but he read with delight. He was near the end when he saw the picture of the man in the story with his finger touching his nose.

The story was a fairy tale but this image was a gold mine. Gary couldn't believe it. Quietly, he tore out the page. Gently, he folded it and put it inside a pair of underwear in his drawer. He had to show Frank, but he couldn't let anyone else see, especially his parents.

***

"Don't be touching yer nose like that." Verna was serious. She rarely took a scolding tone with Sister Georgia. Verna grew up in a time when a person respected her elders in every way and that surely included how you spoke to them.

"I picked at my nose all my life. Ain't nothin' you ain't seen before."

"I know. I know. But, Sister Georgia, we ain't supposed to be doin' that no more. No face touchin'. Them's the rules."

"Well that's just silly. I have t' blow my nose, I have t' get dirt outta my eye, I have t' pick the wax outta my ears. Just silly."

"I know. I know. Seems like they've gone too far. But they has bred these new germs and they done got away from 'em. And these germs just love sneakin' in us through our eyes and nose and mouth. Took me awhile to stop. Oh, I still catch myself lifting a finger toward my nose especially, but I try not to touch my face. If you ever got outta this holler you'd see how important it is these days. Folks'll point and whoop and yell from clear across the street if they catch you touchin' any part of your face."

"Don't say."

"Mm hm. You can even get arrested for it. Though our boys in blue ain't done that yet. Ain't been no arrests in MacDowell County and that's been noticed up there in Charleston. Last night's paper said everyone had to do their part. Said they was calling all the sheriffs together to make sure they weren't downplaying this thing. Said it came from the very top."

"The Governor?"

"No, the President or maybe the Surgeon General, I can't rightly remember, but someone there in War-shington."

"Well I never."

"I know. It's quite a change."

"Well I never go farther out into the world than this porch. So I reckon I'm pretty safe scratchin' my nose."

"Oh, 'course you won't be arrested. It's just...we all have to start making this change. It's evidently mighty important."

"Did you say they *made* these here dangerous germs?"

"Don't know they intended to, but it's somethin' about the way they been growin' crops, you know, on them great big farms. Something to do with that somehow."

"Playing God then, is that what they been doin'?"

"Kinda sounds like it. But I didn't understand all of it, so don't go a quotin' me on it."

"Didn't I always say there weren't enough god-fearing men among us anymore?"

"Yes, ma'am. You surely did. You're a righteous woman, Sister Georgia."

Sister Georgia had grown old gracefully, rocking on her front porch, greeting visitors as they passed. Back in the hollers of West Virginia what money there was had always been needed for food and coal as far back as Georgia could remember. "Never been plenty of nothin'," as her pappy use t' say. But Georgia wasn't a complainer. Her kin had dwindled back in the '80s when all the mines shut down and the working-age folk left for jobs up north. When they'd first left they'd sent checks regular-like, then for special occasions, then not at all. They never had written much, not that it mattered since she couldn't read a lick.

Neighbors were like kin in these parts. She had a couple who tended her. Old Mr. Klinker brought Sister Georgia excess from his garden in the summers. Oh, neither of them thought of it as excess. She thought of it as God's bounty. He thought of it as the way you did for folks. And Verna, she carried groceries to Georgia twice a month and took her to the clinic when she needed.

It wasn't until those darn germs came full on that she'd taken to spending most of her time in bed. Verna or Verna's daughter, Betsy, came by to check on her with some regularity when it first began. They'd brought groceries and stories of what was happening. The stories were important to Sister Georgia. She used to listen to the radio, but it had cut off one day and never cut back on. She'd thought to ask if anyone knew of a radio wasn't being used, but she hadn't done it, not wanting to be a burden. Most folks had cable TV these days, but Georgia didn't have the money. She'd heard tell that some even had something called *why-fight* that they hooked their computers up to. Georgia didn't believe in fighting, but she could tell it didn't have nothin' to do with that anyway. It was beyond her in so many ways she couldn't even begin to imagine and she didn't try. Now being a burden was exactly what she'd become. If she'd a only asked back then, maybe the radio would bring her some comfort now. It was too late for that. And so much else.

The stories they'd brung along most recent was tales of woe, every one. So many had died, were dying. Stories of diarrhea for this one and fevers for that one. Tales of blood that poured out of bodies like no tomorrow. True enough. There weren't no tomorrow for any of 'em that had the blood running away from 'em like tryin' to outrun a tornado. Couldn't be done. There were people she was just as glad were gone and people she was gonna miss. She cried when they told her Old Mr. Klinker had died alone trying to seed his garden for the coming crop. Always a worker, that man. Right till the end.

RED RAIN CONFIRMED IN HAWAII

Honolulu, HI—Homeland Security today announced a threat to national health and safety. In consultation with the CDC and the Surgeon General, the scientific community announced the credible threat of Red Rain.

Red Rain contains harmful elements to human life, not unlike the acid rain of the '80s, referred to as Black Rain. It is believed the recent heavy rains experienced throughout the South Pacific, especially the Hawaiian Islands, were seeded with bacteria by those who would seek to harm the U.S. and its citizens.

Herman Shields of the CDC explained it this way: "Think of the rain as a delivery coming from an unknown source, much as the U.S. post was used to mail anthrax shortly after the turn of the century. However, an individual opened an anthrax package, and only those who came in direct contact with the spores could be contaminated. Red Rain could be much more deadly because it falls on anyone who is outside."

It's currently unknown how long bacteria in rain could remain deadly, living inside puddles and waterways such as streams or the ocean.

While seeding clouds is a longstanding practice for changing weather, there is no evidence it has been used for terrorism. Evidence that the recent storm carried bacteria is unproven, though government officials cite several reasons for today's unprecedented announcement.

First, tests of the windward coastal waters the week following the rains contained high levels of *E. Coli*, resulting in warnings for residents to stay out of the waters.

Second, intel recovered by Homeland Security indicated the possibility of a wide-spread bio-hazard on the horizon. While the phrase "on the horizon" often indicates a time reference, in this case experts believe the usage was intended to mean that bacteria or another biological weapon of mass destruction could be delivered "at the horizon," referring to the widespread effect of the method of delivery: rain.

Third, CIA intel showed multiple rockets fired into the air from various Southern Pacific locations on the fourth day of the rain event. This increases the terrorism concern since cloud seeding did not make it rain, but may have used an already active storm cell to deliver bacteria to the islands.

Fourth, the number of *E. Coli*-borne illnesses in Hawaii was higher than expected for normal contamination, such as sewage overflows. This evidence is most difficult to assess. Because Hawaii is a tourist destination, many who were exposed may not have sought clinical treatment while still on the islands. Additionally, incubation periods vary by individual due to the health of individual immune systems, which further complicates the assessment. However, the number of illnesses in the entire Hawaiian Island chain, and in particularly Kauai, increased greatly during the month following the storms.

At this time, there is no way to be certain if the rain of February 24 - March 5 was actually Red Rain. Nor is there certainty that rain can deliver bacteria successfully. However, Homeland Security considers this threat credible, until and unless investigation proves otherwise. It has warned the nation that remaining indoors during future rainstorms may be required if evidence of a terrorist threat is present.

Gary had the page in his pocket. He made sure not to look at the man touching his nose when anyone else might see, but he stole peeks at it, excited by the prohibited behavior. He carried the picture around for a couple days, waiting for the right opportunity. He had to be sure no one but Frank would see, and he had to be careful not to tell that he sometimes did just what the man in red was doing: touch his nose. He'd wondered if he should even show it to him. Frank might tell his dad. He'd done that before, when they were little. Gary had confided that he wasn't taking his AB pill every day. He'd thought it was an act against his mother, not swallowing the pill she so carefully doled out every morning. He didn't have any reason for not taking it other than to act independently of her and be funny. So he'd told Frank, to get a reaction. He'd gotten one all right, but not the one he'd expected.

"That's not smart," Frank told him.

"It's funny though, right?"

"It's dangerous."

"Seriously? It's just a pill."

"I'm gonna tell my dad."

"Why?"

"It's against the rules."

"Yeah, that's why it's funny."

"No, that's why it's dangerous. My dad says it's important to always tell when someone breaks the rules. Well, he usually says the law, but we're kids, same thing."

"Don't tell your dad. I'll get in trouble."

"You'll only get what's fair. What you've got coming."

"Please, Frank, don't tell. I'll take them from now on. I didn't know it was such a big deal."

Frank told. *Surprise.* And Frank's dad called his dad who told his mom. And the next thing Gary knew he was on restriction. He wasn't allowed to use his cell except to contact his mom, and his computer Internet connection was killed for two weeks.

As he remembered the story, he hoped this wouldn't be a repeat. But they weren't 7 anymore. They were 12 and this was something that had to be shared. It wasn't breaking a rule, just showing it. This was just a funny "artifact," that's what Ms. Gleason would call it, an "artifact of the past." He was sure they tried to hide things like this from kids, that's why he hadn't told his mom he found it. But it couldn't hurt anything. This was just a piece of paper with a silly man doing something stupid. OK, what he was doing was outlawed, but still...

***

Distracted by a movement in the crowd, Trevor noticed an older spectator swipe his fingers under his nose, touching himself and whatever was on his face. It still happened among that generation. *Habits learned late, do not take.* That mantra was an abomination to Trevor. In moments of distraction older people were prone to "accidental touches," as his parents labeled them. The habits they learned early—catching a sneeze in their hands, wiping grime out of their eyes—were bad habits for life. His parents had asked him to ignore incidental touches and begged for his leniency, offering that they were prone to it themselves.

To Trevor it was illegal, immoral and dangerous. Trevor looked around for a police officer.

Perhaps he could let it slide. He refocused on the Tulip Festival dancers, appreciating the boys' small black caps, the girls' large pointed white wings. But he couldn't stop thinking about the touch he'd witnessed. It wasn't just that he was a good citizen, Trevor truly saw FaceTouching as the devil's funhouse. He looked across at the old man again. This time the man looked around and then rubbed the edge of his nose vigorously. It was deliberate!

That was it. The man had to be reported.

Trevor had a habit of informing on rule breakers. His father used to suggest he pipe down because no one liked a tattletale, a truism that didn't affect Trevor. For more than a year he had a nearly standing appointment reporting to his high school principal. The transgressions he recounted were welcomed at first, but as Trevor focused more and more narrowly on the smallest of infractions, he was finally told he was being petty. It was suggested that he didn't need to be so serious, he should have some fun.

Perhaps it wasn't fun in a typical sense, but Trevor was compelled to notice the stupid, the mean, the rule-breaking activities of his peers. He learned to stop reporting them, though he never stopped keeping track. He kept his record of transgressions on his handheld, always ready for an entry. It wasn't hard to hide this activity, the other students ignored Trevor. They might have been meaner had they known about the list. They could have hazed him, beaten him, or even set him up to take a fall for a far bigger crime than he reported.

But they did none of those things. From their perspective, Trevor simply didn't exist.

Trevor scanned the crowd again. There, near the man, was an officer who clearly hadn't noticed the man's behavior. They were across the street, both of them. Trevor couldn't disrupt the dancing. He moved down the block, carefully avoiding touching anyone, worrying that all people carried bacteria that he didn't want to rub off on him. It was difficult to not touch others while keeping an eye on both the man and the officer as the crowd pressed forward to see the dancers. By the time he reached the corner he couldn't see either of them anymore. He crossed the street and moved toward the man until he regained sight of him. When he reached the officer, Trevor cleared his throat to get his attention. Music, clogging and laughter drowned out his attempt. Finally, Trevor stepped between the policeman and the street so the officer's gaze fell on him.

Trevor reported what he'd seen, pointing out the old man. The officer thanked him, and made his way toward the man. Just as the man raised his hand toward his face, the officer caught the man's arm in his own gloved hand, stopping him abruptly. "I wouldn't touch my face, if I were you."

"Oh, I wouldn't, officer."

The officer nodded toward Trevor. "Young man over there reported he saw you do just that." The older man tried to see his accuser but the officer intentionally blocked his view. "What matters is what you did."

"I have an itch. Perhaps I didn't realize what I was doing. I grew up before the Bans. If I scratched my nose, I shouldn't have. I'm sorry, officer."

"Sir, you're out here among a lot of young people, not just the dancers, parents watching have babies with them and small ones. Not one of them is touching themselves. You need to take a lesson."

"Yes, officer. I realize…"

"Given this crowd, I should run you in. You're putting all these folks at risk."

"I never intended…"

"The best of intentions don't matter, actions matter. What's your name, sir?"

"Alto Dijkstra."

"And what village do you live in?"

"Grand Haven."

"I will record this infraction, Mr. Dijkstra. It you're caught again, it won't be just a warning you'll get."

"Thank you, officer. That's mighty kind."

"Just keep your hands from touching yourself. That's what the law demands. It's what safety requires."

Dijkstra nodded as the officer walked away. Then he sneered after him. Dijkstra didn't believe in abstention. He believed his face should be his own domain. *If he wanted to touch it…* Just not in public. Clearly not in public. Not anymore.

Fomite Assessment Team Releases Results: How Bacteria Spread

The Fomite Assessment Team (FAT) today released data from its yearlong study of how bacteria breed and spread. Funded by the National Institute of Health (NIH) and published in this month's edition of the *Public Health Watch Quarterly*, FAT's study reports how bacteria attach themselves to surfaces (fomites) and then infect individuals who come in contact with those surfaces.

The research should be of great use to scientists and public health officials working to assess the risks of contact with particular bacterial strains. The ultimate objective of the FAT is to identify ways to improve human health through monitoring and awareness of the function of fomites.

Health risks are assessed according to the following factors: 1) the types of dangerous bacteria, 2) the possible depositing agents (not only people, but animals, insects, and natural resources like wind and water), 3) the surfaces available for transmission, 4) the frequency of face touches, and 5) the factors influencing compromised human immune systems.

Scientific Background

It has been known for some time that bacteria can be deposited on a surface, making that surface a fomite (Williams et al 2011). It follows that individuals can later pick up those bacteria from fomites and become ill. To date, studies have focused on particular bacteria (Cohn 2013; Hatheway 2024; Wheelis et al 2033), on the environmental factors that keep bacteria alive (Ehrenberg 2035; Breed et al 2035), and on particular kinds of surfaces that tend to collect massive quantities of bacteria, such as cell phones (Famurewa and David 2009). The route bacteria follow to enter the body (Doherty 2032) and the frequency of face touching in the population (Mears 2010; Buckthorn 2029) have also been studied. Recent studies of compromised immune systems (Lamoureux 2035) and the overuse of antibiotics (Nobre 2034; Leone 2035) have also provided data useful to public health officials. Hospitals have recently come under scrutiny for their lack of sterile procedures, making them a primary interest of further fomite research (Weinstein 2034).

New Discoveries

What has not been scientifically recognized until now is the number of combinations of factors that create a far more lethal environment than was heretofore imagined. A supercomputer has been used to analyze rich data collected from research studies conducted around the globe. A complete list of the studies is included in the *Public Health Watch Quarterly* issue devoted to fomites.

By using the supercomputer to link, combine and cross-reference studies, data integrity is maintained while varied studies can be examined in combination. Making this data available online is crucial to continued scientific research.

Because bacteria breed and spread so rapaciously, the NIH has had to develop special protocols for use with these data.

Hope for Future

A vast range of professionals are being encouraged to join this research project, not just health officials and biologists, but social scientists, civil engineers, and politicians as well. The NIH hopes to not only learn more about bacteria and fomites from the research, but to help shape public policies that will keep Americans safe from bacterial diseases in the future.

Gary's mom found the book while cleaning. It was sandwiched between the mattress and the frame. When she saw it wasn't pornography, she almost put it back. *He wouldn't hide something that wasn't dangerous or embarrassing.* Lightweight, more cover than pages, the pictures bright and fanciful, it was so obviously a children's book, incongruous, hidden within the bed. As she began reading, she smiled in recognition. She'd heard this often as a child. When she found the missing page, her mind raced. The sing-song rhyme had a way of sticking. She read the lines preceding the page ripped from the binding:

> He spoke not a word, but went straight to his work, And filled all the stockings, then turned with a jerk.

"Then turned with a jerk," she repeated, until suddenly she had it, "And putting a finger inside of his nose." *Oh my god, no! That couldn't be right. Could it?* She typed the phrase into the search engine on her computer. Immediately she saw what she wanted: "And laying a finger aside of his nose." *Aside*, what did *aside* mean? Maybe it wasn't really touching the nose. Dictionary.com would know: "Aside: next to." Most definitions sounded like they were to the side of or a distance apart. And yet with a nose, how could it be anything but touching the nose? She imagined it with her mind's eye, she didn't raise a hand.

It must be a way of saying *outside* rather than *inside* the nostril, but the more she considered it, the more she was convinced it meant touching the nose. How could touching someone's nose be part of a children's story? That's what it was, right? *The Night Before Christmas* was a children's fable, a supposedly innocent story meant to teach the young to be good. *This wasn't good. This wasn't good at all.*

She had been a young adult when the Touch Ban was first instituted, but this story came from her childhood. She had memories of the story, the line had come back to her. When she left home, her parents must not have followed the mandates to get rid of all touching references in the home. Maybe they thought this Christmas story was exempt. Maybe they didn't think of it at all. Her parents weren't resisters, but they wouldn't have cared much about the details. "Life had been fine before government fucked everything up" was their frequent lament.

Now her son had this page, this contraband, in his possession. She hoped against hope that he hadn't taken it out of the house, especially not to show Frank, the son of a Special Forces Officer. Before the thought had fully formed, she realized she was too late. She picked up her cell to text Gary. But what could she write that he'd understand without it being detectable? "Eyes, nose, fingers, toes" would communicate to him, but censors could pick up those words for sure. "Stories of the past should stay in the past." No, the "past" would get their attention, too. "Please don't share what's not yours." That was innocuous. Families must text that kind of thing all the time. But would he understand? She'd have to hope so. She thumbed it in and hit send.

***

As a biologist, whether working for Big Pharma or teaching at the university, I tended to work late. When I was home, I usually read, I rarely watched TV. In my generation, TV-viewing was still a common entertainment. I tended to watch the evening news before bed. It was a ritual that relaxed me. Other than that, it was rare for me to sit down and watch a program. The wife liked TV. She'd spend a couple hours in the evening watching dramas or occasionally reality TV. Back before the Touch Ban there was a show for a couple seasons called *Risky Business*. Sometimes she'd even call me in to see a segment. It was a lot like the old candid camera. Hard to believe they could pull that off with all the public cams everywhere that could be called up on the Internet. But evidently they could. I never was sure how much *reality* was in reality TV and this was no exception. The premise of *Risky Business* was that they'd catch people doing things they shouldn't. As I say, it was before the ban on touching our faces, but germs were already a threat of a lower magnitude. So while some episodes offered norm-breaching opportunities that didn't involve germs, some did.

The one I remember most vividly was this guy standing at a mushroom bar. For a while, mushrooms were all the rage among the foodies. This guy was waiting to order and there was a sampler cup sitting in front of him. It held something popular like chanterelle, porcini or morel. The important thing was it was sitting there when he walked up. The barista said he had to eat what he had before she would serve him another variety. He told her it wasn't his. She said a sample was a sample was a sample and she could only serve one at a time. "Did you put it there?" he asked. "I'm the only person working," she answered evasively. "I don't know who might have touched it," he countered. "There could be germs." She laughed. "It's a mushroom, a fungus—it doesn't get any more dangerous than that."

By this time the audience could see a line forming behind the guy. Tensions were rising and the next person in line started making a show of waiting. He hurrumphed or said something, I can't recall. But the next thing we knew the barista was offering that same sampler to the next person in line, who took it and started to put it to his mouth when suddenly the first guy knocked it out of his hand. The second guy had no idea what had gone on. He just saw red, he thought the first guy was an asshole who needed to learn a lesson. The second guy draws back to punch the first, when suddenly the first yells, "It was contaminated! I was trying to save your life." That stopped everything. Cold. The guy preparing the punch halted, and asked, "Really, man?"

Then the barista broke into laughter and the star of the show stepped out from behind the counter and directly between the two. He was holding a microphone—actually *holding* one, so old-fashioned it was anachronistic. "Risky Business," he proclaimed with a big show of his arms reaching wide to fill the camera. The first guy just stood there stunned. The second guy joined the barista in laughing. I've always wondered if he was a plant, that second guy.

The TV star put his free arm, the one without the mic, around the first guy's shoulders and pulled him in. "Good man!" the star intoned. "You're a winner. You didn't fall for the bait." Then the music underscore shifted, another reason I always wondered about the "reality" of it all, that they took the time to lay sound tracks underneath. Anyway, the score shifted to a downward set of notes that they used to suggest someone wasn't fun. "Looks like you'll live a long, dull, risk-free life," said the star. The segment ended with a beautiful young woman delivering that day's prize.

I have no idea what the prize was. I was too taken with the juxtaposition. The guy gets called a winner and gets a prize, but his life will be "dull" and "long" and the music told us that wasn't what we should want. The show needed risk-takers. That's what made us watch, being voyeurs rather than engaging in behavior we were too afraid of to try ourselves. That was the drama.

I always thought that episode would have been on the cutting room floor except for the strong visual of knocking the cup away and the near-fight that ensued. That made good television. Funny what passed for entertainment. That segment went viral, as I recall. In fact, that may have been when I learned "going viral" had come to mean that a piece of video or some other cultural artifact had been viewed on the Internet by millions of people. Seeking out such pieces of Americana was a favored pastime. It was a way people filled the hours when they weren't sleeping or working.

There were bacterial epidemics cropping up all around us, but "going viral" was a good thing.

***

Sister Georgia lay in bed trying to remember when someone last visited. She thought it was more than a week ago. Verna came. *Or was it Betsy?* That was right, it was Betsy 'cause she'd said Verna was sickly. Georgia had sent her prayers. Now she worried maybe Verna didn't make it. It wasn't like her to not check in.

Yesterday, no, it was two days ago, she was pretty sure that was when she ate the last saltine. That was it—no food left. The day before that she'd spent what energy she had digging through her drawer and a box she kept what-all in. She found a single half-full plastic box of them old green tic-tacs. Couldn't remember how long ago she'd had a liking for those, but it must'a been years. That had been her supper that night. Wasn't bad either. They tasted minty and there was a definite crunch to each little BB. She mostly sucked 'em to make 'em last and not get 'em stuck in her dentures. She couldn't resist, though, and bit each one as it got tiny so she'd have more of a sense of eating something.

Sister Georgia stopped and recited, "The Lord is my Shepherd, I shall not want." She knew the passage by heart. She tried to imagine the restful waters, which always brought her a sense of peace. When her stomach began to growl and tighten, she reminded herself, "The Lord provides." He'd been a comfort to her all her life. When she was joyful, she thanked Him. When she was angry, she asked that this pass. When she was anxious, as she was now, she gently told Him that she was in His service and would do His will, a gentle reminder of her devotion. With a whole world to worry about and so much destruction going on, she knew the Lord had more important things on His mind. She just wanted to make sure He remembered her, that was all. She was familiar with hunger, if not its friend. She could endure.

***

Frank was the teacher's pet. But Gary's mom referred to Frank as "a real threat." By which she meant Frank would get Gary into big trouble.

Frank wasn't close to his dad anymore. He complained about what a dweeb his dad was. Gary wasn't sure what "dweeb" meant, but when Frank said it, there was a little scowl that appeared in the corner of his mouth. It was clearly not something Gary wanted to be called. The tone of Frank's voice said "don't ask," so he never had.

Gary saw Frank walking toward him. He couldn't see anyone else. This was his chance. "Frank!" he called and waved. Frank smiled, gave him the sign, and sauntered over, acting much older than he actually was.

"Hey, Garbles! How ya doing?"

"Frank, I need to show you something." Gary pulled the page from his pocket and unfolded it. Before opening the last fold he looked Frank in the eye. "You can't tell anyone about this. Not Ms. Gleason, not Jimmy, and certainly not your dad. Do you promise?"

"You know me, Garbles, I'm your bud. Whacha got there?" Frank reached out and tried to grab the page, but Gary saw it coming and dodged.

"My hands only," said Gary. "Look, but don't touch."

"OK, OK. Open, sesame."

"I found this in our garage, in my mom's old stuff. It's out of a book."

"I can tell that. Let me see what makes it worth all this dancing around."

Gary opened the page and held it where Frank could see it. "Man, oh man!" Frank screamed. "This is fantastic! Why is he touching himself? That finger's right on his nose. Man, oh man!"

"Shhhh!" Gary looked around. Luckily they were still alone. "Can you believe it?"

"You could get a lot for that on Re-Buy."

"Don't even think about it. I don't need my mom finding out."

"Or the police."

"Why would they care?"

"It's about touching."

Gary shrugged.

"You hid it from your mom," Frank said. "You made me promise. You clearly think it's dangerous. You can't play innocent with me. I know you."

"What should I do with it?"

"Give it to me for safekeeping."

"Funny," Gary said. "That I'm *not* doing. I don't know what it's worth, but I know it's valuable—somehow." He carefully re-folded the page and stuck it back in his pocket. "Are we gonna go or not?"

"You bet, I wasn't the one holding us up by pulling contraband out of my pocket."

***

Cathy couldn't stop herself. She was always telling stories. It wasn't merely reminiscence. It wasn't exactly educational. Mostly, it was the extrovert in her. She liked to talk, and the easiest way to do that with Maggie was to talk of times gone by. Cathy believed every story revealed something new. When Maggie tuned out or jumped to the conclusion, Cathy was embarrassed, but she just kept talking.

"I remember giving platelets at the hospital when I was just a little girl. By that time no one was donating just for the good of humanity, but we still donated for family. They hadn't perfected bloodless blood yet and when it was someone close, no one wanted a loved one to be the guinea pig. This donation was for my uncle Tomás, who was dying from HUS.

"Anyway, the phlebotomist who drew my blood was careful to put on her rubber gloves. She checked to ensure there were no holes. She popped the end of each finger so it made a tight connection on her hand.

"Then she proceeded to push her hair back behind her ears, repeatedly. This was before the Touch Ban, but it was disgusting nonetheless. The gloves had been sterile, at least that was the idea. Then she threw something away and, in the process, touched the trashcan. It didn't have a foot pedal. Not like today. She touched everything—the tubing for the blood of course, but also the remote for the entertainment station, the paperwork I'd handed her ungloved, the swabs and antibacterials, but also another phlebotomist with an itch. Mind you, the other blood worker had the good sense not to touch herself while gloved, but mine was more than happy to help her out. I wanted to scream, 'Stop it! Just stop touching everything!' But I feared the reprisals if I made a fuss. I said something to my dad, but he told me to keep still. That's what he always told me. You know me, I fade into the background when I can. Don't give me that look."

"Look? What look?" Maggie said.

"I never draw attention to myself."

"No?"

"No. I talk to people but they enjoy that."

Maggie shook her head.

"Oh never mind," Cathy went on, "I lived to tell the tale so she didn't transmit anything to me. Maybe it's not much of a story. Giving blood wasn't much use anyway. Uncle Tomás didn't live very long."

"Was it bean sprouts or spinach that killed him?"

"It was *E. Coli*, but it was on bean sprouts. But back then we all thought fresh veggies were healthy. Salads were popular. We'd been told we could get the most vitamins and minerals that way. We were told antioxidants and fiber and such were stronger in uncooked produce. They were supposed to provide heart health and prevent cancer and keep you slim."

"All those lies to get you to do what they wanted you to," Maggie said.

"If only Tomás hadn't gone to Germany."

"It's not like there weren't ample opportunities to contract *E. Coli* here at home."

"True," Cathy said, "but it still seemed rare then. I remember the family became very anti-German, anti-foreign. We hadn't been before that. But after..."

"A common story, mother. Wasn't there a raw foods movement?"

"There was, but Tomás wasn't that extreme. He ate for health, he said. I told him it would be the death of him."

"Oh, mother!"

"I never meant it. Heaven help me. I was only a little girl, 10 or so. I wanted to enjoy myself and I always loved eating. Couldn't see why I should deprive myself of things I loved, whether that was ice cream or a juicy steak or whatever."

"That's something I've always liked about you, mother. You've always known how to appreciate what you have."

***

The professor was a biologist, working for Big Pharma. He'd been playing racquetball with one of the young technicians from the lab. They decided to stop and have a bite at a fast food place before heading home to their wives. When they walked into the restaurant, the techie reached for the AB wash. Before he could squirt it into his hands, the professor began his rant. "Don't do it. Don't use their antibacterials. They're all broad spectrum."

"Yeah," the young technician said, "that's good, right? They'll kill everything."

"That's bad—they kill everything. There are many good bacteria."

"I don't have any friends among 'em."

"Oh, but you do," the professor said. "Take *E. Coli* for example."

"I'd rather not. It's deadly."

"It's gotten a bad rep. Can't argue with that. What I can argue with is thinking of *E. Coli* as evil. You and I both have *E. Coli* right now."

The young tech got a horrified look on his face. He was clearly worried the professor was referencing something that had happened at the lab. "Shouldn't we do something about that? Go to the emergency room? Take antibiotics?"

"Not at all. *E. Coli* is part of our digestive systems. We couldn't break down food without it."

"No, professor, that can't be. *E. Coli* comes from cow shit and it's deadly. I saw it in the news."

"I bet you did. The news is full of fear mongering."

The tech shook his head. He took the news at face value.

They were just inside the swinging doors. Someone brushed past them, mumbling about how inconsiderate they were. The professor moved them out of the way to continue the conversation.

"A particular strain of *E. Coli*—*O157:H7* to be precise—has crossed the species barrier and is dangerous to humans. That's a fact, if not news, exactly. But that's *one* strain."

"*E. Coli* is *E. Coli*."

"That it's not, my friend. Let's call *O157:H7* bad *E. Coli* for simplicity sake and that which we carry in our gut, good *E. Coli*, OK?"

"Sure, whatev. Mind if we order?"

"This won't take long, I promise."

"I know you, professor. You can talk endlessly about shit. But go ahead. You've got me curious. Just remember I'm hungry."

"OK. So good *E. Coli* you don't even know about, and that's OK, because it's good—good for you and good at doing its job, which is breaking down your food so you can get at the nutrients. Bad *E. Coli*, on the other hand, invades your system. It used to arrive via feces, so the bad was obvious. Now it often comes in on our food, not obvious at all. When we eat it, it starts to digest us instead of our food. It traveled in on our food, but why eat its host? And yet I'd classify it as parasitic, so..."

"You lost me."

"Sorry, bit of a tangent."

"Already? Curb the tangents or I'm ordering."

"You got it. Point is, some bacteria, even some with the same common name like *E. Coli*, come in good, useful forms and in bad, harmful ones. Let me try an analogy. Let's say bacteria are like people."

"OK."

"There are good people and bad people. Those you want to be friends with and those you wish to never see, never encounter even. None of us want to be near murderers, for example."

"Right. Gotcha."

"But even if you're in favor of the death penalty, even if you want murderers and rapists dead, that doesn't mean you'd want to kill all the people you didn't like."

"Well, no. Not liking them doesn't make them bad."

"Exactly. And just because some bacteria are bad, doesn't mean we should fear and kill all bacteria. See where I'm going here?"

"Sort of," the tech conceded. "It rubs me the wrong way, though. I mean, a bad person I can recognize as a bad person.

I can see the look in the eyes, hear the anger in the yelling, fear the gun in the hand. But I can't see any bacteria, let alone distinguish which are good and which are bad. So if I use AB wash I know I'm killing bad ones."

"But there's collateral damage, like when an army accidentally kills civilians in a bombing. With antibacterials in your soap, or in AB wash, you're killing the good bacteria, too."

"I'm OK with that." The techie was focused on the menu.

"We'll eat in a moment. You want clean hands before we do." The tech nodded. "I believe you'll be safer if I get to finish explaining this to you. Then you can make an educated choice."

"OK," the young man nodded begrudgingly. The professor was smart but also longwinded. The smell of fried meat was attractive.

"You should want the good bacteria to do things for you—to aid in digestion, to increase mineral absorption, to strengthen your immune system, to create antibiotics, to develop yogurt and cheese, like the cheese you'll likely want on the burger you're gonna order."

"Bacteria makes cheese?"

The professor nodded.

The tech sighed. "You make the world too complicated."

"The world's already complicated. I didn't have anything to do with that. This is just an area where I want you—well, not just you, everyone really—I want everyone to recognize the complexity of bacterial life rather than destroy all of it."

"You've gotten me to think about it. But signs are everywhere telling me to wash my hands after I touch anything. Even offering me AB wash right here in the fast food joint."

"Wash your hands. Yes. I agree. But just use hot water, not 99% bacteria-killing soaps and washes."

"What good's that gonna do?"

"Hot water and friction will eliminate the bad bacteria from the outside of your hands and leave the good bacteria intact. That system's been working for thousands of years."

"Wow," the tech said. "I hadn't thought about it that way. You're fighting an uphill battle, professor."

"And I'm losing. But I'm going to keep fighting. I believe people are prejudiced against bacteria."

"If you say so. Mind if I wash my hands now?"

"Go ahead. Use the bathroom."

"I will," the tech said, heading into the men's room. "And I won't use AB wash. How's that?"

"One down, millions to go!"

***

Sister Georgia sat at her kitchen table, watching out the window. She wanted to go out to her rocker, but she was unstable. Several days had passed since she ate the last cracker. She had searched, as energy would allow, for any other lost bits that might be hiding, but had found nothing after the tic-tacs. She'd always made sure to empty pockets of candies and such so bugs wouldn't invade. Now she wished she'd been less careful about that. Up the road, leading out of the holler, she saw Betsy and got herself up so she could open the door and call to her. Betsy waved her free hand. Georgia could see that she was carrying a small bag.

By the time Betsy arrived, Georgia was standing on her porch.

"Sister Georgia," Betsy said in a tone that merely acknowledged.

Georgia could see the girl was sick. *Girl?* Funny she still thought of her that way at 30-some years of age. But she was Verna's girl, always would be. Betsy handed the paper sack up to Georgia, who took it gratefully.

"Thank you, Betsy. I've been wondering after you. It's been awhile. Can you sit?"

"Mama died, Georgia. I'm sorry to just spring it like that. But there ain't no reason not to just tell it."

"Not Verna! Not my Verna!" Georgia sank down onto her rocker and placed the bag at her feet. She hadn't even looked into it yet, hungry as she was.

"It happened quick. At least there's that. But then I was supposed to stay under quarantine. Them's the rules now. I stayed more than a week. I got her buried myself. Ain't nobody'll take bodies no more. Junebug helped dig the hole. He wouldn't help carry her and I didn't blame him for that. But as long as I stayed in the house he was willing to dig."

"That was a blessing. Having Junebug to help you."

"Yes, ma'am. That's one way a looking at it." A moment passed as both women considered this death so close at hand.

"I'm supposed to still be stuck in that house, but I couldn't see it. As many germs inside as out. Why should I stay there?"

"It's good you got out. You look a little peak-ed. You feel OK?"

"Good enough to walk to Henry's store." Betsy didn't look directly at Georgia. She was not ready to admit she was sick. She didn't want to think she could infect Georgia. But then Verna could'a infected her too. She was here right before it hit her hard.

"The Lord provides," Georgia said.

"There weren't no one at the store," Betsy continued, "and almost nothin' left on the shelves. Looked almost like locusts had gotten to a mid-summer garden. There was a piece of paper people had writ down what they took, but clearly, only some folks did that. Can you imagine? Takin' from Henry without no never mind?"

"No 'em, I can't imagine. Henry's always let folks eat on credit. That's no way to do him."

"He may be dead. Or gone. Weren't no sign of anyone, like I said. And the mind does wander about these days, thinking the worst things might a happened to the best a people. And that was Henry."

"Yes 'em, sure enough he a good man."

"So there's not much there for you, but I did what I could. Had to keep some for myself."

"I thank you for your kindness. Anything is appreciated. I haven't eaten in awhile."

"Georgia, I'm sorry. I know mama took good care a' you all these years."

"She has indeed. Just like a daughter to me, your mama." Georgia sniffled and wiped at her right eye, catching a tear as it rolled out.

"Don't be touchin' your face, Georgia. I know mama told you that. And now mama's gone."

"The Lord bless and keep her."

Betsy looked off into the hills. She wasn't dealing so well with God these days. "I'll do my best for you, Sister Georgia. But I gotta warn you, it may be awhile and it may not be much I can bring. My trip to Henry's has left me a little fretful of what to do next."

"I'll pray for you."

"Thank you. Tho' I'm not sure what good that will do."

"Betsy, when did you lose your faith?"

"I'm losing it day-by-day, Georgia. This superbug, this germ or bacteria or whatever, is enough to destroy my faith. How could God create something like this? Even if man made it, how can He let it kill like this?" Betsy turned away from Georgia. She got to her feet.

"Honey, you can't question. Ya just gotta trust in the Lord."

"Georgia, you pray for my faith and you pray for me to return. And if the Lord sees fit for that to happen, we'll talk about it further."

"The Lord bless you and keep you, Betsy. And thank you for your kindness. My old body's gonna be mighty happy to enjoy this food you brung."

Betsy was already off the porch before Georgia finished speaking. She turned and gave a small nod of her head and walked back up the road, away from the holler. It wasn't like Betsy to not let Georgia finish speaking, it was impolite, but nothing was like it should be, so it shouldn't surprise.

Georgia struggled to get out of her rocker. When she got to standing, she wobbled into her house, careful to step over the doorjamb. She'd tripped on that recently and almost fell. She sat the bag on the table and opened it. Inside she found four small plastic packages that felt like little bricks. Looked like they had to be cooked in water. She'd never tried them before and they didn't feel like much. *Beggars can't be choosers.* The Lord was providing. She was thankful. There were three cans. One had something brown and smooth looking. It wasn't familiar and she couldn't read the label. Another was mushrooms which she'd never cared for. And the final can, at last, a good one, a can of green beans. *Thank you, Lord.* Sister Georgia looked up and laid her right hand respectfully on her chest as she bowed her head.

She looked the items over. She was hungry and the sight of this food, even food she wouldn't like the taste of, made her stomach growl. She needed to eat. She selected one of the ramen packages since there were several. She put the rest of her meager goods away. It helped her feel normal. For a moment, she was hopeful. She heated a pot of water and dropped the noodles in. She was surprised when a small foil packet fell into the pan. She got a large spoon and fished it out. She tore the end of it open and held it to her nose. It smelled of salt and something else. She touched it to her tongue. It had a strong, but not entirely unpleasant taste. She looked at the pan of water and decided to add part of the packet. If she liked it, she could add more later.

The noodles expanded and softened. Georgia smiled at the quantity. That could be two meals, she decided. There were seven items in the bag. Verna always brought food every two weeks. Hopefully Betsy would do the same. She decided that meant half an item a day. It wouldn't be much, but it would help get her through. She spooned half of the noodles into a bowl and poured in some of the liquid, too. That'd help her feel full. She put the lid on the pot and sat it back down on the stove. She carefully carried her bowl to the table. She reached back for the spoon she'd used earlier. She gave thanks for this bounty. The word curled the edge of her mouth. For the briefest moment she realized that bounty was a rather large word for the slim pickin's in front of her. She took a bite.

Kind of bland, but chewing on something was real nice.

No Survivors Found

Klawosk, AK — A HAZMAT team completed its search of a small southeastern Alaska island devastated by *Cha-Cha MRSA*. Officials expected to find a portion of the small population still alive from last fall's outbreak, but after two weeks of scouring the local forest, they found no survivors.

"It appears that a small number of people did escape the initial outbreak and retreat into the woods," said Jerry Saunders, HAZMAT Project Head. "Unfortunately, it was a very hard winter. We suspect the snow pack made hunting impossible and the winter was just too much to bear."

"Our hearts are with the families of those lost in this tragedy," said Alaska Governor Katrina Friese. "Had the Lower 48 cared, relief might have arrived earlier and the outcome may have been less bleak."

Today's discovery adds fuel to an already heated debate in Washington, where concerns about *Cha-Cha MRSA* continue to mount. Several Big Pharma CEOs were called to the Surgeon General's office to report on progress in the development of antibiotics capable of diminishing the death rates from all forms of *MRSA*, now with heightened interest in the *Cha-Cha* strain. While the death rate from most *MRSA* strains ranges from 8-36%, the as-yet-unique *Cha-Cha* strain discovered in Alaska appears to kill all humans who encounter it.

Neither the Surgeon General nor any of the CEOs were available for comment, but speculation from lab techs in three Big Pharma operations told reporters that very little lab space is being devoted to this project.

One source, unwilling to allow his name to be used for fear of reprisals, said his company's public relations releases state they are working on an AB product to treat *MRSA*, but he personally knows no one who is working on the project. As a Project Director who meets monthly with all PDs, he found this odd, and suggested it meant very little is being done on the project.

Gary's mother called out the moment he walked in the door. "Didn't you get my text?"

"What text?" Gary pulled his cell from his pocket and saw the blinking signal. "Sorry. Frank and I were busy. I had the volume down. Please don't share what's not yours. What's it mean?"

"Frank? You were with Frank!"

"Yeah, I told you that. I told you we were gonna go skateboarding after school."

"Skateboarding? Where?"

"Oh, mom. Over near the tracks where there's that lumber pile."

"I don't like that area. It's dangerous. But you're almost a teenager, I can't run your life. I know that. I have to trust you, trust you to start making adult decisions."

Gary pointed his phone at his mother. "What did you not want me to share?"

"I was picking up your room today and discovered a book." Gary's eyes got big. "There was a page missing." He nodded slightly. "Gary, I know what's on that page. The book was from my childhood. There's nose-touching, isn't there?"

"I was just going through your old toys."

"That's OK. I'm not mad. I'm worried. Who did you show it to?"

"Frank."

"Of all people, Gary! You know his dad..."

"But he hates his dad. He won't tell."

"Today he won't tell. Today he's your friend. But what about tomorrow, or next week? You two are always having fallouts. He's such a threat."

"You're always saying that, mom. But he's not. He's not seven anymore like when he told his dad about the pills."

"This is nothing like the pills, Gary. That was about your health. This is about the world we live in. FaceTouching is outlawed."

"Like I don't know that? I know that!"

"But do you know that what you have is considered contraband? Do you know people get jailed for it? Do you know how dangerous it is? If you did, you'd never have taken it out of this house! The question now is what to do. We could burn it, but you've already shown it to Frank. We're already vulnerable. If he turns you in—turns *us* in—and they come looking and don't find it… He's the son of a special forces officer. Who do you think they'll believe?"

"No, mom. First, Frank won't tell. Second, who would believe him? He lies all the time. Third, I'm sorry. I'm so sorry." Gary disappeared into his room. He removed the page from his pocket. He was scared. His mother had succeeded in that.

He looked at the picture. He still thought it was funny to see a man touching his nose. *Habits learned early are habits for life* was the mantra meant to keep children from FaceTouching. Now he saw why it was needed. Evidently, this book had taught his mother to touch her nose. *How weird was that?!*

***

Trevor walked into his bathroom, opened his fly, paused, and washed his hands. He peed, guiding the stream into the toilet. He didn't shake off, he touched a piece of toilet paper to the drops, ensuring no urine got on the floor or on his hands. He tucked himself back in, washed his hands, zipped, washed his hands again. He used the towel to open the door, a simple white hand towel he could bleach. He deposited it in the laundry, pushing the opener with his foot. He washed his hands, wishing he had an air-dryer at home. *Add that to the purchase list.*

He looked at the clock. Time to brush his teeth. He loved the feeling of clean teeth when it was over, but the ritual took time and had to be scheduled. He began the procedure by covering his hair with a surgeon's cap and putting a large bag of the same sterilized paper-thin cotton over his whole head. It was protection from bacteria that might become airborne during flossing and brushing. He performed this ritual at the kitchen sink. It made the sanitizing easier. He was careful to run boiling water and lots of antibacterial down any sink before and after use. He had a ritual:

1. Floss teeth.
2. Pour boiling water over toothbrush.
3. Add antibacterial paste to brush.
4. Brush one tooth at a time, each face thoroughly.
5. Circle the mouth, top set, then bottom.
6. Pour boiling water over toothbrush.
7. Swish with AB mouthwash.

He tried to make sure his rituals had seven steps or three. Twelve was a good number, too, but it was too large to hold that many steps in mind. Everything had a number. Numbers were important. *Numbers create habits and habits keep me safe.*

Yesterday in Holland he had noticed that people were wearing several kinds of masks. There had been talk of masking the Tulip Festival dancers. But at a Holland town meeting, the mayor had deftly ensured that didn't happen. After outlining everything that goes into the festival, the mayor had led a visualization activity.

"Close your eyes. See the dancing." He paused dramatically. "Hear the wooden clogs. Feel the joy. Now imagine, if you will, that the dancers are wearing masks."

After that, the council vote against masking the dancers was hardly a surprise.

Even if the dancers had not been masked, many in the audience were. Some had kerchiefs across their nose and mouth, which, Trevor realized, still exposed their faces when the wind blew. *What do those people think they're accomplishing? Why bother?* There were also simple cone-shaped white or blue paper masks that had been around as long as he could remember. They were decent at preventing bacterial penetration, but they didn't last long. He noticed a few people were trying newer models. Some had plastic-fronted, wraparound masks much like his dental gear. Others were wearing thin films that adhered to their faces and had additional bulbous nose cups to allow oxygen in and catch potential nasal discharge. *Are those nose cups deep enough to keep the drips from the upper lip? That might diminish the hassles and dangers of my runny nose. Research,* he thought, making a note.

No one was wearing a gas mask yet. No one was carrying a personal supply of oxygen.

Trevor was grateful for the quarantine that had moved everyone into their own homes. He felt safest in his own environment, which he kept much cleaner than anything in the public realm. Obvious, right? People have been dying from bacteria. Clearly others don't take sanitation seriously enough. The Confinement—that's what the local press was calling it—was issued last night, and was followed by looting.

"Habits learned early are habits for life," he intoned aloud. He'd been seven, the age of reason, *a good number*, when the FaceTouch Ban was instituted. His parents only had to tell him once not to touch his face. It had made perfect sense to him.

Trevor was all about cleanliness from the very start. *Fastidious* was the word his mother used. *She said it affectionately, but I saw the little tilt of her head.* She had no idea how he came to be this way. Neither she nor her husband was high strung. They'd spent their youth smoking pot and hanging loose. They were laidback by most any standard. They weren't slovenly, it wasn't that. They were just surprised by a son who took everything so seriously, especially cleanliness. Had Trevor been ADD, they'd have understood better, it fit boys. But the OCD characteristics he exhibited caught them off-guard. *They made me who I am. Had they been better at keeping the rules, I might not have needed to be so attentive. My parents get the credit for who I am.*

Trevor thought of this as Day 1 of the Confinement, time for a new start. *My habit will be cleanliness, it will save my life.* He got out the AB cleanser he bought just last week, in bulk, 12

large bottles, in anticipation of this future. He began at the top
and cleaned methodically, down his walls, across all surfaces.
He had no clutter to worry about, but he did have the necessary
materials for living: pans, silverware, a computer. He refused
to have a cell phone. *I think the cell phone waves may actually
create simple-celled bacterial life.* He realized others would say
that bacteria accumulate on cell phones as it does anywhere the
face comes in contact. His computer had a condom, of course,
and it cleaned easily. His kitchenware was kept immaculate.
But today he cleaned every piece again, just to be sure. He
frequently used cotton swabs to make certain he got AB wash
into the smallest of crevices.

When he was through, he removed his no-longer-sterile
gloves and threw them in the trash, closing the bag. He double-
bagged the trash, replaced the trash liner, and walked to his
back door. He turned the knob three times to the right and
then pulled. He tossed the trash bag as far as he could, closed
the door and locked it. He washed his hands, took an AB
towelette—*the safest way to handle the job*—and wiped down
the doorknob and the edge of the door he feared the trash bag
may have touched. The towelette went into the trashcan. *Why
can it never stay empty more than a few minutes?* He washed his
hands again. He looked at his hands, they were blotchy red.

"The price of a sanitary environment," he said aloud, and
sat carefully down in front of his computer.

He checked seven conservative news websites, in order.
He had an order for everything. *Habits learned early.* He read
quickly, scanning the top headlines, selectively drilling deeper
here and there, following links but only within the sites. He

had no interest in a computer virus from some left-leaning liberal fascist who might be trolling for him. He had up-to-date protection on his computer, but he knew not to trust the Internet. He was careful where he went. He wiped his history every 12 minutes. He suspected that he still dropped breadcrumbs occasionally, but he was as attentive as possible. He tried not to worry about it.

Why is it that everything that can hurt me is invisible? From bacteria to computer viruses!

He could see that people were looting. Obviously, many people were not prepared. *Like I couldn't have predicted that!* What he was reading suggested that others were thinking as he was. *This is the beginning of end times!* Just the thought of it sent him to his basement, his hideout, his bunker. All his neighbors had basements, many of them remodeled in recent years, turned into home theaters and man-caves. They were nice places to hang out, watch a movie, or drink a beer—so he was told. His was nothing like that.

He turned the door handle three times to the right. He opened the door, walked downstairs and stopped to let his eyes take in what years of preparation had wrought. *Beautiful.*

Shelves lined one wall filled with canned goods, water, and foodstuffs with long shelf lives. Another wall was lined with cabinets. They were filled with medical and cleaning supplies, blankets, a biohazard suit complete with an oxygen tank (though only one), and limited armaments. Along the third wall was a sanitation station with running water, a double stainless steal basin, counter, and stainless steel one-piece toilet. The final wall contained the stairwell, so there wasn't much space. Under the steps he'd built a small desk with a setup for his laptop—Control Central, he called it. He also had a stationary bike there. The recommendation was a weight set, but he wasn't really the bodybuilding type. He thought the bike was better because it would help maintain cardio.

He'd never joined the Michigan Militia, but he followed the blog. He knew what to buy, what to store, how to protect himself. He was proud to be an American.

***

Once again, Georgia had run out of food. The cupboards had been empty for several days. She sat at the window and watched out. She hadn't seen anyone on the road since Betsy came nearly three weeks ago. *Can everyone be gone?* She refused to think that. When images came into her mind from the stories she'd been told about this illness, she asked the Lord to carry the burden for her. She knew she was weak. She was old. She was alone. She was hungry. And she didn't have the strength of will she needed to endure this much longer. Yet what choice did she have?

She spent much of her time in bed. There was no reason to get up. No one to talk to. Nothing to eat. She tried to avoid thinking of food. But every little while an image or smell or taste stole her attention and dragged her down that painful road. In late afternoon, she often imagined the taste of potatoes. She had no idea why. She could visualize a nice plate of collard greens. She could smell the fatback and onions. Of all the assaulting sensations, the smell of fatback was the worst. Sometimes it even led her to salivate, which made her stomach gurgle loudly and hurt that much more. She refocused by praying. She still prayed for Verna's soul and asked that Betsy return to the faith—and that Betsy return.

Sister Georgia went in and out of consciousness. When she was lucid, she prayed. It didn't bring comfort exactly, but the familiarity relaxed her, passed the time. She recited Bible verses. Occasionally she remembered days gone by. She thought about her nephew Burt, who moved to Ohio. She saw him as a boy breaking her window with a ball. She looked across the room from her bed and wondered why the window wasn't broken. She fell asleep again. When she woke, she called for her mother. No one answered. She started to pull off the covers and was confused by her adult body. She wasn't a little girl. She was an emaciated old woman.

Georgia awoke with a start. In her dream, a nightmare she realized, dark red boils covered her body. The pain was excruciating. She breathed in slowly. She knew she was alone. And had been. And would be.

Lord, she prayed, *take this cup from me.*

INSECTICIDE LEADS TO INCREASED BACTERIA

Baltimore, MD — Johns Hopkins Medical School announced today that a study of insecticide-carrying GMO seeds has created a niche for new bacterial growth. By killing insects, which reduced the bacterial growth on corn silks, a new strain of *Salmonella* has evolved. The strain has mutated unchecked for years due to a patent held by AgriBiz.

GMO technologies have patented "new life" in the form of genetically altered seeds. Due to the courts' decisions, farmers have been forced to buy GMO seeds or leave fields fallow. This has exacerbated the bacterial growth due to the lack of botanical variety in cornfields.

The original study, funded by AgriBiz, sought to demonstrate that engineering insecticide-treated genes provided advantages for growers of feed and seedcorn. In early stages of the study, crops grown with insecticide-laced genes grew faster, with fuller heads of corn that could be harvested more easily due to a drying quality that occurred in the tassel.

The drying tassel led scientists to explore corn silks more closely. Silks act as the stamen carrying pollen down the tassel to each kernel. Examination of the silks showed how bacteria makes its way to kernels. Though present in the original study, bacterial growth was then dismissed as anomalous. Today, the lead researcher claimed the dismissal of that detail was due to it not being the focus of the previous study. Pursuing it at that stage would have meant unnecessary delays from the perspective of the funders, AgriBiz.

However, early results published on the Internet were noticed by independent bacteriologists at Johns Hopkins. They were looking to identify the cause of recent sweet corn recalls. While it was seed corn, not sweet corn, which carried the GMO insecticide modification, the spread of such factors by wind and pollen-carrying insects is well documented.

At this stage, bacteriologists are only halfway to a possible link between recent recalls and insecticide-laced GMO corn seed. They have proven that corn provides a rich environment for growing this new strain of bacteria. They have yet to document a link between the GMO seed and recent recalls due to food-borne illnesses. The new bacterial strain has similar properties but is not identical to a strain documented by the CDC. More research is warranted.

The Surgeon General's office was unwilling to comment at this time and requested additional time to study the results of the Johns Hopkins research before speaking to the matter. A spokesperson for the CDC admitted that if the two bacterial strains are from a common source, warnings about corn consumption could follow.

Before she got close to the store, Stacy saw people running with their arms full of groceries. Clearly, she hadn't responded as quickly as others. Even now, her instinct was to run away. She'd never liked crowds or panic of any kind. But the latest quarantine meant this was the only opportunity to get food, for god knew how long. And though her pantry wasn't bare, it wasn't very full. Fast-forward, she decided.

Stacy began to trot, not run, not really. She wasn't athletic. She saw people taking carts down the middle of the street, like in the movies. It was hard to get into the store with so many people exiting. Stacy wanted to demand order, as she would of her students, but knew that wouldn't work in this situation. She positioned herself behind a large man and slipped inside.

Hands were grabbing. She couldn't think. Her left arm automatically became a basket as her right hand reached for a box of tuna helper. *She hated boxed food. Would she be able to get tuna?* Stacy moved down the isle, loading up her arms. She picked up items she'd never eaten in her life. She dropped a bag of rice, which split open, making the floor slippery. Stacy hurried toward the front of the store realizing how much emptier the shelves were already. She dodged a man grabbing for something she carried. As she struggled toward the exit she dropped something else. She had no idea what and she no longer cared.

Stacy could feel her erratic heartbeat and realized she was breathing hard. *Survival,* she reminded herself, *if I die here, it won't matter.* She kept moving forward until she was outside. She moved determinedly in the direction of home, keeping herself focused even as she was bumped and jostled.

Turn key. Open. Close. Lock. Stacy slid to the floor and leaned against the wall, letting the groceries fall from her tired arms. She closed her eyes and concentrated on her breathing. She created a vision of Lake Michigan. Ocean air blowing her hair. Fragrance of salt and sand. It was her safe place. It didn't exist. Lake Michigan was not the ocean. And yet, this imagined landscape calmed her. Saved her.

When Stacy finally opened her eyes, the sun had set. She got to her feet. Turned on a light. Looked at the mess spread across the floor. *What a mish-mash. Like her pantry wasn't random enough.* Ever since the pigs had all been slaughtered, she had felt at loose ends in how to put together meals. She was not alone in that. Most Midwesterners were at a loss without their favored pork items: chops, ham, and especially bacon. They still loved their cows and chickens, but it just wasn't the same.

Stacy carried her scavenged items to the kitchen and put them away. She turned on the TV. A banner ran across the bottom announcing Marshall Law had been declared. The story was about looting. With a shudder, she realized she was a looter. *A looter? How could that have happened?* She suddenly wondered what Jared was doing. For the last three hours she had only thought of herself. As a twin and a teacher, she liked to think she wasn't as narcissistic as her contemporaries, but maybe she was wrong. Or maybe this was the time for narcissism.

Jared answered on the second ring. "Hey, sis, how are you?"

"How am I? I can now count looting among my accomplishments, that's how I am."

"Good girl!"

"What?"

"I'm proud of you. These are the times that try men's, er, women's souls. But not my Stace, she does what needs to be done. I repeat, good girl! I didn't think the little schoolteacher had it in her."

"Me either. And you? Have you been out looting with the masses?"

"Yes. Yes, I have. But weren't no ordinary looting for me. No siree. I made for the pharmacy."

"You didn't?"

"I did. Got myself a good stash, too."

"I bet."

"It was hysterical. Everyone else was grabbing Band-Aids and antibacterials. The damned pharmacist had left the building. I was behind the counter in a flash. Grabbed a big-ass bag and filled 'er up."

"No way!"

"Way. There wasn't exactly time to choose."

"I noticed. Drove me crazy."

"I bet it did. Not me. I focused on one idea: wouldn't want just uppers or downers. So I went for the assortment. Let's call it the chef's salad, a little of everything."

"The curry, the masala, the korma."

"What?"

"Indian food. In the states, we think each of those words means a particular Indian dish, a specific flavoring, but they all mean mixture."

"Stop. Don't do that. Don't get all intellectual on me. I'm telling you I scored. I scored big."

"Congratulations. I should berate you. I would berate you. But I feel disoriented."

"Sorry, Stace, need to get online and figure out how to move all these good drugs during a quarantine."

"That does sound like a problem. Call now and then, OK?"

"Will do, sis!"

Stacy woke and lay in bed. She'd been dreaming of swimming in Lake Michigan at the State Beach in Grand Haven. At the end of the pier, the bright red lighthouse was shining through a morning fog. How long had it been since the lake was safe to swim in? There'd been postings about *E. Coli* dangers and the hundreds of thousands of alewives clogging the shoreline. The beaches were closed and open and closed until it became permanent. No swimming, period.

She looked at her clock. *Why get up at 6 when she wouldn't go to school?* No pupils to teach. No lessons to plan. Lessons, oh, there would be new lessons when they reopened. The school board was probably already at work planning them. What would they be? No doubt there were new antibacterial primers to be produced. Kids already didn't touch their faces. And they rarely touched each other, though now that would cease completely. *That should make the playground a much better lunch duty.*

Stacy pulled a book from her nightstand and started to read. She thought about her stack of books. Hardly a stack: three. She hadn't been to the library or the bookstore for a while. She was trying to make herself read the things she already had. *Guess that'll happen now.* Within a page she realized she wasn't comprehending. She began again. She wondered what Jared was doing. He would be sleeping, it was only 6 in the morning.

Was she kidding? She put the book down. It was no use. She looked at her clock. 6:06. *Crap. This was going to be a long day.*

When Stacy turned on the TV, they were showing footage from New York City. A police officer was taking down a female looter. Then several looters jumped the officer. One removed the officer's AB mask and they all touched his face, their hands wrapping around his head, enclosing it with bacteria-carrying fingers. The officer howled and immediately folded into a fetal position. As this was happening, the original looter who'd been detained rose and ran. As she did so, the rest of the looters took heal and followed, leaving the officer screaming and touching his own face, with gloved hands admittedly, but touching himself nonetheless, in an instinctive, but no longer protective, move.

The news reporters were aghast. They explained that other officers responded to an SOS call, but they refused to touch the downed officer because he wouldn't let go of his face. There was footage of the officers forming a circle around him, each of them facing outward, protecting him and avoiding him simultaneously. An ambulance appeared onscreen and picked up the officer, who was reported in stable condition.

The officer became emblematic of a larger problem, the need for better security, better protection from bacteria, and better defense from FaceTouching attacks. Reporters said this as if such attacks were common, but Stacy was certain this was the first one she'd seen or heard about. Maybe it was a New York phenomenon.

The news shifted to a press conference with the President. He explained that with the National Guard deployed overseas keeping the peace abroad, a new service branch was being put into action by Homeland Security. The new detail, initially an offshoot of TSA, would be called Antibacterial Enforcement. The role of AB Enforcers would be to ensure that all bacterial ban protocols were followed and to "subdue and capture" those who endangered public health with their behavior. Stacy was stunned by the language.

The position "Enforcer" struck her as military or para-military. At home in Michigan, she was well versed in how one didn't have to be a soldier to be militarily charged, even if that was only by one's own sensibilities. But "subdue and capture" stuck in her head. There were no details of what "subdue and capture" would mean in practice. Pundits offered speculations, but she knew not to take them too seriously. More often than not they just thought they were smarter than anyone else and tended to miss the big picture. This was clearly big picture.

***

"It wasn't Valentine's Day or anything, not our anniversary." Cathy was telling a tried and true tale of wonder. "We'd just gone out for our usual Friday night date to our usual place, not even a nice restaurant. Oh, it wasn't a hole in the wall, but it wasn't fancy. Howard suggested we skip the appetizer so we'd be hungry for dessert. I should've realized something was up right then. I was the one who liked desserts. Not that he didn't, but he loved their artichoke spinach dip. Of course, neither of us had a regular order or anything. We went to the same restaurant all the time 'cause we enjoyed so many of their dishes, not because we were stuck in a rut.

"Anyway, on that particular night when we finished—I think I had pasta of some kind, probably the special, I often did that, and he had a steak—and were ready to order dessert, he asked, 'Chocolate?' I *always* wanted chocolate. Another clue I missed. But your father didn't recommend the mousse. He was savvy. He knew it was my favorite and he waited patiently. I said, 'I know you don't really like mousse, but we haven't ordered it in a long time. We could always get two desserts.' 'What a good idea,' he said and then he ordered a blueberry crumble for himself and a mousse for me.

"I ate slowly, I liked to savor dessert. I noticed he was antsy. I asked after his crumble, thinking maybe it wasn't fresh or crunchy enough. He just kind of shook his head. But he watched me intently. Then I spooned a bite of mousse and bit down on something hard. I started to grimace and he started to laugh and if I hadn't had my mouth full I would have given him what for. Luckily that didn't happen, 'cause you know what was in that mousse? A diamond ring. That's how he proposed. Can you imagine?"

"I really can't," said Maggie. "Every time you tell that story I try to imagine a world in which coaxing your lover to eat bacteria-ridden mousse is romantic, and it eludes me."

"It was a different time, dear. It couldn't have been dangerous. I'm here to tell the story."

"I still struggle to see the romance in it. It sounds like you were hopping mad when you bit into it."

"Well, you never were proposed to were you? Can't you imagine wanting something so bad and for so long that the moment it arrives you're just giddy with joy?"

"I don't know, maybe romance is dead. Or maybe it's me. I don't get it."

"I had wanted your father to marry me for years. He was slow to commit. That was common enough. It was sort of like when you wanted a child."

"I remember what that felt like. I wanted a baby more than anything."

"You were able to shop the sperm banks and make it happen all by yourself. But remember when you were waiting for the fertility tests, how anxious you were?"

"Oh, it was horrible. I was so afraid they wouldn't inseminate me. And it took weeks and weeks for all the tests and paperwork."

"Remember when you got the news that it would happen?"

"It was one of the most exciting days of my life."

"That's what a proposal was when I was that age. A proposal of marriage meant not being alone, like your decision to have a baby. A proposal meant making your family happy. A proposal meant you could plan the wedding of your dreams, your future. It was something every woman looked forward to. And in my case, I'd been with Howard for years. I'd waited and waited. We were already living together. Some people didn't bother with marriage anymore, but I wanted a wedding. I wanted all my friends and family gathered around to celebrate. I wanted a promise he'd stay. Of course, marriage doesn't guarantee much. I know that now. But at that age I thought it did."

"Mother, he couldn't have promised not to die. It doesn't work that way."

"In sickness and in health…oh, let's not talk about that."

CONTROLLING BACTERIA

Philadelphia, PA — "Science has tried repeatedly and with varied methods to contain any number of bacterial strains," said the Surgeon General. "To date, they have been unsuccessful at every turn. The clock is ticking and is about to run out."

Government officials refused to comment on whether the Surgeon General's remarks indicated an impending end to scientific research. But given the medical upheaval, speculation is rampant.

Researchers have tried to trace numerous strains of bacteria to their sources, but that has not yet led to comprehensive elimination of even a single strain, since bacteria tend to have multiple hosts. The rapid mutation of strains also complicates eradication.

"We've tried sound reverberations, which didn't work. Antibiotics have only had successes after an infection has occurred. Long-range studies are inconclusive to date, but treating the young with probiotics is being tested. We continue to work on the problem," said bacterial researcher, J. Smith.

The bacterial strains the authorities are most concerned about include *E. Coli O157:H7, Listeria, Salmonella, C-Diff, MRSA* (especially the recent mutation *Cha-Cha*), and even *Botulism*, a bacteria once associated with canned foods.

Food sources contaminated with bacteria have caused recent outbreaks resulting in mounting death rates. Animal sources, thought to have been the primary agents of contamination, have been examined at length. But produce sources of bacteria continue to increase.

Mandates to cook all fresh produce to 165 degrees and PSAs aimed at increasing vigilance about cleanliness have not stopped the outbreaks. Habits ingrained tend to remain.

I was still in industry then. It was just before I moved to academe to become a professor. Big Pharma was determined to find solutions to the common cold, which presents obvious problems when people can't touch their faces. Colds weren't bacterial, but they led to the forbidden behavior of FaceTouching. Additionally sneezing or coughing meant sharing germs, and neither could be stopped. Or could they? It was all about mucous. At least that was the theory. If we could dry up mucous, the body would have no reason to sneeze or cough. But that was a tricky matter because you had to dry the fluid without drying the membranes.

I worked on that project. It was one of the final nails in the coffin for my tenure at Big Pharma. Those of us on the biology side of the equation knew the importance of maintaining membrane moisture. While too much moisture led to drowning, too little led to decreased oxygenation, a potentially permanent condition.

There was a race to get products on shelves. The Touch Bans were in place and cold season was fast approaching. Trials were needed to arrive at the delicate moisture balance. Trials were needed to assess how humans would differ from our test animals—ferrets. No matter how vehemently my team argued for human trials, our voices were muted. The wheels were on the car, it was on a downhill trajectory, and the brakes hadn't been checked.

Shortly after the product hit the shelves, a child died after using the inhaler. The death was labeled an "unexpected and unfortunate result." Then a rash of deaths threatened a recall and the meager test data was altered to look more convincing.

Some Washington bureaucrat defended Big Pharma, saying the product was necessary, if not flawless, and that the rush to production was warranted. Then sales tanked. I guess consumers still had the vote of the mighty dollar. That finally caused a recall. There was a large show made of the "proactive response." There was nothing proactive. Pro-business. Pro-sales. Pro-reputation. But proactive? Hardly.

We kept our mouths shut in my unit. No reason to lose our jobs at that juncture. Though I wasn't the only one who started looking for other positions. Not that we talked about it. But there'd be a job ad circled in the break room or a sudden brief illness of a healthy lab worker who no doubt had an interview—after all, he'd been wearing his best clothes under his lab coat when he punched out early.

To solve the problems with colds, tech solutions were tried. Masks with a vacuum capacity that could be activated by the touch of a button. Masks with antibacterial linings. Cough receptacles. And nasal drainers, can't forget those. They were all the rage until it was discovered that like their predecessor, netti pots, they created an increase in bacteria while eliminating mucous, not a healthy exchange.

The common cold, allergies, and other respiratory infections all became dangerous beyond discomfort. People, even close relatives, would shy away from an afflicted person. It was impossible to know what was causing an illness, and the illness caused symptoms that became shunned. A kind of stoning occurred when infected individuals ventured out into public with an audible cough. You could have called it a beating—it would have sounded more contemporary, less ancient—but the fact was no one wanted to touch an infected person. So throwing things—bricks, chunks of concrete, anything you found that was heavy and safe to pick up, though not garbage, obviously—at someone who coughed or sneezed was a safe way to eliminate a contaminating source, who happened to be a person, a person who ignited your deepest fear, the fear that a cold could kill you. After that, people with colds quarantined themselves, sought medical attention and called in sick. It was that or face the wrath of a terrorized public.

***

Trevor was again living under quarantine. He didn't really mind. He knew he was safest at home. He overheard an announcer on the news who revealed a plan to create a new branch of Homeland Security that would enforce the bacterial bans as they developed. He was cleaning his bathroom, but he paused, uncharacteristically, to walk out to see the TV, his hands still gloved. He rarely left a job like that before it was finished, but this sounded like just the opportunity he'd been waiting for. Unfortunately, he only caught the end of the piece. He went back and completed disinfecting the dirtiest room in any home, at least that was his moniker for the bathroom. He didn't cut corners in the process, even though the new position had his attention. Still, he maintained his own strict protocols, ensuring a sterile and safe environment.

Once online he went to three top news sites to find out both what information had been released as well as what his favorite pundits were saying about the new positions. *Enforcing*

AntiBacterial rules, who could be better suited? The blogs made it clear he would be fulfilling his destiny if he was hired for this post. They'd even created links to the application process. *What could be easier?* Trevor filled out the application. When he got to references, he stopped and saved. He picked up the phone and called his old high school, but it was closed because of the quarantine. *Duh? Of course!* He knew a recommendation from his principal would go a long way toward helping him get this job. He did a name search and found two local men of similar age who could be his principal. He got on a social network site and found photos that made it clear which one to contact, but when he didn't find a home phone number, he decided to write on his Wall. Trevor was amazed when he heard back from the principal in a matter of hours and arranged to talk with him by phone.

When the phone rang, Trevor took a deep breath to relax himself and picked up on the third ring. "Mr. VanderHaven, good of you to call me. Thank you for taking the time."

"Certainly, Mr. Kashnikov. Pleased to hear from you. I trust you are doing well?"

"Yes, sir. I'd like to be doing even better."

"Wouldn't we all…wouldn't we all."

"Sir, I contacted you because I'm filling out an application for the new government role of AntiBacterial Enforcer. I figured if anyone knew my tendencies to follow the rules and hope others would do so as well, it would be you, sir."

VanderHaven chuckled. "Oh, Mr. Kashnikov, how I've missed you since you graduated. Yes, indeed. I can testify, under oath if necessary, to your desire for all of us to be exacting in meeting, if not surpassing, the letter of the law. But I don't know anything about the position since I'm not keeping track of news these days."

"It was announced today, and I'm jumping on the opportunity. Homeland Security is expanding."

"Not surprising."

"No, I guess not." Trevor worried about the principal's principles, but he needed this reference, so he decided not to follow the political barb. "It has to do with enforcing antibacterial protocols."

"Does this require a medical background?"

"It's more law enforcement."

"If it involves following rules and holding others to standards, especially of cleanliness, the position is meant for you."

"So I can use you as a reference?"

"Yes. Certainly. You now have my email and phone number. Do you need anything else? Is there a letter of recommendation involved?"

"No, nothing like that. It's a government job."

"Yes, so they'll likely want to talk to me."

"I think so. That's not clear. I was in the middle of filling out the form when I ran into the need for references."

"Not to worry, Mr. Kashnikov. Unlike some of the students who pass through our hallowed halls I do not remember, you will never be forgotten."

"I doubt that's all good."

"It's fine. It means you can get a thorough reference from me even without my ability to access the paper records in the office. So even while quarantined, I can provide a reference for you."

"I hadn't thought about a need for school files. Glad you remember me. Guess our frequent meetings served a purpose after all." Trevor chuckled slightly.

"They served many a purpose, young man. Among them, my learning that I value a certain amount of leniency. You made that perfectly clear to me."

"But you can give me a positive reference?"

"I will, or I wouldn't say to use my name. While we don't see eye-to-eye, I believe students deserve a chance to use their talents, and it sounds like this new position would clearly put yours to work."

"I don't want to take up any more of your time."

"With the quarantine, all I've got is time."

"It's kept me really busy cleaning my place."

"Of course it has. Good day, Mr. Kashnikov. Best of luck to you."

"Thanks, Mr. VanderHaven. I appreciate your support."

Trevor finished the application, which included sending a link to Principal VanderHaven to fill out a form online. Trevor could see the form. Mr. VanderHaven's answers would make him look good, he was sure. But for extra measure, he drafted a quick email to the principal reminding him of seven of the "incidents" he'd reported over the years, especially the early ones the principal had acted on, thus demonstrating that Trevor "made a difference" through his "attention to detail" and his "ability to follow the rules regardless of consequences."

Trevor was more than surprised, he was actually *shocked* when his phone rang the next morning. He jumped. No one ever called him. It wasn't like he was popular. The caller ID said: Government. Trevor waited until the third ring and stood tall as he answered, but he didn't think of the job. He thought: *I'm here if needed.*

"Trevor Kashnikov?"

"Yes. That's me."

"A moment for the Secretary of Homeland Security."

Trevor shook his head. *Did he hear that correctly? Surely not.* He read the spines of books on his shelves as he stood there, making sure the books were in proper alpha order. He pulled one book to the edge of the shelf so he could figure out where it belonged. Its author's name began with a "C" and the one before it began with a "T." Then he realized the "C" book was the first in his non-fiction category, so the order was correct. He needed to put in some kind of marker signifying the change in category. That would make his organization all the more clear. Before he could decide how best to do that, someone spoke.

"Mr. Kashnikov?"

"Yes. Trevor."

"Mr. Kashnikov, this is the Secretary of Homeland Security."

"Mr. Secretary. I'm honored." Trevor hoped he was using proper etiquette. He really didn't know how to talk to someone of such importance.

"It's Madam Secretary, Mr. Kashnikov. Rarely do I call new hires. But I must say, your reference from your principal was the finest. And the speed of your application—less than two hours from our posting—was extraordinary."

"Thank you, ma'am. Did you say, new hire?"

A chuckle escaped the Secretary. "Yes, Mr. Kashnikov. I am pleased to hire you as the first person to fill the role of AntiBacterial Enforcer."

Trevor squealed. He didn't recognize the high-pitched sound that emerged from his lungs. "Thank you, sir, I mean, thank you, ma'am." Trevor was embarrassed. It wasn't smart to make that kind of mistake. Not at this juncture.

The Secretary just laughed. "Stay on the line, Mr. Kashnikov. The Recruitment Specialist will fill you in on the details. Welcome to the AntiBacterial Enforcement Team. Keeping the Homeland secure is our highest priority."

"Thank you, M— " Trevor could tell the line had been put on hold or transferred. He walked to his computer to pull up his application. He wasn't sure what the recruiter would need, but he wanted to be prepared. While his application was loading, he heard the recruiter's voice:

"Mr. Kashnikov? Trevor Kashnikov?"

"Yes, sir? Ready, sir. How can I help you, sir?"

"Do you have your planner available?"

"Yes, sir."

"You're in Michigan, right?"

"Yes, sir. I'm in the middle of Michigan, in Cadillac actually."

"We need you in Chicago for the first training. Can you get there by next Tuesday?"

"Well, sir, we're currently under quarantine."

"Yes, that's true of the general populace. You're above that now, Mr. Kashnikov."

"Oh, oh, of course. Ah, Tuesday. You said Tuesday?"

"I did. Tuesday, the 12th."

"Are the trains running?"

"On a limited schedule. Government purposes only."

"Can I catch the Pere Marquette in Grand Rapids?"

"It runs on Mondays and Thursdays."

"Will thruway bus service be operative in Cadillac?"

"I wouldn't know," the recruiter said. "I can, however, send you the numbers to find out. You'll need a government clearance number as well as a direct phone line to the scheduler."

"OK. Where do I go in Chicago? What time on Tuesday?"

"The Homeland appreciates your enthusiasm. An email will be sent with the specifics."

"Got it."

"We look forward to you joining the team, Mr. Kashnikov."

"Thank you, sir."

Trevor hung up. He almost couldn't believe his good fortune. And yet, he could.

He turned his attention to packing. He realized the recruiter hadn't told him what to pack for. He wasn't sure if he'd be returning to Cadillac after his Chicago trip. He called up his email hoping it would make this detail clear. He actually hoped it would answer several questions, all of which were popping into his head so quickly they felt like popcorn exploding.

In Chicago, Trevor rode the elevator past his floor and back down so he could push the requisite number of buttons: three. As Trevor exited the elevator and approached the conference room he noticed that guards stood watch at either end of the hallway. In front of the door was a table with a simple blue modesty panel reading "Homeland Security" in red lettering. White papers littered the top of the table, completing the patriotic array. At the table sat a rather obese woman with a clipboard. She wore a floral-patterned shirt that barely contained her large bosom, cleavage tumbling out of the scoop neckline. On her left wrist was a man's gold watch, large and clumsy. Before Trevor reached the table, she sized him up and barked, "Kashnikov?"

"Yes, ma'am," Trevor said as firmly as he could manage. The dissonance between her slovenly appearance and her sergeant-like voice caught him off-guard.

"Don't be fooled by packages, Mr. Kashnikov. If you are easily fooled, you will not fulfill this job as anticipated." Trevor looked at her. *What does she know that I don't?* In this situation, he wanted to be on his toes, he wanted to shine, he wanted to stand out as his application obviously had. "Please sign by your name, pick up a packet from the box, put your name badge on your collar, and help yourself to a cup of Joe. Then go on in and have a seat. You're the first one here."

"Thank you..." Trevor paused hoping for a name.

"Nice try. That wins you points. Not that it matters. Not with me. I'm just the hired help."

Trevor smiled, feeling better about his earlier mistake of prejudging this woman, even as he wondered if he'd made a mistake at all. *Didn't she just indicate she was no one of consequence? Wasn't that my assessment?* He followed all her directions, though he counted out the folders until he reached seven, the very best one. He grabbed a coffee, even though he didn't like the stuff.

It was in the list he was given and it was culturally mandated at times like this. He was careful to fill his cup less than half full and add milk and sugar to soften the taste in case he was compelled to sip.

Inside, he took a seat toward the front on a side aisle. He didn't want to appear too anxious, but he didn't want to miss anything. He opened the packet and scanned the contents. Most of it was material he had received in the email. *Why the redundancy? Is it the nature of government work?* He looked yet again at the schedule for the day. It wasn't very detailed. In the morning they'd learn more about the position. In the afternoon, "interactive scenarios." *I don't like role-plays. Maybe I shouldn't pre-judge.* He glanced at the rest of the week. The schedule looked innocuous on the page. *What did I expect? Espionage training?* Trevor took a deep breath and noticed he was no longer alone.

Trevor was an excellent observer. As the room slowly filled, he noticed when people arrived, where they sat, and whether or not they engaged others in conversation. One extrovert sat two seats away and immediately started to talk to Trevor. He didn't introduce himself, didn't ask about Trevor, just started yattering on about getting up this morning and a problem he encountered on the El and then asked where Trevor got the coffee because he hadn't had a chance to get his morning caffeine. Trevor merely pointed out the door and exhaled a sigh of relief as the man trundled out of the room. *Paid no attention when he signed in. Is this who I'll be working with?*

At 8 a.m. on the dot a man stepped up to the microphone in front of the room. He cleared his throat and the room went silent. Trevor looked at the clock and relaxed into his chair. *Any organization that began exactly on time was his kind of group.* The man welcomed them all, provided a few brief housekeeping details, such as bathroom and lunch locations, and then proceeded to introduce their speaker for the morning. He said he was delighted to present a woman who had been with the agency since before there was an agency. He said many would know her name, but few would know her face because she kept to the shadows, and then he laughed at what was evidently an inside joke. He provided a list of accomplishments that caused heads to nod and many in the room to sit a little taller, straining not only to see the microphone but also maintain perfect posture in the presence of greatness. "Without further ado, Commander Triniti Snopek."

Trevor shook his head. He smiled. It was the woman from the table. She had changed clothes. *Had she changed makeup, too?* "Impressive," he said aloud, though no one could hear him with all the applause. She took the podium and scouted the room. Her eyes bore into Trevor's. She pointed the first two fingers of her right hand and gestured from her eyes to Trevor's. He smiled and gave a single, firm nod of his head. She raised her hand to quiet the crowd.

"New recruits, welcome! I'm pleased by your punctuality and enthusiasm. If you look toward the doors, you will notice they have been closed and locked. Latecomers will not be tolerated. The rules are the rules." Eyes met eyes around the room. They were all in the right place.

"I must tell you," she continued, "we didn't expect the rapid, overwhelming response to our job posting. Holding the line against bacteria and against those who would use it for nefarious purposes is our job. The Homeland must be secure. The Homeland must be patrolled. The Homeland must be safe. Enforcement is the key to an antibacterial Homeland. Your job is to ensure that enforcement is carried out in every city in this nation. In ban after ban, you will ensure the rules are followed. The rules are the rules. Am I right?"

A clamor rose throughout the room. In hour one, they had not yet uncovered the language of their agreement. They had not yet achieved a single voice. But they knew their purpose and they would toe the line. Rules were their friends, their family. Rules would keep them warm at night.

AGRIBIZ DEALT AN ECONOMIC BLOW

Sacramento, CA — AgriBiz finds no relief amid a barrage of negative factors tanking profits and stock.

While recalls are nothing new, the frequency and impact of recent agricultural recalls have spiraled out of control. Last month spinach and cantaloupe were pulled from shelves in nine Southwestern states.

Last week alone, bean sprouts, leaf lettuce, onions, apples, and peanuts were removed from grocery stores, restaurant chains, and bars in states all across the South. Monday tomatoes were removed from Taco Bell and McDonald's nationwide. Yesterday two varieties of tomatoes—grape and beefsteak—were pulled from shelves in the Pacific Northwest.

Final damage reports won't be in for some time, but this month's recalls are mounting. The spinach recall hit $260,000 and the "cantaloupe catastrophe," as it's being labeled, topped half a million dollars. Last week's recalls, too numerous to recount individually, collectively hit $2 million, and the tomato removal by Taco Bell and McDonald's is expected to run into seven digits, with lost revenues well beyond the retail level of the chains.

Though Recall Insurance has become common, there are industry rumors of increasing rates yet again, or even elimination. AgriBiz may need to approach Lloyd's of London and similar high-brand insurers to carry agricultural recall risks.

The Raw Foods Movement, an adversary of AgriBiz for many years, has folded up shop. While this would appear to be good news for the agricultural industry, the reasons for the movement's demise, namely the dangers of raw produce, only further damage the credibility of AgriBiz.

Additionally, the death toll in California has been declared an epidemic and state borders have been closed. In California alone, AgriBiz produces nearly 25% of the national vegetable and fruit crop, so further financial repercussions are expected.

Reasons for recalls range from contaminated water and soils to mishandling during packaging and transport. Contagions have included *E. Coli*, *Salmonella*, *Listeria* and other less-known bacteria. Government has tried numerous means to reduce these risks in recent years, including more stringent safeguards at the farm level, closer monitoring of packaging facilities, and better tracing of recalled products. However, their failure to manage the risks effectively has dropped consumer confidence in food safety to an all-time low.

Frank was no longer part of Gary's life. Frank had been caught dumpster diving. His father hadn't stepped in to help. If anything, his father made it worse, and now Frank was incarcerated for a two-year stint. At first Gary visited, but then he realized Frank's anger wasn't healthy. He didn't need it.

Gary moved to San Diego to attend college and become a registered nurse. He'd always loved being in hospitals. He didn't mind the sight of blood. But most importantly, he liked to take care of people. But nursing wasn't culturally acceptable for men. His friends teased him he must be gay. But they all appreciated that he would cater to them when they called complaining of a cold or flu or worse—bacterial infection. He asked about symptoms, caregivers, household supplies. He showed up with treatments ranging from over-the-counter pharmaceuticals to Campbell's chicken noodle soup. His friends were grateful for all of it.

He always teased them that the soup was actually deadly, having nothing fresh, too much sodium, and can liners made with cancer-causing BPA. Gary wished he could make the soup himself or buy it fresh at the local mercado, but he didn't have the time or the money for that. He tended to his friends, believing it kept him focused on the purpose of his studies, but he needed to study every minute he could.

It was during his nursing program that he met Samantha, the love of his life. They were both doing their clinicals. Though attending different colleges, they were assigned to the same ward of Scripps Mercy Hospital. It was a late shift and they'd both been on duty for over eight hours. A code blue sounded and they raced from opposite ends of the hall to room 2112.

As nursing students, there was little they were allowed to do, but they were encouraged to observe procedures and always do as doctors instructed, as long as it wasn't beyond their skill set. Gary and Samantha stood out of the way as the team rolled in equipment, performed CPR, and used the paddles to shock the patient's heart.

Samantha was only months away from graduation while Gary still had a year to go. When the team failed to save the patient and asked if Gary and Samantha would remove the equipment and prepare the body to be sent to the morgue, Gary hesitated. He'd never been to the morgue, let alone prepared a dead body. Samantha nodded as she elbowed him, and whispered she'd teach him the ropes. When the room emptied of medical staff, she stepped forward to begin procedures.

As they removed tubes, took apart equipment that would need sterilization, and cautiously cleaned the body, they began to talk. Samantha informed Gary that this was only her third body, but demonstrated through her actions that she knew what she was doing. Her confidence impressed him.

She asked what brought such a burly, handsome man to nursing. Then she smiled, not so much self-consciously as to invite a response. She knew her questions were blunt, but she also knew others responded to her warm, open expressions of genuine interest. While many men were now in the profession, the female nurses tended to think of the male nurses as wimpy guys who chose nursing because they lacked masculine physical qualities. Gary was surprised and pleased by Samantha's direct approach. He turned a bit red as he admitted that he liked to care for people. She stepped back and sized him up.

"Well, you're not gay, so how did that happen?"

"That's what everyone wants to know. Sorry, but it's confidential information."

Rather than assume he was serious, Samantha laughed. "OK, and confidential it shall remain." She winked at him, which confirmed the flirtation he was sensing.

By the time they took the body to the morgue, their shifts were nearly over. They walked to the desk on their floor to see where they were needed. The shift supervisor told them they could leave a few minutes early. They went and gathered their respective belongings and headed for the elevator, which they reached at the same time.

"Want to get a bite?" they asked simultaneously. They smiled and Gary pushed the button for the ground floor. As they exited the hospital, they turned in unison and headed for a local 24-hour dive. They didn't speak much as they walked, but there was comfort in the silence. At the diner, once they sat down and ordered, they couldn't stop talking.

They had their differences. They didn't order the same meal, share any friends in common or like the same music. But they also had a lot in common. They both came from North County, San Diego, though she inland and he coastal. They were only a year apart in age but had graduated high school the same year. Each came from a two-child, three-parent family. Neither had lived anywhere but San Diego and neither had desires to leave. They were both surfers. Most importantly, neither was involved in a relationship, having been firmly focused on their studies.

They went to Samantha's studio apartment, which she rented alone, rather than Gary's flat shared with three other guys. Though they were tired, the sex was hot. Gary spent the night, a night when neither slept much, as one or the other initiated a nearly endless evening of stimulation. They were both passionate, enjoying the foreplay—the licking, the touching, the kissing—and the exploration of erotic zones with tongues, fingers, and lips. When Samantha finally looked at the clock and announced it was 10 in the morning, Gary pulled her to him and nuzzled her ear.

"I have class at noon. Mind if I shower before I go?"

"Be my guest."

"I think I have been."

From the first, it was the most comfortable relationship either of them had known. She didn't smother him. He didn't possess her. They maintained their focus on their studies but found time for each other every few days. They moved in and out of each other's space with ease. When Sam—no longer Samantha to Gary—graduated with her nursing degree and got a job, they decided to live together. With Gary still in school they couldn't afford anything bigger than Sam's studio, but that would save them Gary's rent and allow them to start saving. Saving for what, they didn't discuss—perhaps a larger apartment, perhaps a wedding. Their future would undoubtedly be shared.

***

Maggie had swaddled her son as she'd been taught. His little hands held tightly to his sides. It had worked easily at first. The boy wasn't a fidgeter. Pele mostly slept and ate. That made it easy enough to keep the blanket tight around him. But now that he was nearing three months, he was awake more, moved more. If she walked away to do any of the hundreds of things she needed to do each day, many of which were for him, he would start kicking and rolling and reaching. Pele couldn't turn over yet, but with every movement of his tiny body, the blanket would loosen and shift. Yesterday, Maggie noticed his movement out of the corner of her eye from across the room, but before she could get to him, his hand was outside the blanket and reaching for his mouth. She'd caught him in time and stopped him, but barely.

She wasn't ready for the next stage. Maggie didn't want to wrap his hands and put the horrid KeepOff on the gauze. It didn't seem right. He was just doing what was natural, exploring his world. Even though she stayed at home all day, she knew she couldn't risk it. *Habits learned early are habits for life.* The mantra sounded friendly enough. She believed it necessary, but she found it anything but friendly.

Maggie had been told by her own mother, Cathy, how hard it was to break Maggie of touching herself when she was little. She'd been 18 months when FaceTouching had been outlawed. Infant Maggie already had the habits: sucking her thumb, rubbing her eyes when she was sleepy, picking at crusty snot in her nose, grabbing at her ears when they itched, tasting most anything she could get her hands on. Cathy's stories were horrific.

To retrain Maggie, Cathy started by putting fish oil on her hands. KeepOff hadn't yet been invented. After a few weeks the aversion had worn off, and Cathy had to try something else.

In the following weeks she went through a long list of awful smelling, worse tasting, bad-for-the-skin alternatives trying to figure it out. There was extract of onion, pachouli, vinegar, super soapy detergent, even gasoline. It had been important to use substances that would deter face contact and stay on the skin long enough to be worthwhile—several hours at least—but wouldn't add any known bacteria to the skin. Plus, with any luck, it would do no harm to the child.

It was a difficult equation. Mothers were constantly on the phone or Internet exchanging stories of what was working. Leave it to the lawmakers to give no thought to how mothers of small children would cope with the anti-human regulation against FaceTouching. It had all happened so quickly that no manufacturers had a chance to create money-making products and get them to market, an unprecedented situation in many ways.

When no odor or taste was keeping Maggie from reaching hand-to-mouth, her mother had resorted to other methods. Maggie's fingers were tied in mittens so she couldn't manipulate anything. Unfortunately, that didn't keep her hands from her face. So her hands were tied behind her back, which left her mobile, but it was hard to keep her tied in a way that didn't hurt her and still kept her securely fastened. Eventually Maggie, like most of her generation, had been tied to chairs.

Maggie couldn't remember most of it. She was grateful for that. But her mother's need to tell these stories had grown exponentially since the birth of Pele. The stories had become so frequent that Maggie was starting to make her mother's memories into her own, complete with sound and picture. She was so overwhelmed by them that she was diminishing contact with her mother, right when she needed her most.

Maggie didn't like imagining her small self tied to a chair. When she saw that in her mind's eye, she shook at the injustice of it. Cathy claimed Maggie was a quiet child and though she didn't like these various methods of control, she didn't raise much of a fuss. Cathy said she was grateful for that. She told of other mothers who had to get earplugs and still couldn't avoid the piercing, pain-inducing, unending screeches of their children. Of course, it wasn't just 18-month-olds going through this re-training. In some households, the clamor was much more defined, in words and deeds, with multiple voices not only crying, but in some cases arguing the injustice of it all. Still, imagining herself in that position, her world inverted without warning. Maggie hated the tears and heartache it generated in her.

It was one more reason she was reluctant to move to the next stage with Pele. She couldn't help but see this as painful for her son. Maggie saw it as wrong, not that she would say so to anyone. She wouldn't risk that. Oh, she'd read the literature. The psychologists condoning the practice, explaining the merits of "gauzing," as it was called. The pediatricians who proclaimed the virtues of KeepOff as if it was a gift to mother and child alike. She was certain those doctors made a killing, by which she only meant they made a lot of money—at least she thought she meant only that—for listing the merits of such an abominable practice. This, too, she kept to herself. As adults, her generation took this for granted. At least the naysayers, if there still were any—and there must be, she thought, she couldn't be alone in her perceptions—were kept away from prominent media outlets.

Last Wednesday, the KeepOff arrived in the mail. Maggie brought the box into the house. She'd ordered only one can. She knew this would lead to more shipping expense, but she just couldn't imagine she would be willing to gauze her beautiful little boy for months. The gauze phase lasted until the child could walk. Then the gauze was removed and a different KeepOff product, a gel next, was applied to the hands. That way children could reach out and touch things, keep their hands antiseptically clean, and still not be willing to put anything near their faces. It meant that children now had to be spoon-fed until at least three years old, when they could manipulate utensils well enough not to slip. Couldn't have fingers making contact with chin or cheek. Oh, no, no, couldn't have that!

Maggie left the box on the floor by the door for two days. Shaking her head, trying to accept the inevitable, she picked it up on Saturday and moved it to the counter.

Now she had a knife in hand and was opening the package. The 10-ounce spray-can looked innocuous enough. What was she afraid of? She set the can on the counter and threw away the box. Pele cooed and she saw that his cute little ball of a fist was in his mouth. Her eyes grew wide and she cried and sat down in a chair muttering, "It has to be today. I've got to gauze him today."

More than an hour passed before she was willing to face what was ahead. Maggie cuddled her baby boy, changed him, fed him and then tightly swaddled him. She was so glad she could nurse, so many mothers couldn't these days. And it wasn't just the gift of bonding, though right now that was foremost in her mind. Most importantly, she prided herself on her ability to pass on immunities to Pele. Maggie was healthy. Her T-cell count was gorgeous and she had antibodies to spare. At least that's the way she liked to talk about it. "I've got so many antibodies, I'm giving them to my son," she would brag. Though she was careful not to say that amid mothers who had to use bottles. Their lives were hard enough. The sterilization procedures alone took half their day, not to mention the guilt they felt.

Finally Maggie picked up her cell and called her mother, who was so thrilled to hear from her that Cathy started talking non-stop as if she herself had placed the call, as if she knew the reason for the conversation.

After a minute, Maggie tried to interrupt. "Mother..."

"...and then I walked right over to him and I said..."

"Mother..."

"I said, if you know what's good..."

"Mother, could you..."

"What? What dear?"

"Mother, can I trouble you with the reason I called?"

"Oh, I'm sorry dear. I was rambling again, wasn't I? I don't mean to do that but..."

"Mother!"

"Yes, dear. I'm listening."

"Could you come over? Today is the day."

"The day for what, dear? Have I missed something?"

"To gauze Pele. Today's the day to gauze him," and with that the dam broke again.

"Well OK! Don't cry. You knew this was coming. It won't be so bad. You'll see. Why when you were little..."

"Not today mother," Maggie asserted between sobs. "No stories about me today. I just need your help. I can't do this alone."

"Of course, dear. I'll be right over. Give me half an hour while I..."

"Whenever you arrive will be fine. We'll be as ready as we can be. See you soon." Maggie hung up without waiting for a reply. There was no reason to continue the phone conversation.

The one in person was going to be bad enough.

RAW FOODS MOVEMENT OFFICIALLY ENDED

Berkeley, CA — Before government could step in, leaders of the Raw Food Movement officially closed shop today.

The announcement was made from Biko Plaza on the UC Berkeley campus. Crowds jeered as Raw Foods announced its website would be dismantled, books removed from bookstores and libraries, and invitations to join would cease. The announcement came as deaths from raw produce reached epidemic numbers in California.

For years, the Raw Foods Movement has attacked AgriBiz moguls as the source of contaminations and death. Raw Foods tried to maintain the practice of eating raw produce, which until yesterday, they argued, was the healthiest way to eat. When it was no longer deniable that it is also the deadliest way to eat, they announced the war lost. In their final words, they chastised Mountain Grown and other GMO producers for their continued alteration of the natural order of growing crops.

"Organic could no longer compete against AgriBiz," they announced. "With Frankinseeds spreading into fields unwanted and with genetic splicing ever more dangerous, there was no longer any place to turn for safe seed, let alone safe produce."

An unnamed spokesperson for Raw Foods said, "An individual can't even be certain of crops she planted in her own backyard garden. It is that insidious.

"With natural, organic, god-given produce," the spokesperson continued, "crops offer the most health benefits when eaten raw. But since natural is no longer an option and since organic doesn't exist, eating raw foods is no longer healthy. The healthiest, safest alternative today is to cook vegetables to 165 degrees."

Many spoke longingly of their forebears' ability to grab a tomato from the vine and eat it on the spot with the juice running down their cheeks. Today, that idyllic image became a thing of the past.

While neither vegetarians nor vegans have any organized movements, individuals on hand at the announcement admitted raw vegetables and fruits have been problematic for years, saying they already cook the majority of the produce they eat.

Daria Global said, "No one talks much about fruits. I still eat blueberries, bananas, and oranges raw and will continue to. None of these fruits have caused outbreaks or been recalled."

Boris Dracon, standing nearby, said, "I will not wait for the outbreak. I will now cook all of my fruits as well as my veggies." He added mournfully, "Breakfast will never be quite the same without fresh fruit in my cereal bowl."

Betsy had been in her home ever since she took food to Sister Georgia. Once she'd gotten there she went to bed straightaway. When she woke, she was sweating. She had it, same as her mama. For days on end, she had no idea how long, she slept and woke in sweats. She'd go to the bathroom, sometimes successfully, sometimes fillin' the stool with blood, uncertain which function she was performin'. Whenever she woke, she drank deeply of water.

Finally, one morning she woke and the sheets were dry. She wasn't shaking. She felt her forehead. She might still be warm. She couldn't be sure. She eased her legs over the side of the bed. She sat for a bit. After awhile, she stood. She was weak and wobbly, but she was also alive. She kept a hand against a wall and slowly made her way to the kitchen. She had the food she'd picked up at Henry's. It was still sitting on the counter in the bag she'd brung it home in. She was hungry and weak. Betsy looked over the odd assortment of food and finally decided she could probably stomach the potatoes. They were dry flakes in a box. There weren't no milk nor butter, but she added water and set the pot on the stove. She sat down and nearly fell asleep again. She heard a sizzle and made herself get up out of the chair to cut off the stove. She opened a drawer for a spoon and collapsed into the chair again. She ate right out of the pan. Betsy fell asleep before finishing. When she awoke, she ate the last dregs of the potatoes and put the pan in the sink with some water. She made her way back to bed.

Sometime later, maybe that day, maybe the next, she heard Junebug calling her name. She hadn't spoken. Her voice was hoarse. She commenced pounding on the outside wall. It worked. He came near the window in her room, which was safely closed. She drew the curtains away.

"You alive!" Junebug was shocked and pleased. He always had a thing for Betsy but nothing ever come of it. "You been sick tho', ain't ya?" She nodded. "You gettin' better?" She nodded and put a thumb up. "You got food?" She nodded. "You need anything?" She shook her head. "I'll check back in a couple days."

Betsy said, "Thank ya."

Junebug saw her mouth move even if he couldn't hear her. He walked away with a little jaunt to his step.

Days passed. Betsy regained strength. She ate what food she had. She used the end of her coal so there was no way left to heat. Spring was comin' on, but the memory of the chills was in her bones and she felt the cold mighty bad. The next time Junebug came by, she asked him for food and coal. He told her he could bring her a little of each. He'd do it right quick. She told him she thought she'd made it. She thought she was gonna live. Junebug smiled real big and she could see the gap where he lost teeth when he hit his head on a rock sliding down the mountain one winter when he was little.

When he came back with the supplies, she asked if she could come out on the porch and talk to him. His eyes got big. He was afeared she could make him sick like her mama did her.

"I tended mama," Betsy told him. "I know the signs. I went past it, Junebug. I done been as sick as she was and now it's gone. I swear. I wouldn't risk giving you nothin'."

Junebug considered a minute. He missed Betsy. He was mighty lonely all 'round. Most of his people were gone, too.

He reckoned Betsy was about all he had left. But he'd seen so much sickness, so much death. Everybody woulda thought Junebug woulda been the most vulnerable, but it wasn't so. He'd come through it without a symptom.

Finally, he said, "I be over there." He pointed beyond the porch to a stump he had always liked sittin' on.

"OK," Betsy said. "I won't leave the porch. I won't touch you or come near."

Junebug nodded and retreated to the stump. Betsy came out on the porch, wrapped in a quilt. "Junebug," she said, "I gotta thank you. Don't know what I'd do without you bringing me food and coal."

"I like to share with ya, Bets."

"You always have."

"I always have."

"Where you gettin' food? Last time I was out there wasn't much left at Henry's."

"I walked to Welch," he explained. "Not much in the stores there, neither. I loaded up the wheelbarrow. It's near gone tho'."

"Do you still have food for you?"

"Some."

"How many still alive at your place?" she asked.

"Just me and Little One." Little One hadn't been little in many a year. In fact, he was bigger than Junebug. But he was youngest and the name got stuck on him. Made strangers laugh, but everybody in the holler just treated it as his given name.

"I'm glad you're not alone," Betsy said. Junebug nodded. "I ain't complaining," she continued, "but this ain't much coal. You outta that too?"

"This is the last. Me and Little One don't need it tho'. We ain't burnt none since the new moon. We warm enough."

"Oh, Junebug, I can't take the last of your coal."

"You can. I brung it. We fine."

"Junebug? What are we gonna do?" Junebug looked at her and shrugged. "Did you run into people in Welch?" she asked.

"No. But it was weeks ago. Most everybody was still obeying house rule. Staying in."

"Is that still in effect?"

"Far as I know," he said. "Radio ain't workin'."

"I should check on Sister Georgia."

"No need."

"She sick?" Betsy asked. "Her people come?"

"She dead."

"You saw her?" she asked. "You're sure?"

He shrugged. "I don't go lookin' that's how I'm still here. But there ain't been lights, nor smoke in the chimney, nor any movements of any kind. She gotta be dead."

Betsy thought it over. "I should check on her. 'Course I got sick right after I was there. I coulda give it to her. How long ago was that Junebug? Do you know when I went there last?"

"I ain't got no way a bein' sure, but there's been at least two full moons."

"That long?" Betsy was surprised. Junebug just looked at his hands and nodded. "How long since you done seen any sign of life there?" Betsy asked.

"Since before the day ya first talked to me through the window."

Betsy nodded while considering the situation, then muttered, "May she rest in peace," as she shook her head gently. Junebug weren't never religious. He just kept his eyes downcast.

Georgia lives—*lived*, Betsy corrected herself—back into the holler, in the opposite direction of any possible supplies. Checkin' on her would be foolish under these conditions, she realized. "We need to go looking for food before we run out, Junebug. By the looks of things, that's gonna be 'fore the week is out."

"Yes, 'em. Sounds right."

"Will Little One come with us?"

"Sure he will. What'd keep him here?"

"Junebug, is anyone else left in our holler? Alive, I mean?"

Junebug looked at Betsy. He hadn't been to the end of the holler in weeks. But he hadn't seen no one come out neither. He considered a minute. Looked in his mind to the road and each person who done lived along it. Lotsa old folks, but some young 'uns. A coupla good providers who likely stocked in.

"Can't say for sure, Bets. But I ain't a'seen no one in a long time. I 'magine somes of 'em might be alive. I hopes so."

Betsy shook her head. Verna knew everyone all the way to the end of the road. Betsy knew 'em, but she didn't know 'em. Didn't feel kinship to them. She was stronger than she had been, but caring for herself was plenty right now. She couldn't go worryin' 'bout everybody else.

"Junebug, looks like this coal'll last me 3, 4 days tops. You brung me food for at least a week, but some of that should go with us. Should still be some gasoline in the car. I kin drive us to Welch or as far as it'll get us. I say let's head up the road in 3

121

days. I'll drive by and pick up you and Little One. Tell him to pack up like we is goin' up the mountain. Gotta take whatever supplies we got. No sense leavin' nothin' behind."

"Alright, Bets. We ever comin' back?"

"Don't rightly know, Junebug. Ever'thin's changed so much I don't know what to count on. Do you?"

"No, ma'am. I rightly don't." Junebug stood then. He waved at Betsy and walked away, toward his shack.

Betsy shivered. It was nice breathing fresh air. If only she could shake the chills.

TTB SPREADS CROSS COUNTRY

Chicago, IL — The Chicago City Council has adopted the Total Touch Ban, the purpose of which is "to establish an end to public touching between individuals for any purpose and in any manner."

Citizens demanded this action in Chicago in the wake of violence against a cougher who tried to shake hands with a city official at a ribbon cutting ceremony last week. Ironically, the incident occurred at the opening of a hermetically secured hospital, where airlocks allow scans of entering individuals, making it possible to quarantine them on the spot if contagion is detected.

No bacterial transfer occurred for the official in question, but the immediate ire of the gathered crowd told authorities it was time to act before vigilantes began patrolling the streets on their own.

Chicago is among 14 urban centers that adopted the TTB today, spreading the new law into the heartland of the country and furthering the call for another national legislative response to the bacterial crisis. "The ban against FaceTouching was a good starting place," said Carlos Zapata, Chief Immunologist at Chicago Hope Hospital, "but it's no longer sufficient."

ISOLATION

The TTB has been dubbed "Crazy Talk" by the hit singer Petroff Jazzy Romansky, whose lyrics, "gonna lick, gonna kiss, gonna touch whoever I want," in the hit single "Crazy Talk," stirred a great deal of controversy recently during public debates of the safety of public displays of affection.

The TTB, part of a larger legislative trend meant to protect citizens from spreading bacterial contagion, is one in a series of bans government officials are pushing into law all across the country. The TTB began simultaneously in New York City and Los Angeles last month and has now been signed into law in 100 municipalities nationwide.

Early concerns focused on city sizes and the extreme nature of the measures. Questions about sexual expression and what would be taken away next, if this inalienable freedom was squelched, were also raised.

Significantly, the science behind the TTB remains under debate. "Human touch is dangerous. Numerous studies document that bacteria is easily passed hand-to-hand. It stands to reason that other body parts are at least as active in the spread of microbes," said James Brown of Brown University's Biology Department.

"We know that humans build antibodies from exposure to bacteria, which increases immunity to disease. There is no science to document what could happen if we end all exposure," offered Dr. Brenda Mallory, author of *Germs-R-Us: A Study of Human-Germ Collaboration.*

The question remains, will federal authorities make the Total Touch Ban national? "It's time to act! Anything less increases the dangers for everyone," said Chicago Mayor Cheryl O'Sullivan as she signed the bill into law.

"Join us!" called City Council Chief, Warren Franks of Lincoln, NE, another city that passed the TTB today. "We're not bumpkins. We're getting ahead of these germs. Washington would be wise to do the same."

For a week Stacy had been cooped up in her apartment. The first full day of the quarantine she spun in place, quite literally. She'd start to walk into the living room to sit and read and realize she wasn't holding a book. As she picked up a book, she'd turn toward the desk to check the Internet news. Before she could sit down at the desk she'd realize the book was in her hand. She couldn't read. Sitting and reading was relaxing—this was anything but.

Stacy typically ran after school, burning off energy, building up endorphins. No way to run now. She put on music intending to exercise, but she couldn't remember any routines. She tried dancing, but fidgeting wasn't the same as rhythm. Dancing was positive, fun, exhilarating. She was scared, agitated, frantic.

Stacy kept restarting the academic history piece she wanted to read as background for her upcoming lessons in the establishment of the American colonies. The school textbooks said little about Native Americans except for the brief bit on Thanksgiving and a mention of smallpox in the blankets. And the one book she'd picked up had nothing more on smallpox, which really interested her now.

She wished she had a hand-held reading device. They were quite popular, but on a teacher's salary, she hadn't indulged in one yet. Right now, it would be far from an indulgence. If she ordered one, she wondered if it could be delivered to her. She hadn't paid any attention to that kind of thing, whether or not packages were being delivered, whether Internet commerce continued or not.

For the millionth time this morning, Stacy looked at her clock. 10:23. The day had barely begun. She hadn't been able to shift out of school mode. Couldn't seem to shake getting up at 6:00. By noon each day she felt like she'd lost her mind. She needed stimulation. Stacy's phone rang.

"Jared, my savior!"

"Thanks, Stace, but I doubt you'd want to call me that."

"This phone call removes the shackles from my eyes so I can see the light."

"Wow, this early and you're already talking that trash!"

Stacy laughed at Jared's response. It felt good to laugh. She couldn't really quote scripture, but she could reference religion in ways that made Jared cringe. She loved to get him going.

"So, what are you up to today, sis?"

"Up to?"

"Yeah, how will you pass the time?"

"Good question. I was just wondering if it's possible to order an electronic reader."

"Why not?"

"Are they delivering? I heard about a terrorist alert or something. Somebody mentioned anthrax."

"Don't think so, sis. I've been able to move some of my pharmaceuticals by FedEx."

"You're kidding me, right? You're not really sending drugs that way?"

"Hell yeah!" Jared said. "Nobody's paying any attention to little 'ol me. Not in this crisis. Besides, all the things I'm sending are still in original medical packaging. Right now, who's gonna question that?"

"Be careful. I'd go crazy if you were in jail and I couldn't talk to you everyday."

"That's right," Jared teased, "if I go to jail it'll be all about you."

"Exactly! Plus there'll be all the negative publicity about the schoolteacher's brother and his drugs. I'd be investigated for selling to kids."

"Still all about you. I feel so loved."

"And you should. I haven't disowned you," Stacy said, "and we both know I should. But it doesn't work that way, does it, my evil twin?"

"Nope, angel on my shoulder, it don't work that way."

"Just be careful," Stacy added.

"Always am. Careful is my middle name."

"Care..f..u..l." Stacy stretched the word out as if in warning.

"Really," her brother said, shifting to a more serious tone. "What are you doing today?"

"Nothing. And then when I'm done with that I'll change rooms and do more nothing. I'm bored, I'm lonely and I'm frustrated. I keep telling you."

"And I hear ya, sis. Let's spend some time in 3-D Life together."

"A perfect waste of time. Just what I need. I don't have an avatar. You know I have to start from scratch."

"I'll walk you through it," he volunteered. "In fact, be my twin there, too. That'll give you a head start 'cause as you know, I've got creds in the game."

"So you've told me," Stacy replied.

"Not that you've listened."

"Exactly," she said, relenting. "When do I meet you where?"

***

Three quick taps on the door and the handle turned—Cathy had arrived. God help me, Maggie thought. Before she could even see her mother, she could hear the mumble. The woman never shut up!

"I see you haven't started yet. I thought you'd at least have him ready."

"He'll never be ready, but it has to be done today. The swaddling isn't working anymore and I don't want him raised to be a clogger with his hands always at his sides."

"Wouldn't want that. No, no, no."

"And everything *is* ready..."

"Oh, now I see the KeepOff sitting there on the counter. Looks like you got the right kind. But the gauze, I don't see it. What kind did you get? At his age..."

"The rest is right here, mother, on the table."

Maggie held it up for her mother's disapproval, but was surprised by a little nod, though the torrent of words did not abate. She had all the equipment, the scissors, the baby tape, the elastics. She picked up the gauze and scissors and handed them to her mother.

"OK, well, what I'd do..."

"Mother, could you just do it this time? I know I'll have to. I'm going to watch carefully. But I just can't do it this first time."

"Oh, dear, it'll be alright. You'll see."

Cathy patted her daughter's shoulder. She picked up a strip of gauze and held it to the baby's hand, measuring enough to ensure coverage, yet not waste any. She knew baby gauze wasn't cheap. She cut one length, measured again and cut the second, being sure each time to tuck the little hand back into the blanket. She didn't want a mishap when they were so close to safety.

Cathy picked up the tape. "Tape like this always makes me think of sending packages in the mail. We used to do that all the time. Today, it's just businesses that get that, uh, that *privilege* I guess you'd call it. But we used to send things all over, to friends and family. I'd save up boxes so I'd have the right size. I remember the time I shipped a whole box of books to myself. I was going away and wanted to read and relax. Didn't want to waste good vacation time searching for books. I sent them ahead and was so proud of myself. I got there fine, but the books never made it. The box did. Showed up empty. Of course that wasn't normal. That's what makes it memorable. So strange to pick up a box that should have been so heavy but was light as a feather. Those books just disappeared."

"Mother?"

"Oh right, sorry, dear."

As she prepared the tape and then the elastics Cathy intoned over and over: "Habits learned early are habits for life." She grabbed the KeepOff and moved it closer. But as she reached for her grandson to put on the gauze, Maggie whisked the baby into her arms and out of the room. "We'll be right back."

Before her mother could argue or ask questions, Maggie was in the bathroom and the door was shut. She released Pele's arms from the swaddling. She put a finger inside of each of his little fists and cooed at him. She looked around to be sure the window coverings were down, to be sure she couldn't be seen by anyone, then she gently kissed each hand. She breathed in his smell and kissed his hands and whispered, "This won't be forever. I promise. I'm sorry. I don't want you to go through this. But not doing it would be worse. *Habits learned early*," she intoned in the singsong way it was always said, "that's what we're doing, teaching you a habit. It'll seem evil, I know it will. But it's for the best."

Her tears flowed and she held him to her, then rewrapped him tightly. She fanned her face and pushed the flush on the toilet, to disguise her purpose, and returned to the kitchen, to her mother, to the over-sterilized world she—and her son— lived in.

DEATH TOLL IN CALIFORNIA REACHES EPIDEMIC LEVELS

Sacramento, CA—Deaths from raw produce reached epidemic proportions in California this week. Numbers have been climbing all month, but in recent days the totals have grown exponentially.

Today the state began comparing the rise in deaths to an 8.0 earthquake, using the logarithmic scale designed by Richter as a metaphoric analysis. "It's something all Californian's can grasp," said California Governor Grace Atwood.

The death toll has not been limited to California; it has spiked in every state where a recall has been mandated. But while limited numbers of recalls occurred in most states, California's recalls outnumber those of all Western states combined.

California has produce from every AgriBiz agent that has announced a recall since February. This stems from the size of AgriBiz in California as well as the large population of the state.

Produce	Reason	Recall States
Spinach	E. Coli	California, Nevada, Utah, Arizona, New Mexico, Texas, Colorado, Oklahoma, Kansas
Cantaloupe	Listeria	
Bean sprouts	E. Coli	California, Arizona, New Mexico, Texas, Oklahoma, Arkansas, Louisiana, Mississippi, Alabama, Georgia, Tennessee, Florida, South Carolina
Leaf lettuce (red-leaf and Romaine, organic & non-)	Salmonella	
Onions (chopped)	Unknown contaminant	
Apples (Red Delicious)	Alar pesticide residue	
Peanuts	Salmonella	
Tomatoes (McDonald's and Taco Bell)	E. Coli	National
Tomatoes (grape & beefsteak)	Salmonella	Washington, Oregon, Northern California, Idaho, Montana

With the death toll rising rapidly, hospitals have been unable to set up enough isolation units and decontamination chambers for the masses assaulting their doors. In response, the state closed its borders to both people and AgriBiz traffic. This is an unprecedented move. California has monitored produce crossing its borders for nearly 100 years, but prior to this latest threat, the state's efforts were aimed chiefly at reducing the number of invasive pests.

However, this new border danger is being closely monitored by California's neighboring states as well, including the nation of Mexico, all of which want to keep Californians and especially California produce out of their districts until the health situation stabilizes. Incubation times and transmission methods for the diseases are still matters of debate by the CDC and other health authorities, making the situation and timeline uncertain.

Trevor's first post as an Enforcer was in his home state of Michigan. Initially, the work was sporadic. When quarantines occurred, he was there to ensure people got off the streets as quickly as possible. He assisted law enforcement when looting broke out, though he mostly watched for those who used quarantines as opportunities for FaceTouching or for trying to get quarantined, not in their own homes, but in the homes of those they wished to touch, especially after touching others was banned. When he found people trying to go into homes that weren't their own, he hauled them away. Usually, the offenders were held for 48 hours and then returned, sirens blaring, to their own domiciles.

Occasionally he was called in to staff the doors at the Emergency Ward when an outbreak occurred. It wasn't always easy to tell who was infected and who wasn't. But it was easy to check identification, call up medical records to check T-cell counts, and ensure the orderly containment of arrivals. No medical knowledge was needed for any of that. At those times he found his habits kept him focused. He kept track of how many people arrived and gave special attention to the third, the seventh, and the 21st. He was careful to ensure the 13th person was moved along quickly, usually sent home.

But the rules, and making others follow them, didn't make him as happy as he'd anticipated. There just wasn't much going on in Michigan. Or perhaps there wasn't much going on anywhere.

At home, Trevor spent time checking his bunker supplies, adding small things that were better, newer. His pay wasn't great, but it was the best salary he'd ever had, and he appreciated what it could buy. He improved his masks, added a second oxygen tank, and increased the canned goods and water supply. He reinforced all the caulking so the bunker would be completely sealed off from possible bacterial intrusion.

Upstairs he kept improving small things. His focus was on increasing the number of tasks he could complete without touching anything likely to carry bacteria. In addition to a touchless trashcan, he installed a touchless faucet, toilet and back door. He was most proud of the back door. It had been such a problem when taking out the trash, which was already a chore he found hateful and dangerous. At least now he didn't contaminate his door in the process. Trevor saw his life as seamless. Off-duty he made his own environment cleaner, on-duty he kept the world safe for others.

During the early days, Homelanders were frequently uncertain what Enforcers did. For that matter, it wasn't always clear to the men and women filling the positions. When family and friends asked, Enforcers gave vague answers that left a lot to the imagination. That was intentional. They'd been warned that since their positions were *emergent*—language used only inside the agency—they were not to be too specific. Enforcers would be used where needed, as needed. They were to remain flexible. They needed to be able to read a list of rules, perhaps even a list with rules contradicted by previous lists, and take the current list, the *emergent* list, and enforce it, enforce every rule present, regardless of what they did last month, last week, last hour. There was never to be any discussion with Homelanders, who would often have an outdated sense of the rules. That was the nature of the situation, the *emergent* situation. Bacteria morphed quickly. Conditions changed rapidly. Everything was in flux.

***

It took Betsy several pumps of the gas pedal to get the cold engine running. It seemed to Betsy the car was just like her. She'd packed up what little food was left, grabbed a few clothes and some blankets. She was wearing a winter coat even though it was nearly summer. She still didn't sense any warmth in her body or the world. She carefully thought through the cooking and living supplies: pans, matches, pitchers of water, utensils for three, and a few tools they might need, like a hammer and a small handsaw, rusted but still useful. All of it had fit easily in the trunk with plenty of space for her passengers and their goods. When the car idled smoothly, she started bumping down the dirt road. Junebug was expecting her, pacing in tight circles as he did when he was anxious, but Little One was just sitting. He clearly thought this idea was crazy.

Betsy started the conversation with Little One. "Do you have any better ideas of how to get food? How to stay alive?"

"No, 'm. But I can't see how galavantin' across the country gonna help much."

"Not positive it will," Betsy said. "Don't see many options though. I'm not fond of the idea of starving to death. I hear it's slow and painful."

"That'll be so whether it happens here or on the road. Won't it?" Betsy nodded reluctantly at Little One. "Then I'd perfer to stay right where I am. This is home, Betsy. My people are buried here. My daddy taught me to tend graves. Said that was important."

"I know it to be true. I just don't want to join 'em in the grave, 'specially when there's no one left to bury me." Betsy looked at Junebug. She wasn't sure if she should leave him here with Little One or persuade him to go with her. Little One was his kin, but she really didn't want to be alone. In the end, she merely said, "Junebug?"

"I tried to talk to him, Bets. Little One ain't a' goin'."

"I got that, Junebug. I'm wonderin' 'bout you is all. You stayin' or goin'?"

Junebug danced around a little. It was an impossible choice. Most of his life others made these kinds of hard decisions for him and told him what to do. His heart was with Betsy. He wanted to protect her, to find her food, give her coal. But his life had always been with Little One, long as Little One had been alive. He looked at the car. A few days ago, he wouldn't join Betsy on the porch. Was he really going to get into a car with her? Was she well? Junebug got a sheepish look on his face and wouldn't look at Betsy. Finally, Little One voiced what both he and Betsy read in Junebug. "He's a stayin', Betsy. We both wish you well."

"You be fine, Bets," Junebug finally said. "You got well when nobody else did. You be fine." Junebug still wouldn't look at her. He wished he could hug her but that didn't seem smart, and he tried to be smart.

"Well, I never. This ain't what I expected. But then, nothin' is anymore."

Both men shook their heads in agreement.

"Alrighty then. Junebug, thank ya fer all ya did fer me. Without food and coal, I'm not sure I'da made it. And Little One, you take care of Junebug, he's special."

Junebug grinned, embarrassed and pleased, and Little One nodded, wishing this moment over.

Betsy got in her car. She sat for a moment, wondering if her plan was still the best. Maybe she should stay right here with Junebug instead of driving who knew where. But she couldn't imagine a future in that. So she drove off. As her tires threw gravel, Junebug finally looked in her direction and waved. She didn't notice. Her eyes were on the road and her mind was on the future, whatever that would be.

***

Before anything could be done about gauzing Maggie's infant son, Cathy started into another story of the past. This time, Maggie held Pele tightly to her, appreciating the delay.

"When I was a little girl, no one even talked about bacteria. It wasn't an everyday word at all. Germs, that's what we talked about, germs. I remember we had this thing we called the five-second rule."

"The five-second rule? What has time got to do with bacteria? Or germs, if you prefer."

"Nothing really. It was just this kid's game. If you dropped a piece of food and grabbed it off the floor quick enough, you could eat it and call the five-second rule, meaning it hadn't been on the floor long enough for contamination, so you could still eat whatever it was. It worked great at home. Guess parents thought of their own floors as clean, or just felt safe at home. That was probably it. But when we were in public, like at a food court at a mall, it didn't matter how fast we were. One of our parents, or in their absence another adult, would knock the food right out of our hands if we tried to eat something from the floor. Can you imagine? A person eating something off the floor? Seems crazy, doesn't it?"

"Yeah, mother, but all your stories from childhood seem crazy."

"Are you insulting me? When I'm here to help you?"

"No, mother, I just mean that things change so fast from one generation to the next that the stories don't seem humanly possible."

"Oh, OK, I thought you were..."

"Just echoing you, mother. You said it seemed crazy and I was agreeing."

"Oh, alright then. I can't remember when the five-second rule ended. Adults stopping it in public must have been part of it. It's not like so many other things, it wasn't legislated. Wasn't them politicians messing with our world, changing it out from under us. Not that time." Cathy paused, tilted her head and turned to look at her daughter and grandson. "OK, can we get this child gauzed so he learns the right habit?"

"Go ahead. I'll watch."

"Well, since there's two of us, you can't just watch. It's so much easier with two people. One of us needs to hold a hand while the other wraps and tapes the gauze. Which do you want to do?"

"Neither," Cathy said, then relented. "I'll hold his wrist. You do the gauzing."

It really was a simple procedure. Cathy took the strip of gauze she'd cut. She wrapped it gently around the little fist. This would get more difficult over the next year as the child grew and wanted to stretch his fingers and reach for things during the wrapping. Before Maggie could worry about that, the tape was on the left hand and the elastic band was snuggly fitted onto the gauze edge at the wrist. Tape didn't hold very well, elastic was the real magic.

"One hand, two hand, red hand, blue hand," Cathy recited.

"Mother! That's an awful rhyme."

"No, it's a required reminder. You always have to be careful to make sure the elastic is exactly the right size so it doesn't cut off circulation. *Red hand, blue hand* keeps that in mind."

"Mother!"

"These little rituals are important. Don't mother me. Now hand me the KeepOff."

"Shouldn't you have done that first so you couldn't overspray it? Now you could get it in his eyes."

"No, you have to wait till it's on. Otherwise you'd wipe it off. Besides you wouldn't get it on the outside of the tape that way. Heck, spray too much and the tape won't even stick. No, you have to do it at this point. They've made the spray nozzle tightly focused, so it won't go anywhere else."

"Show me."

"I will, I will. Now you're the one hurrying. I'll be! You take off the cap. It doesn't need shaking. You just extend his arm so you can go all around at once, like this." With a flourish Cathy sprayed all sides of the right hand. "Now you try."

"Can't you?"

"No, you're gonna be doing this, best to do it once with me here." Maggie picked up the can and gently took her son's left hand, which looked more like a paw now. She sprayed one side, careful not to get any on herself or Pele. Then she rolled his forearm around and sprayed again.

"Not bad for your first time. For the next few days you'll need to watch. Since his hands have been kept down, he'll likely be waving them all over. You'll need to see his reactions. About 99% of kids will make faces and learn after the first lick that they don't want KeepOff anywhere near their mouth or face, but every now and then there's a smell gene missing or some such and the regular KeepOff doesn't offend them at all. If that's the case..."

"I know, mother."

"What will you do if he's one of them irregulars?"

"Mother!"

"Well, it doesn't mean anything bad about him. I just wonder what you'll do?"

"I'll kill that bug when I get to it. I'll be vigilant. God knows I was raised to be vigilant. But I'm not planning for the unexpected."

"If it does happen, I'd recommend going back to swaddling until you can get him tested. Though they make a Super KeepOff, I think they also make individualized ones. I'd try for that if you need to go that route. I don't think it's designer, I think it's not just one genetic mishap that causes the irregulars."

"Enough, mother! For now, this is plenty for us to deal with."

"You're right, of course. You know best. I just always like to be prepared. That's how I try to live my life. Guess it's the Girl Scout in me. When I was little, I remember selling cookies door-to-door. Can you imagine? Handing strangers things, taking money from them? It was another time, that's for sure. Wouldn't do that today. Send a child out to exchange things with strangers who could be carrying all kinds of bacteria."

"Mother, thanks for coming today." Maggie smiled. It was a forced smile. She wasn't happy about gauzing Pele. She wasn't happy listening to her mother's stories. But she was genuinely pleased to have the help. And she was often so abrupt with her mother, *so mean* she thought to herself, that she wanted this visit to end on a positive note. "Would you like to hold Pele before you go?" A peace offering combined with an invitation to leave. Maggie was proud of her rhetorical skill.

"That would be nice dear." Cathy took Pele and sat down in a chair. She looked into her grandson's eyes and immediately began telling him a story. Maggie left the room. She could do without another story, and she felt the need for a breather. This was her chance to release today's stress before her mother left. She went to her room and laid down on her bed. A tear formed in her right eye and puddled in the corner before gently rolling down her cheek. There was no urge to wipe it away. She was used to this sensation, it was part of every sadness in her life.

***

So much bacteria, so little food. Didn't have to be on the botany side of biology to be interested in what was happening to our food supply. As a professor, I found it useful to be able to connect the work of biology to the real world so my students understood the impact of what we did. After my years with Big Pharma, I was keenly aware of the ethical and life-threatening implications of our research.

For years, the FDA released emails announcing recalls. I got on the mailing list and read them religiously. Many were innocuous: misbranding and undeclared allergens—milk, walnuts, soy, peanuts; foreign materials in the product; foreign meat that wasn't presented for re-inspection at the border; or meat making it to market "without benefit of inspection." Their wording, of course, not mine. I could never come up with anything so specious. As if it were a big plus when meat actually was inspected. Though in retrospect, maybe that's closer to the truth. They tested so little and so infrequently as to defy the concept of protection. There were also notices of the more frightening recalls: animal drug contaminants in fully cooked beef patties, sausages with *Staph*, *Listeria*-contaminated cheeses, *Salmonella*-contaminated eggs, *E. Coli*-contaminated beef. And that was just the animal recalls.

Fresh fruits and vegetables became entirely suspect: spinach, bean sprouts, melons, lettuce, tomatoes, olives, apples, pears, strawberries, and on and on and on. In some weeks, there could be several dozen recalls, running in the hundreds of thousands of pounds, packaged with dozens of labels for each product, distributed in multiple states often stringing clear across the country, and with few of the recalls making news. There would be small notices on bulletin boards in grocery stores and occasionally a label where a potentially life-threatening product had been removed from the shelves. But for the most part, the information was only distributed to those acknowledged paranoids who needed to know what was happening in Washington in regard to "food safety"—an oxymoron by that point. No food was safe, at least not to the level of a guarantee. I wasn't one of the paranoids, but I was on the list. I wanted to learn rather than monitor. I wasn't checking the labels in my pantry and fridge. I was just watching the increase in the numbers of products and frequency of recalls. And I was noticing how no one was talking about it. Few were paying any attention at all. We'd been inured to it, and there was no horror.

We had plenty of fear, but that was mostly reserved for potential terrorists, foreigners who didn't look like us, think like us, or act like us. Our fears shifted from one front to another, always moving, always growing, always announced by the media. Fear of anthrax in the mail, car bombs under federal buildings, Arabs anywhere anytime, aerosols in a subway, liquids on an airliner. But rarely a fear of guns in the hands of your middle-class neighbors, or fear of the lack of inspection by government lackeys doing any number of menial jobs, or fear of food produced in ways that made it cheap and deadly.

This was misdirection on government's part, no doubt. "Watch out! The sky is falling." And while we peered up into the heavens, the rug was pulled out from under us, the rug of oats and wheat and sweet grasses, the carpeting of green we lived on.

It's not that there wasn't plenty of food in terms of quantity. There was. In fact, we seemed to live in the land of milk and honey. The problem was, the milk was filled with bovine hormones and mechanical bees pollinated the honey. When I say there wasn't much food, I really mean variety. Oh sure, there was corn and soybeans and potatoes: one kind of corn for human consumption, shot full of a bacterial treatment, BT; one kind of soybeans, carrying herbicides, a kind of Agent Orange in its DNA; and five kinds of potatoes, just the situation that brought on the potato famine in Ireland a century before.

In Peru there were thousands of varieties of potato, and in Mexico hundreds of varieties of corn. That's biodiversity. When a crop fails due to drought or infestation or any other problem, other variants live on, continuing to provide food. Between the economic interests shipping food nation- and world-wide, and their partners in crime, the biotech engineers— like I had been, splicing genes that often reduced rather than increased yields—well, with all of that, it only *looked* like a lot of food. It weighed in tons, but wait awhile, and that amount would diminish beyond expectation. We diminished nearly proportionally, killed by the very food meant to feed us.

TOTAL TOUCH BAN

Washington, DC — The Surgeon General announced today, "Bacteria must be stopped dead in its tracks. Therefore, there will be no human-to-human physical contact. A Total Touch Ban, or TTB, is the only reasonable option."

The announcement was met with questions from all quadrants. What about sex? Infant care? Taking care of the sick?

"Obviously, there are many implementation issues to resolve," said the Homeland Security Secretary. "We do not anticipate a rush to arrests. What we need is for Homelanders to take this seriously and begin habits for life."

"They can't stop me from touching my wife," said Jeb Tree of Miami. "I've got a legal piece of paper says she's mine to touch. If I have to do it behind closed doors, that's OK. Makes the wife happier that way."

"It's the next logical step, right?" offered Dr. Jody Forrester of Chicago. "Our faces aren't our only orifices and our own fingers aren't the only ones carrying deadly bacteria."

"Don't babies need touch?" asked Tory Spruce of Louisville. "I'm not due for three months, but I can't imagine not touching my baby. That's wrong. The government will realize this is crazy. They have to."

Parents won't have to worry about not touching their children, claims famed child psychologist Dr. Emily Croft. "Recent research indicates that eye contact is perhaps more important in child-parent bonding than physical contact."

According to the Surgeon General, babies will respond to human touch even if gloves are worn. "The human infant is an amazing collection of receptors, genetically predisposed to respond positively to all sorts of touch. Putting gloves on mothers' hands will not significantly alter the natural relation of mothers and babies."

Sterile glove manufacturers reported that production will increase but they anticipate a gap between the quantity they can bring to market and the numbers that will be sought by consumers. "We were aware that a TTB was under consideration and have stepped up operations. Gloves are available, but we've been directed to ensure certain areas are supplied first: hospitals, childcare workers, cleaners, diplomats."

Healthcare workers are already used to preventive gloving. "Once you get used to gloves, it's just like you're not wearing them," commented Nurse Bob Jones of Cedar Memorial Hospital.

Stacy was unfamiliar with 3-D Life, but Jared was unprepared for what they found there. Typically, you could lounge around, make the wrong kind of friends, have virtual sex, become part of a get-rich-quick scheme, and even take classes from real-life professors. Not that Jared had ever taken a class. To him, that would be a waste, too real.

But today the game didn't feel like a game anymore. There was looting, just like real life, noncommercial public spaces were empty, just like in Muskegon (and the whole country from what they'd heard), but most surprisingly, there were avatars dying from bacterial infections. Someone had infected the game's organic market. Somebody marketed an AB product that wasn't anti- at all, it was pro-bacterial, carrying germs into every home that tried to be clean. Even the hospital was a dirty zone. Jared and Stacy got out as fast as they could.

Jared IM'd Stacy on the periphery of the game. "Sorry, sis. Thought 3-D Life might be overpopulated with everyone bored, but didn't imagine it would have gone viral, not like this. Evidently someone is striking back."

"Striking back? It's a game. What do you mean?"

"I'm not sure what I mean. Makes me think there's more than meets the eye. Makes all my conspiracy theories come alive. Makes me wonder if someone in the game is a bio-terrorist."

"In the game?"

"On the street. 3-D Life is escapism. Why make it so real? Unless what's real really isn't."

"Huh?! Bro, that was more confusing than normal. You're spending too much time alone."

"Aren't we all?"

Tuesday night, just before bedtime, Stacy got a call. Her principal told her to be at school by 7:30 the next morning. He told her the quarantine would end Friday.

"If it doesn't end 'til Friday, I can't go out tomorrow, can I?" Stacy asked, wanting to leave her apartment more than she could believe, but worried about getting arrested. She blamed that fear on Jared. He took enough risks for both of them.

"You aren't likely to be stopped, but I've been assured the school ID will act as a hall pass." He chuckled at his joke.

"What will we be doing?"

"Checking out the property for vandalism or looting."

Stacy remembered the grocery store, but turned her thoughts away quickly, not wanting her principal to get even a whiff of her illegal experience.

"I'm sure you all have lessons to prepare and students to contact."

"Thanks, Mr. Castignoli."

"See you tomorrow."

Stacy put down the phone and stared at it. She couldn't believe it was over. Or was it? She wondered about the history lesson she was in the middle of. She decided in preparation for Friday, she'd do a bit of Internet research. She needed to learn what she could about how the Indians contracted smallpox. Everyone talked about the blankets, but she wanted more detail. She was suddenly certain there were reverberations in the current situation. She paused for a moment and considered the school board. They hate it when teachers *go off the reservation*. The perfect metaphor. She smiled at the way her brain worked.

She'd never done drugs like her twin, but she had her own ways of rebelling. If she could make solid links to the current crisis, she knew she could hook her students, get them thinking. Of course, that inevitably led to them telling their parents, which led to reports to the principal. With any luck, everyone else was too anxious to get back to everyday life, too busy picking up the pieces, to notice what she'd be up to.

The school year was almost over. She should probably keep her nose clean for the remainder. Ah, keep her nose clean, another funny cliché. She didn't agree with her English colleagues who wanted to end the use of clichés. She thought they carried the culture in ways that taught us something about our history. They also colored the language in ways she appreciated. She guessed she wasn't sophisticated enough. With that, she got up and moved to her computer to start her research. En route, she texted Jared: "Out of jail."

"I am?"

"No, me. Back to school tomorrow."

"And the rest of us?"

"Friday."

"Excellent. Thanks, sis."

QUARANTINE BOUNDARIES IN FLUX

Lansing, MI — The *E. Coli* scare in NW Michigan came to a close today as children returned to school across nearly a quarter of the state. Simultaneously, the botulism outbreak in SE Iowa was officially designated "concluded," with that quarantine to end at midnight.

Just across the Mississippi, in Moline, IL, *Listeria* cases mounted in local hospitals. Enforcers, the latest homeland security team meant to address quarantines, have yet to reach the area, so police immediately began enforcing a mandated quarantine by patrolling the streets with loudspeakers demanding people get inside or face arrest.

Iowa governor Jedediah Grassfield affirmed his confidence in letting people from Davenport to Keokuk return to their jobs tomorrow, saying, "The river is a natural barrier. Always has been." Reporters could not reach Illinois governor Blanchet for comment.

Quarantines are becoming commonplace across the country, though the constantly changing boundaries and timelines continue to cause confusion. In Iowa City yesterday, an Enforcer was arrested when he was reported for knocking on a friend's front door. This lackey had just finished a shift in nearby Waterloo enforcing a quarantine there, but was unaware that a quarantine had been imposed on his city during his shift. He was released when his identity was uncovered, but fined $500 for the infraction.

The uncertainty created by the shifting quarantines means that consumers have begun hoarding supplies. Grocery store owners say they can't keep water, batteries or canned goods on the shelf. Pharmacies report shortages of masks, gloves and other antibacterial over-the-counter necessities. After last week's shooting when two cars collided in a race to a gas pump, gas stations have hired armed guards to enforce perimeters to ensure cars do not form waiting lines.

Though print and broadcast media continue to make announcements, they have proven inefficient in getting word to the public about the ever-changing boundaries of quarantines. Therefore the government has employed technicians to create Robocalls, socialcasting, and spamming, which reaches people far more effectively. Getting people to retreat to their homes happens more quickly with each outbreak. But gaining the trust of quarantined individuals and convincing them it is safe to leave their homes becomes ever more challenging.

Cathy's friends were gathered at her home. Senior citizens all, they sat in armchairs, on a couch, on table chairs pulled into the living room so they could talk easily. They gathered for a potluck, something the young would never do, not trusting one another with the deadly activity of food preparation. However, in a world that boasted habits learned early were habits for life, this group enjoyed the variety of foods and the community built through sharing as they'd done since they were young adults. The meal over, the time to leave approaching, the talk had turned to bacteria and death, as it so often did these days. Someone shifted the conversation, and they were off and running, reminiscing about the dangerous habits of the past.

"I rarely washed my hands after peeing," offered one of the men.

"I took out the trash and then served dinner without washing in between," countered another.

"I ate food off the floor when I was cooking," challenged Cathy.

"Yeah, but did you pick it up and put it on a serving tray? Huh? Huh?" Cathy was not sure if they meant tonight. Before she could respond, someone laughed and the competition continued.

"I ate while working in the garage. Didn't matter whether my hands had paint on 'em or grease, or even insecticide. If I had cookies or a chicken leg or chips, I'd just pop 'em in my mouth and go right on workin'."

"It didn't hurt. Here we are." Everyone laughed, washing away the tensions raised by the discussion of bacteria.

"Can you remember when we didn't have any cleansers that were antibacterial? We didn't even have that word."

"I remember when we simply rinsed off cutting boards no matter what we'd used them for and put them away. They collected bacteria with every slice into the wood. But we didn't die. Did we?" Mouths grimaced and heads shook.

"I recall my grandmother getting upset when I asked her not to cook food she had dropped on the floor. She was Depression Era. She wouldn't waste food no matter what. She'd let things just sit on the counter even if they had meat or mayo in them. She grew up with just a small icebox. That was her worldview. We couldn't shake it. Finally we had to stop eating things she cooked."

"You all know the story of Howard's proposal, how he hid the ring in my mousse at our favorite restaurant," Cathy said. "I usually emphasize how romantic he was." Everyone nodded at Cathy. "But think about it in today's context. Hiding a ring, a ring he bought from a jewelry store. They may have cleaned it with alcohol, they may not. A diamond ring has lots of little crevices, well, mine does. Good places for bacteria to accumulate even if they did wipe it off. And there's no telling how many hands touched it in the store. Then Howard handed it over to someone at the restaurant, probably the owner because they were friends. Maybe not friends, but they talked every week when we ate there. The owner would have given it to someone in the kitchen who put it in the mousse. That ring moved through all those hands and probably was laid down many places in the process. It was probably breathed on as someone or other held it up to his eye to get a closer look or try to judge the diamond quality. No doubt someone along the way used it to scratch a mirror or window to ensure it was real. And then bacteria from all those sources traveled with the ring into my mousse. I discovered that ring in my mouth, of all places! We've always thought Howard wanted to marry me, but maybe he wanted to kill me!"

Laughter pealed around the room. Most knew Howard, all knew the story, but Cathy had delivered a nice twist in this telling that held their attention and garnered their appreciation.

"When I was a kid," another guest added, "I was a nose picker." There were shocked looks on a couple of faces, others nodded in recognition. "Didn't know that about me, did you? It's true. There were two satisfactions in it. The first was a cleaned-out nose. I always hated being stuffed up. The second pleasure is hard to describe to non-pickers. Maybe I can liken it to chefs. There's deep satisfaction in eating what you've made." Several guffaws circulated around the room. "Oh, don't give me that! I knew none of you would understand. I was in my 20s before I stopped picking."

"Do any of you remember when that doctor, or maybe it was a researcher, made those claims that we should all eat our snot?"

"Oh yeah, wasn't it something about building up antibodies?"

"Didn't they compare it to breast milk?"

"Exactly."

"Funny that idea never caught on." Laughter circulated the room.

"I read that in some Asian country, or maybe it was Arabic..."

"Asia and Arabia? Not that similar."

"OK, there was an *A*, that's what I remember."

"How old are you? Memory's already going?" Snickers arose, mostly in recognition.

"The point is, somewhere in the world it not only caught on, but it became big business. They started marketing high-immunity snot. Think they put it in capsule form so there wasn't taste or texture."

"I thought it was supposed to be genetically connected, biome-related or something."

"Does it really matter? We didn't go there."

"Right. We kept thinking of snot as dangerous, as carrying bacteria that would kill."

"And we weren't wrong. The spread of bacteria can involve the nose, the mouth, any moist surface really."

"There you go, the mouth. That was my zone. You know how kids used to put everything in their mouths? We even had a theory for it, called it the oral phase, purported it was for exploration and learning. Kids today don't seem at a loss intellectually for not having tasted the world. Do you think?"

Although it looked like someone might respond, the speaker thought it a rhetorical question and quickly continued, "But that's not the point. The point is, I was a licker. Honest."

Heads shook in disbelief and disgust. A few people said "No!" aloud.

"No, really. My mother was a nurse, so she worried about oral cleanliness before it was mandated. Well, me and my mom didn't get on so well. She was gone a lot and I suppose I resented it. Anyway, I used to sidle up to the most disgusting things I could and lick them. I didn't do it for pleasure exactly. It wasn't a sickness, I didn't have pica or anything. But if my mother could see me, I'd lick stuff. It started with simple things—the spoon she'd been using, my brother's plate before dinner, a pen I was handing to her. But then it got a little out of control."

"That's not out of control?" someone objected, but the speaker continued, unabated.

"If I was upset with her, I'd lick whatever was nearest that I thought would bother her most—her toothbrush, the countertop after she'd been cooking but before she wiped up, a doorknob, the steering wheel, the phone receiver. Can you imagine the amount of bacteria on some of those surfaces? I remember when the news came out about cell phones being one of the dirtiest things we touched. The report caused my gag reflex to kick in as I remembered licking the phone receiver. Cell phones people wipe off occasionally, but the old landlines? Those receivers were never cleaned. I like to believe this behavior has kept me alive by developing quite the immune system."

Someone chuckled, someone else nodded, one man flexed his bicep turning his fist outward and inward repeatedly.

"OK, but did any of you ever eat raw beef?"

"Yowsa! No."

"I frequently ate steak tartare. I took regular ground beef and marinated it in wine and Worcestershire sauce, if you can imagine. I served it with onions and capers. To top it off, I ate it chilled. I think I ate it right up until mad cow disease made it to this continent. Don't shake your heads, we all acted like we were immune."

"From my country, Ethiopia, butchers serve kitfo, right after killing the cow. We chop beef and add clarified butter and spices. We eat it, like all else, with injera bread, which soaks up all the blood. Can you imagine? Of course, right from the animal at least there is no chance of more contamination, not like your ground beef, which gets processed and packaged and shipped, and may or may not be kept cold enough. Oh, ours may sound more disgusting, how you say, *vulgar*, but it is also safer." He nodded emphatically as others looked away, avoiding eye contact. No one wanted to insult his culture, but they couldn't begin to imagine eating flesh that emanated the warmth of life.

"Not beef, even more risky, we ate pork."

"Not raw."

"Almost raw, not completely. In Germany we had what we called *mettwurst*. It was considered master craft because ingredients had to be first rate due to risks. We knew that much even then. Ground pork put in sausage casing. What don't we put in sausage casing, ya? Then it was smoked for few days. So not raw, not cooked. Trichinosis always possibility. Small danger, part of the excitement."

"A young person listening in would think us crazy."

"They'd have us arrested."

"Could they do that?"

"They could try."

"It was a simpler time, wasn't it?"

"Simpler. Safer. Yet, less sanitized."

"Indeed."

"How did we learn to live like we do now?"

"It was adapt or die."

That sobered the room as each person stopped to recall a loved one, many loved ones, and friends who had died from bacterial infections. A moment passed. Eyes slowly rose to meet one another. No one spoke. A couple people nodded as they made eye contact. One woman brushed her tears onto her sleeve.

"Habits learned early," someone intoned in an attempt to lighten the mood before they departed.

"Thanks for hosting, Cathy," said a woman who stood to leave.

"Oh, don't go," she said, disingenuously. They all knew. The spell had been broken. Smiles returned to a few faces. Others couldn't shake the sense that death was again among them.

Individually they stood and moved toward the door, which stood open already, Cathy standing there saying goodbye, reminding some to take their dishes. No hugs, no kisses, no handshakes. Touching was forbidden. Touching was unsafe. As the last man approached, he looked at Cathy and said, "The times, they are a changing." Both smiled.

"Thanks, my friend," said Cathy holding up her hand in the Vulcan symbol. "Live long and prosper." He returned the gesture.

It was a ritual they could keep when so many others had been lost to them.

AGRIBIZ TO DISSOLVE

Des Moines, IA—In a joint announcement from the Department of Agriculture, the FDA, and the Securities Commission, the conglomerate known as AgriBiz will be parceled out to local community governments.

In the wake of massive deaths due to bacterial strains ranging from *E. Coli* to *Cha-Cha MRSA*, a dramatic increase in lawsuits against AgriBiz has led to catastrophic financial losses. Insurance companies are begging for mercy.

Additionally, class action wrongful death suits and even murder charges are pending against AgriBiz. Court dockets are backlogged beyond the foreseeable future, threatening a collapse of the entire legal system.

AgriBiz profits have been dramatically reduced since the end of meat production. Conversion of CAFO land into safe ground for the production of crops has proven far more expensive than AgriBiz had planned, due to regulations requiring cleanup of both feed and antibiotic treatment areas.

The dissolution of AgriBiz will break the giant agriculture megalith into small farms run by local government lackeys. Each farm will produce, package and distribute food products to an area not greater than a 50-mile radius and to not more than 5,000 people. A 10-mile radius was initially proposed but it quickly became clear that urban areas would need immediate dismantling for that to work.

The largest concern remains bacteria elimination from the food chain.

Even with the breakup, officials warn that stricter guidelines will need to be instituted to restore safety to the food supply.

Faith in the integrity of the system is not likely to be regained easily. However, the end of AgriBiz sends a serious message that the cleanup is, at long last, underway.

RESERVES TO FEED THE NATION

Chicago, IL — During the dismantling of AgriBiz, farmland will go fallow for one year to cleanse soil of bacteria and other deadly parasites infecting the nation's food supply.

Americans will be forced to live on reserves during the fallow period. It will be a lean year, said the acting head of the FDA, but with population reduction, it will be manageable. Officials at every level are hammering out a distribution system for reserves.

Priorities are being developed with considerations to health, balanced diets and location. Above all else is the importance of safety. Reserve food supplies are not necessarily free from contamination. For that reason, while priorities are being determined, FDA lackeys will trace the sourcing on each and every food lot in the reserve system. The speed at which this inspection can occur may become a factor in the battle for priorities.

Among reserves, officials listed the following foods: aged cheese (pre-dates the end of beef production), rice, flour (all containing gluten), soybeans (all genetically modified), turkey jerky (pre-dates elimination of fowl), pasta, and oatmeal.

Discussions have begun about repurposing corn for a protein and fiber source rather than as a sweetener, biofuel, and obsolete pig fodder. Geraldine Brown, Secretary of the Department of Agriculture, said, "Corn was once a dietary staple. It can once again be an important part of a balanced diet. I am today proposing that we immediately stop the use of corn for purposes other than direct consumption."

The Secretary acknowledged that this idea has not been vetted by the manufacturing sector and is likely to raise ire there. She indicated that in the future her team predicts corn and wheat will again become staples for the American diet as they were in the 19th century.

Meanwhile, concerns raised about the GMO status of both crops have led independent scientists to suggest oats or rice as more likely central components of the new American diet. Scientists speculate that both the genetic alterations and lack of bio-diversity among corn and wheat seed will eventually lead to a rejection of those crops as safe for human consumption.

While GMOs originally reduced bacterial dangers, resistant strains have emerged, infecting crops and those who eat them. Further concerns were raised about the reduced yields of GMOs, which becomes more significant with the limitations of uncontaminated farmland.

One locus of my cynicism was my prediction that meat would disappear. My only question had been the order of disappearance. We academics are prone to focus on such unanswerable questions. It keeps our brains nimble, keeps our argumentation skills acute.

Before the turn of the century, there were stories of chicken contamination during processing. That hit me hard because I'd been eating only poultry as a way of maximizing proteins, a la Frances More Lappe. It wasn't about the cholesterol, not about my personal health, but the health of the planet. Though poultry was still readily available, the reports made me squeamish, and I stopped eating chicken. Then mad cow came along and I was certain beef would disappear.

I knew that Concentrated Animal Feeding Operations, CAFOs as we called them, would not only be the death of the beef industry, but of humankind. Corn-fed beef! When I was growing up that was the best, what mother wanted to buy. It wasn't till I became a biologist that I realized cows weren't meant to eat corn. They were ruminants with multiple stomachs meant to eat grass. Feeding cows corn leads to acid-resistance, which, along with the crowded feces-ridden conditions in the CAFOs, meant *E. Coli* grew more and more prevalent. How could it not? Perfect conditions. All of which led to more antibiotic use for feed-animals, which in turn led to more human resistance to antibiotics—a viscous cycle.

Not that I didn't hope a Polyface farm—you know, an old timey farm where crops and animals rotated and roamed so fertilization took care of itself—would come along and change the world, but then again, as I've said, I wasn't an idealist. I'd allow myself a day or two of unabashed hope when I'd read an article from the Michael Pollan followers or watch a documentary that called us to action. The wife would renew her commitment to buying organic and buying local. I appreciated that, though I didn't attend to it myself. Bottom line, I didn't hold out hope for a conversion of our agricultural system, not when that would have meant a change in capitalism, which I was confident wasn't happening. The mighty dollar was here to stay.

I had watched AgriBiz grow, just like every other megalithic multinational capitalist conglomerate. It had been so adept, pushing one type of farmer out of business, buying up, changing up, reaping the profits, running the markets, making the cash. Always under the radar. Legal action never yielded anything substantial—an out-of-court settlement here, a payout there. Nothing the company couldn't afford with pocket change. Hell, investors never felt the slightest pinch of their portfolio. So it all kept moving forward.

It was amazing how something so large could be so limber, so lithe, to move with such grace. Sometimes it almost seemed God had blessed them, but that's hubris shining through again. AgriBiz wasn't growing crops or raising animals, it was producing—not food, but money, capital. It appeared invincible.

But with a cyclical concern about the nation's meat sources, focused on poultry then on beef then back to poultry, with one seeming more likely to disappear before the other in alternating waves, I was shocked when overnight pork became history. No warning shot was fired across the bow with that one. I mean, Jews and others had eschewed pig consumption forever, and there were the periodic health warnings, not so much about trichinosis as about the high sodium content or curing. All of which were minor points, raising hardly an eyebrow of the average bacon-loving American. In fact, just before pork disappeared, there was a wild year or two when bacon was in everything: chocolate, cupcakes, you name it.

Yet pork was the proverbial canary in the mine if we'd but paid attention. Turned out pigs were the "mixing bowl" of bacterial disease. As disease after disease crossed the species' barrier—hardly a barrier by that time, another misnomer—it was discovered that pigs were the vehicle for strains to pass from one host to another. A particular strain of bacteria could get into pigs from any number of sources—say monkeys or bats or chickens. Those bacteria could live in the pig until they could combine and mutate into a new bacterial strain that could afflict humans. The science had been hinted at for some time but hadn't been replicated. Couldn't be replicated since funding wasn't there to retest, now could it?!

Finally, some rich guy who'd gotten religion a la the healthy foods movement was persuaded to underwrite multiple studies, each replicating an earlier buried report. Bing, bang, boom! Proven beyond a shadow of a doubt, totally reasonable. While the report was winning one of those big international prizes, the Pulitzer, I think, suddenly pigs were being destroyed by the hundreds of thousands a day. For once, the CAFOs served a useful purpose—the wholesale slaughter of a species.

What happened in the grocery stores was a thing to behold. The stores I shopped at pulled all pork from the shelves immediately. These were the upscale markets in middle class neighborhoods. But in poorer areas, there was a run on all things pork, from chops to bacon to pig's feet. Prices were hiked! It was a sellers' market. Rumor had it that the upscale markets secretly moved the supplies to such stores rather than destroy the meat as promised, which only made sense—dollars and cents.

Pigs were the mixing bowl. The mix had to start somewhere. Before you knew it, poultry was on the chopping block. This time there was a tussle over it. There wasn't a definitive report showing poultry as bacteria-ridden. The studies showed that sick birds could pass bacteria onto pigs, but pigs were gone already.

Unfortunately for chicken and turkey farms, at that moment avian flu made a resurgence in China. Where else, right? It was discovered in chickens during a routine inspection at a plant where results were often misplaced. But as it happened, a novice on the job handled this inspection, the son of a high-ranking official who mentioned the findings at a state dinner. That was that. Too many overheard his story to bury the results. With China slaughtering its stock—a news story not to be missed, complete with gruesome visuals and deafening squawks—the U.S. had to respond.

For 48 media-hyped hours, AgriBiz attempted to suggest that American birds were safe. The delay tactics didn't work because an independent reporter for a radical group was able to get national attention for footage she'd collected, footage showing birds dying in large numbers inside the CAFOs by day and being hauled away by night. That was all it took. Poultry was history. Chickens and turkeys were gone within weeks.

Oddly, cattle were last, and by a long ways. The beef lobby in Washington ensured that. They could see it coming and were well prepared after decades of the small shocks they'd endured. Mad cow disease made it to our shores. *E. Coli* was repeatedly linked to beef, even as it began to appear on any number of vegetables, but that was also cow-related, since it was contamination from proximity to a CAFO.

Beef didn't disappear all at once or as quickly as other meats. First, ground beef was pulled from production. It was obvious that CAFOs, slaughtering facilities and packaging plants each played a role in the contamination of hamburger. Ground beef was said to contain parts of as many as a thousand cows in a single pound. Plus there were reports of ammonia being used to reduce the dangers, but that created pink slime, which was neither tasty nor appealing. Ground beef ceased.

New cuts appeared when ground beef disappeared, and for a brief time this excited us. These obviously inferior cuts had previously been ground, but the new types of steak fed our need for the novel, so craftily built up by ad agencies for nearly a century. These new cuts fit the "new and improved" bill to a T—they were neither new nor improved, so Americans, never having recognized this paradox, bought them with gusto.

Soon that also came to an end. The beef industry really couldn't fight the bacterial tide for long. They hiked prices, made a killing selling steaks to us, then killed all the cows "for the health of the nation." There weren't really many left for that ceremonial slaughter. They'd arranged with Washington to diminish their stock and get most of their cows into our stomachs before beef went belly up.

***

Another quarantine had just ended when Trevor was called to New York City. He'd never been there, but was excited at the prospect of more Enforcement duties. He boarded the plane like any other passenger. He was in plain clothes and seated in coach in a middle seat. The woman on the aisle had her handheld open. The plane backed away from the terminal but sat quietly on the tarmac. Trevor was attentive to all those around him. The guy in the window seat was already asleep. *How could he do that? Sleep when others were no doubt sharing bacteria freely?*

"Please stow all electronic devices. If it has a battery, it must be turned off."

The woman in the aisle seat kept texting on her handheld. It looked like she was finishing so Trevor waited. She sent one message and started another.

"You need to put that away, ma'am."

The woman glared at Trevor. "Little pipsqueak," she said without looking at him.

"Now, ma'am," he said firmly. "Stow that electronic device, as requested."

She kept typing. Trevor reached over and confiscated the handheld. The woman was stupefied. She tried to retrieve her handheld but couldn't with her seatbelt buckled. She glared at Trevor. She rang the call button for the flight attendant and sputtered, "You'll be sorry, buddy."

Trevor held his cool. When the flight attendant arrived, she reached out her hand and Trevor presented the device. Before the passenger could utter a word, the flight attendant turned and made her way down the aisle with the handheld.

"But that's mine," cried the passenger.

"You'll be able to retrieve it when the plane lands. Until then, it will be held for you." Trevor withheld the smile he felt. He'd been taught not to incite people to anger. He knew well that people prized their devices like life itself, perhaps beyond that, since many had been infected due to poor bacterial habits where electronics were concerned.

"But I'm allowed to use that in flight."

"Rule-abiding passengers are allowed that luxury. I'm afraid you lost that privilege by not turning it off when instructed by a crew member."

"TSA?"

"No, ma'am. Homeland Security AntiBacterial Enforcement." Trevor's eyes flashed pride. He was still excited by his position. And now he was being given a better post. He was sure more opportunities would come his way.

"Oh, an Enforcer. I should have known."

Trevor was used to the tone of derision often applied to his position. He suspected if he had as little control as Homelanders did, he might get testy, too. Then again, this was an obvious rule, a longstanding rule. It wasn't like getting a curfew wrong or trying to use the Emergency Room for a compound fracture when it was only seeing bacterial cases. Those were changes. That was understandable. Not following a verbal command? No excuse.

***

Every morning like clockwork, she'd reach out and touch my lips. Then my cheek. I'd push her away. Whether I was enjoying a dream or just relaxed in my sleep, I didn't want to be awakened. I wanted to appreciate the last vestiges of being prone in bed without gravity pulling at my spine. It was no use. She wouldn't take no for an answer. She didn't know "no." That's the beauty of domesticated pets, they live in the moment, not understanding more than wanting to be fed or petted or to jump into our laps. She pawed my face, I got up to feed her. It was a ritual. It was intimate.

I'd thought that domestic pets would go the way of cattle or pigs. I'd thought it would be obvious they carried disease. Dogs licked their owners with those slobbery tongues. Cats pawed in the litter box and dragged it all over. I expected the call for a wholesale slaughter. But it never came.

Morning after morning my cat—Ghost was her name for her love of hiding—would come and wake me from my slumber by pawing my face. No doubt I was to blame for this behavior. I'd head-butted her to make a connection when her sibling had died abruptly years before. And I'd responded to her pleas. Had I ignored them, had she not had this morning behavior, perhaps I wouldn't have worried so much about her carrying deadly bacteria.

Each morning Ghost would paw my lips, then cheek. She'd circle me in the bed, laying out her territory. She'd lay down by my head and reach out and put her paw right on my mouth. I'd move it, usually gently, but sometimes with a bit of force when I really wanted another hour. Every few minutes she'd return and replay the routine with a variation or two. As I'd become conscious, I'd start thinking about where that paw had been. I think we were between the FaceTouch Ban and the Total Touch Ban at the time. You can imagine how those events would invade that liminal space between sleeping and waking. I'd hear her peeing in her pan and then hear the scratching as her paws moved the litter to cover the smell. The same paw would touch my face. Sometimes I'd wonder about the disease pregnant women could get from litter so they were never to clean up after cats during their gestation period. I didn't know if that disease was bacterial. I hadn't heard of any particular bacteria that cats carried. AgriBiz wasn't playing with my cat's food, at least I assumed as much. But the species barrier no longer existed. Were pigs the only possible mixing bowl?

Well, you can see how my thoughts ran. Over a period of months I convinced myself that my cat, my Ghost, was a danger. Putting animals down was common enough. Vets had always done the deed. Walk in with a living pet, walk out empty-handed or with a small burial box or even have ashes delivered to your door. We loved our pets. Even in death we treated them like humans.

I found I didn't need to explain why I wanted Ghost dead, and that's the truth of it, my fear had won and I wanted her dead. I'd become afraid of her. This sweet, soft creature only wanted my love, but I'd come to see her as a bacteria delivery device and I couldn't even bring myself to pet her anymore. That wasn't good for either of us. I discovered, to my relief and chagrin, that I could buy a lethal injection at the pet store. Evidently I wasn't the only one in this predicament.

I'd been shunning Ghost for so long that when I made the decision, she was hungry for my attention. I prepared the injection, fed her a favored treat, and invited her into my lap, which she jumped into with abandon. I held her as her heart stopped and she began to stiffen. Oddly, given the fear that led me to this, I petted her and even kissed the top of her head. I was going to miss her. I couldn't know then how much I'd miss her. My wife was still alive, there were still students in my life. I wasn't quarantined. Today, I would give anything to have Ghost with me. She'd be a comfort in so many ways. I'd happily share my meager allotment with her.

Sometimes when I awake I can still feel the ghost print of her paw at my lips. It's a memory of touch I keep close, problematic as it was. It was such an innocent touch, as most were. Innocence and danger, we were taught, go hand-in-hand, literally. Or in this case, hand-in-paw.

REDUCING CITY SIZES

New York, NY — AgriBiz farms are being cut up into smaller units to decrease contamination. Each farm will feed only small local populations. Urban zones will be problematic since there will not be enough area for small farms in close enough proximity to the large urban populations.

For the past 18 months, government's fear of urban areas as breeding grounds for bacteria has been a growing concern.

Examining the rates of death in large urban areas like New York City compared to smaller cities like Des Moines, Iowa, or rural areas like the entire state of West Virginia, it is evident that it is more dangerous to live in an urban area with high population density. Population centers of 50,000 or less have statistically significant lower death rates. The factors that contribute to soaring urban death rates cannot be altered while maintaining populations over a quarter of a million.

Forced relocation goes against the very grain of our national identity. It is much better to encourage people to move on their own.

Kwitten, Bond and Porter, a Madison Avenue advertising firm, has been hired by government to assemble a team and develop a campaign to entice people to leave urban areas, particularly New York, Chicago, Los Angeles and Washington DC. It is believed that if people can be lured away from these centers, the movement will spread across the nation much like the urban movement of the 1900s or the suburban movement of the 1950s.

"If everyone moved out of New York or Los Angeles at once, it would be a disaster. The more evenly people disperse, the safer the food will be and the cheaper the transportation will be," said Kwitten, Bond and Porter CEO Henry Bukowsky. "Advertisers invite and consumers buy into the idea. The challenge of this ad campaign is to get people moving in different directions at the same time."

The Secretary of the Interior could not be reached, but a staff member said he has complete confidence in the Kwitten Group. "It is our best option at this juncture," said Interior staffer, Jake Jarvis.

Kwitten, Bond and Porter Advertising

Press Release

Distribution: Social Media, E-Banners, Crawls, Skywriting, Print, TV, Radio

Moving on Out

Hired by government to move citizens out of populated urban centers into rural areas, Kwitten, Bond and Porter is putting not only creativity but collaboration to the test. This Madison Avenue advertising firm has hired an assortment of specialists, including social media creators, wedding planners, social scientists specializing in snowball theory, and algorithm data specialists, to create a team that will forever change the structure of America's cities.

Please contribute: *If you have an idea of how to get people to migrate out of cities in a distributive way, post your ideas on the social media of your choice.* "Let's start talking about it," said Twizzler CMO Mayer Scissons. "There's no reason that the handful of us being gathered by Kwitten, Bond and Porter are any more likely to come up with the best ideas than you or your next-door neighbor. The power of social media is in the collective. Together we are smarter than we are individually."

Tell us what you think using http://twit.dys/MovinOut.

"Urbanites, get out your contact lists. Who do you know in a small town? Get out your maps. What part of the country have you always wanted to live in?" asks Kwitten, Bond and Porter CEO Henry Bukowsky. "Don't be the last man or woman standing. Move out while the moving is good."

"Don't just look at your contact list, start calling, texting, Facebooking. Check out where your friends are now and where they're going," says snowball theorist Meghan Burdis. "Small towns aren't just quaint," adds wedding planner Bridgett Shankman. "Rural areas have sex appeal. They are safe, and there's time to stop and smell the roses."

The challenge: vastly decrease the population centers of NYC, LA, DC and Chicago

The method: assemble a diverse think tank

The timeline:

Week 1:	Planning
Week 2:	Campaign strategy
Week 4:	Campaign slogans and designs
Week 8:	First targeted release of ads
Week 12:	Blanket niche markets
Weeks 16-24:	Gather and assess data
Week 26:	Provide report to government

# # #   # # #   # # #

When the Total Touch Ban came, when we were told that all human-to-human contact must cease, a cry went up to the heavens. It wasn't possible. It was inhuman. It would end the human race. Like everything else that has happened, most people went along. They bought up each new device that solved a problem where touch had been previously needed. The tongs that had become so popular were of no use between humans. Many kinds of gloves were developed, some of them equipped with technology to simulate touching different body parts. *Can you imagine?* New larger condoms appeared, not because penises had grown, though advertising for that abounded, but rather, condoms covered more than just the penis. After all, stomachs and asses weren't allowed to touch, either. The condom-bra was meant to allow the touching of breasts, but without tongues involved the magic was lost as far as I was concerned. None of the devices lasted long. It was hard to find the pleasure, the relief and the comfort without flesh-to-flesh contact.

Did couples or mothers and children still touch one another in the privacy of their own homes? Perhaps. But the habit of non-touch had to be learned to survive the years between the Total Touch Ban and the irregular quarantines of the Transition. During those years, it wasn't the possibility of arrest that stopped people as much as the fear of contagion. Fear grew in us like a plague of its own. No one wanted to die of bacteria. One day you were healthy, the next you were gone. Bacteria seemed to be an equal opportunity killer. While some strains focused on the young and old, those groups we traditionally thought of as vulnerable, there were just as many strains that took healthy adults in mid-life. There was no built-up immunity from bacteria the way there was from viruses. If anything, exposure to antibiotics made you more vulnerable as you went through life.

People learned to not reach out to comfort one another. No hands on shoulders. No hugs goodbye. Women were already getting artificially inseminated. Suddenly there were blogs extolling the virtues of a sex-free marriage, the delights of courtship without the challenges of sexual encounters, the pleasures of masturbation. I laughed at that. After a lifetime of being told hair would grow on my palms if I pleasured myself, it was suddenly not only all right, but an important release of testosterone.

Of course, that's not the full story. There was also an enormous increase in rape. Something needed to be done and done quickly. Accused rapists were isolated from the general population in the prisons. They were tested for all kinds of diseases, STDs of course but also bacterial infestations that might be killers. When disease was inevitably found, they were made into public examples.

Oh, we still had laws and courts then, but we also had a media that followed the leader and fed on gore and grief of any type. So it wasn't hard for government to marshall public opinion into an outcry of rage and fear. Some of the rapists died horrible bacterial deaths in front of our eyes, broadcast everywhere from cable to the Internet. While no reality TV shows were created, per se, it became a standard of special news programming to feature the stories of rapists disfigured, bleeding and dying. Rape victims took solace in the deaths while also being tested. Mass resources were used to save the victims from deaths similar to their perpetrators. In public view, the rapists died, the victims lived. I doubted the veracity of that story, too simple, too useful, too ridiculous. All that press attention led young men to line up for their shot at fame. Rape was the last bastion of sex, and death was not too high a price to pay for the notoriety it brought.

Once the story became men who raped, not for the sex, not for the contact, but for the fame, suddenly not all the rapists were dying. Some lived. They were put to work in chain gangs cleaning up toxic bacterial sites. For these stories, the cameras pulled back. There were no longer individuals getting the limelight. Instead, there were horrid conditions depicted where bacteria raged through prisons, schools, and hospitals, any and every contained public space. The chain gangs sometimes collapsed in the midst of the cleaning with the dead chained to the living. The cameras were at a safe distance. No more close-ups. Now the horrors came mostly from the sounds, the clink of chain, the roar of power scrubbers, the screams of those falling in the midst of agonies beyond imagining. This footage didn't last long. It didn't have to. Rape slowed even before the final quarantine, when opportunity utterly ceased.

***

When he arrived in NYC, Trevor assumed the post given him without question. He performed his duties as assigned. He caught and detained many Homelanders who were taking or causing risks to themselves or others by their casual behaviors regarding potential bacterial situations. Trevor never failed to notice. Trevor never failed to stop the "perp," as he had come to think of them. Anyone bacterially ignorant or casual was perpetrating a crime on humanity, a crime against the U.S., a dangerous crime against life itself. No one commended Trevor. Nor did anyone reprimand him. No one questioned his motives or actions.

Not quite true. The Homelanders, the perps, they sometimes questioned what he was doing. Trevor took that in stride, took pride in his ability to stop a face-toucher, an other-toucher, a causal sneezer, and those who allowed spittle to jettison from mouth to surface fomenting potential disease and even death to the unsuspecting. Trevor carried the current AB spray at all times. It hung in a holster from his belt. It was a small bottle with a powerful concentration and a fine mist sprayer that offered maximum coverage. When he was off the job, for personal use, he kept AB wipes strategically located so he was never without AB protection.

During his second month he was put on subway duty. Then moved to a monitor center where he watched live-action cams all over the city. He could activate the earpieces of Enforcers all over the East Side to announce or confirm a broken rule, a bacterial infraction, a dangerous perp. He developed a shorthand, a verbal code to communicate quickly so he could report on as many acts as he could witness and track. He passed the code on to his superiors, who dispatched it to feet-on-the-ground and eyes-in-the-centers. There was no commendation, but he wasn't expecting one. He was doing his job and was pleased he'd made that job more efficient for all involved.

One Saturday, he arrived at his telescreen cubby to find that a street hockey game was in progress, a company picnic underway, a piñata party in full swing, and several other large-group events filling over half his screens. He took a deep breath, relieved the previous Visual Enforcer, or VE, and sat down to begin work. As he radioed the Enforcer nearest the piñata about a nose-toucher among the teenagers rimming the children's circle, he noticed the picnic had been logged as starting three hours earlier. Several dishes on the table contained mayonnaise, meat, or egg products. They hadn't been picked up and a line was forming of newly arrived guests who intended to join the feast. He ensured the food was confiscated before anyone could scoop up another morsel, while also having several guests, whose names were on the bottoms of dishes, arrested for not removing the potentially deadly food in a timely manner.

On screen after screen he found infractions, not equaling the picnic, but where danger lurked or was thrust upon others in the form of invisible, deadly bacteria. By the end of his Saturday shift, 176 people had been detained, 45 warnings had been issued, 29 pounds of food confiscated and destroyed, and 13 people rushed to Emergency. No word on how many of those 13 lived or died. Trevor seldom knew the end result of his life-saving attempts.

On Thursday, Trevor received a text. He was to report to the high command before assuming his VE duties. Trevor quickly reviewed his workweek. He couldn't recall any major mistakes, but then he wouldn't recognize them or he wouldn't have made them. When he'd been posted in NYC and when he'd moved from street duty to subway to VE, he'd received an email detailing the changes, so a text struck him as odd and raised the fine hairs on his arms. It made him stop and consider. *What are the autonomic responses?* He was trained well enough that he didn't reach out to touch the goose bumps, but their mere presence was an annoyance, and a reminder of how the body could betray even the most attuned Enforcer.

Inside high command he stood at attention in front of a desk. Behind the desk sat a tiny, fussy man. Trevor knew well enough not to assume the demeanor meant the man had no power. Trevor would not slacken his resolve to be the best Enforcer possible. He stood tall and proud. After a few minutes, the mousy man with the goatee motioned for Trevor to step into the office behind him. Trevor advanced, knocked and entered. Before him sat Commander Triniti Snopek, the woman he'd first met outside his training room in Chicago. Today she was once again in a billowing blouse, which made her look less than authoritative.

"Commander!" Trevor didn't salute, it wasn't the custom, but he ensured his tone conveyed his knowledge of her rank as well as his admiration.

"Mr. Kashnikov, we meet again. Thank you for answering my text to meet here."

"Yes, ma'am."

"Trevor. May I call you Trevor?" He nodded firmly even though this informality caught him off-guard. "Trevor, I was alerted to the service you provided last Saturday from the VE."

"A busy day indeed."

"Not just a busy day, Mr. Kashnikov. You've handled many of those. But a day in which the code you designed was essential. Without it, you never could have achieved the numbers you did."

"I suppose that's true. There were a couple hours in there when I barely had time to generate the code."

"How do you see so much?"

"I don't know. Is it unusual?"

"Very."

"I've always been attentive, especially when it comes to rules."

The commander laughed. "I see. Yes. Well, obviously you don't know just how extraordinary your gift is." Trevor shook his head. "I've called you here to offer you a promotion."

"A promotion?"

"Yes. It won't take effect for a couple weeks. We need you in the VE until then. Do you pay attention to the news, Mr. Kashnikov?"

"I try. Occasionally my shifts make that difficult."

"Are you aware that Agri-Biz has folded?"

"Of course."

"And that hospitals are shifting to AB work alone?"

"Yes."

"Have you surmised that an Outdoor Ban is imminent?"

"An Outdoor Ban?"

"Yes. A permanent quarantine, if you will."

"Permanent?"

"I'm afraid so. The quarantines have been on-again, off-again one too many times. Bacteria can no longer be stopped. Once someone is infected, they die. It's become a simple equation. We need to do everything we can to keep people away from each other, away from all possible contamination. The Homeland must be safe. Enforcement is the key to an AntiBacterial Homeland."

"Enforcement of rules is key." Trevor spoke his line firmly, but he felt tentative. He wasn't sure what this new Outdoor Ban had to do with him. Why was he being told this news before it hit the media?

"To date, we've worked in conjunction with other law enforcement."

Trevor nodded. As Enforcers, they depended on police, National Guard and TSA. Without coordination, breaches would occur. Breaches could be deadly. The line had to be seamless.

"When we move inside, their roles will cease and ours will increase." The commander paused to let Trevor take in the information. "We will begin carrying out all Enforcement, from catching perps to punishing them. Some police and National Guard will no doubt join our ranks, but none of them understand rules the way we do. They are used to stable rules. Right is right, wrong is wrong. Enforcement against bacteria is more complicated, more diverse, ever changing."

Trevor followed her reasoning. "Emergent."

The commander nodded.

Trevor understood some of the changes that would follow the new ban, but he still had no idea why he stood in the commander's office. Finally his training kicked in. "I'm here to serve. How can I help?"

"Good man. I knew you'd be on board. California has been devastated, Mr. Kashnikov. I need Enforcers who can not only see the infractions, but ones who can respond quickly to the changing needs, as you did when you created the communication code used by VE officers. I need someone who knows not to judge a book by its cover." Trevor cracked the edge of a smile at the commander, remembering again their first encounter. "I also need someone who can mete out punishment."

Trevor's eyes grew wide. He had dreamed of this day. He'd always wanted to drive the point home to perps, make them learn their lesson. "I'm honored. Yes. I welcome the opportunity to take rules to the next level."

"That's just it: the next level. I knew you would understand. We considered CIA training for you and others who will fill this post, but we don't want to repeat their mistakes. Torturing antibacterial rule breakers will not lead us anywhere. Serious offenders can be trained as Cleaners, the rest must be made to see the error of their ways. Quickly. Unequivocally."

Trevor nodded. He couldn't agree more.

"There will be no training. You will report directly to me. Until you are moved, you will say nothing of this conversation to anyone. Not even other VEs. Do you understand?"

"Of course."

"Pack a single bag. Be ready to leave with a few hours' notice. A text from Homeland Security, the Director's Office, will inform you what transport to catch. That will happen after the Outdoor Ban is implemented. The streets will be empty when you make your move. A new communication system is being established. By the time you arrive in California, we will no longer use phones, texts or emails. Our system will be off the mainline grid. Of course, that grid may degrade rapidly with no caretakers. Many things will fall apart. I digress. Trevor you do make me hopeful. I'll miss your presence in the city."

Trevor was touched. Rarely in his life had anyone appreciated him. Usually he'd been seen as a nuisance. He breathed deeply.

"This is an important posting. The Homeland thanks you for your continued allegiance and unquestioning service." She held up her hand and Trevor did the same while she locked eyes with him, clearly trusting him in a way that made him puff out his chest with pride.

As Trevor reached for the door handle, he removed an AB wipe from his pocket, cleaning the handle in a swift movement and exiting. He deposited the wipe in the trashcan under a desk. The fussy man watched his every move. There was no clue on his face whether he approved of Trevor's endeavor to maintain cleanliness, even here in Command Central. Trevor was beyond worrying what others thought of his AB habits. He had been rewarded for those habits.

Trevor had, thus far, been able to travel with enough possessions to maintain his oral hygiene rituals. He was able to acquire, usually through work channels, the cleaning products he needed to maintain the motels and apartments he had stayed in. Now he was being asked to prepare a single suitcase. That was traveling a little too light for his taste, especially if he was staying very long, and it sounded like he was. He didn't miss Michigan, but he did miss his bunker. It had served him well in the days of quarantines, the days before he joined Enforcement. While in Chicago and New York, it gave him comfort to know his bunker was still prepared, should he need it, should things turn. From California, he couldn't imagine it would be of any .se. If the worst happened, he couldn't imagine getting there healthily. If everyone went indoors, wouldn't transport stop? Could he have things moved west? No one in Homeland Security had ever suggested he should have things moved, or even that it was possible. His new job was a step, or more, up the ladder. It sounded like his move would be sudden. And he wasn't allowed to reveal his knowledge of the impending transition to anyone.

Let go of the desire to move your bunker. It isn't healthy. Let go. A few repetitions, three to be exact, and he would diminish the hold his possessions had on him.

It isn't healthy. Let go. It isn't healthy.

OUTDOOR BAN PASSED, NEW JOBS CREATED

Washington, DC — The much-anticipated Outdoor Ban was issued today by the Touch Ban Committee. Public health and safety were cited as the primary reasons for the latest and most wide-reaching ban, which is in effect a permanent quarantine.

Healthy citizens will not be exposed to further bacterial fomites. Health officials believe this will mean those already infected will die in their homes, thereby creating automatic containment. When deaths are reported, bodies will not be removed. This will eliminate the severe casket shortages and increased deaths caused by exposure to infected bodies.

A new type of government lackey was also announced. Cleaners will seal off homes of the dead. They will also deal with all other sanitation issues that arise from bacterial contamination. They will be charged with cleanup of the desolation wrought by recent outbreaks—burning bodies and cordoning off toxic sites. "Where bacteria has wreaked havoc, Cleaners eliminate concerns by cleaning up," said EPA spokesperson Jorge Muerte.

The new role will be filled by those who

were not telecommuting and are now in search of work. This position will start immediately and be a necessary role well into the future. Precautions will be taken for the safety of Cleaners. They will be provided with HAZMAT BioLevel 5 uniforms and given training in bacterial elimination.

"This is not a disposable job, but a job disposing of waste," clarified Muerte.

Trevor's orders arrived as he finished a shift one afternoon. He was to be at La Guardia at 4 a.m. with one suitcase. A car would pick him up. He would be on a military transport with several other Head Enforcers bound for California.

Trevor was surprised by what felt like special treatment. Then again, the Outdoor Ban had moved everyone inside earlier in the day. Catching the subway or even a cab was, no doubt, out of the question. Ditto commercial aircraft. His bag was already packed. Though he had less than 12 hours, he went through his usual routine, disinfecting his teeth, showering, eating. When he finished, he had 7 hours. Good. He carefully folded his clothes, even though they would be left behind, and got into bed. When his alarm went off, he sprang up, dressed in the clean clothes he'd laid out the night before and awaited his ride, which arrived exactly on schedule.

There was no security check, no antibacterial screening, nothing and no one between the arriving Head Enforcers, each in a separate vehicle, and the Marine aircraft that would spirit them across the country. Quiet enveloped the whole scene. Trevor had been out in other quarantines, to travel to locations, to assist with operations. But somehow it was clear that more planning had gone into the Outdoor Ban. *Maybe it's just the organized transport. Or that I knew this was coming.* Yet something seemed drastically different. None of the Enforcers knew each other. They nodded hello without speaking. No handshakes, obviously. No small talk. No questions about where they were headed or what was next. Like Trevor, they each had foreknowledge of the impending event, and all had been instructed not to speak of it. No directive had yet removed that rule.

Inflight they were briefed. Each would be heading security at a different AntiBacterial Center, or ABC. These would all be former hospitals. Staff was already in the process of reorganization. Medical was over, Sterilization was the need of the day. While their new roles were still *emergent*, government expected that to end soon. This was a brave new world and each of them would be expected to enforce the highest of AB standards for everyone employed in each center. These would not have to be standardized, not yet, perhaps not ever. "Let's be clear, if you don't hold the line, the line will disappear in the sand."

Metaphor was not the best communication for Enforcers. The Briefer tried again. "This is the final stage of the human performance." A few lights went on, he could see, but not all. "You're the last hope of human survival, if I must be so blunt." The words were not met with surprise. As Enforcers, they'd been waiting for this day. By the time they were hired, most of them realized it was likely too late, or at least the brightest among them realized that. Pandora had opened the box, the one marked Bacteria—Do Not Open, and chaos was loosed upon the world. That allusion would not have worked any better. Though attentive, though intelligent, Head Enforcers were not classically educated.

"Permission to speak?"

"Sure, what do I care?" The person sent to brief the Enforcers was merely someone close enough to the top to know what was happening, but expendable in case anything happened en route.

"So basically, you're telling us that we, the group of us here, are now THE Enforcers. We'll pretty much be *making* the rules, rather than just enforcing them."

"Basically. At least within your centers. There will still be directives which will give you the latest information, the latest science, the latest protection mechanisms, but how you implement those directives will be your individual call. The most important enforcement zone for you will be the employees who work at the ABC, especially the Sterilizers. If AB management is to be effective, the Sterilizers must be above reproach in their attentiveness to protocols."

At this, they exchanged glances. None of them was old enough to realize that in a former time, they'd have punched each other in the arm or shouldered one another in a comradely fashion. Eye contact served the purpose. They knew they were special, each and every one.

"We expect current communication systems to fail. We're implementing a computer-based notification system, known as the Enforcer Unit, which will allow Homeland Security to communicate with you and, if necessary, for you to communicate with one another. It will offer secure exchanges outside the purview of Homelander eyes. We encourage you to give up all other sources immediately: texts, emails, phones. While they may still work, they are not secure and cannot be trusted by anyone at your level."

"At *our* level," Trevor and others murmured. Though they had been informed this shift was coming, none allowed themselves to admit to the excitement of the rise in rank. Rules in their former lives had been the bane of their existence. Trevor was not alone in that. Now rules ruled and so did they. *Sweet!*

"You will be greeted by a Transition Liaison who will introduce you to your team, the Enforcers working under you. You'll be given a tour of the facility and a chance to select an office location. You'll meet the Head Sterilizer, who reports to you as well. Whether your directives go through the Head Sterilizer or directly to the men and women who perform human cleansing will be your call. Be aware that Sterilizers are an emergent field. You all remember when your jobs were new, it's the same for them.

"There are choices about your living quarters. Sterilizers will occupy pods. You can choose to live there as well, or have rooms developed within the facility so you needn't leave. You could even choose to live away from the facility, as you will be among the few allowed passage outside."

"How would such transport to and from an outside dwelling work?"

"Will streets still be patrolled?"

"What services will be maintained?"

"How will food distribution work?"

"Will food safety continue to be an issue?"

"My, my, my," said the Briefer, "aren't you all suddenly full of questions? Thought your jobs were not to question, but to answer with rules." He smiled at what he considered humorous. The new ABC Head Enforcers awaited answers that weren't coming. "Sorry, I've told you what I know. The situation is, shall we say—"

"Emergent," they said, nearly in unison, as they snickered.

HOSPITALS TO REMAIN OPEN

Washington, DC — Public hospitals will remain open during the Transition, officials announced today. "The infected need somewhere to go," said the Surgeon General. "Personnel are shifting from Medical to Sterilization jobs, diminishing staffing concerns."

According to hospital administrators, HR Departments are backlogged, as would be expected, but they maintain that all services will continue seamlessly. "We have ensured that priorities were set before the Transition began so the most crucial areas would be the least affected," said Dean of Medicine Azra DeSai.

Juan Mendoza, husband of a patient at the Emergency Room at Bethesda General, reported, "We had to wait, but not any longer than usual."

Another patient, who declined to be identified, said, "I observed several doctors walk out in a huff." She said she worried about what their specialties might have been, and hoped it wasn't anything she needed.

An orderly who removed reporters from hospital grounds admitted he was excited about the changes. "The more medical personnel who leave, the better chance I have of moving up the ladder," he confided.

Dr. Jones, a physician no longer with the hospital, said in a phone interview that she was worried priorities would shift and treating illness would no longer be central. "With the uncontrolled fear of bacteria, it appears the only goal of the next regime will be to clean up. That's really not what physicians do. We heal people."

Ambulances will continue to monitor 911 calls and carry the sick and dying to hospitals. It is not clear whether ER facilities will change in a way that impacts delivery of those patients.

The last privatized hospitals closed last month, leaving only government-run operations to face the latest changes. "No one pays anymore," said the former director of Mercy Hospital in a phone interview. "We couldn't stay open, even if we wanted to."

THE DANGERS WITHIN

There was no fanfare. If anything, there was utter chaos when Trevor arrived on scene. People were milling about, some were screaming epithets, others were carrying out boxes. A supply truck was parked blocking the walkway into the building. There was a pungent odor on the air, as if someone had burned plastic. Trevor hoped it wasn't bacterial because he wasn't masked. He immediately realized that was a mistake, opened his rolling bag on the spot and donned the best mask he had.

The Transition liaison couldn't be found. *Or perhaps, hadn't been named. Emergent, as it was.* Trevor asked for the Head of the Sterilizers. That, too, received a blank stare. Finally, he asked the person at the front counter to tell him who was in charge.

"Good question. Dr. Estrailia was in charge before the Transition. She's as good a place to start as any."

"Fine. And where will I find Dr. Entrails?"

The receptionist laughed. "That's funny. Entrails, like intestines. Funny. No, it's Dr. Estrailia."

"Fine. Dr. Estrailia, where can I find her?"

"Another good question. You are full of them. I could page, that's what I'd have done last week. I don't think it'll do any good now. I'd suggest you try her office on the third floor. Go right when you get off the elevator." She pointed toward the elevators and immediately turned her attention to someone on the phone.

Doesn't know who I am, clearly. Trevor thought of Commander Snopek. Ah, he missed her already. He took the elevator up. When he got off on the third floor there were more people with boxes. More anger was spewing forth, though Trevor couldn't locate the cause. No one was in the process of firing anyone. No one was pushing. Trevor maneuvered around people who paid him no attention. He made his way to the right.

"Dr. Estrailia?"

"Hardly. Do I look like the doctor fucking everyone over?"

"Have you seen Dr. Estrailia?"

"No man, not since this morning when she canned my ass. 'Scuse me. Gotta get this shit outta here before someone decides I gotta stay."

Trevor kept walking. He looked into offices as he passed. All were small, simple rooms with a single metal desk in each, a comfortable executive-style desk chair facing out with two arm chairs facing in. Most offices had bookshelves with volumes in disarray. All had diplomas on walls, or frames where diplomas had recently hung. He walked by a break room that was glaring white and glaringly empty. Finally he came to a large office at the end. In front of it sat a tiny reception desk. No one sat at reception. On the office name plate was "Dr. Estrailia." Trevor knocked. No answer. He stood for a moment. He thought he heard movement inside.

"Dr. Estrailia? Are you here?" When there was no answer, Trevor cracked the door and looked in. He saw a woman in her mid-50s, sitting in a white lab coat behind a beautiful oak desk. She looked up, startled.

"Who are you?"

"Trevor Kashnikov, Head of Enforcement for this ABC."

"Ah. The AntiBacterial Center begins." She stood and grabbed a small bag out of a drawer. "I was just leaving. Don't let me get in your way."

"Please. Don't leave. I'd like you to bring me up to speed."

"Of course you would. For the last 48 hours, this has been a war zone. Medicine is what this hospital was built for, to treat the sick. Not that we didn't attend the dying, but our purpose has been life. Until now. Death is not my business, sir. I'll leave that to you." With that she walked from behind the desk. She leaned back across the desk and pulled out a huge ring of keys. She walked past Trevor and pushed the keys into his belly as she walked out the door. "These are yours now. I wash my hands of it."

"Wait. Please." She didn't pause. "Can you tell me the name of the Head Sterilizer?"

"Sterilization, a term that once referred to ending a person's reproductive capacity. And now? What does it mean now?"

"It's antibacterial, ma'am. Sterilization means clean. It's the only hope for us."

"My point exactly. Sterilization isn't hope. Sterilization is the absence of life. Sterilization is death."

"I follow your thinking, but I need the person in charge of cleanliness, not death. Can you tell me that?"

"You'll need to check with the mayor on that. Or maybe the town council. Perhaps Homeland Security. I really don't know." Dr. Estrailia pushed the button for the elevator. "I can tell you that roughly half my medical staff signed the allegiance documents. Half of them are being processed to become Sterilizers. I'd put my money on Joan Jiltson, if they choose among those who stay on. Joan would be the turncoat most likely to fit the mold."

The former head of the hospital stepped into the elevator and pressed the button to take her to the parking ramp. She didn't look at Trevor, who wondered how it was that so many people were still here, out in public, rather than under quarantine. *Evidently transitions take time.*

Trevor walked back into the head administrator's former office. His first thought was how elegant it was. He slid his fingers along the oak surface of the desk. *Elegance doesn't say "enforcement."* He walked out onto the third floor. No, he needed to be closer to the main doors, near the action. His days as a VE were over. Sure, CCTV could feed him images, but that wouldn't allow rapid response when it was needed.

With no liaison, with no Head Sterilizer, he decided to tour on his own. He wanted to get a sense of where he was maintaining AntiBacterial containment. *Check out the territory. Take possession.* Trevor decided since three was a good number, he'd survey the floor he was on. But before he could start, he was overwhelmed by the sense that starting in the middle was wrong, even if three was positive. Believing that at the end of the tour he'd need to begin his command, he decided to start at the top and work back down to the main doors and reception. He stepped into the elevator, pushed three buttons, the last of which would take him to the top. As the elevator climbed, stopped, opened, and climbed again, Trevor counted the number of keys on the ring. Thirteen. *No wonder the woman was so edgy.* Trevor took six keys off the ring, leaving a fortunate seven. The six representing two sets of three could be placed on other rings. The keys needed to be organized with labels. He was struck at how shoddy the hospital organization had been so far. *Could this be the reason bacteria is winning?*

By the time Trevor had walked the entire building, he'd met a handful of former medics who were staying to become Sterilizers. Once he reached reception, he informed the woman still staffing the desk that he was now in charge. She giggled. He stood his ground. He didn't bark at her. He needed working staff.

"You're serious," she said when he didn't move or laugh. "OK. What's next, boss?"

"Has anyone arrived with new communications devices?"

"No, but there was a strange call saying the Enforcer Unit will be here tomorrow. Is that it?"

"Good work. Yes." Trevor realized that amid the chaos of more than two days, this woman had operated in a business-as-usual manner. She was loyal, if not the brightest. "How is it you're still here?"

"When the quarantine went into effect, I was here. So I stayed."

"But you were given 12 hours to get to a destination of your choice. You were informed this was the Outdoor Ban, not just a quarantine, true?"

"I guess."

"You guess?"

"As I said, I was working. Here in the hospital the Transition began *before* the Ban was announced. Sick people were still arriving and had to be rerouted. Staff was quitting right and left. The media was swarming the front of the building, taking shots, interviewing anyone who would talk. I was asked by my supervisor to stay late and ensure we didn't look available to looters."

"And?"

"And, as I just said, by the time it quieted down and I realized I should leave, the Ban had begun. I didn't think I could leave. In quarantines we're told to stay put."

"So you followed the rules as you knew them?"

"Of course. Who wouldn't?"

"There are others who continued to come and go. They're still moving out boxes."

"But the rules said not to leave."

"Good. Good. We'll be turning the 7th floor into lodging. You can select a room."

"Thank you, sir. What do I call you, sir?"

"What did you call Dr. Estrailia?"

"Chief."

"Call me Chief Enforcer." Trevor knew the more that stayed the same, the smoother the Transition would go.

"And your name? May I know it, sir?"

Sir. He liked that. Such respect. "Of course, Kashnikov. Trevor Kashnikov."

"Chief Enforcer Kashnikov, thank you. I'll select a room, and then what would you like?"

"I think we're done for today. But tomorrow, bright and early, I need your help to get this ABC into shape."

"ABC?"

"AntiBacterial Center. I'd like you to continue to staff your desk and phone. But your duties will change to some degree. I'll need you operating as a bit of an executive secretary for at least awhile. Can I count on you to make calls for me, inform me of arrivals and deliveries, and generally send all those needing decisions my way?"

"Absolutely, Chief." She giggled again. Trevor worried about her skill set, but he trusted her ability to follow the rules, and right now that was the most crucial habit to possess.

Trevor rolled his suitcase to the room he'd chosen for himself between the elevator and the stairwell. He made a list of the lead roles he would need filled immediately: Sterilization, Facilities, Technology, Cleaning, Food. The first two of these needed several sub-lead roles filled quickly as well. He made those lists. He tried to organize what changes needed making and began to prioritize them. He needed a list of hospital staff. If he could find those who had filled these roles before he'd have a good start on interviews. He stayed up late and rose early, sleeping little.

It took months to get the ABC into shape. Setting up a triage area for bacterial cases was the first and most difficult order of business. Without Sterilizers in place, trained and ready, it was nearly impossible to handle the onslaught. The media had ensured the public that former hospitals would be available to all bacterial cases. Luckily, there were no huge outbreaks in progress, yet any digestive or bleeding case was potentially bacterial, and since Homelanders still had access to cars with gas and even though the Outdoor Ban was clearly mandatory, running to the Emergency Room had become a habit for many. Ambulances were also still on call. All this meant the number of people arriving was beyond the ABC's capacity since there was virtually no staffing.

Trevor appreciated that Dr. Estrailia had mentioned Jiltson's name. At least he was able to get someone busy at hiring, training and reorganizing. Dr. Estrailia had clearly not appreciated Jiltson, but her comments sounded more like endorsement to Trevor than she'd intended. And while Jiltson had more ambition than talent, the ambition served to drive her to work long hours.

Trevor was catapulted into being more of an organizer and decision-maker than he'd ever imagined possible. AntiBacterial Enforcement was a small part of the picture at first. Trevor had never imagined his OCD would serve him so well. His parents would be shocked, but he had no contact with them, no certainty they were even still alive. He was too busy to give any thought to personal matters.

***

Cathy knew she'd been slowing down. She realized her memory

was starting to fail, though she didn't know when that had started. Homelanders died at any age these days, so she'd forgotten that once upon a time, not so long ago, aging out was common. Oh, there were a variety of ailments of the old that were recorded as the official cause of death: heart attack, stroke, cancer of this or that. But basically, people outlived their bodies' ability to continue. Systems shut down. It happened all the time with computers and technologies. System failure was common. Often, viruses were the source, so contagion was blamed. And it was true, a computer didn't have to be old to suffer a system failure. She stopped. Her thinking had run into a dead end. No, more of a…of a what? Oh, what was the word?

"Maggie? Maggie, can you help me? What's the word for a place where you get stuck and can't get out of it?"

"A dead end?"

"No, no, no. I'm trying to think of the word for a kind of puzzle-like place where a person gets lost inside."

"A labyrinth?"

"Right idea, wrong word. Too fancy. No, we used to say… Oh what was it? Rats! Rats got caught in a…just like rats in a…"

"A maze?"

"Yes! A maze. Thank you."

"Why were you thinking of mazes, mother?"

"I wasn't."

"But you wanted the word…"

"Oh, my mind had gotten stuck and it made me think of a maze, but I couldn't think of the word."

"I hate when that happens. Glad I could help." Maggie walked back into her room, anxious that the conversation not continue. She needed to log a few more hours of work if they were to get their full allotment next week.

Cathy tried to remember why she actually wanted the word *maze*. What had put her in mind of a maze? It was no use, she had no idea. She sat down by the window and peered through the blinds, lifting the corner. Why did she do that? Nothing happened outside. When she was a child, she played outside, people walked outside, drove cars, mowed grass, had picnics, rode bikes, went to the beach. There was no end to what people did outside. Now it stood empty, abandoned. How had this happened? How could leaving the house be so dangerous? But it was, wasn't it? She couldn't see the reason. But that was part of the problem, wasn't it? Germs were so small. She preferred the word *germs*. It drove Maggie crazy so she tried not to say it. Maggie said it was a made up word of her generation. But it wasn't. It was from earlier than that. Maggie said it was a catchall. What did that mean? A catchall? She got up and walked to Maggie's room. She stood at the doorway.

"Maggie?"

Maggie kept looking at her screen.

"Maggie dear, I have a small question. What's a *catchall*?"

"Mother, you could look that up. You can find it online."

"I know dear, but I'd rather have you tell me. I like hearing your voice."

"You can get it to speak to you. You don't have to read, you can listen."

"It's not the same. Even with a choice of voices, I find them impersonal. I don't know those voices. Can't you tell me?"

"I'm trying to log my hours. I have more debugging to do for the week. I'll answer this one more question, but then I'd really like if you didn't interrupt me. The work period closes in a few hours." Turning toward her mother for the first time, Maggie asked, "OK, so what was the phrase you wanted to know about?"

Cathy stood there stunned. She had no idea. Maggie's anger had eliminated it from her mind. She tried so hard not to bother Maggie, and here she was bothering her again and evidently with no reason at all.

"Oh, dear. Now I can't remember. You scared it right out of me."

"Oh, mother. I'm sorry you can't remember, but I didn't scare you. Please!"

Maggie turned back to her computer and continued, leaving Cathy to stand there bewildered. Cathy watched Maggie for a minute and realized she'd been told to go. She began to shuffle back to her room when she caught her toe on the edge of her wrap and stumbled. She'd never liked the wraps and lately she hadn't been good at keeping hers around her without dragging it on the floor. Cathy thumped as her hips hit the floor.

"Mother!" Maggie shrieked as she came running. "Are you OK?"

"What, dear?"

"Are you OK? Did you get hurt falling?" Maggie helped Cathy back to her room, careful to touch her wrap and not her exposed flesh. That's why she tripped, Maggie thought. She never keeps her wrap tied properly any more. Maggie tried to get Cathy into bed.

"I don't want to sleep."

"But if you're tripping, maybe you're tired."

"I just caught my toe. I'm fine. I just..."

Maggie waited. "Mother? You just what?"

"Huh?"

"You started to explain something and then you just stopped."

"Did I?"

"You seem confused, or maybe just not yourself. Are you feeling OK? Not in terms of the fall. Just health-wise? Is anything wrong? Diarrhea? Fatigue? Fever?" She reached toward her mother's forehead, but stopped short of touching it. "Anything at all? I noticed you've been giving more of your food to Pele. I know he appreciates it, growing as he is, but maybe you should eat all of your own allotment."

"I'm not hungry. And that food, if you want to call it food, is so boring. I'm not interested. If I could have a salad with lettuce, tomatoes, a nice balsamic—then there'd be a reason to eat. Perhaps a nice chicken leg."

"Stop living in the past. That just frustrates all of us who remember. And it's not good for Pele for you to talk like that. This is his world, his life. We can't talk like the past was nirvana. And chicken? Why would you mention birds? It was birds got us into this mess. He doesn't even know what birds are, let alone chickens. Oh, now you've got me going. If there's nothing wrong, I'm going back to finish my session."

She looked at her mother. Maggie was frustrated, but she could sense something wrong with Cathy, even if she couldn't name it. She needed to be kinder. "When I'm done we'll all eat and maybe play a game. You can pick. How will that be?"

"Fine, dear. Thank you. I'll leave you alone. I'll just lay here awhile."

Maggie walked away before Cathy could tell another story from the past. She wondered if she should worry about contagion. She saw none of the usual signs, but that didn't mean some dormant bacteria that had been living quietly in the recesses of her mother's body hadn't decided it was time to reproduce. Perhaps after the evening meal it would be good to decontaminate just to be sure.

***

Homeland Security had in no way prepared Trevor for what lay ahead. While he'd been excited he would be in charge, be the one actually making many of the rules, he hadn't realized the chaos that would ensue, nor how long the Transition would last.

The Enforcement Units, meant to provide a secure backchannel, were slow to become fully operative. The delay was exacerbated by the decision to put Enforcement Units into every occupied home—all the better to monitor Homelanders.

More importantly, food reserves were insufficient during the Transition, which ended up being more than two years rather than the promised 4-8 months. ABCs were seen as essential sites receiving priority shipments as food dwindled in the warehouses. Shipments to Homelanders were uneven at best. Certain neighborhoods received more, others less.

Trevor could do nothing about how slow communications were reestablished, nor could he imagine that Homelanders were starving. What he could do was keep his workers safe from contamination. At other ABCs, top-level workers who still had family in the Homeland insisted on commuting. This was sometimes tolerated for those in key roles, but it lead to enormous inequalities among staff who felt the ultimate power of the Head Enforcers and saw their decisions as capricious. At Trevor's center, staff could not complain because he allowed no one the luxury of commuting. Trevor believed in containment and insisted that all who worked at the ABC live at the ABC.

Sterilizers, like everyone in the population, were required to generate electricity to meet daily energy quotas. With no ability to exercise outdoors such generation had been built in as daily cardio routines. A portion of the ABC's cafeteria remained an eating area for staff, but the majority of it was converted into a generation space. Sterilizers could eat and generate after work before returning to a pod.

Trevor insisted that Sterilizers not be allowed capsules of their own. That way, no debris or personal belongings could accumulate that might harbor bacteria. When scourbots were invented, Trevor installed them in the operating theaters set up with observation areas. That way, he could keep the Sterilizers as distant as possible from contamination.

Trevor knew firsthand about the peer pressure to conform. He knew its virtues and its detriments. To increase the benefits, he ensured those who followed rules were celebrated in small ways: names on a plaque were added monthly, short interviews in the videos shown in the generation center. To decrease the problems of peer pressure, he set up systems and spaces that diminished interaction. When handhelds and other devices failed, he confiscated them. He installed large screens in the rooms where Sterilizers ate and generated, the only spaces where they gathered in numbers and the only locations where they had unaccounted for free time. The screens delivered the equivalent of news, mostly ABC statistics. When new equipment arrived, whether it was scourbots or a new type of generator, he played training videos. He allowed select videos from the past, most of which provided good examples of successful AB behaviors and some of which demonstrated the follies of not following AB protocols.

***

At mealtime, Maggie nuked each allotment separately. That way she was sure each got to the proper temperature. Even with current safeguards, she wanted to make sure food wouldn't kill her family. It was orange week. Some of the colors weren't very appetizing. It didn't matter what she was told in terms of nutritional content—puke yellow and barf brown were unappetizing. Those were Pele's names and she agreed with his labeling. To avoid the gruel oats and soybeans would become if cooked into a porridge, allotments went through production, as if that hadn't been one of the problems with contamination in the first place. Making a variety of colors and textures was the reason production continued.

First Maggie nuked Pele's plate, piled with orange strings. She tested it with the heat shield to ensure 165 degrees F. She handed him the plate immediately. Then she put in her mother's portion, much smaller due to her age. And finally, she put in her own mid-sized portion. Last night, as she'd set the plates on the table, her mother had compared their meals to the three bears. Maggie didn't remember the story, but she appreciated the idea it would be "just right."

Sitting down, fork in hand, ready to eat her orange strings, she saw Cathy hadn't started. "Mother, please eat while it's in the safe range. I don't want to nuke it again. The texture will change, and not in a good way."

"Oh, sorry dear." Cathy put a forkful into her mouth. Slowly she chewed and swallowed. Maggie watched. It looked like it might be painful.

"Does it hurt to eat?"

"I'm a little dry. Maybe if I drink my water, dear."

Pele watched his grandmother, too. He'd been watching her for a couple days. He was worried she was losing weight. He knew that was a bad sign. She'd been giving him most of her food lately. That could be bad for both of them. "Is it weight night?"

Maggie shook her head as she chewed. "No," she finally said, "but I was thinking we might make a precautionary chamber visit tonight. You two up for it?"

"Sure!" Pele enjoyed the ritual of decontamination. It made him feel safe and loved.

"If we must," Cathy said. She never liked the process, but recently she'd had trouble staying focused while following the procedures. It was starting to make her nervous.

"It's not a must. This isn't a required day. But to be honest, I'm worried about you, mother. I can't put my finger on it, but you don't seem like yourself. I'd feel better if we ensured no bacteria has gotten to you."

"As I said, fine with me." It wasn't fine with her, but it wasn't worth an argument.

"Then after, we can play a game. What would you like to play, mother? Three-dimensional checkers? Domination? Mancala? Any game you want. Pele always gets to choose. It's your turn."

"How about Rummy?"

Pele started to make a face but his mother caught his eye and he turned away. "I guess so." He said it without passion, but Cathy didn't always notice tone, especially when it was one she wouldn't appreciate.

When they finished eating, Pele loaded all the dishes, glassware and utensils into the sterilizer and pushed start. Maggie opened the doors for their decontamination system as they passed through chambers 3, 2 and 1. Pele would go first. That was one of his favorite parts. He felt special going first. He dropped his wrap on the floor and entered chamber 2, shut the door and closed his eyes. When the bell chimed he opened his eyes and held his breath. He liked to turn slowly while the spray did its magic, reeling as if dancing. He held his arms high and low, he spread his butt cheeks and giggled, and as the spray penetrated his open mouth he gurgled and spit. Where else could he do that?! When he'd exited, the chamber cleaned itself.

Cathy entered. She didn't move. She tried to stay focused. When she opened her eyes she breathed in just as the first spray hit. Immediately, she started choking. "Mother? Are you OK?" When there was no reply except more choking, Maggie hit the emergency button. The doors unlocked on both sides. Maggie entered to find her mother leaning against the wall, head lowered, elbow in front of her mouth, coughing repeatedly. With her hands covered by her wrap, Maggie tried to lift Cathy so she could breathe, but she wouldn't budge.

Maggie told Pele to put on a mask and then hand her a mask and gloves. Then she sent him to his room. Maggie quickly and expertly masked and gloved herself before helping her mother sit down on the floor. Cathy kept coughing as if her lungs might emerge through her lips. Maggie sat with her hand on her mother's back. She didn't speak. She thought. She worried. She wondered, is this it? Was I too late to recognize the signs? Her mind headed down an ugly path where her family began to dissolve. Before her thoughts became too morbid, she realized her mother's cough was finally subsiding. Maggie tried to remain calm.

"Damned spray!" Cathy coughed again from the effort of speech.

"Did you breathe in spray? Is that what happened?"

"Of course. What else?"

Maggie didn't respond to Cathy's question. She couldn't tell her mother what she'd been thinking. Her greatest fears would remain her own.

"When you're ready, I think we should repeat the procedure. I know that's not appealing, but after all that coughing, decontamination is essential."

Cathy looked at her daughter. Who was this person? More concerned about proper procedures than the fact she'd almost coughed up a lung. This is what the world has come to, she thought. Cathy gave a small nod, but remained sitting. Maggie stood up. She stayed in the chamber. A minute or more passed. When Cathy looked up, Maggie extended her gloved hand, wondering how long it had been since she'd had flesh-to-flesh contact with another person. With difficulty, Cathy got to her feet, but the exertion of it caused another spasm. Maggie waited, patiently this time.

"Let's get this over with," Cathy asserted in an aggravated, breathless voice.

"I'll step back into the waiting chamber." The door closed behind Maggie. She removed the mask and gloves, contemplating what might happen next, not in that instant, but in the coming days. She hoped she was wrong. Losing her mother was inevitable, but if her mother took Pele down in their own private outbreak, she'd never forgive her.

But then, she wouldn't need to worry about that, would she?

The seconds clicked by. Cathy, attentive now with a body overrun with adrenaline, was able to move through the UV and spray cycles without a hitch. Her breathing was still labored and holding it wasn't easy, but she could focus on the light and only breathe when no spray was shooting. Finally the outer door opened and she stepped into the dressing chamber. She lifted a wrap from the stack, wound it around herself and plunked down on the bench. She breathed as deeply as she dared without causing another spasm. Then she tried to relax. Before she knew it, Maggie stepped into the area and wrapped herself quickly.

"Still up for a game?" The enthusiasm was gone, but maybe they could still have a little enjoyment together.

"No, I think I'll just turn in. It's been a long evening."

"Do you need anything?"

"No, dear. I'm just going to catch my breath here a bit longer and then go to bed. You needn't wait for me."

Maggie hesitated briefly and then went through the door. She walked straight to her son's room. "Pele? You can take off your mask now. No worries."

"Oh good. Thanks, mom."

"Pele, can I ask, have you noticed changes in your grandma lately?"

"Is she OK?"

"She just inhaled some spray. It happens sometimes. You did it once when you were three. Do you remember?" Pele shook his head. "That's for the best. Habits learned early..."

"...are habits for life," Pele finished. Maggie smiled at her son. He was a good boy, a smart boy. Pele continued to look at his mother with concern, waiting patiently for the answer to his question.

"Yes, she'll be fine. Have you noticed grandma changing?"

"She's been giving me most of her food. She looks thinner. I'm kind of worried about the weigh-in."

"She hasn't been eating. Can you tell why?" Maggie asked her son.

"She doesn't like it. She always starts talking about *real food*. I'm not sure what she means, but it's like she thinks what we eat is boring."

"Good point."

"Should I not eat her food?"

"No, we don't want to waste it. You're growing. They expect you to put on weight. And I think they expect her to lose it, but this may be a little fast. I'm not going to worry about it and you shouldn't either."

Pele nodded. When his mother spoke like this, she was worried. She always kept her real worries to herself, but he could tell.

"Are we still playing Runny?" Pele didn't like the game. It was old-fashioned. But it gave him an excuse to use a dirty word.

"Pele!" Maggie chastised him, but she also smiled. She thought it was a good pun. "No, grandma is going to bed. We could play something else if you like."

Pele grabbed his 3-D checkers set and headed for the table.

***

As a Sterilizer, Gary slept in a pod. Capsule hotels served as Sterilizer housing since they'd been built near hospitals for families who brought infected people in for treatment, hoping they'd be cured, but often leaving their dead behind. Tiny tubes that a person crawled into for sleeping were plenty since they spent long hours holding vigil. The tubes were tall enough for most people to sit up and roll over—the same commands given dogs in the old days. Originally the tubes had been outfitted with entertainment consoles, but compact cameras had replaced them so Enforcers could see in but Sterilizers could not see out. Being watched meant Gary was seldom comfortable masturbating. Besides, at his height, he found the pod a difficult place to beat off.

The contents of a pod were kept bare to reduce the possibility of contamination, especially with Sterilizers living in them. This also maximized observation, there was no place to hide. There was no pillow, which would imply comfort and be a nest for possible infestation. Instead, a head lift of inflatable AB plastic and a covering made of the same material comprised the entire contents of each pod. There were no personal belongings of any kind for Sterilizers. This allowed the capsules to be used to maximum efficiency, with Sterilizers always taking the next open pod. Since the shifts were 12 hours, it meant every pod was used twice a day.

Like all Sterilizers, Gary had no belongings and no place to call his own. Oddly, it wasn't hard to sleep in the pods. Though pharmaceuticals were hard to come by and frowned upon, seen as a remnant of a dead society, a slow deep thrumming sound tumbled through the pods 24/7. In a nearly silent world, the sound was reassuring. It quickly lulled Gary to sleep, recharging his physical body for the next day. The intent was that it also dulled the mind so Sterilizers didn't seek personal fulfillment, relationships, or a life unique in any way. Sterilizers were an important, highly skilled, necessary workforce.

In the beginning, Gary found it a gift that he no longer needed to do laundry. Wraps and cover-ups were kept in the hallway where one was exchanged for the other, whether coming or going. Chutes were available for dirty clothes, clean clothes were piled and waiting.

Each pod was entered from a single hallway that provided constant surveillance. Capsules were open for the four hours between shifts and locked down during the eight hours of expected minimum sleep time. If Sterilizers arrived too late, they were left to their own devices on the streets. Gary, like most Sterilizers, had never experienced a lockout. Why would he? The pod, his shift, eating, generating, the pod, his shift... It just kept rotating, with no variation and no reason to deviate. He no longer gave much thought to the fact that he was on camera. In the scheme of things, it really didn't matter.

There were few common areas where conversation might take place. Sterilizers' allotments were distributed at work. The place where they ate was perfunctorily referred to as the Lot, never *a lot*, as all were well aware that the irony of meager portion sizes was too painful to laugh at. There was, on occasion, an opportunity to interact with other Sterilizers in the Lot, ever so briefly, over a meal when things were slow.

Things were rarely slow. Homelanders were always dissolving and dying, keeping Sterilizers occupationally secure, but bereft of time for personal considerations, like friendship.

***

Nothing much changed in the coming weeks. Cathy continued to pass on most of her allotment to Pele. She would forget words and interrupt to ask about them. She refused to go online and socialize. She had more missteps and falls, but she didn't break any bones. Maggie continued to worry and Pele continued to observe. They also started closing their bedroom doors at night. It was irrational. Bacteria were not nocturnal. If Cathy was sick rather than just old, it was far too late to protect themselves.

When weigh-in day arrived, Cathy had lost five pounds, more than a pound a week. Pele had gained weight, but at roughly the rate he'd been gaining for the last year or so. The red light didn't flash for either of them. No announcement was made, which made Pele feel less anxious. Maggie looked at Cathy and thought, *maybe she's just getting old.* Look at her—gray, thinning hair, drooping jowls, wrinkles, loss of energy. It must still happen, people must die just from the accumulation of years. There'd been no fever, no other breathing problems, no diarrhea—though with her scant food portions, that wasn't surprising. She was losing words, but she wasn't suffering mental losses that *Listeria* or mad-cow could cause.

In the coming days, Maggie paid more attention to her mother. Pele did, too. Maggie responded when Cathy had questions. She held Cathy's elbow when she was walking the length of the house to a meal. Pele offered to play Rummy, but Cathy couldn't keep track of what she was trying to collect and couldn't count what few points she did get. Since the coughing jag, Maggie listened to Cathy's breathing, which thinned to a whisper. Maggie wanted to do another cleansing, but she knew it wouldn't help and she couldn't put Cathy through that again. Cathy didn't seem to be aware of the changes in herself or her family. She slept easily and long. She thought about the past all the time, but stopped telling stories about her childhood, using all her energy to relive them in her mind. That way the colors were brighter, the people more friendly, the food tastier. Maggie noticed that occasionally Cathy would sit with a distant look in her eye and smile gently. She didn't ask.

The day before the next weigh-in, Maggie called her mother to come eat her allotment. She was walking toward Cathy's room as she called and a chill went down her spine.

"Mother?"

She peered into the room. Cathy lay there, eyes open, staring toward the window. Maggie gasped. She'd never seen death up close. Usually bodies were whisked away, suctioned up, dissolved and disappeared. Maggie walked into the room and sat on the bedside. She reached up instinctively to close her mother's eyelids and then realized she dare not touch her face, even in death, especially in death. She didn't cry. How could she? This was peaceful. That thought touched her heart and she smiled faintly and reached out and laid her hand on top of her mother's, despite the ban against it. The skin was already cooling. Maggie called to Pele, who came immediately.

"Your grandma has died."

Pele looked at the body. It didn't look like his grandma anymore. He stood next to his mother and watched as she wrapped their side of the blanket over Cathy's body, including her face. She moved to the other side and did the same so her mother was shrouded head to toe.

"Are you OK, Pele?"

"I guess. It seems strange that she's just gone. It's so sudden. What happens now?"

"I'm not exactly sure. I'll call the Enforcers to notify them. I'm sure they'll remove the body. But I'm not sure what, if anything, they will do to us."

"What do you mean?"

"Well, I don't know if every death in a home leads to any kind of bacterial testing. I suspect fear of contagion is involved. I'm sure they'll check our decontamination system for frequency of use. Maybe we should decontaminate before I call. What do you think?" Though Pele was only 10, she liked to ask his opinion. Now that it was just the two of them he should have a voice.

"I don't feel like decontaminating now. I enjoy it but I'm a little sad right now."

"OK, but I suspect they'll want us to decontaminate after they come. Once I call, we will be at their mercy."

"I understand. If someone else tells me to do it, I will. I won't resist or act like a baby. But you gave me a choice, and I don't want to."

"OK. I'll go call. I don't want them thinking we delayed for any reason." With that, Maggie walked to the Enforcement Unit and pushed the contact button. It took no time at all, presumably they were waiting for such calls.

"Reason for the call?"

"There's been a death."

"Name, age, cause of death?"

"Cathy Okelana, 79, old age."

"Sorry ma'am, old age is not a cause of death."

"Heart attack or stroke. Or maybe no cause. Can I report no cause?"

"You can, ma'am. Is that what you want to report?"

"Yes, I mean, 'no cause.' I'm not a medical. I don't know what happened."

"I've alerted the team nearest your home, ma'am. The system reports that you and your son also live there. Anyone else in the home?"

"Only my mother's body."

"Of course, ma'am, but I was asking about the living. Before the team arrives, I'd ask that you and your son go to decontamination and wait in the outermost chamber. The team will meet you there."

"Is there anything I should know?"

"You've reported 'no cause of death,' ma'am. I'm afraid you'll just have to do everything the team requires."

"Was 'no cause' the wrong answer? Couldn't you have said? Couldn't you have helped?"

"Ma'am, at this stage, you'll just need to wait for the team."

Maggie walked to Pele's room. She wanted to warn him, but warn him about what? She felt apprehensive, but she knew no more now than she had before. The ominous conversation with the lackey hadn't changed that. Why hadn't he accepted old age as a cause? Why didn't she stick with heart attack? Why didn't she assert something? Anything? Why had she said "no cause"? Why should they even ask? She had no medical knowledge, no experience with death. It was a trap. That's what it was. Pele looked at her anxiously. She smiled, unconvincingly. "Let's go."

"Go? We don't go anywhere."

"I mean, let's go to decontamination. That's where I was told we should meet the team. I'm not sure who the team is, but Enforcers, I guess. That's who I contacted."

"Can't I just stay in my room? Can't you meet them?"

"No. A death involves everyone in the home, no exceptions. They took the time to ask if it was only the two of us here."

"OK, mom." Pele was a little scared. He'd never met an Enforcer in person. But he got up and walked with his mom to decontamination.

Maggie thought she heard movement outside. There were no sirens on official vehicles as there was no one to get out of the way. They moved stealthily among the Homelanders, visible, but silent. Before she could stand or speak to Pele, the door was yanked open and two people covered from head to toe in black cover-ups walked in. The smaller one carried a large plastic bag. The bigger of the two barked, "Where's the body?"

Maggie pointed into the home. Where else? "Second door on the left." But wouldn't the corpse wrapped in a shroud of blankets give it away? Both black figures tromped through the home. Pele's eyes were wide open. Before the door closed completely, five figures dressed in white cover-ups swept in the door as well. Each carried multiple pieces of equipment, all of it slick, shiny silver. Before they could ask, Maggie pointed.

When they were again alone, Pele questioned, "Who were those people?"

"I'm guessing the first pair are Enforcers and that second group must be Sterilizers."

"But why do we need Sterilizers? Grandma was just old, right?"

"Yes. But they have to be sure that's all there is to it."

"How could bacteria even get to us? We don't go out. No one comes in."

"There's the allotment delivery, and pickups of our wraps after decontaminations, and the few other deliveries we get now and then. Things like your 3-D checkers."

"But everything goes through decontamination or gets put in the sterilizer."

"I know. I know. But it still happens that bacteria get in through all our defenses. There's nothing to worry about, Pele."

"But you're worried." Pele decided this was the time to say it.

"Not worried. Apprehensive. I've never been through this. I don't know what's going to happen. I don't like that. I like to be prepared." I sound just like my mother, Maggie thought with embarrassment.

The Enforcers stomped through, carrying what Maggie could only assume was her mother's body. It was zipped into the large black bag the big Enforcer had slung over his shoulder while the small one was speaking into a recorder. They acted as if Maggie and Pele weren't there. When the door closed, Maggie exhaled, not realizing she'd been holding her breath.

The inner door opened and two of the white-clad figures appeared. Maggie assumed she and Pele would be asked, told, perhaps even ordered to decontaminate. She was about to ask whether it was time for that, when one of the Sterilizers spoke. "Come with us."

"Come with you? Where? What do you mean?"

"We have to take you in. There's been a death, cause unknown."

"Old age. She died of old age. I tried to—"

"Ma'am, the official report is in my hand. It says 'cause unknown.' In such cases remaining Homelanders must be put into isolation while the body is examined. Follow this member of the team. Do exactly as you are told. Do not question us again."

Pele looked beseechingly at his mother. He couldn't remember ever having been beyond these walls. True, his grandma used to tell him stories that included him playing outside, ones where he traveled somewhere called a mall, ones where he interacted with other children face-to-face. But he had no such memories. He thought his grandma liked make-believe. She even told stories of his mother touching her own face. That had to be a lie, so he figured most of her stories were made up. Maggie nodded at Pele and tried to give him an encouraging look. She wanted to say something, but at this stage, she figured silence was the better choice.

Together they walked behind the short, overweight figure. How was it possible for someone to weigh that much? Did Sterilizers get more food? Surely not. Did they steal? Weren't they weighed regularly like Homelanders? Could metabolic conditions cause such a difference? Maggie focused on anything she could to avoid thinking about what was happening, to avoid worrying about her son who hadn't been outside, who hadn't encountered other people in nearly his whole life.

When they reached the van, the Sterilizer behind them, the one who had started this movement, told them to halt, raise their arms and close their eyes. Both Sterilizers pointed rifle-like spray guns filled with the latest mix of full strength AB fluid and shot full force at Maggie and Pele. They were pushed back by the power and surprise of the blast, but neither fell. Next their heads were bagged. Pele began to panic, having always been told to keep everything away from his face. "Breathe normally," came the order. "Oxygen is flowing in your mask even though it may not inflate." When he continued to hyperventilate, the other Sterilizer spoke for the first time in a most soothing tone. "Observe your mother, son. See. It'll be fine." Pele looked at his mother, who was clearly frightened, but she wasn't struggling to breathe. Next their hands were bagged, each separately. Unlike the clear head-coverings, their hands were now pastel blue blobs. It reminded Maggie a bit of gauzing Pele when he was an infant. She wished she could tell him the story, one Cathy had told many times, as a way of telling him he'd lived through something similar before. Instead she smiled, in a way that looked to others, Pele included, a bit demented, but she gave it her best shot.

At last they were put into the back of the van. Each of them had their own padded cage-like area, with nothing in it. These kept them separate and kept them as clean and safe as could be on the way to the AntiBacterial Center. The ride took half an hour. It was bumpy, no longer any reason for pothole repair, but it was fluid, no stopping for other traffic.

When they arrived, Maggie and Pele were helped out and then told again to follow. Obediently they walked up to a multi-story structure of glass and steel. It sparkled in the bright sunlight, no doubt meant to project an image of cleanliness. It put Maggie in mind of a cross between an office building and a hospital of the past, with the former's glitz and the latter's functionality. She hoped it wasn't the teaming cesspool of bacteria and disease hospitals became in the final years before the Outdoor Ban. A large glass door slid aside as they approached and closed again behind them. Pele tried to turn to see the closure, but the Sterilizer nudged him with the spray gun to keep him from dawdling.

***

The three Sterilizers left behind went right to work at Maggie's house. Each started in a different room. It took a couple hours for the three to do the bedrooms. They collected air samples: 110 parts per million consisting of 100 run-of-the-mill microns, 8 fungal mycotoxins, one mold spore, and one mite fecal, none of it abnormal, none of it bacterial. They opened every drawer and door. No space was left un-inspected. They ran small swabs over every surface, collecting residue and fomites and then read the results on handhelds that kept track of all data collected. 63:10,000; 23:100,000; 790:1,000,000. The numbers were nearly endless strings. Each surface had a unique signature with recurring patterns based on the humans living in the home. As each data sample was collected it caused a twang from the handheld. Were they to encounter dangerous bacteria, it would start chattering just like an old-time Geiger counter. The inventor thought that a funny anachronism, but since none of the Sterilizers was old enough to remember the fear of radiation, they knew the increasingly fast tick-tick-tick as the sound of bacteria, a potentially lethal substance.

When he had examined every surface, the Lead Sterilizer tabulated the results. "AB 100%," he said. "Odd. This was the death room."

The three convened in the living room after they finished the bedrooms. "I haven't found anything," said the first.

"Me either."

"Ditto."

"Let's work on the kitchen together. Since the death room revealed nothing, the kitchen is the most likely culprit."

Each took a portion of the room with no discussion. It was routine. This is what they did. When any particular area was completed, an announcement was made.

"39 parts per million, no bacteria."

"Spores, mites, minute numbers of other microns, no bacteria."

"Sterilization unit clean."

"Remaining allotment properly packaged, no contamination."

When the kitchen was finished they still had no evidence of bacterial intrusion. From there, one Sterilizer moved to the living room with the expectation of an easy job; another to the decontamination chambers with calibrated equipment to check functions as well as cleanliness; and the third moved to the bathroom to continue to search for the killer. Usually they found the bacteria, closed the residence permanently, and conveyed the news to the Sterilizers scouring the Homelanders who had been removed so they could be monitored, in the best-case scenario, or destroyed, in the worst.

***

Once inside the ABC, Maggie and Pele were turned over to new personnel. Their personal data was exchanged, and they were seated in a small room alone. They were told that before scanning and scouring could begin, their data needed to be tied to the file of the deceased removed by the Enforcers. With so many government lackeys doing so many different jobs, interagency communication could be faulty, and it was important for them to not be separated from that which landed them here. For a while Maggie and Pele sat quietly, not looking at each other. Finally, Maggie ventured quietly, "Are you OK?"

"Yeah, I think so. The mask is scary. At first I didn't think I could breathe. But it's OK now."

"That's good."

"Mom, what is scouring?"

"I don't know exactly. Do you know the word—to scour? It's a verb."

"I think I've seen it in old ads for cleaning dishes. But it doesn't make any sense because I just put our dishes in the sterilizer and it removes everything. So is it like sterilizing?"

"Scouring is a physical act of scrubbing. It's not one we have much use for in our daily lives. We have decontamination for us by both spray and lighting, and we have sterilization for objects—which uses a similar process utilizing UV rays. Our air is filtered coming into the home."

"That's a list of what we have, mom. Scouring? You were explaining it."

"Well, that's just it. We don't have any need for it. Scouring is to rub vigorously. Those ads you saw probably involved a scraper or sponge of some sort that a person would put detergent on, like AB wash, and then use the scraper to rub against plates and pots, to scour them. Pots were used to heat food before nuking existed. It was inefficient and didn't protect against bacteria very effectively."

"So scouring happens to things? It sounded like they were gonna do it to us. Maybe scouring is what the Sterilizers still at our home are doing there." Both Pele and Maggie imagined the three remaining Sterilizers were thoroughly decontaminating every surface of their home. Maggie figured the devices they'd lugged in would decontaminate in some way. Each device had its special use, she imagined, cleansing what could be seen and what couldn't. Maggie thought they might hook up a special purifier to recycle all the air. The Sterilizers were known for putting the "anti-" in AntiBacterial. In a contaminated zone, a slip-up could cost them their lives, so they tended to be very good at their jobs, or they were no longer around to do them.

Pele had focused Maggie on their home, which she hadn't even considered. Before she could wonder what scouring might mean in this context, two Sterilizers dressed in white cover-ups with red hexagonal markings on the centers of their chests designating their role in the ABC entered the room. "Let's get you both run through the scanners. Then it's on to scouring. You follow me, ma'am, and son, you follow Gary." They left the room and the two Sterilizers separated to go to different scanners that sat in the hallway. "You can leave everything on, this scans all levels at once, inside and outside. Just step inside.

Put your hands above your head as shown on the diagram. This will take 90 seconds. Please don't move or we'll have to start over." The machines made clunking noises but were innocuous. Both Sterilizers watched monitors as the scans occurred. "Clean data," they both announced.

"One of our scourers is out of commission today. We'll have to take you one at a time. Son, you just go back into the room and wait. Ma'am, please come with us." Pele walked by them to return to the room. Maggie tried to give Pele an encouraging look, but he could see by her eyes that she was terrified.

The Sterilizers took Maggie to another room. Since the TouchBans, robotics had been developed for many services that formerly used human hands. Unfortunately, with scouring, it didn't work very well because bodies were so many different sizes and shapes. The RedHexes removed the gloves and mask from Maggie. Then they ordered her to remove her wrap and put it through the incinerator chute. Though she was regularly naked for decontamination, no one had seen her naked for more than a decade, Pele's birth was probably the last time. She told herself to think of this as medical, after all, many medicals had become Sterilizers when given the choice of that or what? She wasn't sure. Were they eliminated? Used as test subjects? Just sent back to be ordinary Homelanders? The important thing now was to focus on this as a medical procedure so she could endure it.

The scourbot had a variety of protruding arms. Each ended in a brush or abrasive pad. The pads ranged in size, texture and material. The pads put her in mind of her father's shop, which she hadn't thought of in years. He had a whole set of grades of sandpaper used to smooth wood, plastic or even metal, depending on the project. The different grades varied in roughness. She recalled her dad started with the coarse sandpaper and as he worked he switched to finer and finer grains to polish a surface from rough to smooth.

She wasn't used to touching, let alone having her flesh rubbed with rough plastic and metal. She was told to use the mannequin stand, a metal cross of thin supports, to keep her arms at 90-degree angles to her body, during the entire procedure. There it was, medical language, "procedure." Everything had been a procedure. Remove a wart—procedure, have a broken limb set—procedure, flood a body with noxious chemicals to kill cancer cells—procedure. This was just an uncomfortable procedure.

Once Maggie was positioned correctly, the Sterilizers stepped into a small booth from which they could manipulate the bot remotely. As the first scour arm approached, Maggie unconsciously pulled back. "Hold still!" barked the RedHex. "Trust me on this, you don't want me to sedate you." Maggie thought sedation sounded like a good idea. Then she wouldn't have to be conscious for any of this—the nudity, the pain, the fact that Pele would have to go through it, too.

When the arm approached again, she stayed still and found the bot actually encircled her, rubbing left and right at the same time. She didn't like it on her arms. It felt alien, but why wouldn't it? She couldn't remember being touched, not her bare flesh. Then the bot shifted to her front and she screamed. The intimacy, the force, the roughness—it was all causing her to feel her body as a body and it was horrifying. It was harsh enough to redden her skin, but it didn't draw blood. The Sterilizers kept the bot moving unabated, with no acknowledgement of Maggie's response. It was merely auditory. She remained physically stable.

Pele jolted at his mom's scream. In the minutes that had passed since her departure, he worried, nearly panicked, and then calmed himself in his usual manner, rocking side to side, gently, arms wrapped around himself. Since he was in a wrap, this didn't count as touching. It was, in fact, encouraged in the young to simulate the touches that no longer existed, touches that were important to human survival. How *that* need had frustrated the powers that be!

When Maggie screamed, Pele jumped to his feet. He walked to the door, but with no window, it wasn't of much use. He started breathing heavily and found the mask was sucking in. He suddenly felt like it was going to adhere to his face. He needed oxygen. He didn't want to suffocate. A monitor he hadn't noticed before began a ticker tape display:

Remain Calm. ...... Sit Down. .... Breathe Normally. .... Oxygen Is Flowing In Your Mask. ..... Remain Calm..... .... Sit Down. .... Breathe Normally. .... Oxygen Is Flowing In Your Mask. .... Remain Calm.

Pele looked around. He could see a small camera above the monitor. It was like the camera on his console. He realized he was being watched. That made him feel better. It allowed him to trust in the mask again, as he had when he'd watched his mom breathing in it earlier. As his panic abated, the reason for it returned to him: his mom had screamed. What were they doing to her? What would they do to him? When would he see her again? All good questions.

The bot scouring Maggie was slow and had to be adjusted repeatedly. Arms had to be raised or lowered, the squeeze needed to be adjusted looser, tighter. Most adjustments were made electronically. However, at one point a RedHex needed to actually enter the room and move the arms manually. This made Maggie self-conscious as it reminded her she was naked. She realized the cover-ups meant she had no idea what sex the Sterilizers were. Did it matter? It was the bigger RedHex who entered, the one who barked orders, probably the one in charge. The voice was deep so he was likely a man, but she couldn't be sure.

The RedHex grabbed an arm of the bot and stretched it out. Pushed a couple buttons. Tinkered with a flexor. And as his hand pulled back from the flexor, the edge of it ran across Maggie's breast. Her nipple responded by hardening while the area around it shrank. Maggie's eyes widened, her breath quickened. The arousal was abhorrent. She didn't ask for this. Her generation was the first to be forbidden to have sex. She'd been just old enough that she'd been touched by a boy. They'd gone to third base, as they described it, each touching the other's privates. But they'd never "done it." For years she felt deprived, wished on that night in the backseat of his car they'd gone all the way, but over the years, as the physical isolation grew deeper, longer, she'd all but forgotten. Now, this Sterilizer's brief touch, if you could call it that, brought it all back. She flushed with excitement and embarrassment and fear. The RedHex seemed to look her in the face, but she couldn't see through the mesh mask, so she couldn't tell what that look meant. What was it? "Don't say anything" or "You liked that, didn't you, bitch?" or merely, "Stand still!" Whatever it was, it passed in an instant, and the Sterilizer went back to the booth and continued the procedure.

Maggie's mind raced. Surely this procedure was being observed. Would that interaction lead to anything? Would she be accused of inviting touch? Though the touch was brief, she knew her body's reaction was visible. Her autonomic responses were intact, if seldom called upon. She willed herself to breathe normally. She tried to distract her thoughts. Focusing on the moment wouldn't work because every scouring motion made her more aware of her nakedness and of her body's possible betrayal. She shifted her thoughts to Pele, but that was too frightening. This would be horrible for him. For him, *all* of this would be a violation. She thought of Cathy and suddenly missed her mother's stories. She'd have a distraction at the ready. Cathy could spin a tale, especially about the past. But now Cathy was gone. There would be no more tales of touching or eating or how changes affected their family. For the first time, Maggie let Cathy's death seep in. She was gone. Her mother wouldn't be at home when they returned. Cathy hadn't left that house in seven years. She'd joked that they'd have to carry her out in a body bag and that's exactly what happened. No joke. Maggie tried to decide if that was irony or just inevitable.

The bot stopped with its arms loosely around her. Was it over? Nothing happened. Then she heard a whirring sound that seemed to be inside the bot. "You're done," came the voice from the booth. "The bot should have pulled away, but it seems to be stuck. Can you shimmy under those arms?" Maggie looked at the bot, especially the locations of each scouring pad. She started to crouch but that made her back into a pad behind. She raised a leg and slid it sideways and started to duck, but again she hit a pad, this time with her forehead. "Wait, wait, wait!" came the voice and then the smaller RedHex entered the room. "Let me remove the pads." The Sterilizer expertly removed all pads, and then stepped back. Maggie again crouched but when she hit the metal of the bot, she pushed a bit and was able to extract herself with several shifts of one arm, then one leg, then a tilt of the head, a movement of shoulder, and so on until she stood alone, no longer embraced by modern technology.

Maggie was pointed to a door, told to go through, wrap herself and wait. She would be taken to an isolation room as soon as someone could collect her. *Collect* her? Like garbage? Like decontamination waste byproduct? Or *collect* her like a favored treasure, like seashells or figurines from days gone by? That was a more pleasant, if distant, meaning. Waiting always made her wonder about the strangest things. It was a good distraction from worrying about Pele. She didn't want to think about his flesh feeling jagged like hers now did, or imagine him going through the embarrassment of disrobing. Maybe taking off his clothes wouldn't matter to him. He was a boy who had grown up entirely in this world. Instead of another indignity at the altar of bacteria, maybe he'd experience being unwrapped as something new. But the bot wasn't friendly and the scouring was a bit painful, so he wouldn't enjoy it.

Pele waited for hours. He worried about his mom. He worried about what would happen next. He worried about the mask, but then he'd read the screen again and remember to stay calm and he'd start rocking side-to-side. Finally the door opened.

"We had to wait for a working scourbot. It won't take nearly as long as you've waited. Let's go." Pele followed the RedHex.

Once inside the scouring room, the Sterilizer reached for Pele's mask. Pele immediately started hyperventilating again. "I'm taking this off. Relax!" ordered the RedHex. With a flourish, the plastic was removed from Pele's face and he took a big gulp of air, which started him hiccupping. "No, no, no," barked the RedHex as he took off Pele's gloves. "This procedure has already been delayed. You need to get rid of those hiccups so we can do this. Stand up against that wall with your back flat to it. Close your eyes. Breathe slowly. Imagine a favorite pastime." Pele did as he was told. Very quickly his hiccups subsided.

"How'd you do that?"

As soon as he'd asked his question he knew it was the wrong thing to do. When he was told to throw his wrap down the chute and stand in the mannequin holder, he did so without another word. This scourbot needed few adjustments. Yet, with the first swipe, the scour pad went too deeply and drew blood from Pele's shoulder. He yipped loudly at the sharp pain and the intrusive action itself. The extreme touching caught him off-guard—he couldn't remember having ever been touched.

One of the Sterilizers came back into the room and placed an AB patch over the wound. "That shouldn't have happened. We've made an adjustment. This patch will protect the injury."

The RedHex left the room as swiftly as she'd entered, with no time for Pele to respond.

Immediately the scourbot began again. When the procedure ended, the bot opened all its arms and slid away a few feet. Pele was told to exit the room and wrap himself. "You'll be collected for isolation as soon as an Isolator is available."

"Isolation? So I won't be with my mom?"

"Isolation. You'll be alone until the autopsy is complete, as you were told."

He hadn't been told. He was good at remembering things. Pele walked through the door. He looked down at the AB patch on his shoulder. It didn't hurt, not any more than the rest of him. He felt kind of raw all over. He didn't like scouring. He hoped he wouldn't have to go through it again. It was nasty. He saw a wrap and clothed himself in it expertly. He glanced around the room. There it was, another monitor, inset in the wall, nearly invisible. Good, he thought, I'm not alone. Then he sat down and instinctively began rocking slowly, methodically, side-to-side. He could sit this way for hours.

Maggie's mind was racing. She pursued any thread of interest well beyond logical conclusions, finding that veering off on tangents kept her from a variety of fears. Hours passed. Suddenly two Sterilizers entered the room carrying a Turbobike. It was newer and smaller than her one at home. They set the bike opposite the monitor and plugged it into a gathering socket. Then they used a key to reset the counter so they'd know whether or not she'd met her quota. Though Maggie was unaware, it was required that ABC residents generate enough power to run the procedures they'd been brought in for, plus 20% for those who were incapable of making their own quotas.

"While you wait, generate."

Maggie made adjustments to the seat height, climbed aboard and started pedaling. This would help. She knew well how to busy her mind while making power. She did it every day.

When the Isolators entered Pele's room, they were carrying a large hollow ball. Inside the ball was a seat and straps. The monitor had shown Pele's rocking motion, so he was being given a Stirball for his generation quota. The ball had a gyroscopic weighted mechanism that kept his head predominantly in an elevated position relative to the rest of his body. They found this allowed a greater energy creation because the Homelander inside didn't become dizzy and stop.

Pele had never seen such a device.

The Isolator strapped him inside and closed the ball. Then they flicked a switch so the wireless would gather the power and feed it to the mainline.

"We'll be watching. If you have any problems just say so out loud and someone will come in." They released the ball and watched for a moment to ensure it was closed tight and Pele wouldn't get upset again. No reason to leave and have to return immediately.

At first Pele rocked the ball tentatively. Then he reached out his right hand and felt the shift from his movement. He added his right leg. He was enjoying the rocking motion and discovered he could make it go faster or slower. He could make it go in many directions. This would be fun.

"No sign of trauma, no accelerated deterioration, no evidence of bacteria at autopsy or in the home. No reason to keep you."

Maggie wanted to say, "See, I told you it was old age." She wanted to ask, "So, was it a heart attack? Stroke? What?" Then she realized they'd said something about no bacteria in her home. "What did you do in my home? I thought you were decontaminating, but that wasn't all was it?" She wanted to scream, "Does this mean I can see my son now?"

Instead, she nodded.

It had been at least a day and a half, maybe two. Who could tell? Food had been delivered twice, but that meant nothing. She didn't know what the feeding schedules were. At intervals, videos had played on the monitor as well as lists of bacteria and the warning signs of contamination. Funny how they seemed to want to both entertain and instruct. She wondered if that was something the Psychs had determined was a useful combination.

"Come with me, ma'am." She was walked to a room where they found Pele sitting, rocking himself. He jumped to his feet and put both hands high in the air in the sign of affection that Maggie participated in as well. They both smiled. Maggie inquired with her eyes how he was, and Pele nodded he was OK. Now that she was with him, he was better than OK.

"You'll be taken home. You'll need to be masked and gloved for the journey. You're currently good and clean, we don't want to ruin that. In your absence your home has been installed with the latest AB mix. That should help."

Help what? Maggie wondered. It's not as if they were brought here because of catching a bug. In fact, they were brought here for no real reason at all. If she admitted it to herself, they were brought here because she said "unknown" as the cause of death. They were brought here because fear ruled. They were brought here because they could be—because it gave the Sterilizers, Enforcers and all the lackeys a purpose in this world.

But she didn't say any of those things aloud. She'd learned to keep quiet. Right now, she was just grateful Pele was OK and they were going home.

"Mom, I got to generate in a Stirball. It was really fun."

"You can tell me all about it when we get home, Pele." Her voice was warm, but it was clear now wasn't the time for family intimacy. It was a time of public scrutiny, but until today, Pele hadn't experienced public anything that he recalled, so he had no idea what the rules were.

***

Gary sat on the Rowathon and imagined the woman from this morning's procedure. She wasn't anything special, just a Homelander in for scanning and scouring. A death in the family, precautionary. If the scourbot had worked properly, this never would have happened. He wouldn't have touched her. Oh, he was wearing his cover-up, so there'd been no actual contact on his part, no flesh touching flesh. But he could see it was a touch from her perspective.

In those gloves his fingers had the sensitivity of a bot. He knew when he connected with something, but he wouldn't say he could feel it. So when the outside edge of his right hand, his dominant hand, brushed against her breast, he hardly noticed the contact with the soft object.

But the changes in her body exploded in front of him.

He saw the nipple shrink, heard a sharp intake of breath, looked up and saw her face flush pink. Her pupils were dilated when he looked into them. He held her stare for a moment, wondering what she was thinking, what she was feeling. He'd hoped none of this was detectable in the booth. He'd finished with the bot flexor so it was positioned correctly and hurriedly left the room.

"Something happen in there?"

"Huh? Did I put the flexor in the wrong position?"

"Looks fine. You just kinda slammed the door."

"Oh, that. I just get tired of these things not working. You'd think maintenance could get it right, wouldn't ya?"

"You'd think."

As always, his reaction caused the greatest stir. He needed to control his emotions. Why did he get angry and upset? No one else seemed to. That ended with the old regime. Life was repetition. There was nothing greater to be achieved. *Do your part*, that was all, *do your part* was the mantra Sterilizers lived by. They were public servants, lackeys as far as Homelanders were concerned, but they were essential to life continuing. Without them, bacteria would rule.

Today's encounter reminded Gary of his fiancé, Sam. They'd been so hot for each other. They had sex everywhere—living room floor, shower, kitchen counters. Clothed, naked, midway between. Little could prevent them from hooking up, that was the language they used, "hooking up." Not "having sex," not "making love," not "fucking," just hooking up. Not that it was nonchalant—they were planning their wedding. They'd both been nurses. When Sam contracted *E. Coli O157:H7*, they both hoped she could be saved because they'd noticed the signs early and gotten the confirming tests. But it hadn't mattered.

By then the strains were so resistant and hearty that it coursed through her in less than 48 hours. He was sure he'd die, too, as much as they shared. He went over and over the day before she died trying to figure out the contaminating culprit: the counter they'd hooked up on, the hamburger she ate, her clinic duty. He hadn't had to revisit her caseload, the hospital had handled that since it was looking to deny an outbreak at its hands. The source wasn't located, which was pretty common then. Whatever had taken her, it didn't take him. He lived. As dismayed as he was by that at the time, since then he'd often wished he'd shared her *E. Coli* as they'd shared everything else.

Now he thought of the woman getting scoured. He wondered if she'd ever had sex. Her body certainly had all the prerequisites. Her response to his touch was so immediate and intense. She was only a little younger than he was. It was possible she'd mated before the Touch Ban. He started to fantasize about her, right there, rowing away, generating his daily quota. He'd found it was the safest time to fantasize. It wasn't detectable. He was in his cover-up. He was sweating. Though there were other Sterilizers generating, they were all hypnotically engaged in the monitor's information scroll. It reported news from their ABC and compared it with other ABCs across the country. He found the endless string of data mind-numbing and seldom paid attention. Others seemed to appreciate that dulling quality. They certainly paid no attention to him.

It wasn't that he made a habit of fantasizing. In fact, it was a rare event. There wasn't much to stimulate him. It was true his work put him in contact with naked bodies daily, but they were there for scouring, hardly a situation that made them attractive. Sixty-seven percent of them would die before leaving the ABC. It was an equation that kept him from thinking much about any of those he worked on.

But this was an exception. The touching was unusual. Had it been noticed, he would have been reprimanded. Or at least that seemed likely. Not that the broken bot situation wouldn't have mitigated any punishment, but it was still an infraction.

And *this* was why. Here he was, now, imagining touching her without his cover-up. That could be dangerous.

***

By the time they got home, Pele was no longer thinking about the Stirball and his mom didn't ask. He wanted to go straight to his room, to be alone and think about all that had happened. But when they walked through the last chamber into their home, everything felt wrong. Nothing looked out of place, but for the first time in his life, Pele could feel that others had been in his home. It wasn't anything like the violations he'd felt at the ABC, but it made him uncomfortable.

"Wonder what all they did here?"

"You mean the Sterilizers, mom?"

"Yeah, those three who stayed behind."

"I can tell they were here. But nothing looks different. Why is that?"

"I don't know how to explain it, Pele. People leave an invisible mark. Evidently even in those cover-ups. People have...they have...well, *we* have...an *aura*, some people call it. Our psyches pick up on it. It's not visible, but it's real. We just sense it."

"Will our home always have their aura in it? Will it always be this way?"

"No. It will fade."

"Good. I don't like it."

"I also think we're missing your grandma. She had an aura, too, and it's gone."

"I almost forgot. Is that bad?"

"That's normal. Death is hard to get used to. We expect people to still be around, especially when it comes to things we did with them. Like you'll miss her when we play games after we eat. I'll find I miss her interrupting me when I'm working."

"You hated her interruptions."

"Yes, I did. And I didn't like her storytelling about the past, but I'll miss that, too. Those absences will remind me she's gone. What was an annoyance, like her interruptions, will become a signal to me that she isn't here any more, and then I'll notice she's gone and I'll miss her."

"I've never known anyone who died."

"You have, but you don't remember. You were too young. And that's good. But it'll make this stranger for you. Ask me questions."

"I always do."

"I know. But this may be different. Her absence may make you sad, perhaps very sad. That might mean you don't want to talk. And that's OK, too." Pele nodded, but he wasn't exactly sure what she meant. "Everything's OK."

"Can I go to my room now?"

"Of course."

Pele walked into his room. It felt odd. The Sterilizers must have been in here, too. Why? He noticed his drawer was ajar. He looked inside. Everything looked the way he'd left it. He walked around the room. Nothing else looked different. He ran his eyes over everything in sequence. He didn't touch anything—he learned early his habits of keeping his hands from the act of fomiting surfaces. He pulled his wrap away from his shoulder and looked at the patch. They hadn't told him what to do with it. He'd have to ask his mom later. He was pleased it didn't hurt.

He lay down on his bed and stared at the ceiling. He replayed the events that had happened since his grandma died. They were a jumble of images and sensations. He started by remembering the bot scraping his flesh off. That led to the fear he experienced inside the mask when they were first leaving home. Then he heard his mom's scream. Before he got too panicky, he saw the monitor in his mind's eye and reread the calming directions. As his heart slowed he saw the black-uniformed Enforcers. He'd never seen an Enforcer before. The full suit of black made them scary. Or maybe just two strangers entering his home was scary. He'd never seen anyone but his mom and grandma, at least not that he could remember. Though they would say he had seen others. He always felt weird when they said things like that. It was as if he had another life he wasn't aware of because the things they told him had no anchors in his reality. He couldn't even really imagine them. Sure, his grandma told stories about the time before the Transition, and he'd read things online about that world, but it was all once-upon-a-time to him.

The Enforcers looked frightening, but the Sterilizers actually *were* frightening. In their white cover-ups they looked OK, but they were the ones who made him put on the mask that threatened him. They were the ones who took his mom away. They were the ones who cut his shoulder. They were the ones who left some part of themselves in his home, who opened his drawer, who touched his things. Sterilizers were evil.

Pele fell asleep thinking about all the horrors of the last several days. He awoke screaming with his mom standing above him murmuring, "You're alright, Pele. It's only a dream."

He nodded that it was OK so she'd leave the room. But it wasn't OK. He wasn't OK. It hadn't been a dream, or a nightmare. It had happened. He had the patch on his shoulder to prove it. He knew with a shudder that his life had changed. He would never be the same kid he was before his grandma died and they took her away, took him away, took his mother away.

On delivery day, Maggie found the food allotment hadn't changed. She wondered if this was a result of the various lackeys not communicating well with each other. She remembered the importance placed on that when they'd entered the ABC. She wondered if she should report this error, but realized the Enforcers knew as well as she did that Cathy was dead. They had the body. If they hadn't properly communicated that to other agencies it wasn't her fault. She said nothing. Pele had been eating most of Cathy's food anyway, so Maggie continued a distribution that meant he was getting a full two-thirds of each allotment. He didn't ask questions and she didn't say anything. She didn't want him worried about the weigh-in, and she didn't know how long it would last. Why not just let him eat while it was possible?

A week after they returned home, the buzzer went off. Maggie ran to the Enforcement Unit. She pushed the acknowledgement button. The lackey asked if there was anything unusual. Maggie stuttered out a "no."

"Are you certain? You don't sound certain."

Maggie answered that she wasn't sure what was meant by unusual. She said they were adjusting to life without Cathy, she said her son's injury from the scourbot had healed well, but she didn't say anything about the allotment.

"Just checking up," said the voice. The transmission ended. Pele entered the kitchen.

"What was that about?"

"I'm not sure. They asked if anything was unusual."

"Everything is unusual. Grandma isn't here. We're not playing Runny. We're not watching after her, answering her questions about some word she can't remember."

"I know. I know. And yet I don't think that's what they meant."

"What do you think they meant?"

"I don't know."

The allotment continued unaltered. Life began to have a new texture, one without Cathy and her stories. During the third month, the allotment was reduced. There was no announcement, no warning, even though Maggie had continued to receive calls. Maggie just opened the package one day to find less—not a third less, since Cathy's portion hadn't been a full third. Maggie didn't say a word to Pele or anyone else.

When a call came following the reduced delivery and she was once again asked if there was anything unusual, she said no and she said it firmly. She still wondered what was sought in that question, but she'd prepared herself to answer smoothly, without hesitation, a simple no.

She'd come to realize her wondering was a problem. They weren't looking for thinkers. Sometimes she added, mimicking one of Cathy's favorite phrases, "same old, same old."

Eventually, the calls stopped.

***

I've been living alone inside these four walls for several years now. OK, OK, I'm not in a one-room efficiency, I have more than four walls. But after a time, it really doesn't make much difference. When you've spent your life driving to work, walking to the park, attending conferences across the country and taking vacations across the world, staying home day in and day out is confining. There's no getting around it. In the early days there were stories about claustrophobia hitting people hard. A few refused to stay in. Some were rounded up by Enforcers, others got "bit"—that's what we called it—they got bit by bacteria and died. Those situations were highly publicized, and we were watching the news avidly then. A lesson to all that staying inside was worth the effort.

Can't say how long hope lasted, hope that life would return to some semblance of normal. By the time we were locked down, we'd been yo-yoing in and out of quarantines for quite awhile. And we'd always gotten out. They'd watch the rise and fall of one epidemic after another and let us out when the death toll diminished. When they announced that this was an Outdoor Ban, not just a quarantine, I don't think we believed them. We didn't have imaginations big enough for what was happening. We'd been conditioned *not* to think for ourselves, sold the idea that individual will was to blame for many a bacterial death.

In the early days there had been legal battles, radical protests, movements to regain our constitutional rights. But leaders got scared, leaders died, quarantines made meetings impossible. The tides were irregular, and somehow none of the attempts gained enough momentum to make it beyond the breakers. It was like novices trying to take surfboards across waves in a rough ocean current, being hit by wave after wave without the knowledge to dive under those waves, without the strength to keep at it. Eventually novices lose their boards or retreat, often getting knocked about in the process.

At least we still have the pursuit of life, that's the primary drive it seems, but there's not a lot of liberty, and very little happiness.

My days are pretty slow. I don't do much. Could be that I'm just old. We all slow down as we age, and I have no comparisons.

It's been years since I've seen a contemporary. I have no idea how old I am. I hadn't yet retired when the Transition occurred, but I don't know exactly how much time has passed since then. It's not that I couldn't know. The Internet still keeps track of time. But I have no reason to pay attention at that level. No schedules, no meetings, no celebrations of time—birthdays, holidays. It's all the same. Every day. The same.

I have to generate, but that's about it. At my age, my allotment is provided. I don't get much. I keep expecting the food to stop, but evidently enough have died that it's feasible to keep feeding us. It's all government-run. Makes me snicker when I think how hard the U.S. fought communism and now everything's equal, everything's government. No free enterprise. No capitalism. No individualized healthcare based on income, no fancy restaurants, no jets for the rich. At least as far as I can tell. I could be wrong, some of that might still exist somewhere, but here...we're finally all equal. Not exactly communism really, just practical, that's what it is.

I'm not sure it's truly each according to his or her means. I mean, who would choose to be a Cleaner, to be exposed to possible contamination? And yet people are doing those jobs. At first it was a post filled mostly by criminals and others who owed something tangible to society. Today? I'm not sure. For a while there were ads trying to get people who would be caught without housing to become Cleaners. But that didn't last long. I suspect they just rounded up the street people and those too poor to find adequate shelter. Why not? Seemed they'd die anyway. Practical. No one would complain about that move, not even back in the day. You see, some people never did have the rights the rest of us held so dear. Some have always been expendable.

I still spend a few hours a day reading things, mostly on the Internet. I follow threads, kind of like a weaver. Following a line of thought is about all I have for entertainment. I don't find the old movies or TV shows of any interest. There's nothing new, of course. No resources for that. I could read fiction, but I just don't find it plausible, the characters uninteresting. So I muse over this and that. Used to be that could fill a day. Now I make myself do a bit of it just as a way to keep the juices flowing.

Before the Transition, lots of people were involved in social media. It never interested me much. I preferred people to be face-to-face so I could look them in the eye to see the spark of disagreement when I provoked them. Lots of folks were tweeting and such. Perhaps some still do, but without a life to report on, most of that has disappeared. You'd think social networking would have been a connecting point. But to what end? How long can electrons effectively connect humans?

I'm gonna write that down. Might keep me busy online for a while seeing if anyone researched that question before it all came to a halt. Hmm. That's interesting.

***

Pele was home-schooled, at least that's what Cathy had called it. It was a concept from a time before. School had no meaning any longer. Learning was still needed, but it wasn't prized, it wasn't scheduled. During the on-again, off-again quarantines, the school districts had rushed to ensure everything was accessible online. Even after the Transition, they kept teachers employed, if briefly, while they ensured the curriculum was complete, in sequence, and had enhancements for interaction. After that, they continued partial employment if teachers were willing to answer student questions, grade exams—especially essays that still couldn't be adequately scored by computers—and help maintain records to move students through the system. But sometime during the second academic year, it fell apart. There was lethargy among parents trying to cope with their children 24/7. They couldn't be bothered to ensure kids did their lessons. And there was growing apathy about the outside world, the world beyond the home, because no one could see *this* ending any time soon.

When Cathy moved in so they'd all be together in this new world, Maggie had put her in charge of Pele's education. Cathy taught him to read, to do simple math. It was how their games of Rummy had first started. It was a way to expose him to numbers and get him to do simple addition. She devised ways to lead him into subtraction as well. For multiplication she had him draw groups of shapes on paper. For division, they drew lines to divide a large group of shapes.

But it was Maggie who determined what Pele would need in terms of the computer and the larger world. While she worked, she made notes of concepts he would need and ways to demonstrate them.

There was no need for team building, for social skills, for interaction. What little his world demanded in this realm he had with his mom and grandma. And now, because there were only the two of them, and very little to stress about, they had few interactions that weren't easy-going. Pele was nearing puberty and Maggie wondered how this would change him, change their relationship. The world was so different from what it had been when she'd grown up. She'd had the urge to run from her mother, to separate. That was no longer possible. The days in the ABC were the first time she and Pele had been separated from each other since he was a small child.

With Cathy gone, their relationship was uncomplicated by others. They weren't friends or neighbors or strangers. But they still had two separate wills. Surely, Maggie thought, Pele would change, make some kind of demand to be allowed to grow up.

He'd been different ever since they returned from the scouring. He had nightmares. She knew, because he often cried out. At first she had gone in to comfort him, as she'd done all his life. But he never spoke to her in those moments as he had before. He would open his eyes and acknowledge her presence, her efforts. Then he would close his eyes and she would leave the room. They didn't talk much about Cathy being gone except when it was game time, and then they usually commented only casually. They didn't share their grief. Maggie wanted to leave it to Pele, and Pele had no words for the feeling of absence. While Maggie missed her mother, she missed much in life, the feeling as familiar as the dimpling skin of a cold shower.

Maggie couldn't help herself, she kept speculating on the possible causes of Pele's quietude. Was it Cathy's death? A response to the pain and terror engendered by the Sterilizers? Was he angry at her for allowing these things to happen? Was he just beginning to grow up? Would self-actualization still be the pinnacle of maturity or would something supplant it?

And what would self-actualization mean now? By the time she got this deeply into her questions, she was lost in a lovely mindlessness that removed the pain of her mother's death and the distance she was experiencing with Pele. She sometimes wondered why she wondered so much. To keep her brain agile? To keep her mind busy? Perhaps just to salve her soul when there was no one to take care of her, no one to touch her.

Pele started thinking about the Stirball to calm himself when the fear took over. Finally he decided it was time to ask his mom if they could get one. He was tired of the Turbobike. Even with the screen tuned to something entertaining, he found it boring. And if he wanted his handheld to be powered fully each day, he had to ride for three to four hours, in addition to his household requirement of two. Six hours a day was a long time to sit on that bike.

"Mom, remember me telling you about the Stirball I generated with at the ABC?"

"Yes, it sounded fun."

"It was. I'd like one for home. It'd be so much better than the Turbobike."

"I imagine it would be. Do we have room for it?"

"I hadn't thought of that." Pele walked into every room. He could clearly see there wasn't room enough to roll with abandon. There wasn't really room to roll. "No, we don't. Is there any way to make more room?"

"No one builds anymore. And though there must be abandoned homes, I've never read of anyone moving. It would mean taking everything outside and risking contamination.

We might be able to make more room, if we're willing to give up things. Sort of like when you have to give up a toy for us to order something new."

"OK. But I like the living room furniture. It's nice to get out of my room sometimes. What other options are there?" They both thought of Cathy's room. Pele wasn't willing to be the one to bring it up. He didn't know what happened to dead people's stuff. Maybe it couldn't leave. But he didn't know why, because they didn't go in there. Neither of them used anything that was his grandma's.

Maggie sat down in a kitchen chair. Pele joined her at the table.

"How important is this to you?" Maggie asked.

"I've been thinking about it more and more. Sometimes you want to generate when I'm on the bike. This way that could happen. Besides, there's nothing to do the six hours a day while I'm riding it. I've seen all our programs a million times."

"We could empty your grandma's room."

"Could we?"

"Sure. It's not like anyone comes to visit. We don't need to keep a guest room."

Pele looked at his mother. He had no idea what she was talking about. He could tell it was old-timey talk. He waited patiently for her to go on.

"I'm not sure how we get rid of furniture though. There's no market for used goods. I suppose we could just carry them outside, but we'd be exposed in the process. We can't leave it for the Cleaners the way we do our wraps. It's too big for that. Let me investigate. There must be a way, but I'm not sure what it is. Tell you what. I'll look into that and you find out how we acquire a Stirball. When we had to start generating, the Turbobike was just delivered and installed. I'm not sure of the protocol. Can you do that?"

"Sure, mom. No problem."

The government was filled with lackeys. Besides the obvious—Cleaners, Sterilizers, and Enforcers—Maggie was sure there were still plenty of bureaucratic lackeys as well. Those lackeys might not work in offices anymore. Like Maggie, they likely worked from home. But there were dealings with the allotment production and distribution, generation modulation, weigh-in supervision. The list was probably very long. There wasn't a private sector anymore. There wasn't business, banking, or commerce. But there also wasn't visible infrastructure. You couldn't just look up say, the parks department to learn about pool hours or the department of motor vehicles to find out where you could get a license. So when Maggie got online to try to figure out what she could do with Cathy's bed, dresser and the few boxes still remaining from her life before, she couldn't figure out where to look for an answer. Amazingly, the first several search terms yielded sites that were more than a decade old, back when people sold used goods. Goods?! She had to laugh at the word. Good, if you could get a few bucks even though you'd used it for years. Good, unless it carried bacteria. Good, unless it killed you.

Maggie was surprised by the abundance of this dreck, these unmoored sites that led nowhere. Maggie's hours—she refused to think of it as a job, but the work she did in order to keep their allotment coming, keep the clean wraps coming and the dirty ones going, keep their water running—her *work* was to clean the web. Her duties were assigned to her. She couldn't just randomly trip upon an anachronism like these sites and eliminate them. She could report them, as could any Homelander, though few bothered, but she couldn't determine her own workflow. Each day, she reported to a queue that listed the tasks to be done. She selected one, logged in and completed it, was assessed based on an algorithm of the expected speed for the number of pages and type of cleanup, and accrued credits for her hours.

Select. Deprogram. Repeat.

Select. Deprogram. Repeat.

An endless series of the same thing, over and over. At least that's how it felt.

Occasionally she was assigned an interesting site where she learned something, like when antibacterials were first invented and why. Or she was given a task that involved actual problem-solving because a site contained both antiquated ghosts of the old world as well as information that continued to be pertinent, and she had to figure out how to eliminate the garbage while keeping what was useful. Or she needed to remove a virus. That always made her smile. She loved that there was a time when going viral was tantamount to one's 15 minutes of fame. *How absurd!*

She loved that the scientists and medics had all predicted a coming virus that would take out the population. They studied plagues of the past. They prepared vaccines. They warehoused pharmaceuticals they thought would save their nation, their people, their friends, all the while making "them," the amorphous other—Big Pharma—piles of money. Meanwhile, they paid no attention to what they were doing with their other hand, the one deep in the pocket of AgriBiz, which created various toxins, ones that were deadly not only to the animals raised and plants grown, but inevitably to those who ate from the bounty—Americans first, and eventually, the world.

When she'd started this work, she knew little about any of this. It had all been kept in the background. But over the years, she'd uncovered more and more of the story. Her endless curiosity meant that as she worked, she accumulated knowledge. She wasn't a mindless drone. She couldn't be. Some days she wished she could. But it just wasn't in her.

So as she searched for a way to get things out of the extra bedroom to make room for Pele's new means of generation, she mused about Re-Buy and garage sales and Craig's List and estate auctions and all the ways that people used to move used junk from one home to another. Cathy had loved garage sales. Maggie remembered that as a child her mom had spent Saturday mornings dragging Maggie from sale to sale. Often they bought nothing. It was more about the rummaging than the purchasing. It gave Cathy an opportunity to talk to strangers. It gave Maggie a chance to think about how others lived. It got Cathy "out of the house." How odd that seemed now.

Maggie smiled at the memory, one that only a few months ago would have made her ridicule Cathy, telling her what an extrovert she was and that she needed to live in the present. Maggie missed her mother. She was grateful that in the final months she'd been kinder to Cathy as she had declined, gotten angry with her less, helped her more. Cathy could be annoying, no doubt, but she was a good mother, faithful and loving. Maggie would have never chosen for the world to be this way, never. But under the circumstances, she was glad Cathy had lived with her during the worst of it.

Maggie got up from her computer. She walked from window to window looking out. She rarely looked out anymore. Now she examined what lay between her home and her neighbors'. She noticed for the first time that there was an old clothes dryer, a large metal sink, and some other rusting pieces sitting next to the former garage, no doubt converted into decontamination chambers. She shifted her gaze to look at the neighbor across the alley. Though some raggedy bushes blocked part of her view, she could see there were a couple pieces of indoor furniture, a kitchen table and an old-fashioned writing desk sitting in the midst of the yard. Maggie chuckled. All she had to do was open her eyes. Obviously, people were just moving things outside when they were done with them. Made sense. The world had dumped bacteria on all of them, they could dump crap anywhere they wanted.

Pele found out it would take his mother working 200 hours for them to acquire a Stirball. That sounded like a lot to him. He wasn't sure she'd be willing to do that. He also wasn't confident they had the proper wireless setup and, if not, he suspected that would end his desire for a Stirball. When he talked to his mom, she said they had the wireless or his handheld wouldn't work. Maggie also suggested that he share the 200 hours of work with her. She would teach him how to do some of the simpler things she did, and he could put in the hours. That way, he'd be getting an education and helping to "buy" the Stirball. He had no idea what it meant to buy something, but he was more than happy to help if it meant he'd get to roll around generating. Besides, with two of them building up the 200 hours, they'd get there that much faster.

It took nearly two months, but time was amorphous. An hour was still an amount people kept track of. Hours filled generation quotas, hours ensured allotment delivery. But days and weeks and months were meaningless. There was no longer reason for a calendar. Every day was like every other. And there was no reason to track the months because the change of seasons was meaningless when you lived entirely indoors. Global warming was no longer discussed. No doubt it had slowed or even ceased with fewer people and huge decreases in fossil fuel consumption, but living entirely indoors, it wasn't a concern that mattered much anymore.

They'd been able to start an account for the Stirball that allowed them to see their progress toward their goal. Each time they worked in excess of Maggie's weekly expectation, they were able to bank the extra hours. As they neared the 200-hour mark, Pele began to get very excited. He talked to his mom about modifications in the new Spinning Room, as he liked to call it. He was worried that it was smaller than the room he'd been in at the ABC. He asked about bumper pads and the possibility of knocking out part of the wall to his room. Maggie thought the pads would be fine, but she didn't think knocking out the wall was a good idea. Surreptitiously, she measured the living room furniture. It wouldn't all fit in Cathy's former room, but

Maggie thought they could probably live without one chair now that Cathy was gone. It would be a lot of work and disruption. She decided not to tell Pele unless the ball arrived and it really wouldn't work in Cathy's former room.

One thing neither of them had thought about was how to get the ball into the house. When it was delivered, they watched as the truck unloaded an enormous box. They looked at each other with eyes wide open. The Delivery called Maggie on her computer.

"Yes?"

"We've got your Stirball."

"I can see that. How does it get set up? Will you bring it in?"

"We can, but we need to decontaminate if we're going to do that. Is that what you want? Some Homelanders don't want us coming in these days."

"I'd prefer you come in to us going out."

"Yes, ma'am. If you set up the de-con for us, we'll bring the ball in with us, in pieces, and then set it up when we've got it all inside. It'll take one of us a couple trips. You sure you have enough AB wash? And what about wraps? We'll put our cover-ups back on as we exit, but inside your home we need something you find safe."

"Plenty of both, wraps in the third chamber, of course. Come in when you're ready."

Pele could hardly contain himself. They'd never had deliveries brought into their home. And to top it off, it was his Stirball. He was jumping up and down. Maggie couldn't remember seeing him this happy in a long, long time. When the first piece was brought in they could see the box must have had lots of packing material. The Deliveries brought it in easily. Three separate pieces. Maggie watched as they assembled it. They asked for the wireless connection details, and then asked Pele if he wanted to try it.

"You bet!"

They strapped him in and showed Maggie how to do it. They told Pele he would need someone to help him in and out. All of them stepped into the hallway so he wouldn't run over them. Pele started rolling around and immediately went upside down. "That shouldn't happen, should it?" he asked.

"No, we forgot to center the gyroscope." They stepped into the room and stopped the ball, making sure he was upright, and then adjusted a panel near the door. They explained to Maggie where she would find the directions online if she needed them. She shouldn't, but a power outage could cause need for recalibration.

Pele started to roll again. He was hitting the walls quite often, but not with much speed.

"Looks like it's working," said one of the Deliveries. As they headed for the de-con he whispered to Maggie, "The room's a little small, ma'am. Could be a problem." She nodded as they exited. She walked back and looked into the room. Pele was already learning how to avoid the walls. "I'll be in my room. Just yell when you want out."

"Thanks, mom. I will."

A couple hours passed before Pele called. Maggie didn't delay. She went right in to release him. "Well? Was it worth all our work?"

"Absolutely! But this room is really small. I spend more time turning than rolling. I'm getting better at it, but it's kind of tricky. Not quite what I expected."

"Think you need the bumper pads?"

"Maybe. That would let me put more speed into it, which would be nice."

"Another consideration is moving the living room in here and letting you roll around out there."

"Really? Is that possible?"

"It is, but it'll take some work. We'd need to move furniture again and maybe get rid of mother's old chair. And we'd have to build some small barrier so you didn't destroy the kitchen table. There wouldn't be any privacy. There might be times I'd want to be in the kitchen without you rolling around. If we do all this, I don't want to switch again."

"Excellent! No problem. Can do!"

"Do you want to spend a few days thinking about it?"

"No. I'd like to make the change."

"How about tomorrow?"

"Sure. I'm a little dizzy right now anyway. Between hitting walls and avoiding walls, I spent a lot of time in awkward positions, not like at the ABC."

***

still full-moon night in a warm comfortable bed something hiding i cant see something bad coming i feel it suddenly a body next to me in bed no one shares my bed this makes no sense no face but someone here a warmth gentle murmurs in a deep voice no words i understand green expansive meadow of clover a fragrance so sweet warm sun on bare shoulders slender masculine fingers reach toward me a familiar voice barking dogs one bark then another and on down the length of the street what happened to the meadow anticipation rises with jagged icy knife points moving up my spine those fingers coming toward my cheek i pull my head back to avoid the touch bright vivid kaleidoscopes of color and an index finger near my face i cant breathe i see a hand attached to no one my back arches my nipples stiffen i need to breathe i need air fingers closer and closer almost touching

Maggie startled awake to find moisture between her legs, her breathing irregular, her nipples erect. Another wet dream. She laid there, hand resting on her inner thigh and struggled to pull back the imagery. What was exciting her? What was she imagining? Who was there? She sensed she was not alone in the dream. Why now? Many dry years had passed. For a decade the only man in her life had been her son. There was no rule against sexual self-touching, as long as there was no face contact. After Pele's birth, she'd spent time bringing herself to orgasm when he was asleep. But after a few months, she found he took all her attention. And as the months passed and her mother moved in and they became captives in their own home, things like sexual excitement fell off her radar.

∗∗∗

Gary warmed his allotment, not that warming it made it taste any better, but bacteria-killing temps had to be achieved before consumption. It was green week. He found the green allotment the worst. Green was not an appetizing color. He'd never been a salad eater, in fact, veggies weren't ever among his favorite foods. So there wasn't even a green food memory for him to use as a stimulant. This week the texture was mushy with occasional chunks. Again, not appealing.

"Hey Izzy, what do you think of this allotment?"

"It's fine."

Izzy was the Sterilizer he worked with most often. They were both RedHexes. It meant they had been medicals in the previous time. It meant they might have knowledge. It meant they might not be trusted.

He'd worked side-by-side with Izzy almost every day for nearly five years. In all that time, he could count the number of conversations she'd started: 3. There was the day they met when she asked his name and several other factoids about him and his medical past. She was the initiator of that conversation, and she had revealed little about herself. She'd been a physician's assistant. She had four years on the job before the Transition— that's how most of them referred to the Outdoor Ban, the Transition, as if it were a simple planned movement from one system to another rather than a terrifying roller coaster ride on faulty equipment.

There was the day that the person they scoured was Izzy's sister. That day she talked more than in all the years combined. She'd told him that her older sister, Martha, had been her idol. She'd taken care of Izzy in all the important ways an older sister does. Martha had protected Izzy from her father's wrath and their mother's drinking. She'd helped her with homework, especially math. She'd explained romantic relationships, though she couldn't explain boys since she was a lesbian. When Martha entered the ABC, Izzy hadn't had much contact with her in several years. As a Sterilizer, she wasn't allowed to live with a Homelander, which her sister was. So when Martha showed up, compromised by a vicious strain of *Salmonella*, Izzy was distraught.

Izzy was careful not to implement any medical procedures beyond scanning and scouring. Electrolytes weren't available, but Martha was encouraged to drink as much water as she could, dehydration being a primary concern. Izzy carefully watched Martha while she was in isolation. Izzy found a way to send personal messages of encouragement through the monitor as she watched from the omnibooth. She didn't go back to the pod that night and risked being caught and punished. It was a typical case, first Martha's body curled in on itself from the severe stomach cramps. Then she began to dissolve from the inside out. What started as diarrhea morphed into a loss of blood and other bodily fluids. There was nothing to be done, no forensics to even hope for, so the room was filled with an AB gas that was deadly to humans as well as bacteria. Izzy had never watched an isolation from start to finish before. She hadn't known that deaths were hastened. Officially, this was an act of hospice, but it defiled the word. In reality, it was a way to diminish the mess and get the body bagged while there was still something to bag. The fewer fluids that had to be dealt with, the cleaner, the safer, for everyone.

It was traumatic for Izzy. Afterwards, she continued to talk about her sister the rest of the day: what she'd witnessed, and the horrors surrounding her in the ABC every day. Most of Izzy's talk had happened in the booth while she and Gary scoured one Homelander or another. But that day she even talked to him in the Lot. He felt close to her then. Gary appreciated learning about Izzy and Martha. The next day he kept talking. She didn't. As abruptly as her need to talk had started, it ceased.

The third time Izzy talked to Gary uninvited was the day that the scourbot lost a pad and actually sliced a Homelander's abdomen. It was already a case where the likelihood of death was extremely high, the Homelander having contracted *C-Diff*, so the error had only hastened the inevitable, but Izzy still reacted by bitching about the technical error. Gary bitched that way often, finding that given the delicate and deadly nature of their work, he believed the powers that be could be more attentive to the maintenance of vital cleansing equipment like scourbots. But Izzy took most problems in stride. The slice hit the same emotion Martha's death had— Izzy was powerless. Worse, she didn't help patients, or rather Homelanders, live—she aided in their deaths. That wasn't what had attracted her to med school.

Now, sitting in the Lot, Gary tried again. "Did you notice anything different about that female Homelander yesterday, the one who came in due to a family death? I think she was our third of the day. The one who was brought in with the 10-year-old son?"

"Different? No. Same old, same old. Why?"

"No reason."

Izzy didn't engage. He knew she wouldn't. That's part of what made it safe to ask. There was no rule against them talking in the Lot. Yet it seldom happened. They weren't monitored.

At least they believed they weren't. It wasn't like their pods where a camera watched them from the moment they entered until the moment they left. Gary couldn't figure out how it was that none of his co-workers had a desire to share their stories. Were there no extroverts among them? Were they afraid? He didn't sense that. It seemed more like their lives had taken on a gray texture of sameness, lifelessness. He had a rich internal life, but he'd like to share that with someone, anyone.

He missed Sam at moments like this. Even though it had been an erotic encounter that started his musings, maybe because it *was* an erotic stimulus, he knew Sam would have helped explore the many parameters of that brief brushing of gloved hand against naked breast. She'd explain what led to each change: the hard nipple, the wide eyes, the breathing, the flushed cheeks. He wanted that conversation. He wanted to understand his part in the mystery.

Or maybe he just missed Sam.

***

Maggie found she liked having the living room in what had been Cathy's bedroom. It was a smaller, more enclosed space, which felt like a hug. Given that she hadn't been able to shake the erotic dreams since her scouring, a hug was just what she needed.

She needed something to calm her nerves. She wasn't anxious or upset, it wasn't that. It was more her physical nerves that needed salve, the balm of touch. At moments, she had almost turned to Pele to ask for a hug. But he knew nothing of that sensation and would be horrified by the idea of such an embrace. Cathy had persisted in patting Maggie's knee, even after the Transition. That would be comforting right now. Maggie knew if her mother were still alive, she could have closed the door to a bedroom and been hugged. Not that she'd done that, not since the Total Touch Ban. In the early days, Cathy had tried occasionally to get Maggie to ignore the rules. But Maggie feared a slip in public and insisted that private be no different. How she longed to change that history. If she could have been more easygoing, she and Cathy could have been touching all these long years in captivity. No one would have been the wiser. If she'd known physical touch all these years, the contact made with her breast would have been just that, contact. She'd decided it was unintentional. Surely there were consequences for a Sterilizer who touched people.

The Stirball had changed the mood in the home. Pele's nightmares had all but ceased. Maggie found it surprising that the Stirball wasn't connected to the scouring in Pele's consciousness. But clearly, for him, the rotations of the Stirball were energizing and positive. She certainly didn't ask why it didn't make him think of all the horrors that trip had entailed. She was smarter than that. The Stirball brought out a childish glee that refreshed his spirit. Interestingly, this flashback to younger playfulness was coupled with a budding maturity. After he had put in hours on the computer to earn the Stirball, he had offered to do more of that. He was also generating more than he could use with his handheld, especially since he didn't use it while generating, which had been a problem when he rode the

Turbobike. This meant fewer hours Maggie had to put in since they had a home collection counter, not individualized ones.

Unfortunately, these gifts of time just left her pondering the touch and wondering, for the first time in years, what she'd lost since the world changed. At first she hadn't had time to wonder about that because the changes came so unexpectedly and often piled up one on top of another. Then, too, it seemed futile. She wasn't capable of changing anything. Before the Transition, she'd paid attention to a handful of activist groups that were proposing to clean up agriculture, to get rid of GMOs, to return to farming on a small scale. They staged actions, mostly symbolic, where they took over plots of unused land. The problem was getting seeds. AgriBiz had a monopoly on so many crops by then. The problem was growing enough to feed more than a handful of people, and there was no way those little bands of dissenters were going to convince the masses to farm for themselves. The problem, the real problem, was apathy. From her current vantage point that was oh so clear. She, too, had been part of the problem.

Loss. Today it made her think of her mother. The lost touches. The lost voice. Even the lost arguments. What she wouldn't give to sit and talk with Cathy about what had been lost. She'd fought the sense of loss Cathy erupted into without provocation. It was almost as if, while Cathy was alive, she'd carried the loss for both of them. She carried it vividly, recalling incidents no one else would bother with, little things, moments in time, a lie she'd told as a child about a watch that didn't work when she'd shown up home after dark, a recipe for scones Maggie had loved but had never been able to duplicate to anyone's satisfaction, and of course the marriage proposal. Some memories she offered up with a repetition that could bore the dead. At the time, Maggie had seen it as mindless yattering. At the time, she'd argued it would create the wrong sense of the world for Pele. At the time, she had shut her mother up every chance she got.

Now she realized, all those reasons were excuses of a sort, they hid a truth Maggie couldn't face—she missed the former world. Sitting in her quiet living room, comforted only by the close walls, gently reclined in her mother's chair—she'd put her own outside rather than Cathy's, what a surprise that had been—she started listing the things she longed for. She wanted to be touched, that was clear. She missed the feel of a breeze across her face, the smell of the air as the seasons changed, the fragrance of her favorite carnations. She longed for the richness of a full food palate—vegetables of every color and texture, chicken and bacon and steak, a choice of starches: potato, rice, bread. Wine, she suddenly thought. She missed wine. A deep red with tannins that bit at the sides of her tongue. A light crisp white, citrus sharp on a spring day under a tree at sunset. Sunset? She could still appreciate that if she chose to. She could open her drapes on the western side and watch the sun go down. It would mean paying attention either to time or the darkening of the sky. She typically did neither any more. But she could. The western windows were where Pele now generated. He'd be willing to let her have the half hour it would take. He might even be interested in joining her.

Pele was more than willing to grant his mom the opportunity to watch sunset. When she suggested he join her, he wondered why anyone wanted to watch the sky. She explained the beautiful changing colors. She said no two sunsets were the same. She said they could be spectacular.

He said he'd pass.

She took it as his youth, his being male, his lack of experience. But as she relaxed and watched the sunset, a rather gray one with little color or change, but one that nonetheless led to a peaceful reverie, she questioned if it might be more about his lack of interest in the outside. The sunset let Maggie continue her list of losses.

She missed friendship. Sunsets were usually spent with people her own age, friends, intimates. It provided time to discuss relationships, take them deeper. Time to explore new ideas, plan vacations. Oh, vacations! She'd had friends who talked art during sunsets, who talked physics, who talked so long the stars came out and then they examined the constellations and considered what it meant to travel by ship, which led to the power of the oceans, which led to the consequences of the social class you were raised in and how childhood experiences like sailing or riding horses molded people into different adults than did busing or riding bikes.

Habits learned early are habits for life. How about that? A truism that crossed the chasm between worlds. Yet, in the former world, it was more of a novel idea, as she thought about it, one someone capitalized on. The moment she thought the word *capital* she thought Madison Avenue. How much was predicted? How much planned? That was frightening. Had this just happened or had it been orchestrated? She peered out the window. The sun was set and darkness was all she could see. There weren't streetlights anymore. Who would generate the energy?

Maggie made a decision. It must be possible to still find someone she knew through the Internet. That was her area of expertise, after all. Well, not friends, certainly, but trolling the Internet, figuring out what was live and what wasn't, knowing what "they" looked for and what "they" ignored. She doubted anyone cared about relationships through the net, but she couldn't be sure. It wasn't like it was outlawed, but then again, that didn't mean it was safe. Perhaps she had just learned the habit of fear. What could possibly happen? She might not find anyone. If she found someone she'd have someone to talk to. If she found someone, it was possible someone doing a job like hers would be given the task of cutting the connection. But she couldn't find a reason for that. Perhaps if the communications looked like agitation, a move toward activism, an attempt to overthrow. But overthrow what? Who would want to be in charge of this nightmare?

She started with the obvious sources she remembered, Facebook, Twitter, LinkedIn. She found remnants of the sites. But clearly there were gaps, likely servers missing. Could that be intentional? Didn't matter. She accessed her old Facebook account but she saw no postings by any of her friends. No activity she could detect. Obviously, she didn't expect to find events, but she thought she might find postings of daily activities. She also thought people might still be playing games.

Games gave her the idea to check 3-D Life. She'd never had an account so it took a bit of her skills as a deprogrammer to get inside. When she did, she just started laughing. Clearly the site hadn't ended until after the Transition. There was evidence of avatars having communicated only from inside their imagined homes. And there was a wonderful banner in the coliseum that read: "Beware all ye who can read this, bacteria has won. Beware that which ye cannot see. It be a killer!"

She searched for something that would tell her when the site was last changed and whether or not others were accessing it. She got inside enough to see that it was more than a year beyond the Transition that the last playing took place. But she couldn't find cookie crumbs to show that others besides her were searching for activity. Chances were someone like her would decommission the site soon enough.

She stepped away from her desk. She went to the bookshelves and extracted her yearbooks, her photo albums, anything she could think of that might bring back names and memories of someone she might search for. She took it all to the kitchen table and grabbed her handheld so she could take notes.

Pele was rolling around. She watched for a moment and smiled. He seemed so content alone. She wished that were true for her. She had accepted her situation—until the ABC. Until she was reminded she wasn't really alone in the world. That other people existed.

Until she didn't have Cathy.

***

I was never much into politics, except as they infringed on science. But I was always clear that I was an American with certain inalienable rights, liberty being one of the highest. Yet with rapid speed our liberties became a dream, and not the American dream, I assure you. In an irony lost on almost everyone, focused as they were on their own survival, the party in power, whose platform was grounded in individual and states' rights, was suddenly making national decisions that would forever displace the Constitution. We were ordered not to touch our faces. Then not to touch each other. Then we were ordered to go into our homes and stay there. That final order was all but moot. By that point most people had sought safety by locking themselves away of their own accord. They had looted, they had rioted, and then they had retreated.

An object in motion remains in motion. The change came on with lightening speed. We went running into our homes full bore. And then we stopped. Halting a moving object takes a great deal of energy and force. Many people spun out in their own homes. They weren't psychologically ready to be quarantined, not permanently. Many of them carried bacteria with them that ensured those they lived with, those they loved, would share the bacteria, sicken and die.

I just keep playing it over and over in my mind. It's like a puzzle, a mystery. I want to understand how it all happened. I can see the whole picture, I can pick up the individual pieces, but I don't understand how they make the whole. Maybe that's not the best metaphor. Pieces are discreet, so it makes an obvious kind of sense. Maybe it's more like a cloth with a detailed design where the threads change colors as they weave through the fabric. I can't figure out how it works. It can't just be top and bottom, back and forth, or it would be a plaid, but it's not. It's a rich mosaic, a realistic tapestry that could hang in a museum. A museum I couldn't visit though, could I?

***

crashing ocean waves the sound lulls me its rhythmic coming ashore whoosh whap whoosh whap splashing water against black lava rock i feel moisture on my arm the moisture touches me i do not touch slip slide of ocean returning under pound of surf crashing water on rocks smell of sea salt air heavy with moisture falling from cliffs and sprinkling gently against face and fingers outside my home at last i breathe deeply of fresh mountain spruce-scented air deep into lungs as i hear beat of eagle wings reverb in the air watching eagles falling through spiraling columns of eagles circling broad wings extended fingers reaching toward me fingers without faces unattached alone isolated coming closer fingers reaching fingers brushing my cheek

Maggie awoke to find her fingers circling her breast, touching her flesh ever so lightly. She flattened her hand across her breast and lay there enjoying the tingling sensations running the length of her body. She cupped her other breast with her free hand and opened her eyes. It was still dark out. She had held onto an image this time, just one, but she could see a masculine hand with the fingers extended toward her. The fingers were close. She didn't think the person had actually touched her, but she wasn't sure. This time she didn't wonder why, didn't ask why now? She just luxuriated in the warmth and let herself fall back to sleep.

***

Trevor had been monitoring Enforcement Unit output closely. While the Enforcement Unit now functioned as the contact point with Homelanders, separate channels were still used by Head Enforcers for discussions and Homeland Security for updates. Though audio transmission was primary, a running record was also kept in print so all communications could be revisited, studied, and acted upon as the need arose.

No one had said much about the problems with scouring equipment or the decrease in bacterial cases arriving at the ABC. Trevor decided it was time to contact Commander Snopek. He had, of course, read directives from her, or perhaps just her office, though he imagined her voice when he read them. But he hadn't spoken with her since he left NYC. Why would he? Sure, he had risen to the level of Chief Enforcer, but he knew there were many at his level, let alone above and below him. And Commander Snopek was in charge of them all.

He walked into the small cubicle where the EU resided and dismissed the Sterilizer and Enforcer who were staffing the unit for potential Homelander calls. He told them to remain outside since this wouldn't take long. He sat down in the chair. *It isn't very comfortable*, he thought. He'd forgotten the care he had taken years ago to select the most comfortable chair for his office. When he thought of those times, what he usually focused on was the way he had eschewed the decadence of the former head of the hospital. He hadn't used her oak desk, nor her office.

He returned his attention to calling the Commander. When did he become someone who would let his thoughts wander?

Had that always been his way? He tapped on the EU seven times, and then he put in the code for the Commander.

"Commander Snopek's office."

"Is the Commander available? This is Chief Trevor Kashnikov of SoCal ABC 27."

"I can read that on the screen, Head Enforcer. Give me a moment to see if the Commander can speak with you."

"Thank you."

Trevor considered the tone the receptionist just took with him. He wasn't used to that kind of treatment. *So condescending.* He adjusted the left sleeve of his black cover-up by tugging it toward his hand, then repeated the procedure with his right sleeve and then once again with the left. Three tugs. It was a ritual he performed when he was uncomfortable.

"Trevor, good to hear from you."

"Thank you, Commander."

"When we last spoke, it was in person, yes?"

"Yes."

"It was your promotion to Head Enforcer."

Trevor realized he had called himself "Chief" to the receptionist. That was only his local title. Why did he always slip up when he was nervous? Maybe that was the reason for the receptionist's tone. "Yes, in New York."

"Enough small talk. I know you, Mr. Kashnikov. You wouldn't contact me without a reason. What have you observed?"

"Thank you, Commander. Yes, I do have a couple observations that prompt questions. I'd like to know what is being done about the scouring situation? While the bots are a safety improvement, no doubt there, they are also horribly temperamental, which causes Sterilizers to adjust them or send them to repair with a frequency that is troubling."

"That problem has been noted, Mr. Kashnikov. Several have complained."

"I saw nothing on the logs, Commander. I wouldn't have troubled you with that had I realized."

"Not to worry. What else have you observed?"

"Well, Commander, I've noticed a reduction in the number of bacterial cases coming into ABC 27."

"Yes?"

"I would never presume to wonder about the larger picture."

"And yet?"

"I'm wondering if others are seeing a similar trend or if it's localized?"

"Why would that matter, Mr. Kashnikov?"

"Well, I guess it makes me wonder what happens next."

"Ah, yes, I can imagine you making such leaps. You are right when you say you should not presume about the larger picture."

"I'm sorry, Commander. I didn't mean…"

"Trevor, please, we have a connection, you and I. Do not worry that you contacted me about this. You were right to do so."

"Thank you, ma'am."

"Consider this a local phenomenon."

"Yes, Commander."

"The Homeland must be secure. The Homeland must be safe. Enforcement is the key to an AntiBacterial Homeland."

"Enforcement puts the anti- in AntiBacterial."

"I appreciate you contacting me with these concerns. It's good to hear from you again. If you find yourself wondering about the bigger picture in the future, just put those thoughts to rest, Mr. Kashnikov. Trust that I am in charge."

"Oh, I do, most certainly, of course, Commander Snopek. You have my allegiance. My faith in you is unwavering."

"Thank you, Mr. Kashnikov. I appreciate that. Good day."

"Good day."

As the connection was severed, Trevor wondered why he had echoed the Commander's words: "good day"? He never said that. *Hearing her voice had made it a good day. Why had the Commander use the phrase "consider it a local phenomenon"? Why "consider"? Didn't that suggest it wasn't really a local problem?*

He suddenly realized he'd just been snubbed in a way he was no longer used to. It echoed his youth when his reports fell on deaf ears. Of course, he wasn't reporting any infraction. Perhaps the Commander *should* be deaf to his curiosity. That wasn't her role. He would let it go.

***

When Gary showed up at my house one night under cover of darkness, I almost didn't let him in. It wasn't that I was afraid of bacteria. It was that with the Outdoor Ban, I hadn't had anyone at the door in years. I didn't even recognize the sound of the knock at first and wondered what had fallen into the house. Then I thought it must be a creature, but there were so few left of any size, that I had no idea what it might be. With the typical Homelander setup of AB decontamination chambers between the living quarters and the door, there was no way to see if someone was there, let alone who. When I finally realized it was a person, I made my way out to chamber 1 and yelled through the door to find out who was there. Naturally, Gary was trying to be somewhat quiet. He really shouldn't have been out. So he said his name, but not loud enough for me to hear. We did that routine a couple times and finally I decided that a guest would be nice, whoever it was and whatever he brought.

When I finally opened the door, there stood Gary. It had been years. Not just since the Transition, I hadn't seen him for some time before that. He'd been busy building a life and I was busy with...with...whatever. We were all *busy with* back then. Busy, busy, busy.

Gary had been a favored student of mine. I'd mentored him the best I could. Not being in actual medicine myself, I could only advise him so far, but I did what I could. He had a good mind and a good heart, a rare combination.

There he stood wearing a RedHex Sterilizer suit. I had a bit of a start seeing that suit when I first opened the door, but he took off the mask as soon as he saw it was me, and he spoke so I could recognize his voice. I moved aside and ushered him in quickly and closed the door. I didn't bother to look to see if anyone had seen him. I assumed, as he did, that they hadn't.

"Need decontaminating?" I asked jokingly.

"Not a chance, you old bugger," Gary smiled, taking the liberty with such a friendly phrase. But I'm sure my appearance said "old man" loud and clear, and Gary wasn't a young undergrad anymore. We were more equals now than we'd been then.

"Come on in."

We walked through the chambers. It was a bit awkward with the two of us at one time. Chamber 2 was so clearly built for one person. But we managed. When we got inside, I'd almost forgotten how to be a host. We just stood looking at each other for a time. Then I regained myself and suggested we sit in the living room. I asked if Gary wanted anything to drink, that was the custom as I recalled. He said he was parched, so I moved to the kitchen. No need to ask what he wanted. There weren't choices. Distilled water was it. For a long while I'd had tea, due to my lust for trying new tastes whenever I'd had a chance, so I'd built up quite a cache. That consumer fancy served me well when the Outdoor Ban hit. But eventually it ran out.

I brought the water, one for each of us. Then I sat down and waited. It may have been my home, but it clearly wasn't my show. Gary just sat there for a while. I let him. I knew it must be important or he wouldn't take this kind of risk. Important takes time.

"I'm not quite sure why I'm here," Gary ventured at last. "It has something to do with a touch that occurred in the unit. Well, not just a touch, *my* touch. It got me thinking is all. I'm not sure what to do with that thinking. So I thought of you, naturally. In my early 20s you were always helping me with my thinking. If ever I needed help with that..." He trailed off.

I took a sip of water. I watched his face. He wasn't making much eye contact. That could be from the way things have changed, but I was guessing it was due to discomfort. When an idea is just formulating we're embarrassed that we haven't worked it out yet, even if the telling is supposed to help work it out. I've never understood that, but I saw it in so many undergrads back in the day that I accepted it as fact.

"The thing is, oh, I don't know. Let me start by telling the story and see where it goes from there."

Gary proceeded to tell me how he'd touched a woman as he fixed some kind of robot. He had gloves on, so I'd call it *contact* rather than a *touch*, and that's not just semantics given the current regime. He told me how the woman's body reacted. Why wouldn't it? She probably hadn't had physical contact in years. And sexually, maybe never. Yet bodies are hard-wired for touch. No government, no bacterial threat, nothing is going to stop that in a single generation, maybe not ever. I realized I'd lost focus. When I tuned back in, Gary was saying something about his workmate, Izzy, who didn't notice and didn't want to talk about it. After that, he went silent again, but it was a spent kind of silence this time, like he was at the end of something.

"I hear three things there, Gary, that might warrant further consideration. One, it sounds like making contact with that woman's breast might have had a sexual response in you as well as in her. Only makes sense. And sex these days isn't common. Two, I hear a fear of someone finding out about it. That's logical. And three, I wonder about the need you clearly express to talk about this event. The event itself could be seen as minor. In fact, the fear of observation suggests you'd like it to remain minor. And yet, for you, it was momentous. You risked a great deal coming here. You could lose your job as a Sterilizer."

Gary scoffed, but I continued. "You could be demoted to a Cleaner."

He looked at me and his pupils enlarged. He clearly hadn't thought of that possibility.

"But you came because you need to talk, you need to think it through. I don't really understand how Sterilizers live. Is there no one in your world to talk to?"

Gary shook his head. "That's part of it. Izzy is the closest thing I have to a friend and yet, we don't really have a relationship. There aren't friends anymore. It isn't outlawed exactly, but no one talks in my world. Perhaps it's all the death we're exposed to. Every day we encounter contaminated people who die. Maybe Sterilizers are numb by profession. They stay inside their own heads, or perhaps they evacuate them with mindless input, I don't know. How could I know? They don't talk. I feel so, so…alone."

"You're not alone, Gary. And you know that. You came here. We haven't seen each other in years. You couldn't have been sure I was even alive, and yet, you took a risk and found me."

"It feels so good to be here. To be talking to you. To sit in an actual home."

"Where do you live?"

"A capsule hotel, all Sterilizers do. We work a 12-hour shift, do our generating and eating, and sleep in a pod. That's life. Can you imagine how dull?"

"But every day for you is different. At least there's that. And you move about in the world. I sit here, day in, day out. Me, myself and I. I'm at least as excited to see you as you are to talk with me."

Gary smiled for the first time, and his shoulders relaxed. He sat back in the chair and took a long drink, emptying the glass.

"Guess the grass is still always greener."

"Wow, has that metaphor lost its mooring."

We both laughed at that and then sat and considered. I was wondering if I could find a more apt metaphor.

"Mind if I get more water?" Gary asked.

"Be my guest."

Gary moved to the kitchen. I got up and followed him. He leaned against the counter facing me.

"So, shall we take your three identified considerations in order, like the old days? Or do you need to head back?"

"I've got all night. I can't get back in once I'm locked out. My shift starts at 8. If I leave here by 6:30 I'll be fine. At least that's my plan, to be fine." He smirked.

"A shift that starts at 8. How civilized! Didn't know anyone still lived on that kind of schedule."

"Schedule, yes. Civilized, I'm not so sure."

"Consideration 1: your sexual response."

"There's a lot wrapped up in that one. Obviously, I haven't had sex in years. I seldom even bother to beat off. In my world, it's nearly impossible without being observed and I was never into voyeurism. So even being stimulated is rare. I guess, in a way, I should be grateful for the excitement." Gary paused. "And as you might imagine, it also reminds me of Sam. You met Sam, right?"

"Sure did. She was a fine young woman. I'm sorry, Gary. You lost her too young."

"Thanks. A lot of that going around, yeah?" Gary paused. Clearly the loss of Sam still affected him. I waited again, not knowing if Sam was a necessary detour in our exploration.

"Rare physical excitement, a reminder of lost love, those are both obvious, common. But it was more, much more. Seeing her response was part of it. I see 8 to 20 Homelanders a day who come in for scouring or sterilizing of some sort. So, yes, I see people. Most of them experience fear in my presence— fear of pain, fear of dying. For some that rises to the level of terror, either because of others they've seen die, because they realize they've been contaminated, or because they haven't been out of the home in so long that just the trip to the ABC has their adrenaline in high gear. For some, sorrow takes over, for others, anger. A few become very subdued, especially Asian women, that must be cultural. My point is I see a wide range of human responses every day. But I don't experience sexual arousal. That doesn't occur."

"Gary, I hear another question lurking. What's your emotional response to all of that?"

He looked at me stunned. It was a familiar expression. Seems he was getting what he came for. This was the magic we worked together.

"Anger. I get angry. I bang around. I slam doors. I break things."

"And your response to *this* contact?" I refused to use the word *touch*, even if Gary did call it that.

"I slammed a door. Izzy pointed that out when I got to the booth."

"Yes. That's your default. What else?"

Slowly words emerged from Gary's lips, "Shock...interest...excitement...fear."

The gears were still turning behind Gary's eyes. Whatever he was considering, he didn't want to admit to himself, let alone to me. But that was why he came. I had to push a little. In the past I wouldn't have. We'd have had time. Not so tonight.

"What is it? What's the thing you don't want to say? Name it."

"I can't. That's the thing."

"You can. It's turning and turning in the widening gyre." He smiled at my oft-cited allusion to Yeats. I like to think that's what dislodged the word, but then, I like to take credit even when it's not my due.

"Connection. I felt connection."

"Did she?"

"I don't know. I looked into her dilating eyes. Yes, yes, we both held the look, the gaze. So yes, we connected. I have no idea what it meant though. Through my mask, under those harsh lights, I don't know that we communicated, but we did connect."

"And now?"

"Now?"

"Yes, what next? What now?"

Gary shook his head, like he was clearing it of cobwebs. He looked at the floor. He shrugged his shoulders nearly imperceptibly. These motions repeated, in no particular order. I watched. I waited.

"Well, for one, we don't have to follow observations 2 and 3."

"No?"

"No. We know why I'm afraid. It's dead obvious. And as to why I needed to talk, that's becoming clear isn't it?"

I nodded. I didn't want my voice to interrupt where Gary was going.

"Evidently what's next is I need to find her. I need to explore what the connection might be."

"And how will you do that? How can you do that?"

Gary's eyes lifted to meet mine. "That my friend, has yet to be seen. But I made it here." He tilted his head, gave a little twist to his mouth, as a twinkle escaped from his left eye. "Mind if I catch a little shut-eye here on the couch? I'll be better apt to pull off my return if I don't yawn all day."

"Absolutely. If I can be of help…"

"You already have been. But, yeah, I'll keep you in the loop to the best of my ability. I have absolutely no idea what that means."

"Just the possibility will give this old man reason to go on." I smiled and got out a blanket and handed it to Gary.

"An actual blanket? I haven't seen one in years. Mind if I take off my cover-up so I can feel it on my skin?"

"Be my guest."

***

floating on air soaring high above an arm reaching toward me brushing past a flush of embarrassment in my red face there are no eyes as fear raises goose bumps on my arms my spine tingles i see fingers reaching my arms flapping to stay aloft how can i fly i wonder as i

*recognize myself dreaming enjoying a green meadow below now blue
ocean white waves colors combining like a kaleidoscope fresh pine
scented air turning sour smell of death of putrefaction of dissolving*

Maggie opened her eyes as she recognized her mother's
body, seeing it as clearly as the day she died. Her mother
hadn't dissolved. Her mother hadn't decayed, not in her
presence. Maggie shook her head to clear it. She didn't like
the nightmare. She didn't want to return to sleep because
of what might await her. She could tell by the darkness of
the room that she hadn't been in bed long. She considered
logging another hour on the Turbobike, but decided it might
wake Pele. She remembered Pele's first steps as a new toddler,
outside on the deck. The favorite memory allowed Maggie to
relax and return gently to sleep.

*fingers closer fingers reaching toward me panic rising my
breathing shallow my heart tightening sweat growing on my
forehead i need to escape i run down an alleyway dark arm with
fingers reaching for my cheek a deep voice i don't understand the
alley ends abruptly my heart races throbs i look but see no one with
legs exhausted saliva mounts in my mouth i smell rotting meat see
blood red splatter stark white background a needle pierces my arm
tied down a man in bed whispers threats fingers move closer to my
face i fall through air off a rooftop see a weather vane spinning hear
wind raging dogs bark i need oxygen i struggle to breathe waterfall
sprays catch in my throat nipples tighten winding cobblestone road
before me irregular footfall behind me bass drumbeat gets faster as
fingers meet my cheek fingers touch me*

Maggie's eyes flew open. She was excited and scared. She
looked around her room. Nothing had changed. If there were

Thought Police, they'd know she'd been aroused by the thought of having her cheek stroked. The mere idea of a man's fingers along her cheek, gently brushing her face, raised her nipples to attention. She brushed her fingers lightly across the left breast and realized with clarity she'd been thinking of the Sterilizer's touch. That was the stimulus causing her erotic dreams. Why hadn't she recognized that sooner? Seemed obvious enough. Repression, she thought with such clarity that she gulped in air and started coughing.

***

In the morning, Gary awoke with the dawn. He'd hoped to be out before light, but obviously he didn't make it. He got up, peed, slipped on his cover-up and quietly extracted himself through the professor's de-con chambers and back outside.

The trees and grass hung heavy with AB wash. Every night since the Transition, either from electrical poles where they still stood, or from ground sprinkler systems, sprayers doused the world with the latest AB concoction. These were believed to be the most effective means of keeping the bacterial populations minimized, though had scientists rather than lackeys been at the helm, they might have wondered if it just gave the bacteria an invitation to alter and repopulate.

Gary wondered if the sprays were instituted in a belief that one day everyone would be free to move about the country. He liked to think that had been the original plan. But he didn't have time for thinking right now, not ponderous, what-if thinking. He needed to get to the ABC and, if possible, do so without being discovered. He appreciated that he wasn't soaking wet with the spray, but he wondered if that would give him away as having visited a Homelander. He dropped and rolled. Just like that. Of course they'd know he was out. He didn't check in at the capsule. But they couldn't know *what he did* while he was out. That was the real danger.

Gary was used to walking the streets, but typically in a short, routine pattern from pod to ABC. And on that route, there were other Sterilizers—RedHexes, Red Suits, White Basics—all tracing the same route to or from. Now he realized how empty outside really was. There was no movement anywhere, no people, no animals. It was quiet, too. In the time before, outdoor sounds had included cars, construction, sirens, jet airplanes, and voices in many levels and cadences. More recently, he could hear footsteps on his short walks to work, occasional whispered conversations, and the sound of the airlock as he walked into the ABC. But today, nothing. It was too quiet. He worried about being seen, and yet there was no one anywhere.

Gary realized for the first time that he had no idea where Enforcers lived, if they were centralized, if they patrolled. Surely they didn't wander the streets. Not at this point, though maybe in the beginning. *Focus.* Last night it had seemed the easiest thing in the world to find the professor's home and yet today, Gary felt like his internal map of the city was failing him. It must be panic setting in about what might happen to him when he arrived at the ABC. He strode with purpose, but he didn't run. He tried to let his feet find their way. Body memory was safer than thought.

He began to notice that debris was massed near many of the homes, piles of odd bits of furniture and household goods. He saw that while trees and grass and some bushes were alive, there was little variety left in terms of plant life. As Gary began to wonder about the causes—lack of rain, too much AB wash, a lack of pollinators—he looked up to see he was getting close. Sterilizers were filing to work a couple blocks ahead. He did what he could to avoid being noticed as he slid in among them. He could see the line was thinning and thought it best to fall in so he wasn't late as well. He breathed heavily, undetectable to others because they were all inside their cover-ups. Gary collected himself. He'd seen someone pulled out of line before as they entered, but beyond that, he knew little of what could happen. Izzy had returned to work the next day after she spent the night with her sister, but she'd stayed inside the ABC. That probably made a difference.

***

Maggie thought she should be able to find someone still alive who would be willing to communicate with her. As she went through her yearbooks, she remembered she hadn't been very popular. She'd forgotten that. It had been a benefit as the Bans emerged.

Maggie listed a few names from her yearbooks. Petros sat next to her at pep rallies during her senior year. He had come from Athens. Classmates were suspicious of him, but she found Petros had an interesting take on all the cliques and stupidity of high school. She had even dated him a few times. They'd kissed and fondled. It was all so easy back then. She added Tracy to her list, her lab partner in biology sophomore year, and George, who helped her with pre-calc. Then she moved on to her teachers. There was a picture of Mr. Thede. She didn't like him as a coach, but he was a great history teacher, so she wrote his name down. Ah, Mrs. White. She'd encouraged Maggie to use her mind. Maggie never would have gone to college if it hadn't been for Mrs. White, which would have meant not being a deprogrammer now. That would have meant an even duller life. Mrs. White was on the list.

Her photo albums, she quickly realized, had been filled by Cathy, which meant there were few people Maggie knew well. Cathy had hosted big parties. A camera in hand was a great excuse to mingle and talk to everyone. Maggie noticed there were few photos of her father. He'd been more like Maggie, happier in the background. Today that comforted her.

She looked up at Pele in his Stirball and was grateful she wasn't completely alone. Yet, a son wasn't a husband, a boyfriend, a partner. She wanted more. She added a couple more names to her list, Cathy's intimates whom Maggie knew well: Doris Berkhard, Claus Heidenberg, Augusta Black. If they were alive, they were likely to remember her.

Oddly, Maggie put off her Internet search for days. It wasn't postponed for lack of time. When she noticed the list was still popping up on her reminders, she knew the truth was she didn't want to discover that she couldn't connect with any of these people. Better to believe they were out there, living, potentially interested. If the search came up empty, she didn't want to imagine the anguish that awaited her.

But in the end, she knew she needed to proceed. She would take it slowly. She would anticipate a bleak outcome. That way any progress would be hopeful. Her plan was to take one name at a time and search for it in multiple ways. She outlined the methods she would use and created a grid so she wouldn't retrace her steps. Her system would help her feel she was doing something productive. She'd start with the youngest, who would have the fewest web ghosts and, hopefully, the greatest chance of still being alive.

She started with Petros, whom she actually hoped to find. She could imagine starting a conversation with him. She didn't care if he'd married, though his wife might not like the intrusion from a high school sweetheart. *Sweetheart* was a bit too strong a term, it had only been a few weeks of fun. Oddly, though, what she did find eventually was a story about Petros' return to Athens. It made the news because his father was an ambassador. She couldn't read Greek, and the translators didn't work very well, so she let go fairly quickly.

George Steinem was next. In the first three passes she found no trace at all. Then she uncovered that George had won an award in real estate. That trace led her to email addresses and phone numbers that led nowhere. She turned up one more trace, which led nowhere, of a George Steinem who was father to a stillborn girl. It shocked her to think of George as a father, but she was a mother, so why not? The article cited maternal *Listeria* as the cause of death. That was common in the early days.

When she searched for Tracy Nelson, she expected she'd find her in the sciences—her lab partner and all—but Tracy was found through her short, but noteworthy career as a pastry chef. She'd developed techniques to get a decent rise in gluten-free French pastries. Gluten intolerance was one of the big allergies near the end. It seemed absurd—humans had been consuming wheat for centuries, but gluten intolerance became so prevalent that businesses from pizza parlors to low-end grocery stores carried gluten-free products. Among the email addresses Maggie found for Tracy, only one didn't immediately bounce. But after a week had passed, it also hadn't been responded to. While the timeframe for responding was no longer a matter of hours, Maggie eventually conceded it was unlikely she'd hear back.

As she shifted to those who were older, her mother's friends and her teachers, she found two obituaries rather quickly, for Claus Heidenberg and Mr. Thede. Both died before the Transition. Claus was taken by an early wave of *E. Coli O157:H7* he contracted from a bad hamburger, and Mr. Thede succumbed to a case of *HA-MRSA* contracted when he'd gone in for a hip replacement.

Searching for Augusta Black proved a worthy chase. Maggie first found reports of her charity work with AIDs patients. Then the donations of her husband's remains after a motorcycle accident. Then she found a website dedicated to a foundation Augusta had started with the inheritance from her husband's family's estate, she being the sole survivor. That website had links to email, phone, fax, social media of all sorts and all kinds of other links.

Keeping track of her grid so she wouldn't waste time revisiting locations was time-consuming in and of itself. At one point she received an automated reply saying the foundation was currently dormant, but it would keep her contact information for future use. The foundation had erected firewalls blocking her attempt to reach Augusta. She didn't know if Augusta, or anyone at the foundation, was still staffing their online presence, but they had done a damn fine job setting up barriers. She took the time to be thorough and was vigilant, even as she moved on, hoping one of the trial balloons she'd sent to Augusta would be received and answered.

Maggie sat looking at her list. Two names left: Mrs. White and Doris Berkhard. She remembered Mrs. White's slim frame, her jet-black hair twisted into a bun, and her narrow rectangular-framed copper glasses that focused the twinkle in her eye. Mrs. White could get even the most recalcitrant students to participate in class. She cared, but she took no guff. It was an unusual combination, one that made her popular. Maggie started digging. She uncovered one email address. She sat pondering what to write. On the one hand, this would likely yield nothing, on the other, if she could connect with Mrs. White, she'd be happy.

To: e.white@evercast.edu
From: magscompserv@Tmail.com
Subject: A blast from the past

Hey Mrs. White,

I was once a student of yours. I want to thank you. If it weren't for you I wouldn't have the computer work that gives shape to my days.

It would be wonderful to communicate with you again. Please respond, even if only to let me know how you are.

Yours,
Maggie, class of '44

The message didn't bounce immediately. The next day, Maggie received this:

To: magscompserv@Tmail.com
From: e.white@evercast.edu
Subject: Re: A blast from the past

Dear Maggie,

I intercepted your email. I'm sorry to inform you that though my mother, Eunice White, Mrs. White as you and all her students knew her, is still alive, she is unable to respond to your kind email. She has Alzheimer's or some similar dementia. She tells stories of teaching, but she is unable to call up particular memories or people.

Amazingly, our incarceration in our home allows me to care for her without concern about finances, something that would not have been possible before the Transition. For that, I am grateful.

Sincerely,
Cody White

To: e.white@evercast.edu
From: magscompserv@Tmail.com
Subject: Re: Re: A blast from the past

Dear Cody,

Thank you for your email. I'm sorry to hear about your mother's condition, but I'm pleased to know she's still alive. She really was an important influence in my life.

I can tell you are taking good care of her. Please give her my best. She may not know me, but sometime when she's telling a story, let her know that the former student she speaks of appreciated her class and her kindness. It needn't be an actual story about me. ;-)

I've been searching for anyone from my past for over a week now. Your email is more important to me than you can know.

Yours,
Maggie

To: magscompserv@Tmail.com
From: e.white@evercast.edu
Subject: Re: Re: Re: A blast from the past

As you can well understand, with my mother's situation, I don't have time for correspondence.

And with that, another glimmer of hope faded. It wasn't that Maggie asked to exchange emails with Cody. In fact, she thought that would be pretty odd since they didn't know each other. Yet they had an important woman in common, which would have been a place to start. Maggie had chosen her words carefully. She didn't mean to imply that she expected a response. She'd hoped the lack of one would leave the door open, perhaps interminably. Now, it was closed.

Doris Berkhard. Maggie turned her attention to the one remaining name on her list. Doris was one of Cathy's best friends. When she was small, Maggie remembered that if she saw Doris coming, she knew Cathy's entire attention would be focused on Doris. They told each other everything, sought council when making decisions, included one another's children in activities as if all were one family.

What had happened? Maggie had no clue what led to the falling out. It was after her father had died. She knew Doris had been there through the long months of chemo. She had brought food after the funeral and stayed through those first restless nights when Cathy didn't sleep. Then she'd disappeared. Suddenly. Cathy would never speak of it, not even after the Transition, when there was nothing but time.

Surely, Doris would want to know that Cathy had died. Surely she would not turn Maggie away. And yet, Maggie couldn't bring herself to start the search. She returned to delay mode. As long as she hadn't looked, she couldn't come up empty, she couldn't be ignored. Hope resided with Doris and for now, with the lack of an attempt to find her.

"Hey, mom, what are you doing?"

"Just a little research."

"Not deprogramming?"

"No, not right now. Why? Did you need something?"

"No. I just got out of the Stirball and wondered what you'd been up to. You've been in here a lot lately. I got to thinking maybe there was something you wanted the way I wanted the Stirball. I thought maybe you needed help putting in the hours to get it, whatever it was."

"You're so sweet, Pele. And so observant."

Pele smiled. He liked to think he paid attention. He liked to think that showed how intelligent he was. His grandma used to tell him he was "one smart cookie." He always thought was an odd phrase. She had explained *cookie* to him, but even then he wasn't sure how a sweet edible treat would make someone smart.

"Since your grandma died I've been a little lonely. That's all."

"Me too. I miss her."

"I do, too. Even her annoying stories. That woman could spin a yarn."

"Spin a yarn?"

"It means that she could make a story interesting. Spinning yarn is a step in making fabric, like our wraps. Once upon a time, long, long ago, even before your grandma was little, people, women mostly, would spin yarn in their own homes to make their own cloth."

"I'll look that up. I can't even imagine what you're talking about."

"Come here. We'll look it up together."

Pele pulled up a seat next to his mother, remaining a safe distance away so they wouldn't accidentally brush into each other. Maggie started by teaching Pele about yarn, and the animals the wool had come from, and cloth and sewing and the many types of clothing men and women used to wear. It was the longest time they'd spent together since Cathy died. Maggie realized she'd been neglecting Pele and his education. It felt intimate to be teaching him. Maybe this could fill the void she felt. Maybe she needed to spend more time with her son.

She closed the notes she'd made in her search. Doris would just have to wait.

***

As Gary entered the ABC, he paused in the airlock for his scan. A red light flashed brightly. *This is it.* As he passed into the interior, two Enforcers casually closed him between them and walked him through a doorway he'd never even noticed. Immediately inside sat an Enforcer behind a desk, one with a more sophisticated hood that allowed full peripheral vision and was clearly a model with a particular purpose, meant to accentuate sight and sound, all the better for interrogation. Gary was placed standing in front of this official, the Chief Enforcer.

"I see you're a RedHex."

Gary remained silent.

"I see you didn't return to the capsule last night. Your cover-up looks wet. We can't have you working in that, now can we?" The tone was at once both derogatory and conciliatory, meant to chastise and elicit connection.

Gary waited.

"Not much of a talker, eh?"

"I don't know the protocol, sir."

"No, you wouldn't, would you? I can see by your record that this is your first outing. For a RedHex, you've been exemplary."

What was that supposed to mean? Did other RedHexes spend nights out? Gary doubted it. But it made him wonder what rules RedHexes were prone to break. They'd been identified for a reason, and it wasn't just their history with medicine, he was pretty sure of that.

Gary simply nodded.

"You'll need to speak, my good man. Head movements aren't easy to read inside that cover-up. But surely you know that."

"Yes." Gary paused. "Yes, I know body communication is compromised by the cover-up. And yes, my record is spotless."

"So now, what would keep a good RedHex like yourself from sleeping in a pod? What could possibly keep you from a timely return?"

Gary had prepared his excuse the night before, "Generating, sir. I must have gotten lost in thought. When I looked up from the Rowathon it was nearly zero hour. By the time I reached the capsule, it was locked."

Gary wasn't sure about surveillance outside the capsule hotels. He'd never had reason to care. And when he'd lit upon the idea of talking through his problem with his old professor, he didn't take the time to research. So he had, in fact, walked up to the capsule and tried the door, which, of course, was locked. He'd waited a few minutes, looked in the door as if trying to get someone's attention, knowing full well that was impossible. Lockdown was automatic, not manual. Finally, he'd tried to look at a loss as he walked away, giving the impression, he hoped, that he was without purpose in his movement.

"Yes, yes. I can see here that you were on the Rowathon until late and you tried the door after hours. Again, let me inquire, why did this happen?"

"How can I answer that? I don't know. I must have gotten wrapped up in my thoughts is all."

"Such important thoughts must be shared."

"They weren't important. That's the thing. I can't even tell you what I was thinking about. I was just distracted."

"Distracted? Interesting choice of words. Distracted by what? Something in your work, no doubt. Sterilizers don't have any other life. So what in your work distracted you? A new co-worker? A Homelander? A mistake?"

"None of those. I don't know."

"So you've said. Let me try another tack. You were in your 20s when the Total Touch Ban occurred, you must have had sexual encounters before that? Yes? I can see you never married, but I can't imagine you never had sex."

"Of course. Yes. In fact I was engaged." Gary stopped there. He didn't want to share Sam's memory with this man, this Enforcer. But he hoped mentioning the engagement would lend his answer credibility, make him sound open and honest.

"So you must still find women attractive, you must have urges, you must be, shall we say, titillated from time to time."

He knows. He knows about the touch. Gary felt his heart racing. But he kept his voice modulated as best he could. "Sure. Sometimes."

"Ever find that to be true when you're scanning and scouring? Does a Homelander catch your fancy now and then?"

"Not really. It's routine."

"How about when you need to adjust a bot?"

"You know, sir," Gary breathed deeply, "if I may say, that happens a bit too frequently. I don't know if you have any influence with maintenance or design, but the scouring bots break down frequently and need so much manual adjustment that I'm not sure just how useful they are to us."

"I'll pass that along. Those manual adjustments, any unusual circumstances with those lately?"

"No, sir. I'm not sure what you mean." Gary wasn't sure how much further he could go with this lie. But if they knew, why didn't they just say? Would it be better or worse if he admitted what happened? "Has there been a report of misconduct?" Gary thought of Izzy and wondered if her silence extended to the Enforcers or whether there was something to be gained if she reported on him.

"No, no reports. Let's put that to rest for now."

Gary sighed inaudibly. Though he worried that with the more open visor, the interrogator might catch it.

"Tell me about what you did all night?"

"What I did? Well, I went to a club. I caught a movie. I had a beer. What I did? I wandered around. It was weird to find myself in that situation. After a while I figured I better get some sleep, so I found a place I hoped would be safe, though

I wasn't sure what I needed to be safe from, still wearing my cover-up. So I tucked myself into a space and fell asleep."

"And where was that?"

"Where? I don't know exactly. Several blocks from the ABC. I didn't check street signs or anything. Are they even still up?" Gary knew misdirection was his best ploy to keep himself calm as well as to try to get the interrogator off-balance.

"You say you tucked yourself into a space. What kind of space?"

"Oh, sort of next to a home, kind of behind a bush. The bush didn't look very green. Made me wonder if the AB wash was bad for plants."

"Yes, I'm sure it did make you wonder about that. You seem to wonder about far too much, I must say. You RedHexes are prone to that, no doubt about it. All the education. Invites you to think far too much."

Gary made no further response. He sensed this might be winding down.

The Head Enforcer adjusted the left sleeve of his black cover-up by tugging it, then tugged on his right sleeve and then pulled the left. "So, tell me how you liked being outside?"

"Outside? I walk outside everyday. I'm not a Homelander."

"No, you're not. You're a Sterilizer. We need to keep you clean. Being outside, unaccompanied overnight, might lead to contamination."

"Outside was outside. Looked like it had gone downhill a bit… Uh, it was quiet, that's what I thought of outside. It was quiet."

"I think you're playing with me, Gary. You're not being very forthcoming. You wonder too much, and I don't trust that. It's not healthy, all that wondering. Ideas, like bacteria, can creep in when you're not paying attention. And you've admitted to not paying attention. Your mind wandered off, and then you did. You want to watch out for that, Gary. You've been doing well here at the ABC. Don't let some idea, some experience, contaminate you."

"I see your point, sir. I'll be careful."

"What do you think would be an appropriate punishment for your little outing?"

"Punishment? For staying out all night? What are you, my father?" And with that, Gary knew he'd gone too far. There it was, his temper flaring up again.

The Chief Enforcer gave Gary a look of surprise, shifting into pleasure, shifting to power. The lecture was over and it was time to impose sentence. This wasn't gonna be pretty.

"Since you like generating so much, and since we're suffering a bit of a shortage right now—too many Incapables coming in the last couple of weeks—we'll start you off with 24 hours in the Stirball. And then when you do return to the capsule, take pod 19, near the end."

"Capsule 19? I didn't know there were numbers. We just take what's available, sir."

"Normally, yes. Your life for the next couple of weeks will be anything but normal. Unit 19, remember that. There will be a surprise waiting for you there. Berta here," he pointed to the Enforcer on Gary's left, "she'll be your warden for the duration. You needn't worry where you're supposed to be. Berta will be responsible to move you from spot to spot. Berta shows up, no matter what you're doing, you're done. You go with Berta. Understand?"

"Unit 19. Berta is my warden. Got it."

"You're quick, I'll give you that. There are choices, even now, Gary, there are choices of how you use your intelligence. Let this be a lesson to you and we won't need to meet like this again."

"Yes, sir."

The interrogating Enforcer pointed to the door. Gary turned and Berta ushered him out. The other Enforcer stayed behind.

Gary was taken straight to an isolation room. The Stirball was already in place. Gary climbed in, and Berta closed it up and left the room. She never spoke. Gary began spinning. He immediately realized the gyroscope had too wide an arc set. He was nearly upside down half the time. It made him dizzy and he couldn't steer. He kept bumping the walls. Knowing he was being monitored, he voiced this aloud, asking for an adjustment. None came. At least not when he asked.

But over the next 24 hours, as he spun, Berta would periodically enter the room, stop the ball, make an adjustment and depart again. Sometimes the gyroscope kept him upright, other times it let him tilt to varying degrees. He couldn't get comfortable. If he slowed down too much, a voice would goad him to speed up. He was glad he hadn't eaten in a while because the nausea was overwhelming. He wasn't a kid. This wasn't fun. He found it did what the interrogator wanted, it kept him from thinking about anything other than what he was doing.

This could be called Zenball. He was "in the moment"—an unhappy, uncomfortable, interminable moment.

When Berta finally released him, he couldn't walk. He had trouble even sitting up straight. Evidently that was expected. She told him to lie on the floor until she returned. He closed his eyes and slowed his breathing. His head was still in motion. He reached out his hands and felt the floor through his gloves. That helped him start regaining his equilibrium. As he calmed, he started to drift off, but that was interrupted by Berta banging through the door.

"Let's go," she barked.

Gary sat up. Then he crawled onto his hands and knees. He kept moving in an upward direction, but he did so slowly. Finally on his feet, he wobbled. He extended his hands for balance, stumbling toward the door. He paused in the doorway, holding onto the frame for a moment. Berta nudged him forward with her baton.

They made their way to the capsule. Gary had no idea what time it was. All he knew for sure was that it was not a normal passing time. No one was walking to or from the capsule. A buzzer sounded to unlock the door. Gary stopped and looked right and left. No one. He looked for numbers but didn't see them. Berta nudged him to the right. He started walking down the hall.

"Can I piss and change?"

"Soon as you know which pod is yours, I'm outta here. Piss. Change. Habit. I'd suggest you follow your habit, that's the safest thing."

Gary found himself looking at 19. Looked like every pod he'd ever slept in. Might have even slept in this one before.

"Stay here till I come for you."

"And when will that be."

"When I get here."

Gary nodded. Berta walked off. Gary waited for the door to close.

He felt a release in his entire body. He dumped his filthy cover-up down a chute. Then he pissed, showered, put on a wrap and crawled into the pod. He had never wanted to sleep so badly in his life. When the pod's door shade closed, a sound started that he didn't recognize. It was a woman's voice. She was screaming, wailing really. Then another joined and another. He could detect children's voices, a few men. *This must be the surprise. How will I ever get to sleep?* At first the screams and cries reverberated emotionally. He felt their pain. Then he noticed that as he began to disconnect from a sound, when his senses had dulled, it would shift, more people, fewer, louder, softer, audible words, just guttural utterances. He couldn't fall asleep. He was dead tired, but he just lay there tormented.

Gary drifted on and off. His nerves were a jangle. He kept waking up in nightmares only to realize his nightmare was associated with the sounds he was hearing. He tried to tell himself this had been put together on a sound stage, but he couldn't hold the thought long enough to construct an understanding of it that might help him tone down the impact. For a moment, he thought, that's what this is for, to keep me from thinking. But he couldn't hold the thought. The technique was working quite well.

For days, perhaps weeks, Gary was irregularly moved from pod to Stirball back to pod. Had the interrogator said two weeks? He couldn't recall. Time was endless. Time had no shape. Life had no shape. It wasn't life. Gary rolled around getting dizzy, or Gary fought to sleep amid the terror-stricken sounds that haunted his pod. He saw no one but Berta. When he was moved it would be day or night, he could never predict which. He was fed in the isolation room where he generated. He didn't think about why he was there. He didn't think about what he'd do when it ended. He didn't think.

One day they walked outside the capsule and he noticed there were others ahead of him going into the ABC. He said nothing.

As they reached the airlock, Berta said, "Return to work," and she walked away.

Gary was stunned. He had no idea what he was supposed to do. He couldn't remember. "Habits learned," echoed in his head as he waited for the scan, then he proceeded to his workboard. There was his name with today's assignment. He was with Izzy, as usual, or at least what had been usual—before. He made his way to their room, and they collected the first Homelander for scouring. There were no questions from Izzy, no wondering looks. It was like he hadn't been out of the loop.

***

I was never a very good husband. Scientists seldom are. No, that's an excuse. Not that I argued with my wife. She and I saw eye-to-eye on most things, especially the big picture. She was a wonderful ally when discussing all the things the feds were doing wrong. We shared that. At a party, we could out-talk almost anyone on the issues and have a grand time doing it. Such debates led others to think we had the perfect marriage. We could lay in an argument with each of us taking different angles and outmaneuver most academics from a variety of fields. My science, her numbers, both of us systems thinkers, yet adept at data. It was fun. Brings a lump in my throat to say that. *Fun.* I can't think about those conversations without smiling, and yet in retrospect it seems cavalier on so many levels.

In public, we were paired, no doubt. But in private, well, in private I tended to neglect her. We both had our careers and we respected that. But I got involved with my students. No, not that way. I wasn't unfaithful. Not sexually anyway. It'd be time for our dinner and I'd still be in the lab. It wasn't my own research that kept me. I think she could have understood that, respected it even. I was always teaching, mentoring. Had it been the struggling students, that, too, she might have tolerated, understood. But I tended to stay and work with the bright students, helping them think through a reaction, test a theory, solve a problem. Maybe I just loved watching a mystery unfold.

My wife, the love of my life, wasn't in the center, but I didn't recognize how off-kilter my priorities were until she was gone. Not that she left me. She'd gripe when I'd finally arrive home in the evening, say the cold dinner was waiting, or had been delicious when warm. But she didn't hold it as a grudge against me. And I guess it got to be habit, so I didn't even notice her tone of regret.

She endured me, but she didn't have to endure permanent quarantine. Don't know which strain got her. By then they weren't bothering to stop and identify. That would have amounted to morbid curiosity since so little could be done about any bacterial infection. I was lucky there were still caskets. I got to bury her. Had the chance to say my goodbyes proper. Had the chance to play the good husband in public one final time. Not that many mourners came. Most wouldn't take that kind of risk. Many of our students paid their respects virtually, electronically, even when they only knew one of us.

She died in early summer. I remember thinking summer wouldn't be long enough to mourn her. I didn't realize I'd have a lifetime alone to recognize all she'd done to make our house a home.

Homesick, that's what I am, homesick.

But not how we used to mean it.

***

Maggie and Pele explored all kinds of things in the weeks following their research into spinning yarn. One of their techniques was to remember a story of Cathy's and then to look up the references Pele didn't understand. The irony was not lost on Maggie that she'd tried frequently to stop Cathy's stories with the admonition that it wasn't good for Pele to think of the past world as the better one, and now here she was educating him on the world before the Transition with a gusto that excited both of them. It was a gift to have Cathy's absence unite them.

Twice a day they sat together, first thing in the morning and immediately after they finished their allotment. They followed Pele's questions into mazes of interconnected concepts, materials and devices. What Maggie couldn't always show him visually were the relationships and organizational structures that supported it all. When those questions arose, they would sit back or even move into the new living room and talk at length. Pele had always been a bright child, but he'd never been overly curious. That was Maggie's niche in the home. But once they re-started his education, all of that changed. He would roll around in the Stirball wondering how things had worked, like everyone having their own cars, or where people bought things, especially grocery stores, because he couldn't begin to imagine having choices of what to eat, or why people traveled on vacation when it was so dangerous. Pele created a way to attach his handheld to the Stirball so he could record ideas as they came to him. That way, after eating their allotment, he was always prepared with questions.

Maggie found that in explaining the world before the Transition, she came to see the new world in ways she hadn't appreciated. Pele couldn't conceive of the need for choices in the way she did, nor could he imagine why anyone would ever want to leave a home, nor did he have any desire for additional relationships. He missed his grandma, but for him that was a singular void, not the edge of a chasm of loss, as it was for Maggie. He took it for granted that bacteria was everywhere and that if he wasn't cautious about it, it would kill him. But it wasn't an overarching fear. He'd never seen anyone die from bacteria, other than on old news clips he found on the net.

It was habit for him to decontaminate, to weigh-in, to wear wraps delivered by Cleaners, to eat his allotment once a day without a desire for more in any way. Most importantly, he never touched his face or his mother. His own arms wound around his young body was the only comfort he knew, and he was perfectly capable of providing it. Maggie envied him that.

While they followed paths to knowledge, they would, with some frequency, run into dead ends. Usually, they just went around the debris they found, there being so many sources for the information they sought. However, on occasion, it would tick Maggie off, and when it did, she'd file a report, quickly, without really considering what she was doing. She never wondered if it would be noticed that she had greatly increased the number of dead links she was reporting. Nor did she consider whether the content of any of the sites was likely to set off alarms. She didn't think about her cyber activity leaving a trail she might not want reported by lackeys to higher-ups. At least, she didn't think about it until they started researching bacteria.

They started with *Staph*, especially the varied strains of *MRSA*, which led them on an examination of hospitals and the prior healthcare system. They moved on to *E. Coli O157:H7*, which led to mad cow disease and CAFOs and AgriBiz. That in turn led to *Salmonella* and *Listeria* and how crops began to be agents of disease. This led to the year-plus of government-warehoused foods, while small farms were redeveloped in the wake of the AgriBiz failure. That was a year of civil unrest—no one would say the word *war*—and to be fair, it was never that organized. Distribution was a huge problem, and in some parts of the country starvations outnumbered bacterial deaths. This was something the government fought to hide, and in the process it dismantled the news agencies, which wasn't difficult since the Transition kept Homelanders indoors.

Each bacterial starting place was a safe-enough educational pursuit, but each inevitably led to enormous, greed-centered mistakes of either AgriBiz or government or both. Discovering government's complicity, if not active role, in eliminating news sources was when Maggie started to glimpse how much she'd never realized. Then she came across a mirror government website, one that covered the administration at the time of the Transition. When government sites were dismantled, this mirror had been forgotten. It provided the names of the top people in all the government departments. Since Maggie and Pele had just been reading about AgriBiz, she recognized several of the names. It appeared that many top seats in the USDA and FDA were held by former AgriBiz execs. Those agencies performed inspections and set regulations for agriculture, so the presence of former execs in government positions struck Maggie as a form of collusion, or at least a questionable situation ethically.

Her discomfort deepened when they learned AgriBiz had been overdosing animals with antibiotics, resulting in the creation of more and more deadly bacterial strains. Wasn't that exactly the kind of thing government officials should have deemed a bad practice, a health risk?

At Pele's age, the combination rang of injustice so loudly that the bells finally sounded in Maggie's ear, and she realized the reports she'd been making and the trails she'd left on the web might be dangerous. She was suddenly careful, not so much in what she said to Pele about the government of the past, but in the need to discretely erase what she still could of their most recent searches. She also believed they needed to stop, or at least slow down for a while. Perhaps pursue other questions.

For the most part, Pele was willing to move his learning into other arenas without Maggie explaining why. But he kept returning to questions surrounding bacteria, especially the role of AgriBiz and the ways government appeared complicit, negligent, or responsible for bacteria growing ever more virulent, able to multiply and kill faster. Maggie did her best to answer his questions without online searches. When she did search, she steered away from government connections, and she erased her path as they went. Pele noticed this change and asked why she was hiding the trail. He pointed out he might want to revisit these sites to learn more, especially since some of it was hard to believe and therefore hard to remember.

Finally Maggie came clean. "When we started examining the role of government, I got scared," she told him.

"Why? It's just information."

"True. But how did that information make you feel?"

"Confused. Angry. I felt a bit lost actually. It's all too big to hold onto."

"OK. So information isn't neutral. Information makes us feel things. Information can lead us to do things, too."

"Like what?"

"Well, in this case, it has already led us to more research. It keeps raising questions for you."

"Isn't that true of most information?"

"Yes." Maggie smiled, realizing how much Pele had been learning and how quickly. "But when information elicits emotions and raises questions, it can also lead to action. Here, let's do a bit of historical research, and I'll show you what I mean."

Maggie led Pele through the successful Civil Rights Movement, through the protests for Gay Rights, including the right to be included in partner insurance, to be "out" in the military, and get married. Through the failed Raw Foods Movement. Through the fast-sprouting and then stagnant Occupy Wall Street Movement. She pointed out the information involved, but more importantly, she showed Pele how his feelings of injustice about how power was used against people were involved in each subject.

Pele went to bed uncertain how his interest in bacteria was parallel to any of the movements his mom had explained. And the next day they went on to other fronts of exploration.

"Mom, mom, I think I get it," Pele came rolling up to Maggie in the Stirball as she walked into the kitchen.

"Get what, Pele? And please, don't run into me with that."

"Why you're erasing our trail on the web."

"I'm listening."

"Wait, I need to get out of the ball."

Maggie repositioned the ball and opened the hatch.

"The people who have power always want things to stay the way they are. If those people saw what we're looking up, they might think we were considering doing something to change how things are."

"Very good. People in power sometimes do want to change things. So that part you still have a bit too simplistic. But yes, my fear is that someone might think we want to protest."

"But wouldn't that take other people?"

"Definitely."

"There's just the two of us."

"True. But we don't know if others might be doing similar research."

"That's possible."

"And you know from listening to your grandma and even to me sometimes that some of us who lived through the Transition wish things could go back like they were before."

"Yeah."

"It's probably irrational on my part, Pele. There's probably no one watching what we're doing. But I don't know that for sure. I don't know much about the world anymore. But ever since we were taken to the ABC, I think about it more."

"Like what?"

"Like wondering if anyone even thinks about changing anything. Like whether many people are still dying from bacteria. Like whether or not it's safe to be outside again. Like how many people are still alive. Like my desire to talk to other adults."

"Wow, mom, that's a lot. No wonder you got scared."

"In fact, for awhile I looked for people through the net. That's part of it, too. If I was being watched, that might have looked like an attempt at organizing. It'd be pretty crazy to think that though."

"Why?"

"Because I only got one email response and it wasn't even from anyone I knew, just a child of someone I once knew."

"I'm sorry. I wish you'd found someone."

"Thanks, Pele. That's sweet."

* * *

When Gary returned to the capsule hotel the first night after his punishment, he moved into the first available pod rather than heading for 19. He glanced down that way but didn't see anyone entering it. The sound in his pod was the dull thrumming he'd heard for years, and he laid back and fell into a deep sleep. In the morning, it was all he could do to pry himself awake. He suddenly longed for a day off. Before his escape and subsequent punishment, he'd gotten so used to his life that this idea hadn't occurred to him in years. Obviously, in the new world a sick day was out of the question.

It took Gary days before he began to feel normal again. Once he started to catch up on sleep, once he stopped worrying that Izzy would say something, or alternately, that Izzy was watching him, once his daily habits became habit again, once all that took place, he was able to begin to let go. That meant he began to think, to consider, to wonder. The reason for his punishment took time to recall. It eluded him. He fairly quickly remembered being outside and going to the professor's. But why? His mind would not pull up a memory of what compelled him to walk outside into the night. *Why had he taken such a risk?* The more he tried to search for the memory, the more frustrated he became. He couldn't force himself to remember. He tried.

Then in a visual flash, he saw the nipple contract and the pupils dilate, and the memory began to emerge. He had touched someone. "You must have urges, you must be titillated from time to time," Gary heard the Interrogator in his head. *Oh god! They know.* Pieces returned to him, all out of sequence. The touch, a random question from the interrogation, the look on the professor's face when he opened the door, Gary's attempt at conversation with Izzy, his longing, slamming the door after adjusting the bot, getting aroused while sitting on the Rowathon, rolling in the grass to wet his cover-up, looking into her eyes.

He stopped. That was it. *They'd connected.* He'd seen it in her eyes. That was what sent him searching.

And now? *He had to be careful.* The moment he used the word *careful*, he realized he wasn't just letting it drop. Like he should. If he valued his life.

But what was life without thought? Without connection? What he'd done the past few weeks wasn't living. Stirballs and sleepless nights were not living. Wouldn't pursuit of the female Homelander lead to more punishment? Shouldn't he avoid that outcome? Shouldn't he go back to the life he'd had since the Transition? It was OK, wasn't it? But that was the thing. The moment the touch occurred he knew it wasn't OK. *It wasn't enough.* Scouring and scanning and working with Izzy, who was little more than a bot herself with her silent working—no, that wasn't enough. If Sam had taught him anything, she'd taught him how to live and love and enjoy life. He'd mourned her loss. Now it was time to start living again, living the life Sam would want for him.

***

At the weigh-in yesterday I discovered I had lost a pound. That's not good. That's happened a couple of months in a row now. I would think it was a reduced food supply, except the allotment hasn't changed. When the Transition occurred, I lost weight for the first several months. I suppose most people did. We weren't eating as much, especially as much fat and protein. Of course we were also exercising far less. Even people like me, who were veritable couch potatoes before, got even less exercise once quarantined.

The amount of exercise shifted again when the government realized it was going to need us to generate power. When my Rowathon arrived, I increased muscle. The first several days, maybe longer, I was sore in my gluteus maximus, aka my ass, and my thighs got tight. Had I been vain, I likely could have seen a decrease in inches.

Funny that. I remember when men paid attention to inches gained from weightlifting and women paid attention to inches lost. Never did achieve equality between the sexes. Even when both partook of the same activities, they had different goals based on body type and cultural expectation.

***

When the Enforcement Unit buzzed, Maggie jumped. Other than their calls following Cathy's death, she'd never known the unit to ring in. She thought of its purpose as an emergency device to call out. She walked over and pushed the acknowledgement button.

"Hello?"

"Just checking in, ma'am."

"Checking in?"

"Yes, wondering if things are normal."

"Yes," Maggie said, trying to exude confidence even though she could feel her breath catch and her hands start to shake. "Perfectly normal."

"Using your decontamination chamber?"

"Of course."

"Levels of AB sufficient?"

"Yes. Would you like me to check to be sure we have the most current version?"

"That won't be necessary. Are your wraps being exchanged regularly?"

"Yes. I haven't noticed any problems. Has there been a change of some kind?"

"Is your allotment on schedule?"

"Yes." Maggie held her next question. Clearly, it wasn't her place to ask.

"Have either you or your son been outside recently?"

The furniture! An Enforcer noticed we put it in the yard. "Only to the ABC when my mother died."

"No additional outings?"

"No."

"Delivery?"

"Yes, a Stirball."

"Ah. And did the Deliveries remove anything when they were there?"

How to answer? Should she lie and say they took the furniture out? Would that be safe? Would it get the men in trouble? She'd learned before not to leave an opening as she did when she said Cathy's cause of death was unknown. Better to be clear and firm. *Stop thinking and answer.* "Yes, the Deliveries moved a bed, a dresser and a chair outside to make more room."

"Neither you nor your son went out with them?"

"That would be dangerous. No, of course not."

"And how long ago was that?"

"I'd have to check. I don't keep track of days. Do you want me to look it up?"

"No, ma'am, we have the records."

Maggie heard the other end go dead. She walked to the window and looked out. She could see Cathy's furnishings sitting there. She remembered carrying them out with Pele. They were careful to do it on a dark night. They had made sure they were masked and had decontaminated the moment they returned. Having been to the ABC, they weren't terrified of the outside, but they were vigilant about their safety on multiple levels. She looked around. Seeing the other furniture outside she wondered if each of her neighbors had gotten calls when they'd taken things out. Suddenly, she wondered about her neighbors. *Did she still have neighbors?* Perhaps if she watched the homes closely she'd notice small changes that would confirm their presence. She'd always assumed they were there. What if they weren't?

"Did I hear a buzz?" Pele asked.

"You did."

"What was it?"

"The Enforcement Unit."

"What did they want?"

"Very good question. When I picked up, I thought it might be about the bacteria research on our home, but their questions were about us going outside."

Pele's eyes got big. He had begun to develop a fear of authority.

"Don't worry," Maggie said. "I told them the Deliveries removed mom's furniture."

"But they didn't."

"I know."

"Do *they* know?"

"I don't know. I don't think so. They asked when it had happened. I said I didn't know but I could check. Then they told me they had the records and hung up."

"Didn't we take the bed and dresser out a day or two before the chair?"

"I think so."

"Will they figure it out? Will we get in trouble?"

"Pele, I don't know. I don't even know what getting in trouble would mean. They may have known when they called. I really have no idea what the purpose was in that contact. I've been teaching you about how the old world worked. That I understand. I don't know how things work now. It's mysterious, kind of cloak and dagger."

"Cloak and dagger?"

"Another cliché for your list. Let's go do some research."

"But, what if…?"

"Don't dwell on it. That'll make us paranoid. We can't afford that. Let's go look up *cloak and dagger*."

***

I have nothing productive to do. When Gary visited, and for a time after, I started thinking again, had a bit of incentive to go on. There was really no way for me to speculate on what happened to Gary. And yet I wondered. I wondered if he was caught. I wondered if it was ignored or if he was reprimanded, and if the latter, did that mean a few more hours of generating for him or some kind of physical punishment. I wondered and I worried about Gary. And that made me care again, but there was nowhere to put that care. It led me to contemplating all the ways I could have made my wife's life easier, happier, better. But that was so painful I turned away from those thoughts.

And yet, what is there but thought? There's really nowhere to turn.

***

Gary became an attentive observer of everything happening in the ABC. He watched as others went through the airlock every morning to see if anyone was pulled aside. Once he saw the light go red as it had for him. The two enforcers book-ended the Sterilizer passing through the chamber. But then a whir swirled through the air and the Enforcers just stepped aside and the red-lighted Sterilizer was allowed to pass. *Curious. So mistakes are made.* Gary filed that information.

329

He paid attention to what was routine and what wasn't. He watched Izzy. He watched others in the Lot. He listened when other Sterilizers talked to one another, not that there was much of that. But he attended to their tones, watched for body language, paid attention to the content of what few conversations there were. He didn't discover anything of much interest.

Information he picked up while generating was nothing more than common topics with no emotional attachments he could detect, either to the information or to one another. He had hoped he might discover someone like himself who wondered about things. If any of them allowed curiosity, they kept it to themselves. Safe. He wondered if he was the only one wondering. *Surely not.* Even with all evidence to the contrary.

He encountered few other RedHexes. Perhaps he needed to explore their conversations. Then he remembered that Izzy was also a RedHex, and he decided it wasn't worth the trouble. At least not at this point.

Sterilizers didn't have handhelds. Their life was sterilization. They had no need for personal entertainment, storage or communication. Until now, Gary hadn't realized this. Generally there wasn't time to utilize a handheld, so it had never occurred to him until now. *Actually, that might not be completely true.* He thought he remembered that many Sterilizers had handhelds when the Transition occurred. But as batteries failed and devices died, they weren't replaced. Had he tried to keep his? He didn't think so. Without a handheld, without paper, without privacy, Gary needed ways to keep track of information. He worked on developing mnemonic devices to fix details in his memory.

One dimension of his strategy was to plan out exactly what he needed to do. He started mentally exploring and mapping the possibilities. He wasn't willing to go outside again without knowing. *Without knowing what?* Without knowing he wouldn't be turned away.

If he was going to risk punishment, there had to be near certainty of a successful meeting. His outing to the professor's had been worth the punishment. At least that's what he told himself. He needed that to be true to carry on with his plan. And it was true that just talking to another person, especially one who knew him well, just talking in a thoughtful way, had brought him back to himself. That was worth a lot. As he regained his memory of what had led to the punishment, he lost the intensity of his sleep-deprived thoughtlessness induced by the Stirball and the scream-loop. The punishment was brutal but fading.

He needed certainty that if he was out all night, it would be worth it. He had to know the female Homelander he had touched would at least talk to him. Who was she? Getting her contact info was first on his priority list, his map. He needed a name to hold on to.

Getting that info meant paying attention to computer usage. No Sterilizers had private access to a computer, let alone one of their own. He had two needs: researching her data on the mainframe and doing so without anyone knowing. From everything he could tell, no one was monitoring usage. Part of his job was to enter data from each day's scours, scrubs and sterilizations. When doing so, Homelander data was available. He tested accessing records from earlier in the week. He started by doing a single search. He waited a day. No repercussions. He did some calendar work to figure out the day the touch had occurred. That gave him a good access point. He noticed that while computer terminals were never empty, at the end of shifts they had the fewest Sterilizers.

He saved up a day's worth of input. He was coy enough to wait until a particularly busy day. He carried his records to a terminal and sat down. When he started, there was someone next to him on one side, but within a few minutes, he had an open terminal on either side. That gave him the physical space he needed to take the next step. Between each input, he would do a single search. First he located her name. He was grateful she'd come in with the boy because that helped him isolate her among possible candidates. Maggie. He liked that name. Maggie. He spoke the name silently, to himself, not wanting to risk anyone hearing him. He must have paused briefly because the next thing he knew a supervisor was standing over him.

"You've been here awhile."

"Yeah, a whole day's worth to enter. Busy day. No time." The supervisor nodded, but with an incredulous look on his face. He pointed to a stack of files Gary had laid aside.

"Done with those?"

"Yeah."

"I'll take them."

Gary handed them over without question. He entered the next file without delay. The supervisor walked away. Gary breathed deeply. He assumed his work would be checked. As long as it didn't show every keystroke, he thought he'd be OK. He did a couple files without additional searching, then returned to his pattern of looking for a single detail at a time, but now did so in the midst of each file. He realized he could make a better argument as to why he wasn't on an appropriate screen. He gathered Maggie's address, luckily in an area of the city he knew well from before the Transition so he could imagine it in his mind, helping him hold the info. He found a couple email addresses for her. He hoped he wouldn't mix them up and created a mental key to keep them straight. He discovered her job involved computers. That gave him hope he might have more ways of reaching out to her.

When he finished with the files, he stood and looked over to the supervisor, who seemed to be watching. Gary raised the files in his hand as if to ask if he should file them as usual or hand them over. The supervisor waved him on. Evidently the supervisor didn't find anything unusual. Gary was going to hold that thought. Perhaps he had passed the first gauntlet successfully.

Gary needed to contact Maggie before he could plan beyond the ABC. But how? His first idea was email, but that could be easily traced. Besides, email was notoriously bad at conveying tone, and the first contact, well, he'd made the first contact with her breast. He smirked. But his first communication needed a kind of tact. *Tactile. Touch.* That would be difficult in email.

Though his memory was returning, he found he could be distracted easily, especially by language. A word would catch in his mind and spin out similar words and ideas. He interpreted this as further demonstration of his need for connection. To think of it as anything else—as brain damage from the punishment, as a permanent disorder, as distractions that would prevent him from living a fulfilling life—made him angry. He couldn't afford to be slamming around the ABC. That would be noticed, and being noticed was not in his plan.

He considered using a computer crawl to make contact. It would leave no trace, but it would also have to be incredibly succinct. He wasn't sure 72 characters would be enough. Besides, she would have to be sitting in front of her computer when he sent it. Even if she saw it, how could she respond? If she bounced a crawl to him and he had left the terminal, someone else could intercept it. Or more frightening, it could come while he sat there but be noticed by a supervising lackey. He wouldn't have to go back outside to end up being punished. No, that wouldn't work.

He could try to reach her through an Enforcer Unit, but there was always a Sterilizer and an Enforcer pulling that duty together. Even if he was the Sterilizer, which was an unlikely assignment for him, he could never imagine getting the Enforcer to leave the room. He pondered his options, none of which stood out as a perfect method.

Gary thought about how to contact Maggie. He thought about the message and the method. Once he had accessed her files and knew her name—*Maggie*, he did like that name—once he knew Maggie worked in computers, he reevaluated using a crawl. It seemed the best starting place, at least if he could find a few words that would get her attention, but ones that would not immediately incriminate him if he were discovered.

"I touched you" was out of the question. He couldn't risk using the word *touch* no matter what delivery method he used.

"I'm sorry the bot kept needing adjustment." No, he didn't want to start with apology.

"I met you at the ABC." He wouldn't dare mention the center.

Days passed without Gary finding an approach he could imagine using. He stopped himself. He realized all his thoughts centered on himself. Understandable, certainly, but maybe that was the problem. Maybe he needed to put himself in her shoes. What might she need? What might she want?

What would interest her enough to pursue communication with a stranger?

"Are you as lonely as I am?" He thought she might be. But a line like that begged the question: *who are you?* That probably wasn't a good way to initiate, even if interest was ultimately important.

He had met her because her mother had died. That could be a starting place.

"Has your mother's death left a void in your life?" Too direct.

"I'd like to express my sympathies on your recent loss." Too distant.

"I'm sorry about your mother." Hmm, that was getting somewhere. In fact, that would be a good initial crawl. As soon as he found the start, he realized he would need a few lines ready.

In his situation, he couldn't sit and think. He needed a clear goal with this first communication. What did he want? He certainly couldn't ask for a date, a fling, a chance to hook up. Hook up? Who was he kidding? Was that an option? Even if they met in person?

Dates. First dates used to happen at coffee shops, restaurants or bars—safe public locations where you could get to know each other. He was hopeful he was setting up chances to get to know her.

He wanted a date, but it only had a few rough similarities to dates of the past. Dating presumed many things: (1) The ability to go out. *Not going to happen.* (2) Two people meeting. *Hopefully.* (3) Talking? *Certainly.* (4) Touching? *Who could know?*

Dating had never been easy, but what he sought was in another league.

He'd start with a crawl, but maybe his first goal would be to change the communication method to email. No, that didn't feel safe to him. If the crawl worked—he knew he was getting ahead of himself—but if the crawl worked, maybe he could establish an arranged time for a second crawl exchange. *Wait, think of her.* Maybe she would have ideas on how to communicate. He was certain she would know computers better than he did. As a Homelander, she might also know of other communication methods.

Maybe they could still send letters. He had no idea if there was still mail delivery, or any delivery other than allotments. But then again, even if mail was an option for Homelanders, he couldn't imagine being delivered a piece of mail, not unread, not following his recent outing and punishment. No, while he wasn't certain what they knew about his reasons for not sleeping in the pod, he was certain they didn't believe he'd accidentally missed curfew. *That couldn't have been the punishment for not keeping better track of time.*

***

My weigh-in showed I'd lost another pound. That's not good. That's happened a couple times in a row now, I think. If I let myself admit it, I suspect I'm wasting away, as we used to say. Don't know if it's old age exactly, might just be a lack of will. I no longer spend days pursuing a line of thought about what led to the Transition. I no longer explore the Internet. I no longer find any thought compelling. I've never been bored in my life. Until now.

Occasionally I still wonder if I'll see Gary again or at least hear from him, and that provides a bit of motivation. But for the most part, I've just stopped caring if I live or die. I know that's harsh to say, harsh no doubt to hear. But what's the point? Even people living mundane lives found purpose when the world was open. Now that it's closed, I can't seem to figure out what good there is in going on. If I had children or lived with someone, if my wife was still alive or if I had work like Gary does, even such minimal interactions and opportunities would likely keep me from the depressive downward spiral I've begun.

I struggled with depression in my late teens and then off and on in my 20s. But after that I always had enough diversity, enough ego stroking, enough...well, just *enough* to keep my mind from wandering too far astray.

Now I sit and stare at my walls. Sometimes I sit there for hours because when I catch myself, that is, when I realize I've just been sitting mindlessly, I notice the quality of light in the room has changed significantly, telling me time has passed, the Earth's rotation has continued, and the sun is going into hiding.

***

Maggie couldn't decide if she'd been having nightmares or dreams. *Was fear or desire the prominent sensation?* She liked the arousal the dreams created. She appreciated feeling the urgency in an erect nipple, the moisture between her legs, the excitement of climax. She disliked how many different fears the nightmares ignited. She feared Pele would hear her. She feared Enforcers might be able to see her from her computer camera. She feared someone might detect she wanted her face stroked. Someone might know she wanted to be touched by fingers other than her own. *Was she unique in that? Didn't that have to be common for people her age and older?*

She sought to end the nightmares. She altered the time she generated in hopes of changing her body rhythms. She tried playing games on her handheld before going to sleep. She tried reading about computer deprogramming techniques, believing she could bore herself into unconsciousness.

Though it took time, eventually she was successful—no nightmares. Then she missed them. She realized they were an unbidden connection with something larger, something older, something missing, something missed. But she couldn't bring herself to seek out the dreams. They felt illicit. Dangerous. Besides, the surprise they generated was part of the allure. She'd just have to wait.

Maggie was sitting at her computer. She'd finished her deprogramming hours for the week. Since Pele had started helping with them, she had more time on her hands, which she couldn't use for much of anything.

She hadn't been actively avoiding the search for Cathy's best friend Doris. Her dreams had distracted her, to be sure, but she hadn't put it off intentionally. She remembered the contact with Mrs. White's child. Cody was it? She pulled up the email and reread their brief correspondence. Maggie hoped Cody would write when Mrs. White passed away. Why would she want that? She wasn't sure. Maybe just because Mrs. White was one person alive in the world who still knew her. But since she couldn't attend a funeral, couldn't share the passing with others, maybe it would be better to never know. Maybe it would be better to live under the delusion she was alive. It didn't really matter. Cody had been clear in cutting communication lines. It would come or it wouldn't. Maggie couldn't control it. That was the story of her life.

As she turned her attention to searching for Doris, a crawl came across the screen. It read:

I'M SORRY YOUR MOTHER'S GONE.

Maggie was stunned. What? Was someone referring to Cathy's death? Who knew? The common courtesy was to thank the person. But who was it? Maggie typed:

THANK YOU. DID YOU KNOW CATHY?

Maggie waited. And waited. What was this about? Was it someone from the deprogramming office? She'd had to explain her absence when she and Pele had been at the ABC. But there had never been a personal, human exchange with anyone there. Maybe it was Pele, trying out a new skill.

After a few minutes, Maggie got up and went into the new living room. She sat down. She thought about her mother. If Maggie had wondered aloud about the crawl to Cathy, she would have reminisced about something. What might it have been? A letter from a long-lost friend? The lost books she so often mentioned? How that must have bothered her. An encounter at someone's funeral? Just then, Pele popped his head in the doorway.

"What are you doing here?"

"Hi to you, too."

"Sorry, mom. I'm just surprised. At this time of day you're usually busy at the computer."

"Ah, so it was you?"

"What?"

"Did you just send me a crawl?"

"A what?"

"A crawl, letters moving across my screen with a message."

"Nope. Don't even know what that is. What did it say?"

"That's the thing, it inquired about your grandma's death."

"Who knows about that?"

"Exactly my thought. I asked if they knew Cathy, but they didn't respond again."

"That sounds weird."

"It was. That's exactly what it was."

After a moment, Pele said, "The Enforcers know she died."

"True."

"You've gotten a couple of weird messages on the Enforcer Unit, haven't you?"

"I have. And the early calls seemed to be connected to Cathy, but the latest one didn't. It only asked questions about us going outside."

"Oh yeah. I remember. We worried they knew we carried grandma's stuff out."

"Yep, but they never contacted us again, so I stopped thinking about it."

"Are we going to do any lessons today?" Pele asked.

"I hadn't planned on it. Is there something we were in the middle of? Something you're wanting to learn?"

"Not until a moment ago. Now I'm wondering about crawls. Can you teach me that?"

"Sure. Now?"

"Well, no, I want to stir for awhile."

"Let me know when you're ready."

"Will do."

***

Gary had started making a habit of saving his data entry for the end of the shift. He and Izzy still split the caseload, he didn't want her to see any changes in routine. She still kept up with hers throughout the day, but didn't seem to notice he didn't. He knew the Enforcer on duty in the computing room had noticed. Early encounters had made Gary aware he was being watched. He hoped creating a habit would lead to less scrutiny, buying him unnoticed contact opportunities with Maggie.

Today was the day. Gary had awakened with an erection that demanded attention. He knew he'd been in the middle of a dream that involved touching Maggie. This time, he had not been wearing gloves or a mask. In this dream, it was almost like being in bed with Sam. But he'd known it wasn't Sam. There wasn't the familiarity, the comfort, the love. There'd been excitement—obviously—but it was an illicit excitement. A forbidden pleasure. The fingers of his right hand tingled with the touch of his cock as he brought himself to climax. Since these dreams had become frequent, he now took bits of paper to his capsule at night so he'd have a way of wiping up the ejaculation. He avoided thinking of what he was doing in words. He didn't want to use the words of the past: *cum, gism, wad.* He wasn't sure if he was avoiding more thought or if it was some kind of magical thinking meant to separate past and present, as if there were choices about that. The two had little in common besides his body, which had aged without much touch, even his own, for a number of years.

Gary knew it was time to send his crawl. He'd followed his routine with precision. He'd kept his emotions in check, allowing a single angry slam of a door, believing that was in keeping with Izzy's expectations. But he hadn't allowed excitement around the edges, no jaunt in his step, no smile on his lips, no glee in his tone. When he found himself in the computer room, he began by entering data from a file. Then another. Then he made sure the settings on the computer were such that if he received a crawl, it wouldn't fill the full screen, nor would it be so fast he couldn't digest it. He entered data on another case. He didn't glance around. That would draw suspicion. He merely typed in his first planned crawl and hit send:

I'M SORRY YOUR MOTHER'S GONE.

He didn't know if Maggie would see it. He didn't know how long she would take to respond, if she did. He was ready with responses, but he also had more data to enter, and he had to remain busy. He began to enter another file when words started across his screen. As he saw "Thank you" appear, an anticipated response, he continued to enter data readying for his next crawl. Then he read:

DID YOU KNOW CATHY?

That wasn't expected. *Who was Cathy? Cathy?* Before he could realize she must be the dead mother, the Enforcer walked up behind Gary.

"Did that screen flash?"

"Not that I noticed. Did it?"

"I thought I saw something from the booth."

"I didn't notice. I switched files a moment ago. Could that—?"

"No. That's normal. This wasn't."

Gary removed his gloved fingers from the keyboard. He tilted his head up with what he hoped was a look of subservience, confusion, anything but the fear he actually felt. Of course, the Enforcer probably could no more read his facial expression than he could the Enforcer's. Gary didn't speak. If he'd learned anything about himself in his encounter with the Chief Enforcer, it was that the less he said, the better.

"We've been having trouble with the monitor over there," the Enforcer pointed across the room. "Maybe this one has a glitch, too." Gary shrugged and waited. "Let me know if you notice anything."

"Will do." Gary immediately returned to entering the file info. He waited until the Enforcer returned to his cubby to exhale a deep, ragged breath. In attempting to regulate that breath, he developed the hiccups. He finished the file he was on, put the finished files into the dropbox and exited the room, carrying the remaining files. He placed his back against the wall and slowed his breathing until the hiccups subsided. During the minutes that took, Gary considered the question about "knowing Cathy" who, he now realized, was likely to be Maggie's mother. How could he respond? The more he thought about it, the deeper his hiccups became. Finally he forced himself to abandon thinking about it. He focused his attention on slowing his breathing, regulating it.

When the hiccups finally disappeared, Gary returned to the computing room. As he entered, the same Enforcer, still on duty, observed Gary re-entering. He walked as casually as he could to the same terminal, sat and entered the remaining data with no thought toward sending another crawl.

Gary spent the next morning thinking about how to respond. As he and Izzy scoured, he formulated language to send in his crawl. But no matter how many times he turned it over in his mind, he was going to be forced to use words that would be dangerous: ABC, *scouring*, *death*. He couldn't find a way to explain who he was without using words a censor would flag.

But as his mind spun, he thought about the Enforcer noticing the crawl. He was very likely to be caught anyway. He was going to do this or he wasn't.

***

It's not like I'm suicidal. Even if I was, what would I do? Stab myself? Not likely. I guess I could slit my wrists. But I've never liked blood much, so I can't actually imagine it. There aren't drugs available. What else? *Starve myself?* That seems to be happening anyway. Weight loss leads inevitably there when you're already below the healthy body index.

But the inevitable isn't suicide.

Perhaps I could go outside. If I were truly suicidal I'd worry that wouldn't be quick enough. There are the nightly AB sprays, so I can't imagine I'd be lucky enough to find a deadly strain immediately. And what would I do once I was outside and alive?

Outside and alive?

I will admit, there is appeal to that. Gary made it here unimpeded. Maybe there's reason to start imagining escape. Though I'm not sure—escape to what? I have no idea what's out beyond my walls. Evidently the AntiBacterial Center, aka the old hospital, is still in use, but beyond that, I have no idea. There's no traffic, no people, no news.

There is a door. I have a door and I could go through it. Hmm. I haven't considered that seriously in many a year. Maybe I should. It appears better than the alternative—at least, it might be better. There's the rub, though, isn't it? It might be worse.

I could see my warning worried Gary when I suggested his foray could lead to him being demoted to a Cleaner. The same fate must potentially await stray Homelanders who wander out beyond the confines of their homes onto the land.

Maybe I'll think on that, though not during wall-staring time. That's sacred.

***

Maggie had taught Pele how to initiate and respond to crawls. Since then, Pele sent her crawls instead of calling out or walking to her doorway. On the one hand, she loved watching him embrace something he'd learned. On the other hand, it meant less face-to-face and that bothered her. She was already starved for human contact.

She kept wondering who might have sent her the crawl about Cathy's death. It was both unnerving and exciting. Could it be someone she knew? Was there someone out there searching for her the way she'd been searching for others? It seemed possible, but she couldn't let her hope live there. It felt at least as likely that it was someone from Enforcement or Sterilization who knew about the death. But why that method of communication? What could they hope to gain? Her trust? Information she hadn't been willing to share when they buzzed the Enforcer Unit? Which would be what? That they went outside? Surely that wasn't important to anyone. No one patrolled the streets.

Maggie decided to start searching for Cathy's dearest friend, her estranged friend, Doris Berkhard. Maggie was no longer living under the delusion that finding Doris was about informing her of Cathy's death, though the crawl made her wonder if by any chance it could have come from Doris. But she hadn't been in medicine or government. She wasn't likely to be in a position to learn about Cathy's death through any official channel.

Between the dreams and the crawl, Maggie suddenly had plenty of excitement in her life. If she didn't find Doris, she could live with it now. It wasn't about learning what happened when Doris and her mother fell out of touch. It wasn't about her own survival. It was about a touchstone, not a lifeline.

Her initial searches turned up minimal references. Doris hadn't been someone who left much of a trail. The email address she found was from a server Maggie knew had been dead for years, ever since the town that housed its central servers burned and caused a breakdown in the grid.

Maggie sat and thought about Doris. What else did she know about her? She remembered what she looked like, always dapper in the latest fashion. She tended to wear greens—lime, avocado, melon—but not grass green. She also wore peach colors, ones that were on the pastel side of orange. Those colors made her dyed red hair shine and her green eyes sparkle.

None of that would be useful in a computer search. She'd used her address, her place of work. She knew Doris was funny in a way Cathy hadn't been herself, but in a way she'd appreciated. The two women could get to laughing to the point that tears ran from their eyes. No problem before the Touch Ban, a bit of a hassle after. Maggie still heard her mother's voice saying to Doris, "Stop! Stop! Don't make me laugh. You know

I can't stand the feeling of tears running down my cheeks." By that time it was always too late. Maggie could still see her mother's shoulder trying to reach her face to dry her tears. She was more successful on the right than the left and sometimes asked Maggie to stand near so she could wipe her left cheek on Maggie's shirtsleeve. Maggie always thought it odd. When she cried herself, she just let the tears go where they wanted. No big deal. Probably generational.

Maggie examined her memory closely. She had a few ideas she entered into the search engine, but none of them yielded anything useful. Hours passed without any notice.

Maggie's stomach told her it was time for their daily allotment. *Funny.* She rarely felt actual hunger. The portions were meager and uninteresting, yet sufficient. It was a perfunctory part of the day to eat their allotment, made pleasant because she and Pele used it as playtime. They'd continued the tradition of playing games after eating, just as they had when Cathy had been alive. It allowed them to reminisce about Cathy, and provided the wake they were denied without a burial, without friends traveling, without obituary announcements.

Just as she was about to get up, a new crawl appeared.

WAS CATHY YOUR MOTHER'S NAME?

Maggie read the screen. *Hmm.* The person sending it had offered condolences for someone they didn't know. And they owned up to that. Surely, it wasn't an Enforcer. Maggie wanted to know who was contacting her.

DO I KNOW YOU?

WE MET AT THE ABC.

Sterilizer or Enforcer then. Could either be good?

WHY ARE YOU CONTACTING ME?

I KEEP THINKING ABOUT YOU.

WHY?

WHEN I ADJUSTED THE BOT, I TOUCHED YOU.

Maggie was stunned. Was this the Sterilizer who touched her breast? Had it impacted him the way it did her? Was this who she was dreaming about? What did this mean? Maggie's thoughts took off in all directions. Her heart started racing. She didn't even think about responding. She sat in front of her computer staring into space.

IS IT TIME FOR OUR ALLOTMENT?

Maggie's face contracted. What? Allotment? Oh, this crawl must be from Pele. Maggie replied:

SURE. GIVE ME FIVE MINUTES.

Maggie looked at the timestamp. It had been several minutes since the Sterilizer, the toucher, had crawled. She decided just to leave it for now. She needed to think. And evidently he was giving her time to do that.

Maggie cleared her cache and turned off her screen. She walked out of her room realizing she didn't want to tell Pele about the latest development with the crawls. She'd keep this to herself, her little secret, at least for now.

When Maggie awoke the next morning, she walked immediately to her computer. Nothing. Since she'd erased all traces of the communication, she couldn't even re-read the crawls, the way she would have re-read texts from so-called friends in high school. She remembered how long she'd keep some of them, pouring over them again and again, trying to decipher hidden messages, appreciating emotional exchanges. What she wouldn't give for that opportunity now.

By the light of day, she doubted it had ever happened. And she'd avoided telling Pele, so there was no one to double-check her reality. She tried to replay the conversation. She could remember he mentioned the ABC, and she was pretty sure the final words across the screen were "I touched your breast." Hadn't he also said he couldn't get her off his mind? No those weren't the words, something about imagining her, no, thinking about her. Something like, "I can't stop thinking about you." Or maybe it was, "I can't stop thinking about touching your breast." She was sure by this point finding the exact words was an illusion. She knew the things she wanted to hear: that he lusted for her, that he dreamed of her, that he'd been touching himself while imagining her naked flesh, that he was going to show up at her house.

Oh, this really was fantasy land.

Maggie stared at the screen, willing a crawl to appear. Nothing happened. She sat there for a while, reliving the touch, remembering how embarrassed she was, how titillated, how vulnerable. Goose bumps raised on her arms. With her left hand she slowly brushed her right arm from shoulder to hand. She shuddered. She made the motion again, this time with more pressure, trying to wipe away the excitement coursing through her flesh.

With sheer willpower she stood and walked to her Turbobike. She hoped generating endorphins would level out her chaotic emotions. Besides, she could see her screen from the seat.

***

Today I opened the door, first thing.

The morning air was glorious. Actually, that's not completely true, it had a foul smell. No, an antiseptic odor on the breeze. Unpleasant smell, but a breeze! Glorious, I tell you!

I brought over a kitchen chair and sat inside with the door open. I didn't venture out. I can't recall a single dictum saying we couldn't open our doors or windows. Odd. It seemed they had thought of everything. They must have taken for granted we would hermetically seal ourselves inside.

The breeze had a kind of dead quality to it. Not just the antiseptic odor, it was also void of other smells I expect outside. The scents of flowers and grass and worms mulching dirt into life. None of that. The air was dead. The breeze was lovely, don't get me wrong. After years without feeling a breeze, it was downright startling, but the lack of fragrance, no smell whatsoever. The odor wasn't lovely, it was dead. It was wrong.

Not that I'm complaining. I sat for an hour or so. It was wall-staring time, but today I stared out the door. With no one passing, no dogs romping, no birds chirping, with none of that, with nothing to interrupt my sight line, it was actually very much like staring at the wall. Not much different really.

***

Gary wondered why Maggie didn't respond after he told her who he was. He was going to ask if she was still there, but right then the Enforcer had walked over saying he saw the flashing again. Gary had pointed out he was on the same terminal as the day before. He'd sat there for just this excuse. The Sterilizer then asked Gary to switch terminals to finish his entries. Gary noticed he'd been put on a terminal where he could be monitored more closely, so he finished his data entry with no further crawls.

Today he was considering what he should do. Give it another day or two before the next contact? That might protect him from Enforcer scrutiny, but it would leave Maggie wondering. Perhaps Gary could return to the habit of entering the files during the day, so he might encounter a different Enforcer and reduce the observation factor. But then he'd be able to send only one or two crawls. At this stage, that wouldn't be enough. Or would it?

When he and Izzy finished their second scouring, he took the file and went to enter the data. He'd guessed right: a different Enforcer. He sat down at a terminal as far away from the Enforcer as possible and immediately sent a crawl:

ARE YOU THERE?

Then he started entering information. He knew he didn't have long and was pleased when a reply came fairly quickly.

YES. WHAT'S YOUR NAME?

GARY.

I LIKE THAT.

THANKS, MAGGIE. ;-) I DON'T HAVE MY OWN COMPUTER. DO NOT CRAWL UNLESS I DO.

Gary knew he could only sneak in one or two more crawls.

OK.

I HAVE TO GO, I'LL CRAWL AGAIN IN A COUPLE HOURS.

UNTIL THEN…

Gary finished his data entry. The Enforcer hadn't moved. Gary dropped the file in the completed pile and returned to work with Izzy.

Gary proceeded to scan the next Homelander. He and Izzy performed the scouring and she took the file. It was pretty routine. He prepped the room and went to pick up the next case. Izzy hadn't returned yet, so he performed the scan and took the Homelander into the scouring chamber. The Homelander was an older woman. She was clearly terrified. She shook as she took off her wrap. It was a simple garb and most Homelanders just let it drop, or removed it cape-like from their shoulders to toss it into the chute for disposal. But this woman futzed with it as if it were caught on her flesh. And perhaps it had been. When she finally removed it, Gary could immediately see she had telltale blotches on her skin, red cavities of bacterial infection surrounded by pus. She clearly had a form of *MRSA*. This wasn't a case where she had come in because she was paranoid. She had to know this would be the end. Though the scan had shown nothing, there was no point in scouring. Gary called a supervisor to come to the booth so they could save her the agony of a scour if she was just going to be put down anyway.

After Izzy returned, after the Supervising Sterilizer pronounced sentence, after the woman wailed and shrieked and unsuccessfully tried to fight off the Sterilizers and the lethal injection, after all that, Gary took her file to enter the data. His thoughts were not on his longing for Maggie. He sat down and entered all the details, including connections from the woman's electronic file to the video footage that was shot from the scour room. Gary shuddered. That startled him. He'd been immune to Homelander deaths for years. This really shouldn't bother him. The emotion reconnected him to Maggie. *Was it because he had started to care about someone else that this latest death touched him?*

Gary had already finished the file, so he knew he couldn't stay long. He sent one quick crawl.

EVEN THE THOUGHT OF YOU IS CHANGING MY LIFE.

***

Each day was the same. I opened the door, placed the chair just outside and sat down. The breeze provided one appealing attribute. It was like I'd acquired a fan that created a gentle breeze to lift the scarce, somewhat long, thin hairs on the sides of my head.

I appreciated the touch of those hairs. It put me in mind of fingers, my wife's delicate fingers, stroking my cheek. She liked to do that before we parted for the day. We'd kiss, and then she'd ever so tenderly place the fingers of her right hand on my left cheek and hold it there a moment, looking into my eyes.

But I'd come to realize that staring outside was different than wall-staring. Wall-staring was numbing. It stopped memories. Painful memories. Not only did I miss her, but I recognized I had taken her caresses for granted. I didn't appreciate them. I didn't luxuriate in each one as I now would, in the love expressed in that gesture.

Staring outside brings it all back. I've started to feel again. It isn't worth it.

***

Maggie was trying to focus on her work. She was scrubbing old websites today, ones linked to the government that had been in office just before the Transition. She wondered why she'd been given this assignment. It was probably random, but she couldn't help but worry, just a little, that it had been prompted by her recent forays onto these sites to teach Pele about the time before. She couldn't think about that. It would mean she hadn't been successful at erasing her trails. That wouldn't be good. She preferred to hope the crawls she was getting would lead somewhere. Well, not likely some "where," but at least to contact, to connection, to interactions with another human being.

Just then a crawl came through from Gary. Nice name that—Gary. Gary was crawling to her.

EVEN THE THOUGHT OF YOU IS CHANGING MY LIFE.

Maggie didn't hesitate to reciprocate:

MINE TOO.

CAN'T CRAWL AGAIN TILL TOMORROW.

OK.

Maggie wondered for the first time what Gary's life was like. Maybe it was because she had his name. Maybe because they'd agreed this communication was life-changing. She wondered about someone who didn't have his own computer. That in itself was odd. She thought Gary's lack of computer and his need to keep their conversations short indicated fear on his side. Perhaps he was being watched. Or he feared it. That made sense. If she was afraid, and she lived in a home, surely a lackey—a Sterilizer yes, but a lackey nonetheless—needed to watch his back. There must be bosses at the ABC, probably Enforcers, who kept track of everything Sterilizers did. It'd be dangerous not to, right? Wouldn't it be important to ensure Sterilizers didn't go rogue with bacteria? They must have access to a variety of strains.

Maggie suddenly realized she was letting her imagination run away with her. She needed to continue the cleanup she was in the midst of. With a complicated government site, she needed to pay attention so she didn't miss any dead links. Not to mention she knew there was information putting government in a bad light, and she no doubt would have orders to eliminate those pages revealing the tentacles of AgriBiz that had infiltrated, as she now knew, the highest government offices before the Transition.

***

Gary had finished his shift without incident. He'd eaten his allotment, rowed, and returned to a pod in the capsule for a solid night's sleep, undisturbed by nightmares and unencumbered by wet dreams.

Before his next day with Izzy had hardly begun, the scourbot got stuck. Since his attention lagged, Izzy was already saying she'd go and fix it. The Homelander being scoured was extremely tall. Gary wondered if lackeys took that into account in allotment sizes. He wondered whether someone that size felt more claustrophobic than the average-sized Homelander, stuck inside forever. Before he could come to any conclusions, Izzy returned.

"Did you see that?"

"See what?"

"The contact? My hand came into contact with that Homelander. Do you think I need to get scanned?"

"It was just your glove right?"

"Right."

"You didn't tear it, did you?"

"No."

Gary shrugged. He immediately wondered why Izzy was telling him this. Was she a spy for the Enforcers after all? He'd given up worrying about that possibility, but here it was again. Why was she asking these questions? It wasn't like her. He looked at Izzy.

"Do you think the Enforcers will find out?" she asked.

"Can't see how."

"Isn't there a rule against this?"

"Probably. There's a rule against almost everything."

With their masks it was difficult to read facial expressions. Gary realized Izzy was already back at the console setting the next parameter. He returned his attention to scouring. Izzy's questions and concern were logical enough, if uncommon from her. Any conspiracy was probably all in his mind.

When they finished the scour, Izzy didn't pick up the file. She typically took the first case of the day. They didn't normally discuss such mundane routines.

"Want me to do this one?" Gary offered.

"Would you?"

"Sure."

Oh no. Izzy was up to something. She must be. She couldn't be that thrown by touching that guy. *Crap. What now?*

Gary realized he didn't want to enter this file immediately. He laid it near the door as he walked out of the room. He wasn't going to crawl today anyway. He knew that now. He felt his timeline constricting. "Safety first" was a motto of Sterilizers, though it had never meant what it did today. As he walked down the corridor his heart raced. He'd imagined there would be time for the conversation with Maggie to evolve at its own pace. He was excited when she'd said he was changing her life, too. He wanted to linger in the excitement of getting to know each other. He longed for the verbal foreplay that led to a first date, whatever that might look like.

He thought his biggest concern was deciding if he was going to sneak out again. Now he realized he might already be targeted. He looked down at the red hexagon on his chest. It had never looked so ominous.

As Gary neared intake to pick up the next Homelander for scouring, he refocused himself on the task at hand. He was worried he was going to start sweating, a dangerous situation inside the Sterilizer cover-up. He was worried he'd give himself away by doing something stupid, like ripping his mask off because the sweat was making him crazy, dripping in his eyes.

He had to calm down, to pay attention, to do his job. And only that. His job.

When his shift ended, Gary took his stack of files to the computer room. As he walked though the door, he noticed the terminal he'd been using had been removed. *Shit! Had he left traces?* He had meant to erase the crawls, hide tracks of his searches, not leave any hints. He'd done some of it. But with the Enforcer's watchful eye, his hiccups and the interruptions, he didn't know if he'd been thorough. He wasn't confident of his computer skills to hide his tracks, especially if the Enforcers were looking seriously. He glanced to the other side of the room. The other terminal the Enforcer had pointed out as flashing was also missing. Maybe the techs were just servicing this room. He could hope.

He sat down at the terminal the Enforcer had put him at last time he was here, figuring that way he'd arouse the least suspicion. It meant his every keystroke could be observed. He opened a file and began. When he finished that file he set it aside and started another. Slowly he made his way through the stack. He didn't want to take less time, so he made sure to make a few errors as he went and then take the time to correct them. He didn't let himself think about Maggie or the possibility of contacting her. He couldn't do that today, not after Izzy and the touch and her talking about the touch and her leaving the file laying there for him instead of picking it up as she should have. His concerns about what today's events might mean, from Izzy to the missing terminal, were more than enough to consider.

When Gary went to the Lot he found he couldn't imagine eating. His insides were churning. Allotments were individualized. Allotments weren't wasted. Ever. The Lot had the usual suspects from his shift, a group of Sterilizers who sat reading the monitor, eating. It seemed like there were fewer of them lately. *Why would that be?* Maybe others were in the GenCenter, generating power for the grid. The rooms were right across the hall from one another. Gary supposed that made it easier to keep an eye on all of them. He'd never considered that before. It had always just been the way it was, but now he saw ulterior motives everywhere he looked.

Gary took his allotment from its container and zapped it to the proper temperature. He looked at the firm brown square. *At least it's not green.* He began to eat, washing it down with more water than usual. He wished it were a softer texture so it would be easier to get down. He inhaled as he swallowed and found himself choking. That got attention from several in the room. But as he cleared his windpipe they looked away again. No one moved toward him. No one asked if he was OK. At least the choking gave him an excuse to slow down. He tried to think of a way of tossing the rest of it, but he couldn't imagine it going unnoticed. Right now that was too big a risk. He got himself more water and just kept at it until he got the entire allotment into his stomach. He hoped he could keep it down. Throwing up was a sure way to be carted off for fear of contagion. He doubted Sterilizers who vomited were ever returned to the job.

When he finished, he made his way to the GenCenter and put in his requisite time. He often spent more time there than necessary, but tonight all he wanted was sleep. So he headed for the first open pod and lay down. He fell asleep immediately, but it was a fitful sleep during which he awoke often to nightmares.

He was chased. He was contaminated. He was in front of the Chief Enforcer again.

There was also one dream of Maggie that started pleasantly and moved toward eroticism and then shifted until suddenly his naked, ungloved hand was reaching out to touch her but instead of reaching toward a woman, his hand was engulfed in flames. His heart was racing, his breath unsteady, as he opened his eyes to find he was still in a pod.

He waited a few calming minutes, breathing deeply, eyes closed. Then he slid out and went to the showers for his morning AB cleansing routine.

***

I didn't eat today. I don't think I ate yesterday. I haven't opened the door. Or did I? I know I sat, but whether I stared at the wall or out the door, I can't honestly be sure. What could it possibly matter which? There's me and the allotment delivery and the walls and the weigh-ins and…that's about it.

Gary hasn't come back. My wife can't come back. Back would be better but it's not an option.

There are no options.

***

Trevor felt like his job had shifted from an Enforcer, ensuring everyone followed the rules meant to keep the population safe from bacteria, to an administrator just keeping the ship afloat. Not only that, he was keeping it afloat without any navigation system. Though the Commander had ducked his question about decreases in numbers, he had since dealt with the reality. He couldn't have Sterilizers just sitting around. It wouldn't do. They'd start talking. They'd get playful. They'd do dangerous, rule-breaking things. He couldn't have that. So as the numbers of Homelanders coming in for scanning and scouring decreased, he began to move Sterilizers to other jobs.

At first he created new levels of bureaucracy—double-checking data entry and supervising jobs that had been previously unsupervised. Both of these further diminished camaraderie, an added bonus. But there weren't enough of such meaningless positions he could create. He had to start changing some Sterilizers into Cleaners.

This meant he'd been picking off both the top workers for bureaucratic posts and the bottom ones to be moved into cleaning, though he tended to put many of the "new" Cleaners in supervisory positions. Since Sterilizers had educations, deride them as he might, they tended to have more analytic skills and were therefore adept at adapting to observing and assessing workflows. Not that he needed more efficiency, he didn't, but he hadn't lost his own predilections. He still wanted a ship-shape operation filled with rule-followers who created a sanitary environment.

Too many Sterilizers wasn't Trevor's only problem, he needed to find ways to keep Enforcers busy as well. Creating new tasks for them was easy, it was why he was promoted to his position. First he sat down with the current set of rules. He read each and looked for implications behind the rule. Often he could come up with several types of tasks that could be added to Enforcer job descriptions to keep them busier. For example,

Rule 21: Ensure that Sterilizers go nowhere other than the ABC and the pods.

Trevor realized that to date, they had enforced this rule by monitoring only between the two locations and only during the hours of typical movement. He increased this security detail in several ways. He made it 24-hour coverage. He ensured that in addition to the main door, all access points received regular physical walkthroughs in addition to electronic camera surveillance. He rotated Enforcers among posts every 45 minutes to disrupt staff. And finally, he made sure he walked the beat in irregular patterns with much more frequency. This made the Enforcers nervous and had the added benefit of giving him back a sense that enforcement was crucial to an AntiBacterial Homeland. The Homeland must be safe. He was there to ensure that.

Enforcers were used to rules being changed and job descriptions shifting. Even after all these years, they thought of their jobs as *emergent*. But Enforcers were only part of the ABC team. Trevor didn't want the decrease in Sterilizers to be noticed by Enforcers or other Sterilizers, so he began to close down parts of the building and cordon off portions of space so the decrease would be less noticeable. He knew he had to make these changes slowly or he could end up highlighting them instead of hiding them. But he was fairly confident that other than the RedHexes, few were likely to pay attention.

Their worlds had shrunk to working/generating/sleeping. There were few stimulants in the equation. They thought about very little and wondered less.

One type of change involved decreasing the numbers of things: scanners, scourbots, computers. Diminishing scanners meant more open hallways, since they'd never fit anywhere. That was fine. He just placed those that were removed into rooms that were being decommissioned. He was pleased to shift a few scourbots into a rotation, so when they inevitably broke down another one was waiting. Removing computers provided a chance to keep a few Enforcers busy. He realized he'd done little to monitor computer usage, and he could easily assign a few of the computer-trained Enforcers to comb through the hard drives looking for irregularities that might indicate contact between Sterilizers and Homelanders. Not that it was forbidden, but it might indicate potential breaches in the offing.

The former receptionist Trevor had met his first day had remained with him. He moved her around to several jobs as needed. Her loyalty was unparalleled, except perhaps for Trevor himself. She never complained, though she still giggled a great deal because she never saw things coming. That made her ideal to be at Trevor's right hand. She would do whatever he wanted, but she wouldn't anticipate, which meant she couldn't try to take over or get in the way. And she had an uncanny knack for noticing when routines were altered or rules bent, which she always reported to him right away.

"I need you to monitor the Enforcers who are flea-combing the computers."

"Flea combing?" the receptionist laughed. "Have they got bugs?"

"Good, yes, it is a type of de-bugging."

She recognized she'd inadvertently made a joke and laughed harder. "How can I monitor something I don't understand?"

"I just want you to look over their work and report any anomalies to me."

"Anomalies?"

"Altered routines—if someone suddenly started emailing, visiting a blog or crawling. If there were suddenly many deletions during data entry or if a Sterilizer was wiping the hard drive trying to erase tracks. Those things. I want to know who."

"You got it."

***

For two days Gary stayed focused on his job. Well, he did his job, flawlessly, without any telltale signs he was expecting to be descended upon at any moment. It didn't happen.

It was a strange combination: the more hours that passed, the more paranoid he became, and yet the more likely it was, logically, that the computers were being repaired, that they hadn't removed them to examine them for clues. So the computers hadn't been removed because they suspected him.

Or maybe they had been, he couldn't be sure. Maybe they were waiting for him to do something that would give them reason to put him in front of the Chief Enforcer again.

Izzy didn't mention the touch of the tall Homelander again. No one mentioned the older woman with *MRSA*, of course, as no one mentioned much of anything.

Gary worked, ate, generated, slept. And repeated the process.

He also thought about Maggie. He wondered if this kind of absence made the heart grow fonder. He doubted it. They didn't know each other well enough yet. More likely, it drew her into paranoia, one where he was the villain rather than the hero. Mostly, he tried to decide when and how he'd be willing to risk another crawl. He wanted more—more exchanges, more knowledge of her and her life, more contact. He'd love to meet up with her in person. He wondered what that would be like. How would it be different than it had been with Sam? When he considered it, he wondered if they'd have anything in common: Sam and Maggie, not Maggie and him.

Then again, what would *they* have in common, he and Maggie? For years she'd been a Homelander living with a son and mother. For years he'd been a Sterilizer sleeping in a pod, living at the ABC, if you called that living. He knew she did computer work, while he was in medicine, or rather, sterilizing. Other than the touch, did they share anything? Perhaps a longing. He sensed that in their limited communication. Clearly they both longed for something, each other at the moment, though he suspected it was more than that.

He needed to stop dwelling on Maggie. He hadn't acted on his urges in days. It would get him nowhere. He needed to do something. He had continued entering all his files at the end of the day. Though the same Enforcer was on duty, the guy seemed to be ignoring him now that the terminal was gone. If all felt normal, *whatever that meant*, he'd crawl to Maggie again tonight and hope she'd be at her computer.

When Gary entered the room, there were two other Sterilizers entering data. Gary, as casually as possible, sat as far from the Enforcer's watchful eye as he could. He entered part of the first file and then typed:

MAGGIE? YOU THERE?

Gary continued to enter data. Within a few minutes a reply came:

GARY? WHAT HAPPENED?

JUST BEING CAUTIOUS.

R U OK?

Gary thought it clever that Maggie began to use text-speak. It was faster than typing words. But Gary had never been good at it. Though it was fast, he was worried he'd get confused and wouldn't want to ask what Maggie meant. He'd stick with English.

NOW THAT WE'RE CRAWLING, I AM. ; -)

GOOD. I WAS WORRIED.

Gary took the time to enter the rest of the first file and start the second. He also glanced to see that the Enforcer's attention was elsewhere.

WHY WORRY, YOU DON'T REALLY KNOW ME.

I FEEL LIKE I DO. OR AT LEAST I WANT TO.

IF THIS WERE A FIRST DATE, WOULD IT BE GOING WELL SO FAR?

INDEED.

Gary couldn't believe he'd asked the first date question. He was moving this along. *At last.* It felt like they were getting somewhere. He continued to enter data. Just then he heard a commotion in the hall. The Enforcer looked up, then stood up, and finally exited the room. The other Sterilizers seemed nonplussed and continued the data entry. Gary was curious. This rarely happened. But it gave him the perfect chance to really talk to Maggie.

WHAT'S IT LIKE TO BE A HOMELANDER?

RIGHT NOW IT'S LONELY.

BECAUSE OF YOUR MOM?

YEAH. SHE WAS A PAIN SOMETIMES, BUT SHE WAS AN ADULT TO TALK TO.

YOU AND YOUR SON LIVE IN A HOME TOGETHER?

YEP.

Gary heard an alarm sound. That meant the Enforcer would be gone for at least a few minutes.

DO YOU CRAWL OR EMAIL OR ANYTHING WITH FRIENDS OR FAMILY?

NOPE.

NO ONE?

I HAVEN'T COMMUNICATED WITH ANYONE ELSE IN YEARS. WHAT ABOUT YOU?

I WORK AND SLEEP.

NOTHING ELSE?

GENERATE.

LOL. :-)

GUESS WE ALL DO THAT.

WHERE DO YOU LIVE?

IN A CAPSULE HOTEL NEAR THE ABC.

THE OLD RONALD MCDONALD PLACE?

WE CALL IT THE POD.

FUNNY. THAT MEANS YOU GO OUTSIDE?

ONLY WALKING BETWEEN THE TWO.

IS THAT DANGEROUS?

NO MORE SO THAN WHEN YOU WERE BROUGHT HERE.

WE WERE MASKED.

I'M ALWAYS MASKED.

ALWAYS?

EXCEPT WHEN I SLEEP.

Gary listened. The alarm continued. The commotion had grown rather than reduced. More time for Maggie.

WHAT MADE YOU CONTACT ME?

I THOUGHT WE CONNECTED.

I THOUGHT SO TOO.

IT SEEMED KIND OF ABSURD.

I KNOW.

BUT I COULDN'T GET YOU OUT OF MY MIND.

YOU CAME TO ME IN DREAMS.

I CAME TO YOU? ARE WE SUDDENLY SEXTING?

NO, YOU DIDN'T COME, NOT SEXUALLY, OR, NOT AT FIRST.

NOT AT FIRST?

LET'S SAY THE DREAMS HAVE PROGRESSED.

THIS IS GETTING INTERESTING.

YES IT IS.

Gary stopped to listen again. No alarm sound. He could still hear loud voices though. That didn't mean the Enforcer wouldn't walk back in at any moment. Higher-ups would probably take over.

I SHOULD GO. CAN I EMAIL YOU?

THAT MIGHT BE EASIER.

YOU'LL BE HEARING FROM ME.

CAN'T WAIT.

Gary wiped the crawls. Then he returned to his files. He typed in the data as efficiently as he could. He picked up the pile of files to drop in the completed box just as the Enforcer walked in the door. The Enforcer turned his head to face Gary, but with the black mesh in the Enforcer's mask, Gary couldn't see an expression. Neither spoke. Gary dropped the files and exited. He walked to the Lot and enjoyed his meal for the first time in over a week. When he finished he got on a Turbobike and pedaled away.

Though it didn't move, in his mind, Gary was riding through the Homeland, heading for Maggie's door.

***

The professor opened the door. He walked out.

It was a gray day. He didn't close the door, didn't look back. He walked away.

He had no goal. No hopes of a better tomorrow. He was tired. After the first day's excitement at the breeze, he hadn't found the outside stimulating. It could just as easily be a wall in his home, worthy of staring at, but not much more.

There was, however, room to walk. He was unsteady. He hadn't walked more than room to room in years.

He walked away, whatever that meant.

***

Gary couldn't stop thinking about emailing Maggie. He was excited about how much he might be able to say at one time. Of course, there was still the Enforcer's presence to contend with, but he thought it would be much easier to email than crawl. There wouldn't be any flashing, just a screen change, and with the right preferences that could look similar to any page change while inputting data. He would miss the back and forth of crawling, which had felt almost like talking, synchronous as it was, but it would be safer and still exciting.

Of course, there wasn't much to tell her. Not at this stage. She had asked about where he lived, so he could fill her in on the parameters of his life. He refused to think of it as a lifestyle. It wasn't like he'd chosen it. And perhaps he could tell her about Sam. But maybe not yet. He was curious if she'd had lovers before the Total Touch Ban. She was old enough, barely. He had the advantage over her of having her vitals, thanks to the data entry after her visit to the ABC. He'd gone back to find that info. At the time, it had been a weird accident, nothing more.

He could certainly fill her in on some of his vitals. How to decide which? Perhaps the ones of hers he found most compelling, like her age and knowing she'd been born before the FaceTouch Ban. He wondered what she remembered of that time. Had her hands been tied behind her back? Had she sneaked touches on the sly, away from her parents' gaze? The more he thought about it, the more questions he had. He'd need to balance his first email with information and questions. Just questions would be rude when he already had more information about her than she did about him.

When Gary arrived at the computing room, he realized it wasn't the same Enforcer. *Nice. This is my chance.* Gary sat down as far away from the booth as possible, yet not next to another Sterilizer. That wasn't done. Besides, he couldn't risk observation from anyone. He entered a file, then set the preferences so email had the same background as data entry. He started an email. Between files, he'd add a sentence or two. He had several paragraphs when he heard a pager go off. Out of the corner of his eye he saw the Enforcer in the booth stand. Though he couldn't see his eyes, Gary could see his face was pointed directly at Gary as he exited the booth. Before the Enforcer reached him, Gary stood and started for the door. He left the files on the table. He hadn't sent the email, nor had he erased it.

"Wait!" the Enforcer demanded.

But Gary didn't stop. As he passed through the doorway, a second Enforcer met him nearly head on. Gary dodged to the left and tried to run. Though he wasn't thinking, he was making his way toward the exit to the building. Before he could reach the end of the hallway, an Enforcer pummeled him with a stun gun. The alarm sounded. It was the same one Gary had heard last week. Within minutes, five Enforcers towered over him. It looked like overkill. *Why would they need so many?*

"Once wasn't enough, eh?"

Gary recognized the voice. It was the Chief Enforcer who had interrogated and punished him when he'd been out all night.

"Sir…" was all Gary managed as the first boot connected with his chest.

***

Trevor's pager vibrated. His assistant wanted him to know about developments. She didn't usually page him since not that much had been happening lately. But she had information she thought he'd want to know.

"There's a walker, sir."

"How do you know?"

"The new patrol spotted him. It's an old man. He's nearing the ABC."

"He's nearby? Is he sick?"

"Can't tell. No outward signs. Though he is weaving a bit."

"Have him picked up, scanned, scoured."

"And then? If he's bacteria-free, what do you want done with him, sir?"

"If he's bacteria-free? No need for more Cleaners. Return him home, as if we had brought him in."

"Right, sir. But won't he walk again?"

"Maybe."

"Thought we wanted to prevent that."

"Keeps us on our toes. Emergent situations rule the day."

"Got it, chief. Change in rules."

"Rules follow the emergent reality. We don't change them willy nilly."

She giggled in embarrassment. While she always followed the rules, and informed Trevor of anyone who didn't, she also thought the rules changed way too often. It was hard to keep track. "Of course not, sir. Just my shorthand. Won't use it again. Note to self: rules don't change, situations do."

"Well put. Is that all?"

"On my end, yes, chief."

"Have the flea-combers finished with all the machines?"

She couldn't help herself and giggled when he said flea-combers. She still thought that was a funny thing to call computer work. "They have."

"No more computer violators found?"

"Just the one, sir."

"Good. We know he won't cause any more trouble."

"No, sir. You took care of that."

"That I did."

***

Maggie hovered near her computer. She'd been waiting for a couple days. Since they'd agreed to switch to emails, she thought for sure Gary wouldn't delay. But then, she really had no clue about his life. She couldn't begin to fathom that he slept in one of those capsule hotels near the ABC. She remembered when they were built and all the hubbub over whether or not Americans would sleep in such tight quarters. The builders, Japanese obviously, had argued that when a loved one was hospitalized, family wanted to spend most of their time by their bedside. Sleeping was a necessity in such circumstances, not a luxury. They argued they could house up to six times the number of people for the same expense. The project went forward.

Pundits continued to rage against the cultural encroachment. But in the end, the capsules filled without delay, because so many were unexpectedly and rapidly hospitalized due to various outbreaks. Though the facility had been meant to house the families of small children, it quickly opened its doors to all who needed respite. Until the beds were full, that is. The rotation of families through the pods could be rapid. More always appeared, ready to use the beds without complaint, just happy for a place to rest between vigils with the dying.

Maggie remembered that the RedHex who touched her, Gary, was a tall man. She imagined he wouldn't have much room to move around in a capsule. Where would he keep things? No wonder he didn't have his own computer. There would be nowhere to put it.

As Maggie acknowledged to herself her reluctance to step away from her computer, she remembered a story of her mother's. Cathy used to tell about her first date with Howard. She would describe how well it went, how excited she was by the prospect of an actual boyfriend. She'd veer off then and talk about her teen years and her popularity among the girls, but not the boys. Eventually, she'd describe how she had waited by the phone for a call.

It was something Maggie couldn't imagine then. First, there was the idea of a landline. Maggie had always carried her phone with her. Second, there was the idea that her mother had not been popular with men. Maggie struggled to make sense of that, given that Cathy had many male friends, some of whom Maggie worried might be more than friends, though her father never seemed concerned. And third, there was the idea that anyone, especially her mother, would just wait for a call. Maggie saw Cathy as a doer. Maggie had had such little romance in her life that imagining someone just wiling away hours, growing more and more concerned that a call wouldn't come rather than picking up the phone and calling that person, perplexed her.

Maggie's generation had not achieved equality of the sexes, but when it came to phoning, she hadn't noticed different male/female behaviors, at least not among her contemporaries. This was one of the points Cathy always made. She derided herself that she'd been so characteristically feminine. She didn't see herself that way. Cathy had been raised to be independent. But when Howard came on the scene, "she melted." That was always the way she described it. That her will had melted away and left a "puddle by the phone."

Maggie didn't want to become a puddle. Puddles were what became of bacteria victims. Was that what this hope of connection was turning into—a bacterial infection? Surely not! Maggie stood up and walked out into the kitchen.

In days long gone, wine was an answer to a mood like this. She missed wine. She could uncork a new bottle, pour a little into a large, thin-stemmed glass and sit out back on a lawn chair and watch the leaves blow in the wind. Yes, that would take care of it.

She pulled out a chair and slumped into it. It had only been a couple days and in their brief relationship, *dare she call it that?*, in their time crawling, he'd been absent like this once already. He'd said he was being cautious. That's probably all this was. She needn't get upset. She just needed to keep herself busy. She chuckled. Nothing new with that.

She picked up her handheld and started a game, one that would take her awhile to complete, one that would tame her brain waves into a dull, lifeless state. She knew how to deal with the need to keep busy.

A week had passed. Not a word from Gary. Maggie no longer sat in front of the computer waiting. She was able to work again, continuing the enormous cleaning job she'd been given for government. The site was old enough that she didn't run across anything that gave her insight into the situation Gary lived in. Nothing interesting, nothing stimulating.

Once or twice a day she'd attempt to learn something about Sterilizer life, but other than ABC statistics, she really couldn't find much. She ran across a few documents setting up the positions, but after their establishment, there was a void. They followed the Transition, so it made perfect sense information was scant, but she had hoped.

She tried not to speculate on what had happened. She tried to let go. Not that she was having much luck in that area. Pele hadn't noticed that Maggie had a secret. He hadn't asked about any changes in her behavior or mood, so she must have been hiding it all well enough.

Maggie walked into the kitchen. She looked at the cupboards. She missed the days when she could alter her emotions by baking a batch of cookies or muffins. She opened a cupboard door and stared at all the kitchenware she still had. There were mixing bowls, measuring cups, soup bowls, wine glasses, coffee mugs. She opened all her cupboard doors and drawers and stared at the wealth of useless dreck. Pots and pans and bakeware, a coffee pot and blender and toaster and toothpicks and ice cube trays.

Why keep all this? Why not get rid of it? What good was it other than to remind her of a past that was never returning? Without considering the consequences, she yanked out a drawer and dumped the contents in the middle of the table. Measuring cups and serving utensils clattered down. The sound was amazingly loud in the quiet home.

"Are you OK, mom?" Pele shouted as he ran into the room fearing his mom might be hurt, just as she swiped her hand across a cupboard shelf and plasticware tumbled all over the floor.

Maggie didn't meet Pele's eyes. She started to shake her head. She didn't know what to say. She didn't have words for the overwhelming sense of loss that washed over her. She burst into tears. Pele stood and watched. He waited, uncertain what was happening. Finally, he asked quietly, "What happened?"

"What happened? Good question. What happened? What did happen?"

Pele waited. He couldn't understand why his mom was repeating his question. It was a simple enough one. Surely she understood what he wanted to know. Why had she dumped out the drawer? He had no idea what most of it was. He'd never seen it used. He couldn't recall exploring the kitchen cupboards. Maybe when he was little. He had a notion that his grandma got into the drawers now and then, though he had no idea why.

As Cathy had gotten old, she had forgotten things, asked questions about the meanings of words, but she'd never gone senile. Pele had no experience of a person losing touch with reality.

"Mom, are you OK?"

Maggie started to sob.

"Mom?"

As Maggie sunk to the floor, her arm dragged across the table pulling some of the metal utensils crashing to the floor with her. She hugged her knees to herself. She could hear a voice, but she couldn't understand what it was saying.

When Pele saw his mom rocking, he recognized the motion he used to calm himself. He had no idea why she would be upset, but that didn't matter, at least now he thought he understood. He walked in front of her. He put both hands high in the air to show his mom affection. But Maggie didn't look at him. He tried speaking. He tried their hug equivalent. He couldn't figure out how to get through to her.

All his life Maggie had been attentive to his every need. It wasn't that he had a need now, not exactly—*she* seemed to have the need—but he couldn't help her if she wouldn't look at him, wouldn't listen. Pele sat down on the floor in front of her. He sat cross-legged.

He had an impulse to reach out and touch his mother. He'd never done that. He had no idea why that idea even came to him. It scared him. Not as much as Maggie was scaring him, though.

With no one to ask for advice, Pele reached out a tentative hand. His fingers made contact with Maggie's shoulder.

Maggie looked up. Pele rapidly pulled back his hand. "I'm sorry. I shouldn't have done that."

"Pele?"

"Mom? Are you OK?"

"Pele, did you touch me?"

"I'm sorry, mom. I didn't know what to do. You wouldn't stop crying. You didn't even look at me when I put my hands in the air."

"You touched my shoulder?"

"Yeah."

"To get my attention?"

"I guess. To comfort you, I think."

"Thank you."

"You're not mad?"

"It's just what I needed. In fact, can you do it again?"

"I'm not supposed to."

"I know. I taught you that, didn't I?"

"Yes."

"And now I'm asking you to break that rule."

Pele thought for a moment. Touching his mom had been strange. It had sent a tingling sensation through his body. He wasn't sure he liked that. But his mom looked so sad.

Slowly, he extended his hand to her shoulder. He started to snatch it away again, but Maggie reached up and placed her hand on top of his. Eyes closed, she held both their hands firmly on her shoulder. She breathed deeply, the touch reaching to her core. Then she looked into Pele's eyes and saw fear there.

Maggie released his hand.

Habits learned early...

ACKNOWLEDGMENTS

T hanks to my Forever Editor, Bob, who read, edited, and gave feedback on this writing with great frequency and endless praise. Thanks to dystopian Brandi Blahnik, who never doubted a bleak future and who offered audience insights at many turns. A special thanks to Karen Baum, who saw the treachery in a young boy with OCD. I appreciate the vast feedback from early readers who assisted in necessary revision and made it clear the story was working, particularly when they confessed their difficulties with hand sanitizers: Anthony, Curry, Deb, Irene, Jane, Karen K, Linda, Robin, Sam, Stacy. Thanks to Shareen Grogan for willingly engaging with this less than appetizing topic during meal after meal.

While a sabbatical allowed me the time and freedom to imagine and write *Isolation*, the ever growing support of my MiraCosta colleagues ensured its publication. I couldn't have done this without all of the interested questions, the classroom readings, and the substantial financial backing—thank you. Through my Kickstarter, 159 people financially supported *Isolation*. I'm grateful to every one of them. The following contributors' reward level includes seeing their names in print:

Amy Bolaski
Anthony Ginger
Carol Peterson Haviland
Carol Wilkinson
Christine Popok
Connie Wilbur
Dana Smith
dara
Deanna Stephenson Gross
Elizabeth Dinamarca Clarke
Eric and Nikki Gross
Familia Pohlert
Ian and Nicole Kenning
Jamie Manley
Jeff and Jennifer Bennett
Jessica Magallanes
Jim Matthews
Joe Silverman
Jonathan Cole
Karl Cleveland
Krista Fedon
Leola McClure
Linda Shaffer
Meghan Burke
Melanie Haynie
Pamela Perry
P D Stephenson
Pilar Hernández
Rica Sirbaugh French

Robin Galen Kilrain
Sam Arenivar
Sandy Williams
Sarah Hochstetler
Sayaka Neal
Solomiia and Gene Zhitnitsky
Susan C. Herrmann
Thao Ha and Raleigh Orias
The Gerold Family
Tom Severance

DENISE R. STEPHENSON resides in Oceanside, CA, but she has lived in all the isolated locales of this novel at one time or another. Her publishing history is primarily academic, though as a member of *Attention Deficit Drama*, she has written and produced monologs and short plays. This is her first novel.

CPSIA information can be obtained at www.ICGtesting.com
Printed in the USA
BVOW01s0555300414

352073BV00001B/3/P